EVERYONE
IN THEIR PLACE

Maurizio de Giovanni

EVERYONE
IN THEIR PLACE
THE SUMMER
OF COMMISSARIO RICCIARDI

*Translated from the Italian
by Antony Shugaar*

Europa
editions

Europa Editions
214 West 29th Street
New York, N.Y. 10001
www.europaeditions.com
info@europaeditions.com

Translation by Antony Shugaar
Original title: *Il posto di ognuno. L'estate del commissario Ricciardi*
Translation copyright © 2013 by Europa Editions

Library of Congress Cataloging in Publication Data is available
ISBN 978-1-60945-143-1

de Giovanni, Maurizio
Everyone in Their Place

Book design by Emanuele Ragnisco
www.mekkanografici.com
Cover photo: Italy. Naples. 1958
© Leonard Freed/Magnum Photos/Contrasto
Digital elaboration: Papirus

Prepress by Grafica Punto Print – Rome

Printed in the USA

To Titto and Vale,
fellow travelers who've gone the whole distance.

EVERYONE
IN THEIR PLACE

I

The angel of death made its way through the *festa*, and nobody noticed.

It passed close to the wall of the church, which was still decorated from that morning's religious celebration; by now, though, night had fallen, and the sacred had given way to the profane. A bonfire had been set in the middle of the piazza, in keeping with tradition, even though the brutal heat of August left everyone breathless, and no one needed those flames dancing over the pile of old wood that every family in town had contributed.

But the flames proved useful to the angel of death, casting the shadows of couples as they danced merrily to the sound of tambourines, guitars, and clapping hands, accompanied by the shouts of children and the whistles of strolling vendors. The angel hadn't foreseen it, but it knew that divine justice would intervene in some way. A firecracker exploded, followed by another. Midnight was approaching. A fat perspiring woman pretended to faint, and the man next to her laughed. The angel of death brushed past him, touching his elbow, but the man didn't even shiver: it wasn't his turn, not that night.

Skirting the edge of the piazza in a nondescript black outfit, there was nothing about the angel that could've attracted notice, save perhaps the sadness of the downcast eyes and the slight droop of the shoulders. That too was something it had counted on.

It reached the front door of the palazzo and for a moment

feared it might have been locked for the festa; but no, it had been left open just a crack, as always. The angel of death slipped inside, shadowlike, as the tarantella built to a crescendo and the crowd accompanied the dance with song and applause and firecrackers crackled, keeping time to the music. It knew just where to hide. It reached the narrow gap behind a pillar, took up a position, and settled in to wait.

Its hand slid into its pocket and touched the cold metal, but it brought no comfort. Nor did the courtyard's solitary shadows bring comfort of any kind.

Nothing did, except the thought of the justice that would soon be meted out.

II

Commissario Luigi Alfredo Ricciardi didn't mind working on Sundays, and that was just another of his quirks. His colleagues came up with excuse after excuse to get out of Sunday duty, every time shifts were being assigned: they had sick mothers to care for, seniority accrued, alleged family emergencies. Any excuse would do, as long as they could skip working the one day of the week that the whole city rested.

But Ricciardi said nothing, as usual, and so as usual he was stuck with the worst assignments. Not that the fact won him any goodwill from his fellow policemen; in fact, they took every chance that presented itself to whisper venomously behind his back.

He was a solitary soul, his hands always in his pockets, invariably hatless even in winter; he never attended parties or drank toasts, he was always somewhere else when people gathered. He let invitations lapse, he failed to form friendships, and he was never open to the confidences of others. His green eyes glittered in his dark face, a lock of hair unfailingly draping across his forehead, only to be swept away from time to time with a sharp gesture. He spoke only seldom, and then with a cool irony that most failed to understand. Still, his presence never failed to attract attention.

He worked tirelessly, especially when he was pursuing a murderer, indifferent to the vicious backbiting of those colleagues incapable of equaling the pace he demanded from all his investigators; the officers assigned to him cursed him under their breath for the hours he expected them to spend in the pouring rain or the hot blast of the noonday sun; he sent them out on seemingly endless and often futile stakeouts. They bitterly noted that, on each case he worked, it was as if someone had murdered a member of his family, no matter whether the actual victim was an aristocrat or a pauper.

On the other hand, nobody questioned his abilities. Without adhering to procedure or following the instructions issued by his superiors, he pursued his own incomprehensible twisting paths and always seemed to catch the culprit. Word had spread that Commissario Ricciardi spoke directly with the devil himself, and that the devil whispered to him the very thoughts that had been in the murderers' heads; this rumor only widened the empty space around him, because superstition was so deeply ingrained in this city's soul. No one knew a thing about his life, or perhaps there simply was nothing to be known. He lived alone with his old nursemaid, Tata Rosa, and no one knew of any relatives or friends. He frequented no women, or men for that matter, and no one had ever run into him at a bordello or a theater: never an evening out on the town. He inspired the same mistrust that always seems to spring up around those who have no vices, and can therefore have no virtues.

Even his superior officers, first and foremost among them Angelo Garzo, the deputy chief of police, were openly discomfited by the presence of a man who, despite his enormous abilities and skills, seemed to lack ambition entirely. It was whispered that Ricciardi was wealthy by birth, the owner of vast estates somewhere in the distant countryside, and that he therefore aspired to no increase in salary. The only thing that seemed to attract his interest was investigation itself.

Not that he ever showed signs of satisfaction, once he finally laid hands on the guilty party. He limited his reaction to a steady glance from those unsettling clear eyes, then turned his back and moved on. To another murder. Hunting new blood.

Ricciardi always came into the office early, even when he was working a Sunday shift. On his long walk from Via Santa Teresa to the end of the Via Toledo, he met fewer people when he walked early, and he didn't mind that a bit; the city slowly awakening from slumber, the occasional fruit vendor or milkman strolling bandy-legged up the hills, the morning songs of the washerwomen gathered around hidden fountains in the working-class quarters through which he walked. In this brutal August—more than two months since the last drop of rain—it was a way of enjoying the last trace of evening coolness that made the walk pleasurable.

In the dim light of the half-closed shutters, sitting at his desk, the commissario gathered his thoughts for the day. Mechanical gestures, bureaucratic details, reports to compile, the roll call of attendance: very few people present that day. The piazza beneath his window was still deserted. A drunk sang raucously: somebody else working the Sunday shift, thought Ricciardi.

He'd left his office door ajar, to create some minimal cross breeze. Blades of light played on the wall, underneath the official portraits of the midget king and the oversized head of state. A seagull sang counterpoint to the drunken melody from below, and Ricciardi decided that of the two, the bird had a better sense of pitch and melody. He idly glanced through the narrow opening of the half-open door, looking down the hallway to the stairs, as far as he could see.

Even in the dim light the two corpses were clear to his eyes. They stood side-by-side, joined for eternity after their ever-so-brief meeting while still alive. A monument to cops and robbers everywhere, thought Ricciardi. But a monument invisible to almost everyone.

From where he sat, a dozen yards away, the commissario could see the broad scorched cavity carved into the side of the robber's head and the tiny entry wound that the same bullet had made in the cop's forehead, the rivulet of blood and gray matter that oozed down his neck; and he could hear the subdued murmuring of both men's last thoughts. The two of you don't work shifts at all, he thought with hatred. You're here every goddamned day, poisoning the air with the useless sorrow of your wasted young lives.

He tore his eyes away and stood up from his chair; the heat was growing more intense by the minute, and out on the street he could hear the occasional engine roaring past, heading downhill to the waterfront. He went over to the calendar and tore off the previous day's sheet. He read the new date: Sunday, August 23, 1931—IX. Year Nine. Of the New Era. The era of black ribbons on hats and high black boots, the era of full-page newspaper photographs of men in shirtsleeves, guiding a plow. The era of enthusiasm and optimism. The era of law and order and clean cities, by government decree.

If only a decree were enough, thought Ricciardi. The world keeps spinning the way it always has, since long before Year One, unfortunately: the same murders, the same corrupt passions. The same blood.

He shot one last look down the hallway, listening to the murmuring thoughts of the dead. He went to shut the door, as if that would be enough to fence his soul off to those emotions, as if he were hearing those words with his ears, not his heart. Before tossing it into the waste bin he once again read the date on the sheet torn off the wall calendar: Year Nine. Yet it's been twenty-five years for me, since my first scorching August. Twenty-five years today, to be exact.

The Baroness Marta Ricciardi di Malomonte was a petite, elegant, quiet woman. In the small town in the Cilento region that was overlooked by the ancient castle, everyone loved her—but from a distance; there was something strange and remote about those beautiful sad green eyes. Something unsettling.

Fate had not been especially kind to the baron's child bride; her husband, so much older than her, had died when little Luigi Alfredo was only three years old. She had chosen not to go back to the city and instead led a life of active involvement in the village, aiding the poorest families and teaching the little children to read and write so that they might be good company for her son, who was so very like her. But social distance is hardly a promising foundation for friendship; indeed, Luigi Alfredo chose to spend his time with Rosa, the *tata* who had been with his family since she was a little girl, and with Mario the overseer, a young man who was a passionate reader of Salgari's adventure novels and who told the young boy stories of tigers and warriors. The child was a daydreamer and he liked to reenact the stories he'd heard as he played in the castle gardens; surrounded by imaginary comrades and enemies, he battled loneliness with his imagination, brandishing the wooden sword that Mario had made for him by nailing together two sections of board in the shape of a cross.

Luigi Alfredo's world was an equal blend of reality and imagination; he used reality to fuel his imagination, selecting the most intriguing and fascinating details and inventing new adventures based on them, to while away his long, solitary afternoons. His mother and the help were used to hearing him murmur in the garden, urging invisible troops into battle and beheading sea monsters with a single blow; it fell to a grumbling Rosa each night to treat skinned knees and mend ripped shirts before giving him a rough but consoling hug good night.

But one day the boy ran into the house screaming, in tears, and told his mother and Rosa that he had seen a dead man who spoke to him. The *tata* had soothed him and that night she'd grimly questioned the housemaids to find out which of them had been stupid enough to tell the child about the murder of the hired laborer, the one who had been stabbed to death in a jealous vendetta the previous winter. The women all protested, swearing that they had never spoken in the presence of young Master Luigi Alfredo about "the Deed." The boy, who was eavesdropping as usual outside the ground floor window, would later use that term, "the Deed," to describe the second sight that he possessed, the ability to feel the pain and grief hovering in the air in the aftermath of a violent death. And to see its source.

He had almost forgotten about that encounter, one August morning when his mother told him to get dressed so that they could go out for a walk; he was six years old and time spent with her was the greatest source of pleasure in his life, even though she didn't have Mario's gift for telling wonderful stories, nor did she envelop him in rough hugs the way Rosa did. She would look at him with her large green eyes, smile at him with gentle sadness, and caress his forehead, brushing aside the rebellious lock of hair. That was more than enough. That day, however, his mother's expression was different, tense and distant. Luigi Alfredo decided that she must not feel well, perhaps one of her headaches.

They had walked together along the road that led out of town. Now, all these many years later, Ricciardi could still remember the suffocating heat and the smells of manure and farmland, as they strolled along, leaving the last few houses behind them. He'd asked his mother where they were going, but she had squeezed his hand in hers and said nothing. The boy didn't sweat much but still the heat drained his strength; he was thirsty and eager to stop walking. But the woman continued along the road. They'd been walking for close to an hour when they reached a house that seemed abandoned. There was a wooden gate hanging askew on its hinges, while weeds and stubble covered what had once been a little lane. From the branch of a great tree, in the center of the courtyard, dangled a rope with a plank, an old swing, now broken. His mother stopped a few yards short of the tree; she looked around her, her brow furrowed, hesitating. The broad brim of her white hat concealed her expression, but Luigi Alfredo could sense her uneasiness. Behind the trunk of the tree, he glimpsed a little girl more or less his age; he hadn't seen her before because she was standing in the shadows, he supposed. He walked toward her with a smile on his face and asked:

"Do you want to play with me?"

His mother, startled, raised one hand to her mouth. The little girl was pale, her dirt-encrusted hair hung loose over a dress made of rough gray homespun. In his memory, Ricciardi could still see her, as real as the portrait of Mussolini hanging on the wall. The front of her dress was some other color, black, it seemed. Luigi Alfredo walked over to her, and looked more closely: the little girl's belly had been torn open by a spray of buckshot fired at point-blank range. Her ribs jutted white from the mess of burnt and ravaged flesh. Staring at him with dead eyes she said:

"*Mamma, run come see, someone's knocked down the front gate, run come see!*"

Luigi Alfredo took a step backward, astonished. He turned to look at his mother, pointing the little girl out to her.

"Mamma, help her! Can't you hear what she's saying?"

Marta didn't move; she stood there like a statue carved in stone. She looked toward the tree and Ricciardi realized that she couldn't see the child, though she certainly sensed something. So he headed toward the house: he'd go himself to summon the little girl's mamma. He'd only gone a short distance when he saw a boy, sitting next to a large stone. At first he thought the boy was asleep, but as he got closer he realized that something was gurgling out of his mouth, like water. He drew closer still until he was able to make out individual words:

"*Papa, Papa, the brigands, the brigands have come!*"

From a gaping wound in the boy's throat a bubbling black liquid came pouring forth, unstoppable. Luigi Alfredo, without realizing what he was doing, began to cry. A dull and fathomless sense of grief swept over him, surging intermittently like the boy's blood, and with every gush he felt filthier and more desperate. From far away he reached out his hand toward his mother, who was still standing motionless next to the tree with a broken swing, her hand covering her mouth. He took a few steps toward the house. At the threshold of the door a kneeling woman, almost hidden by the shadowy interior, was stretching her hand toward the courtyard.

"*Lucia, Gaeta', run!*"

From throat to belly, the woman's body was ravaged with knife wounds; her tattered dress left the dozens of cuts that had been inflicted upon her open to view. A large puddle of blood was spreading across the ground between her legs. Behind her the little boy glimpsed a man, and he too was on his knees; half of his face was gone, eradicated by a close-range shotgun blast. The other half was the very picture of terror. From the one staring eye flowed tears, from the mouth twisted into a grimace poured an incessant mumbling:

"*Have pity, have pity, take anything you want, take the girl and the boy, have pity . . .*"

Luigi Alfredo felt a hand clutching his shoulder and he screamed: it was his mother dragging him away.

He looked at her and saw that she, like him, was crying.

"What did you see? How many, how many of them did you see?"

The boy held up his hand with four fingers extended. He'd never forget the words his mother spoke.

"All of them, then. You see them all. You're cursed, my poor little boy. Cursed."

The same suffocating heat enveloped Ricciardi twenty-five years later, in his office in police headquarters. A cop, he thought. And what else could I have done for a living? Infected by pain and grief, lost in the corruption of rotting passions, what other kind of work could I have done? And work that, perhaps, does no good at all, except to put a belated patch on all that suffering.

He had scrupulously kept himself at a safe distance from all passion. He'd walled emotions out of his life, keenly aware as he was of how love could destroy and corrupt. Every grave in every cemetery is full of love, he thought. And so the best thing to do is to remain alone and observe love from a distance; as far away as possible.

And yet for the past few months this distance had been growing narrower, in a worrisome and unexpected fashion. Ricciardi threw open the shutters and let in the sun; the first shaft of light illuminated the heap of documents on his desk, waiting to be filled out. With a sigh, he began writing. Better to work: God bless the Sunday shift.

III

God damn the Sunday shift, thought Brigadier Raffaele Maione with a snort of annoyance as he headed downhill from Piazza Concordia toward police headquarters. The heat was already hellish, and it was only eight in the morning. God damn the summer, too.

The brigadier was furious, and he really shouldn't have been. But he decided that he had perfectly good reasons. Actually, he was having a good moment, the best in the three years since a thief had stabbed his son Luca to death. This horrible event had not only broken his heart, it had also driven a wedge into his family, separating his wife from him and the other children, and leaving her closed up in a silent, inconsolable grief.

Until the miracle happened that spring, just when he was beginning to despair of ever seeing her enchanting smile again. Man and wife had come together, united again the way they had been so long before, and at age fifty Raffaele had been given another unhoped-for chance at happiness. Once again, the Maione household rang with the bright laughter of mother and children, once again the father good-naturedly allowed himself to be mocked and ridiculed; once again on Sundays Lucia's legendary spaghetti sauce opened stomachs and hearts to optimism. And so, why was the brigadier striding off with a grim expression of discontent toward his Sunday shift? And above all, why had he intentionally accepted that shift, swapping with a colleague who could hardly believe his ears when Maione proposed the trade?

This is how it happened: a week ago Raffaele had gone out for a stroll, arm in arm with his pretty wife, their five children trailing after them. Just a short distance from their front door they had walked past the shop of Ciruzzo Di Stasio, vendor of fresh fruit and vegetables, one of the brigadier's old school-mates and longtime official purveyor to the Maione family. The man had stepped forward, doffed his cap, and had proffered a gallant compliment to Maione's wife:

"Donna Luci', you're simply enchanting. There is gold in your hair and your eyes are the color of seawater. One of these days I'm going to write you a song, you know how much I love to sing. But what are you doing with this burly bear, is what I'd like to know?" And he'd reached out to give an affectionate pat to the jacket of the police uniform, comfortably stretched over the prominent belly.

Lucia had laughed and thanked him. Maione however was hurt, and a stab of jealousy had pierced his heart. He preferred not to show it however, swallowing bitter gall when Lucia commented that Ciruzzo too was holding up well, still thin as a nail at age fifty. Maione, who weighed a corpulent 265 pounds, now felt even worse; actually Lucia's comment was due only to her concern for her husband's health. His father, after all, had had the same physique and had died a young man, of a heart attack.

And so it was that, from that day forward, every time he took a bite of food, his mind ran to Ciruzzo and Lucia, which put him in a bad mood. And so he decided to lose weight, and right away; he'd teach that oaf of a grocer to court his wife; he'd show him who was still the luckiest husband in the Spanish Quarter. So there he was now, cursing under his breath and going into the office on a Sunday for a reason he would never have confessed, not even under torture: to avoid eating Lucia's wonderful spaghetti sauce.

From behind the shutters, already half-shut to ward off the ferocious sun, Lucia was watching her husband leave for the police station. On Sunday. Just when she'd finished cooking the finest pot of beef ragu in the city: nine pieces of meat, nine different varieties, sautéed in lard and then left to simmer for a whole day in tomatoes, onions, and red wine. This was impossible, she knew her husband too well. He'd never give up his ragu. There could be only one explanation: Raffaele had another woman on his mind.

That was the only possible explanation for the silences and unhappiness of the past few days, ever since they'd gone out for that stroll with the children; it was unmistakable, he'd met another woman and it had altered his mood.

Stirring the terra-cotta pot with her wooden spoon, she remembered that her mother used to tell her that the cook's mood altered the food that she prepared: to cook well, you had to be happy. This ragu would no doubt be bitter as wormwood, she decided.

A sharp stabbing pain in her chest: jealousy. She was not going to let destiny deprive her of someone that she loved so dearly. Biting her lip, Lucia walked away from the window.

Enrica Colombo liked to wake up early on Sundays, so she had plenty of time to prepare the midday meal while the rest of her family lazed away in bed, taking advantage of the fact that it was a holiday. Her methodical personality required order, and order required time. She laid out on the table all of the ingredients for her ragu, and wondered what her parents and her brothers and sisters would have thought if she suddenly burst into song. Certainly not because of the dawning Sunday—considering the heat, already blistering in the early morning—nor because of the family stroll that would come later in the Villa Nazionale, with the traditional purchase of peanuts for the little ones by her father. There was another reason entirely.

Enrica was twenty-four years old and she'd never had a boyfriend. You couldn't call her beautiful, but you couldn't call her homely either, because she possessed an utterly feminine grace and kindness as well as fine delicate features. A little too tall, perhaps, and reluctant to open up to strangers; from behind her tortoiseshell rimmed glasses, her eyes were perfectly capable of chilling the ardor of anyone ill advised enough to try to bridge the distance that she put between herself and outsiders. This attitude was a source of great concern to her parents, who were afraid their firstborn might be looking at a future as an old maid; after all, her younger sister had already been married for two years, while she seemed unwilling even to meet anyone. She'd had her suitors, but she'd discouraged them all, turning down invitations courteously but firmly.

Truth be told, Enrica was not indifferent to the subject. Quite simply, she was waiting. She was waiting for the man she had slowly fallen in love with over long blustery winter evenings and then during the sweet mild flower-scented nights of springtime, to finally step forward in some fashion.

After waiting for a year, she'd had an opportunity to speak to him. The occasion was hardly what she'd been dreaming of: she'd learned that the man of her dreams was a commissario in the police department, a discovery that had come when he'd questioned her about the murder of a certain fortune-teller she'd been to see a couple of times. The interview hadn't been particularly friendly,—he sat there in silence and she was furious at how unprepared she'd been for the meeting;—but at least the ice had been broken and now, in the evening, when she sat stitching her embroidery by the kitchen window, she'd tilt her head ever so slightly in his direction, and in return she'd receive a hesitant wave of the hand from him. It might not seem like much, but to her it was a great deal.

Now she had to wait for Commissario Luigi Alfredo Ricciardi, for that was his name, to find a way to be introduced to her father and ask his permission to pay a call on her. That, too, might take time, but she was certain that he'd manage it; because otherwise why would he come to his window, every night between nine and nine thirty, to watch her embroider? It was only a matter of time.

Enrica Colombo had a quiet, determined personality. And she knew how to wait.

Livia Vezzi, née Lucani, and now widowed, believed that she'd waited long enough. That was why she was now sitting in the central Rome train station waiting for the *direttissimo* to Naples, where she planned to take an extended holiday. The choice of destination was no accident, of course; and of course it had caused concern and worry among her friends and relatives, becoming a topic for the gossips who inhabited the high society of Italy's capital.

Livia Vezzi was in fact a prominent personality: she was beautiful, dark, and feline, her buxom figure and symmetrical features embellished by a dimple in her chin and a dazzling smile. Moreover, she had been married to the nation's most famous tenor, Arnaldo Vezzi, an absolute genius, the leading man in the society pages for a decade; she herself had been an opera singer, endowed with a lovely contralto voice. Her promising career had been interrupted by marriage. Her husband had had plenty of lovers before being murdered in his dressing room at the Teatro San Carlo in Naples, just four months ago; and Livia, too, had had fleeting affairs that had left her untouched except perhaps for a deepening of her loneliness. As for her marriage, Livia couldn't remember it ever being a happy one.

When she was left a widow, there were plenty of men who stepped forward; her beauty aside, she possessed an attractive position in society, and plenty of money, too. There weren't many women who could boast among their friendships the daughter of the Duce, and she was invariably invited whenever *he* entertained. But she didn't seem interested in new relationships; she showed the world a calm and smiling face but kept everyone at arm's length. It was said that she had other things on her mind.

Putting on a show of indifference to the two men who were trying to strike up a conversation in the train station waiting room, the woman admitted to herself that what they said was true: she had other things on her mind. What she had on her mind was a pair of extraordinary green eyes, whose gaze she had met at an absolutely inappropriate moment, during the investigation into her husband's murder.

A pair of eyes that had remained indifferent to her allure, which was something she was unaccustomed to; and yet it was no mere whim that had led her to take a train back to the city of blinding lights and deep dark shadows. She'd told her girlfriends, who were eager to determine whether there was a love story behind her apparently macabre decision to return for a holiday right in the city where her husband had been murdered, that her decision was an attempt to exorcize that ghost, once and for all. The truth, however, was that she wanted to understand what lay beneath her uneasy dreams. And if she wanted to understand, she'd have to see those eyes again.

As she watched the *direttissimo* come puffing into the station, offering a smile to the two men who'd offered to carry her luggage, she decided that she'd waited long enough to understand this thing about herself.

Perhaps she'd waited too long.

IV

The door of Ricciardi's office swung open and the broad sweaty face of Brigadier Maione appeared.

"Commissa', *buon giorno,* and good Sunday to you. You too among the lucky few working today?"

Ricciardi gave him a half-smile.

"Ciao, Maione. Come in, come right in. How is the day shaping up?"

Maione walked in, mopping his brow with his handkerchief, and dropped into a chair.

"Just like yesterday, Commissa'. Hot, a scorcher. It's still early morning and already you can hardly breathe, and personally I had a lovely night, tossing and turning in my bed like a cutlet being braised. At a certain point, I had to sit down out on the balcony so I could get a breath of air: no matter what I tried, I was awake, and awake I remained. Can you believe it, Commissa'? I couldn't wait for morning to come so I could get up and come into the office."

Ricciardi shook his head.

"I don't understand what makes you do it, coming in on a Sunday. You have a lovely family, and for all I know your wife even made ragu today. Shouldn't you be at home with your children?"

Maione's face tightened into a grimace.

"Let's not start talking about food, Dotto'. I've decided that I absolutely have to lose weight: the jacket on my summer uniform won't button and, as you can see, I've had to put on my winter jacket and I'm about to faint from the heat. If you want to know the truth, it's precisely because Lucia made ragu that I've decided to take the Sunday shift, otherwise, I know myself, I wouldn't be able to resist, I'd gobble down three bowls. No, no: better if I stay here. After all, it ought to be a quiet day, don't you think? Who's going to have the energy to start trouble in this heat?"

Ricciardi had stood up from his desk and was looking out the window with both hands in his pockets.

"I don't know about that. You can never say. You see, people are strange: their passions gain energy at the most unexpected times. The heat makes them lose their minds, makes them intolerant; things you'd put up with in the winter or spring irritate you in the summer. Believe me, the craziest things happen in this season."

Maione gazed tenderly at Ricciardi's back. He was the only one in police headquarters and, he suspected, in the whole city to be fond of the commissario. He liked the way that Ricciardi took the grief and pain of the victims and their families as his own, but also the way that he could understand, if not justify, the motives behind certain murders, comprehending the emotional turmoil of the guilty parties as well.

There were times when he'd also worried about the commissario's loneliness and the suffering that he could sense formed a permanent background to his life. He'd even talked about it with Lucia who'd said, with an enigmatic smile, that every type of fruit ripens in its own season. Who knows what she had meant by that.

Well, one thing is certain, he thought to himself, you could say anything about Ricciardi except that he was an optimist.

"Well, what can I tell you, Commissa': let's just hope that no one gets worked up today. Let's hope that instead of killing each other or beating each other up they just go for a nice dip in the sea at Mergellina, and they enjoy a nice bowl of pasta—

damn them because they can eat pasta and I can't—and then fall asleep in the bright sunshine. And that they leave us in peace, the few of us that are in here dripping sweat."

He hadn't finished the sentence when there came a knock at the door. Through the half-open door, the hawk nose of Ardisio, the policeman manning the switchboard, appeared.

"Commissario, Brigadie', forgive me. A call has come in from Santa Maria La Nova, someone's found a corpse."

Maione got up from his chair with a look of misery on his face.

"And just once, they could've let us be. Of course, Commissa', if someone actually decides to invite trouble in . . ."

Ricciardi had already thrown on his jacket.

"Don't try to be funny, and let's do our best not to be superstitious, at least in here. Ardisio, send for a photographer and the medical examiner, see if Dr. Modo's in, give him the address, and ask him to join us there. You, Maione, get a couple of uniformed men: who's on duty?"

The sun was high in the sky by now, and it was taking no prisoners. The part of the piazza in front of City Hall not shaded by the crowns of the holm oaks was deserted, except for the occasional automobile which drove through without stopping. The few pedestrians sought the shade of the taller buildings, such as the Teatro Mercadante or the Hotel de Londres, even if it meant walking an extra two hundred yards. No noise came from the port, either, except for the quiet lapping of the waves.

The mobile squad usually moved on foot, given the chronic shortage of motorized vehicles. But their destination wasn't far away and by now, according to the information taken down by Ardisio over the telephone, whatever may have happened was over—there was no longer anything to put a stop to. Ricciardi knew perfectly well that without being there himself there wasn't much hope of keeping the crime scene intact; in a city where everyone spent their lives peering into other people's business, no one would admit to having seen a thing, but they'd all do their best to help by moving objects, gathering evidence, and fiddling with corpses. So they might as well arrive with calm deliberation and in considerable force, to gather as much information as possible according to the particular procedure required by Ricciardi.

To reach Piazza Santa Maria La Nova they had to take Via Emanuele Filiberto di Savoia, which the populace who never read the marble plaques bearing the street names continued to call Via Medina, the name it had had for centuries. The shaded part of the street ran alongside ancient and aristocratic palazzi, behind which unfolded a tangle of narrow alleys running down to the waterfront. The population of these lanes, which were dark even in broad daylight, was ignored by the census takers, didn't know how to read and write, and lived like so many mice, according to codes unknown to the law.

As the team led by Ricciardi and consisting of a huffing and puffing Maione and the two uniformed cops, Camarda and Cesarano, moved slowly by, you could see shadows moving frantically in the narrow passageways between the buildings to conceal whatever business they had in hand.

The other side of the street, in the harsh bright wash of sunlight, was deserted. Or almost. Ricciardi saw the image of a dead man standing outside a large street door. He remembered the case: the corpse had been found one morning a few months back, beaten to death by fists and feet and some blunt object, perhaps a club. The killer, or more likely, the killers, had worked the victim over for a long time. Incredibly, though perhaps it wasn't all that unbelievable given the times they lived in, the family hadn't filed a criminal complaint, claiming that the man had simply fallen down; as if it were possible to fall from a standing position and split your forehead open like a watermelon. But, as the deputy chief of police had commented as he signed the order for the police to drop the case, if two family members, a brother and a cousin, were both present and gave eyewitness testimony to that effect, there was little point to investigating further. Cimmino, Ricciardi's senior colleague who was assigned to the case, had been happy to go along with Dottor Garzo's instructions, both to please his boss and because the dead man, who was unemployed, also had a reputation as an anti-Fascist activist.

Now, as he walked hastily through a veil of heat that made the façades of the buildings shimmer, Ricciardi saw the man standing motionless, vivid, his face swollen with bruises, his shattered forehead dripping blood into his eyes, his teeth broken. From his mouth, a black gash in the middle of his face, came an infinite litany, an endless repetition of a single phrase, surprisingly clear:

"Buffoonish clowns, you're nothing but four buffoonish clowns. Four to one, for shame, for shame, you buffoonish clowns."

They reached their destination just as the church bells were summoning the faithful to the nine o'clock mass. The little piazza still showed the signs of the festivities that had taken place there the night before, with a heap of burned wood in the center of the square and crumpled paper littering every corner. Ricciardi shot Maione a quizzical glance, and he explained:

"It was the festa of Santa Maria Regina, Commissa'. It's a tradition, this is the month for the festas. Look at that, all the brown paper cones, what those scoundrels must have gobbled up last night!"

Directly across from the church was the front door of an ancient aristocratic palazzo. It was obvious that the crime had taken place there: if nothing else, from the small murmuring crowd that had gathered there awaiting news, as was customary. The church bell went on ringing but no one was moving off to mass. Mass, after all, was said every Sunday, while a murder was much rarer. Perhaps.

The arrival of the police sent a shiver of discomfort and curiosity through the mass of people; everyone wanted to see what would happen, and everyone had something to hide. Maione went first, pushing his way roughly through the crowd.

The front door stood slightly ajar. On the threshold, screening the interior from intrusive eyes, stood a little man in livery. As soon as he saw Maione coming, he greeted him with relief.

"At last, at last, please, come right in, this is where the horrible thing happened."

His voice was shrill, almost feminine; from the midst of the crowd a young man imitated it mockingly and here and there people laughed. The man seemed not to notice: from under his oversized hat, which settled down around the crown of his head until it rested on the base of his nose, he was sweating profusely. He looked upset. Maione asked him:

"And who are you?"

The man stood to attention and snapped a salute that in any other context would have been comical.

"Giuseppe Sciarra, at your service, Brigadie', building doorman, in the employ of their graces, the Duke and Duchess of Musso di Camparino."

The effect of the pompous introduction was spoiled by the ridiculous high-pitched voice, once again promptly mocked by the anonymous comedian in the crowd who set off another round of laughter, this time more widespread. Maione spun around with an angry glare:

"So we think it's funny, eh? Then let's see who wants to come down to police headquarters and do their laughing there. Camarda, take some first and last names in that crowd, I'm really feeling like having a laugh myself. And I laugh hardest when I see someone crying."

A worried silence fell and a few people backed away. Ricciardi spoke to the little man.

"I'm Commissario Ricciardi. Let us through."

Sciarra doffed his hat, uncovering a thinning head of hair and to some extent emphasizing the prominence of the nose that practically filled his face.

"Come right in, Commissa', if you please; in the courtyard you'll find my wife, the maid, and the housekeeper, and they'll show you to the place where . . . where it happened, that is. I'll stay here and make sure no one gets in."

But Ricciardi wanted to have everyone present who might be able to provide information.

"No, I'd like to have you accompany us, actually. Don't worry, the policemen will stay here, by the front door."

The little man made a face; he would gladly have skipped the chance to return to what must have been an awful sight.

"At your orders, Commissa'. If you please, I'll lead the way."

V

Water. With this horrible heat the plants need lots of water. All of a year's work, all the tender care and hard work can be wiped out if you forget to make sure they have plenty of water in these pitiless days. The sun, such a necessary ally in other seasons, becomes your worst enemy: it sucks the life out of the leaves, just as it does out of the muscles of human beings.

And you, my sweet little friends, can't cry out for help: if it weren't for me, you'd die, singed, desiccated, your branches extending toward the heavens and begging for a refreshing drop of rain. It's been seventy-six days today since it last rained. Seventy-six days that your lives have been in my hands: leaf by leaf, bud by bud.

I am the one who waters you, and I water you in the morning, before the sun gets too high and starts ranging across the terrace in search of damp spots to bake dry. I wish I could sleep, or even lie sprawled out in my bed, eyes wide open, thinking. Remembering. Planning things that may prove impossible. But I love you, my dear silent friends, and love, as everyone knows, means sacrifice. So I get out of bed, I get the bucket, and with trip after trip down to the fountain, I give you the gift of another day of life. None of you can move, your place is here on this terrace. And I who can move, I take life and give it to you.

It's wonderful to see the way you thank me, with new scents and new flowers. And you give life yourselves, just listen to the insects, the festival of buzzing in the air. This is the miracle, life as it multiplies, dividing itself into a thousand parts. Every one of them in its place, every one of them playing its part.

It's a marvelous thing to be able to give life. You become God. And you're God when you take life, too.

Ricciardi and Maione, after giving orders to Camarda and Cesarano not to let anyone in or out through the street door, followed the tiny doorman into the courtyard. Along with his diminutive stature, shrill voice, and enormous nose, the way the man walked was ridiculous too: he took short, bouncy steps, like a series of halfhearted leaps; his oversized uniform billowed on his back and with every movement his hat slipped to one side or another, only to be straightened with both hands, the tips of his fingers protruding from too-long sleeves.

The courtyard was hardly as vast as those that Ricciardi had seen in other aristocratic palazzi; then he realized that the space was restricted by a huge flower bed in the middle of it, planted with hydrangeas. Noticing that the policemen were admiring the flowers, Sciarra said without slowing his pace:

"The flowers, eh? He's obsessed, the son of the duke . . . that is, the young master is quite fond of them, he insists that we have flowers all year round."

Ricciardi took a look around, making a mental note to undertake a more thorough examination of the place later, and noticed four large columns, one at each corner of the court-yard. Quite handy, in a pinch they could offer shade and shelter. To an overheated tradesman, for instance. Or to a murderer.

On a line with the street door, but at the far side of the courtyard, a broad staircase led upstairs. Just inside the entrance, on the right, was a little doorless room containing a small table and a chair. Maione spoke to the doorman:

"Is that where you sit, when you're on duty?"

"Yessir, Brigadie', exactly so. Whenever the street door is open, I sit there without fail."

At the foot of the staircase two women were walking toward them; one was enormous, both tall and broad, with a white apron over a light blue smock, hair tied up into a bun behind her head. Her face was pale, with a patch of red on her neck, and she was wringing her hands; there was no mistaking the fact that she was overwrought. The other one, younger, was skinny and angular, and she wore the black work dress of a scullery maid; she was sobbing, dabbing constantly at her eyes with a filthy handkerchief.

"This is Signora Concetta, the housekeeper," said Sciarra, making the introduction by extending his dangling sleeve in the direction of the huge woman; "and this is my wife Mariuccia, who cleans house."

Maione touched his visor.

"Brigadier Maione, from police headquarters. Commissario Ricciardi, commander of the mobile squad. Concetta: and your last name would be?"

The big woman replied in a whisper. She had been instructed always to speak in a low voice in the palazzo and, overwrought though she might be, she could hardly break the habit.

"Concetta Sivo, at your service. As Peppino just told you, I'm the housekeeper here in the palazzo. Her grace the duchess . . . I was the one who found her, that is, who saw the deed that had been done. The horrible thing."

At the housekeeper's words, the maid burst into another series of hiccuping sobs. Her husband touched her arm, as if to support her. Ricciardi broke in.

"I'll need all three of you to remain on call, make sure none of you leaves the palazzo for any reason whatever. By the way, are there any other exits besides the street door? Tradesmen's doors, cellars, any other points of egress, in other words."

"No, no, Commissa', no other exit. You either leave by the

main door or inside you remain. Unless you jump out a window, but the lowest one must be twenty feet off the ground."

Ricciardi raised his eyes, and as he looked up the stairs, he sighed imperceptibly.

"Well, let's go up. Signora Sivo, show us what you found."

The jasmine hedge is a wonderful thing in the summer. It's not just the perfume, though I could never tire of inhaling it, sweet and light as it is, a smell that stays in your nose for an hour after you've left. It's the color, that dark green punctuated with white, the little pointed leaves. I like the fact that it's thick, I like that it covers the terrace from view, that it ensures that from the outside world, even from the bell tower of the church across the way, the picture of this house is one of greenery and flowers. That everyone may think it's a beautiful place. A place without sorrow. That no one may know that this is a place filled with death.

After the first flight of stairs, there was a gate on the right enclosing the entrance to the main floor, and behind it could be seen the open door. The gate swung ajar, and from one of its bars hung a heavy chain, with a padlock fastened shut at one end.

On the left, the staircase continued upward. Ricciardi asked: "Where does it lead, this staircase? What's upstairs?"

The housekeeper replied under her breath:

"First there are our bedrooms, mine, then the doorman's and the maid's with their children, four little ones. Then above that is the apartment of the young master, the son of the duke."

"Then who lives on this floor?"

"Only the duke and the duchess live here. The duke is bedridden, he's very sick. His bedroom is at the far end of the palazzo, all the way down, while the duchess's bedroom is on this side."

There was shade on the landing but the heat was intense all the same. The bells had finally stopped ringing; the silence was now broken only by a woman's voice, singing somewhere in the distance. Ricciardi asked:

"Where did you find the dead body?"

At the sound of the words "dead body" Sciarra's wife sobbed even louder into her handkerchief. Her husband gripped her shoulder with one hand, his hat askew over his forehead. The housekeeper replied:

"Right here, in the first room. The anteroom, really. On the little sofa."

"Have you touched anything? Is it all just as you found it?"

The woman furrowed her brow.

"No, I don't think I did. That is, I touched the duchess, I called her. Then I called Mariuccia, and Mariuccia called Peppino. We tried to wake her up, then we saw . . . we realized . . . well, now you just come in and you'll see what we saw."

Ricciardi looked toward the half-open door. It was one thing to run into the Deed by chance, while walking down the street or by happening to pass by the site of an accident; it was quite another matter to go looking for it intentionally. This was the real sacrifice that he made: choosing to take onto himself all that pain and grief, allowing the last terrible shudder of departing life to coil around him and through him like a bloody mist.

He nodded to Maione; the brigadier was accustomed to the commissario's working methods, which never varied. He'd enter the scene of the murder alone, he'd stay there for a few minutes, and then he'd emerge. Simple. As for Maione, he needed only to guard the door, and make sure that no one else came into the room.

He'd never be willing to be the first to enter the scene of a murder with the commissario; nothing on earth could persuade him to do it. Maione might be a big, strong brigadier who wasn't afraid of a thing, and he might be fond of his superior officer, but he'd never have the guts. And that was that.

At the far end of the hall, stretched out in the bed where he'd certainly die before long, Matteo Musso, Duke of Camparino, listened to the silence that was broken only by the rattle of his breathing. It wasn't normal for there to be all this peace and quiet, not on a Sunday. From the tightly fastened shutters, he should have heard the laughter of the children playing in the piazza, the chattering of the housewives emerging from mass, the shouts of the strolling vendors selling *spasso*, the blend of walnuts, hazelnuts, and lupini beans that would brighten the dining room tables after Sunday lunch.

In short, he ought to be hearing the sounds of life. The same life that was abandoning him now. Instead: all this silence.

And solitude, of course. But that he was used to. Aside from the nurse who came twice a day, to give him those useless injections: as if you could stop death, instead of just putting off its arrival.

What silence, thought Matteo. The silence of death. Perhaps after all death had come to the house before its time. Perhaps it came in through another doorway: a door that no one expected.

Wheezing and gasping, the elderly duke smiled an obscene smile.

VI

Behind the door was a proper room, not at all the ante-room that the housekeeper had described. It was swathed in dim light, the shutters pulled to, as if to let a sleeper sleep, but the figure that he glimpsed on the sofa wasn't sleeping.

Ricciardi stepped forward, shutting the door behind him. He could make out the silhouettes of the furniture, the chairs, a writing desk. Paintings on the walls, a soft carpet underfoot. Odors. Lavender, sweet smelling, a sparkling clean house. But also the smell of cordite: gunshots had been fired in that room. Perhaps just once, the smell wasn't overpowering. And something else: blood. Clotted blood, that characteristic odor, like rusted iron.

The commissario gazed at the form of the corpse, which he'd take the time to examine more closely, later, in the light. He identified the direction of the face, well aware that the Deed would set the image in the place where the victim had last looked: this was the strange physics of his power, one of the rules established only to be broken. There was no exception to the rule that time, however: in the corner exactly opposite the couch on which the dead woman lay, perfectly visible to Ricciardi's mind's eye, in spite of the darkness, the Duchess Musso di Camparino went on repeating her last living thought.

She'd been a very beautiful woman: death could not conceal her height, her prosperous shape wrapped in a black silk nightdress. She would have been forty, more or less, but she must have carried her age with all the pride of wealth and the confidence of her resources. The image stared straight ahead, proud and motionless. Ricciardi sensed none of the most common emotions: fear, rage, horror. Instead, he sensed surprise, something approaching curiosity: the woman never thought that she was about to die, right up to the end.

Still, now she was dead; in fact, to be exact, she had been murdered. At the center of her forehead, sharp and precise, above her half-closed eyes, was a round hole: the entry wound, a bullet hole. Her face was reddened, her black tongue protruded from her lips. But her features were also fine, high cheekbones, dark eyes, a mouth with large, very white teeth.

As always, the commissario focused his attention on what the Duchess di Camparino had to tell him, the message that she was leaving; the portion of thought that death had interrupted, the snapped thread.

"The ring, the ring, you've taken the ring, the ring is missing."

Like a prayer, murmured endlessly, repeated until it could dissolve into the air along with the simulacrum of a mouth that was uttering it. A simple phrase, as clear as if it had been screamed in silence.

"The ring, the ring, you've taken the ring, the ring is missing."

Ricciardi had no need to memorize it: he'd hear those words, and the suffering that lay behind them, over again many times. Head down, he went to open the shutters and let in shafts of pitiless sunlight.

Maione had stayed outside to sweat with the Sciarras, man and wife, and the housekeeper. Two children had come laughing down the stairs, a boy and a girl, the girl brandishing two large hunks of bread. The brigadier's love of children was sorely tested by that sight. Sciarra, in a firm voice, hushed them both and halted their progress by seizing each by the nape of the neck, as if they were a couple of puppies. The little boy loudly protested:

"Papà, listen, that Lisetta took my bread, you tell her to . . ."

The doorman pried one of the hunks of bread out of his daughter's fingers and gave it to the boy. The little girl whined:

"Papà, Totonno ate my cheese, we'd made a trade and now he wants to eat the bread too!"

Sciarra smacked them both hard and threatened them: "If the two of you don't cut it out, I'll take the bread away from both of you and give it to the brigadier, here, and he'll gobble it up for himself. Now get out of here, and shut the door behind you!"

Maione inwardly prayed that they'd keep it up, and that, strictly for educational reasons, let that be clear, he'd be forced to eat both pieces of bread. Possibly, to wash them down a little bitter, dipped in a nice tomato sauce. But instead, the two children, duly frightened, shot back up the stairs, each clutching his precious chunk. The brigadier heaved a sigh.

"Sweet. Are they yours?"

"Yes, Brigadie', two scourges of God. And there are two others upstairs, an older boy and a little girl. But these two are the worst stinkers."

Mariuccia had started up the stairs after her children, but Maione had halted her with a wave of the hand.

"No, Signo', you'll have to wait here until the commissario says otherwise, and allows you to go. And while we're waiting, tell me something: just how is the duke's apartment divided up? Are there personal rooms, shared rooms, and how many?"

The housekeeper struck a stance that seemed strangely defensive to Maione.

"No, you understand, Brigadie', each of the three has his own rooms, they don't actually see each other much."

Sciarra grimaced, wrinkling his enormous nose.

"No, for that matter, they never see each other at all. The

duke stays in bed and never moves, while young master Ettore is always out on the terrace, him, the flowers, and the plants, and the duchess . . ."

Concetta blasted him with a murderous glare.

"It would be best if everyone just stayed in their place, that's what would be best. You won't learn, will you, that we're the servants and what the dukes do is none of our business."

"Why, what's the matter, Donna Conce', what have I done wrong? All I meant to say is that each of them keeps to himself, to try to answer the brigadier here—that they might have common rooms, but they weren't used."

Mariuccia broke in; she'd never stopped sniffling into her handkerchief the whole time.

"That's right, no one ever goes there, but the duchess insists that the room be kept clean and tidy, she checks, and if she ever finds anything out of place, she calls me and gives me a lecture. That is, she used to. Now, she'll never give me a lecture again . . ." and she started in again, sobbing in despair. Her husband intervened:

"Now, what a fool you are, it almost sounds like you're sorry the poor duchess can never scold you again."

Once again, Concetta thought it her duty to explain to Peppino how matters stood.

"No, you're the ones who don't understand that now, with the death of the duchess, the way this house is organized might change, and maybe there's no more need of us, and we find ourselves kicked out into the street."

Sciarra shrugged his shoulders.

"Eh, when would that ever happen? If anything, now the young master and the duke will need us more than ever. After all, who's supposed to keep all this household running, otherwise?"

Maione listened to the exchange of remarks, with apparent distraction but actually letting nothing get by him. He'd understood that in the palazzo there lived not one single family, but five different clans: the Sciarras, Concetta, and the duke, the duchess, and the young master, who had as little to do with each other as they could. He made a mental note to inform Ricciardi of the situation, just as the commissario stuck his head out the door again and told him to come in.

Now sunlight had filled the anteroom, and the temperature was rising noticeably. Ricciardi and Maione looked around at the wallpaper, the paintings, the furniture. Their expert eyes detected an abundance of silver objects, fine artwork, two Chinese vases, and an ancient bronze statuette: there had been no robbery, or if there'd been an attempt, it had been thwarted before it could be completed. Nor did they see any signs of a struggle; nothing was broken or even overturned. The only visible sign that anything had happened was a square cushion on the floor, at the corpse's feet, with a hole in the side facing up. Ricciardi didn't turn it over, because he didn't want to move a thing until the photographer got there, but he was willing to bet that on the other side there would be unmistakable burn marks on the fabric, the very same signs that had been missing on the dead woman's forehead. The murderer had fired through the cushion.

The duchess, if you didn't look at her face, might have been sleeping, languidly stretched out on the sofa, just slightly relaxed, legs extended and hands in her lap. Ricciardi drew closer and noticed that she had no rings on her left hand, though there were marks of a ring on both her middle and her ring fingers. The middle finger actually seemed broken or at least sprained, though he saw no signs of bruising. He'd have to wait for the medical examiner and the photographer, before moving the corpse; but there was no mistaking the cause of death, the bullet hole in the forehead, right between the half-open eyes.

Maione, huffing and puffing and sweatier by the minute, had squatted down by the sofa and was trying to look under it.

"Where are you, now where are you, you damned little . . . ah, there it is now. Commissa', here's the shell, it was right under the sofa, exactly where I expected it to be."

"Nice work, Raffaele. Don't touch it, though; let's wait for the photographer. And while we're waiting, why don't you call the housekeeper, let's hear what she has to say."

The Sivo woman entered the room, silent and bulky. She shot a quick glance at the duchess's dead body and quickly looked away, her face turning pale but with no change in her impassive expression. Ricciardi, standing with his hands in his pockets, watched her sweat for a long moment without speaking, seeking any other signs of discomfort, but he saw none.

"Now then, Signora. Tell me how you discovered the corpse of the duchess."

"I rise early, around six. When I don't have to go to the market or run other errands out of the house, like today, since it's a Sunday, I stay in my room for a while. I tidy up my own things, in other words. Then I go to the first mass, the seven o'clock mass."

"So this morning you left around seven, too?"

"No, this morning I wanted to look around a little. Last night, I don't know if you'd know this, but it was the Festa of Santa Maria Regina. Those people get up to everything imaginable, there's garbage scattered outside the front door, they light a bonfire in the middle of the piazza. I wanted to give Mariuccia instruction to start cleaning up a bit."

Ricciardi tried to reconstruct a time line.

"And in order to go out, you go by way of the anteroom?"

"Yes, I have to. At night, when I go to bed, I shut the padlock on the gate outside here. The Signora, who comes home late, leaves the keys on the chain in that drawer," and she pointed to a console table next to the door, "so in the morning I can open up and let Mariuccia in to start her cleaning."

"And you close the padlock with a key of your own?"

The Sivo woman shook her head.

"No, no. I don't have the keys to the lock. I snap it shut, and in the morning I take the keys from the drawer. I take a look at the room, and usually I find it's tidy and clean. But this time I found . . . I found the duchess."

"And what did you do?"

The woman's tone of voice remained subdued but her expression betrayed deep emotion.

"I thought that she'd fallen asleep on the sofa, fully dressed. It had happened before, more than once, the duchess . . . sometimes she came home tired, very tired."

Ricciardi decided to call a spade a spade.

"Do you mean drunk?"

The Sivo woman had no intention of uttering words she didn't feel authorized to use.

"I couldn't say, Commissa'. It's none of my business, and when something's none of my business, I look the other way."

Ricciardi looked her straight in the eye.

"But this time you couldn't look the other way. What did you do when you realized that the duchess wasn't sleeping?"

"I stuck my head out over the courtyard and I called Sciarra. I told him to come upstairs and stay close to the duchess, and I went up to the top floor to call young master Ettore."

Ricciardi tried to reconstruct events with as much precision as possible.

"And was the gate already open or did you open it?"

The Sivo woman seemed surprised. She furrowed her brow.

"It was open. Now that you mention it, the gate was open and the padlock was shut, the way I leave it in the daytime."

"Go on. Was the young master at home?"

"Yes, he was already out on the terrace, watering the flowers. He wakes up early too."

"What did you say to him?"

Concetta looked down.

"I told him that I thought the duchess was dead. That she had a hole in her forehead."

Ricciardi kept pushing:

"What about him, did he come downstairs with you immediately?"

After a moment's hesitation, the woman replied:

"No. He said that he's no doctor. And he went to call the police. But he didn't come downstairs."

There was a long silence. Ricciardi processed the information.

"How long have you been in service with the duke and the duchess?"

"Twenty-five years, Commissario. Ever since I was twenty-one. First as a scullery maid, then as a cook and for ten years as housekeeper, since the duchess passed away."

"What? What do you mean, since the duchess passed away?" asked Maione, staring at the corpse.

"The first duchess, I meant to say. The duke was married before, and young master Ettore was the son of his first wife, Signora Virginia. The Duchess Adriana is . . . was . . . his second wife."

Ricciardi decided to dig a little deeper. He meant to understand just what relations there were between the two women.

"So when the duke remarried you were already here. And did you get along with the duchess?"

The woman shrugged.

"The duchess was almost always out. Practically speaking, the house runs itself, there's not a lot to do. I do my work and, more importantly, I mind my own business."

Ricciardi didn't miss the implicit condemnation in the Sivo woman's reply and he made a mental note to explore this matter further.

But there was one thing he wanted to see immediately: he

went over to the console table and pulled open the drawer. And in the drawer, just where the Sivo woman had said it would be, was the key to the padlock that was used to fasten the chain on the gate to the landing.

You can see the street through a gap in the bougainvillea hedge on the south side of the terrace. I left it there intentionally, since there's no way anyone can look in from that side. And the street outside the front door is full of people. Rubberneckers, passersby. Who knows what they expect to see. Don't they already know what's happened? But as soon as one person stops, another one stops and stands next to them; in this city no one minds their own business.

I remember when I was still attending the university, four or five of us would go to the Villa Nazionale or to Via Toledo and start looking up at the sky. Two minutes later, there's be at least ten other people with their noses in the air, and no one would ever ask, "Youngsters, what are you looking at?' No one. Then, as soon as we'd had enough of that game, one of us would say: "Well, let's go now, it's clear that the flying donkey won't be coming today after all." And back home I'd tell my mamma, and she'd laugh, even through her pain.

I still see you, you know, Mamma, in your bed, smiling, because now you're too weak to laugh. I see that you don't want me to see that you're suffering, in your heart and in your soul.

Because you'd already figured out what that whore dressed as a nurse was planning to do.

But now that woman's dead, you know that, Mamma? She's dead too. And not like you, in your own bed with a rosary in your hand and with my tears. No, she died the way she deserved too. Murdered.

Like the bitch she was.

VII

By now everyone was up and about in the Colombo home, bent on creating the disorder of a typical Sunday morning. Enrica was resigned to the loss of the lovely peace and quiet she'd won by rising early; to make up for it, once breakfast was over, she'd expelled everyone from the kitchen with the excuse that she had to wash up and go on with her preparations for lunch.

As she went back and forth in the large room, every time she went by the window, she shot a fleeting glance across the street at another window. It was still Sunday, after all, and she hoped to catch him giving a chance look back at her, in broad daylight, for once; but she failed to spy the object of her interest. Instead, she saw the elderly woman who lived with him, as she was tidying up the apartment. In a strange fashion, she had learned that this was his old *tata* and not, as she had supposed for almost a year, his mother.

The one who had told Enrica was Signora Maione, the brigadier's wife; a genuine angel who had come to tell her about the commissario's introverted personality and his loneliness; and about his sadness.

Luigi Alfredo. She let the name roll off her tongue, alluring and slightly mysterious, like the man it belonged to. She uttered it to herself, at night before falling asleep or while taking a bath in the new metal tub that her father had triumphantly had delivered to the apartment. It had been Signora Maione who'd persuaded her that nothing was lost, that it was worth waiting because, certainly, even if he wouldn't admit it, he was actually interested in her.

With a smile on her face as she took the long way around, for no good reason, to reach the sink, the long way around that took her past the window, Enrica decided that it was worth waiting. For as long as it would take.

Livia decided that it wouldn't take long.

When she'd come to the city during the winter, summoned to indentify her husband's corpse, she'd been unable to book a seat on the *direttissimo* that ran on the new line via Formia, and instead she'd been obliged to take the train that followed the old line, the one that ran through Cassino. She remembered a long, exceedingly tedious journey of more than four hours, interspersed with numerous stops, level crossings, and even flocks of sheep blocking the tracks, so that the engineers and firemen had to get out and chase them off. All the same, on that occasion she'd been glad of the extra time it took; she was in no hurry to come face to face with Arnaldo, even if he was dead. The longer the trip the better.

This time, instead, she'd have flown, if she could. Since she'd made the decision to go see Ricciardi, to find out why she couldn't get him out of her mind, every day had been pure torture.

While the *direttissimo* rattled through the countryside, Livia, ignoring the conversation that was taking place in the first-class compartment, fantastized about meeting him again. The other seats in the compartment were occupied by two married couples, and the husbands were gazing at her rapturously while the wives stewed in angry silence; as far as she was concerned, they could have been dancing naked, and she wouldn't have noticed.

Out the window, blending into the sea that she could just begin to glimpse and in the shimmering heat that was suffocating her, she could only see a pair of green eyes. And she thought about what a strange thing love is.

The door swung open and in came Doctor Modo, followed by the photographer with his camera, tripod, and magnesium flashbulbs. Beneath the broad brim of his white hat, the doctor was sweating freely. Without a greeting, as if he were simply continuing a conversation begun previously, he said:

"Now, I'm not saying that there are better times or worse times to be murdered, of course not. Still, once you've made up your mind, how are we supposed to do what's necessary, on a Sunday, with a temperature of 105 degrees? I wonder if someone would be so kind as to explain that to me?"

Bruno Modo was a hospital physician, a surgeon, and, when needed, a medical examiner. He'd been an officer on the Carso front during the Great War, and he'd developed an exceptional body of experience, invaluable for police investigations; but he had no difficulty voicing his opinions and his clear anti-Fascist leanings made him a dangerous person to know. As a result, despite his outgoing personality, he had few friends. What's more, a number of officials at police headquarters avoided using his services.

Not Ricciardi—he sought Modo out whenever he needed a doctor. He had the highest opinion of the man's extraordinary expertise, and found him to be profoundly humane. Moreover, he had the gift of irony, as did Ricciardi himself; and so they had a working relationship that, while you might not call it friendship, was certainly something that verged on it. He was the only person who addressed the commissario with the informal *tu*.

"Oh, Ricciardi, and who else would it be? Tell me the truth, did you murder this lovely lady, with the sole purpose of making me sweat through my clothes and ruining my Sunday? Next time, I'd advise you to try suicide, just for something different: in that case, I'd even promise to come out and work the case free of charge."

Ricciardi shook his head.

"Ciao, Bruno, *buon giorno* to you, too. I felt sure you'd enjoy this little social occasion as a way of killing time on a boring day off. You'll certainly appreciate the Signora's company, accustomed as you are to the cheerful denizens of the morgue."

The doctor was fanning himself with his hat, and sweating profusely beneath his unkempt mop of fair hair.

"Well, at least, from the look of things, I can say that the duchess didn't leave us because she'd been beaten to death by some damned squad, like the guy we found in the Via Medina. I've drafted a forty-page report on the effects of the man's 'trip and fall,' which is the finding you all came up with at police headquarters. You're shameless, the whole lot of you. I often think life was easier in wartime."

Ricciardi protested:

"Look, they didn't even ask me to take a look at the crime scene. If they had, official complaint or no official complaint, someone would have wound up in jail. So, what do you have to say about this?"

Modo had removed his jacket and rolled up his sleeves, and now he was kneeling down by the corpse.

"Well . . . judging from appearances, I'd opt for a myocardial infarction. Or perhaps she simply died of boredom. What do you say?"

"I'd say that, to the best of my knowledge, they're looking for a new vaudeville routine at the Salone Margherita. Have you ever considered it? A new line of work might spare you the indignities of internal exile."

"Fine, fine, I'll go talk to the stage manager and see if they're looking for a duo. I always work best with a partner, and you have such an infectious laugh. Now let me do my job, please, and I'll have something for you in a couple of minutes. I've already alerted the morgue, and they're sending an ambulance; in this heat it's not advisable to leave a corpse out in the air for too long."

In the meanwhile, the photographer, sweating copiously, was punctuating the scene with flashes from all angles: the dead woman, the cushion, the door. Maione, who had stepped away to inspect the stairs, came back in.

"*Buon giorno*, Dotto', what a pleasure," he said, touching fingertips to visor.

"And here we have him, another comedian. A very good morning to you too, Brigadie'. Next time, though, perhaps we should meet at a trattoria somewhere, if you really want it to be a pleasure."

Maione sighed.

"Eh, if only we could. Now then, the courtyard offers plenty of hiding places, Commissa'. The four columns, various nooks and crannies, the doorman's booth. There's nothing wrong with the padlock, the chain wasn't tampered with: whoever opened the gate did it with the key. The stairs lead up to two other floors, which must have been installed at some later date: if you ask me, when they built this palazzo, it must have had ceilings higher than the Naples cathedral. Right above us are two doors, one of them is closed, and that must be where this famous young master lives; the other door is open, and inside are the Sciarras' children who, I hardly need tell you, are eating. And then there's a narrow little staircase that leads up to the terrace."

Ricciardi listened intently.

"And have you talked to any of the spectators, downstairs in the street? No one heard a thing, no, of course not? But we do know that someone fired at least one pistol shot."

Maione ran an already drenched handkerchief over his face.

"No, Commissa', when has anyone ever heard anything? Still, this time there's a justification, the festa was last night and they danced and sang out front until three in the morning. The main event is a tarantella that lasts for an hour, with the dancers spinning around a bonfire of old wood, you can still see the debris outside, they're cleaning up now. Can you imagine, a bonfire with this heat? People are crazy."

The photographer coughed discreetly.

"Commissario, I'm done here. I'll get you the prints tomorrow night or, at the very latest, the day after tomorrow. *Arrivederci*."

Ricciardi gave a little farewell wave and lifted the cushion. It was a foot square, fringed with gold frogging and with little tassels at the corners. Made of silk, with a floral motif, stuffed with goose down. Just as the commissario had guessed, the side that had been turned toward the floor had a vast burn mark more or less in the center, while on the other side there was a large depression matching the duchess's face, with the exit hole made by the bullet.

As he leaned forward to see more clearly, Ricciardi saw signs of moisture: saliva, perhaps a little blood as well. The pillow had been pushed down violently.

As he laid it back down onto the floor he noticed that, partially concealed by the cushion, there was also a mark on the floor. Getting down on both knees, the commissario looked closer; it seemed to be a murky stain left by a shoe, not exactly a footprint. As absurd as it might be, since it hadn't rained in forever, it might have been a mudstain left by a wet shoe: he could just glimpse minuscule fragments of gritty dirt. At the far corner of the room, at regular intervals, the dead image was repeating:

"The ring, the ring, you've taken the ring, the ring is missing."

Ricciardi spoke to Doctor Modo.

"Bruno, forgive me; could you tell me something right away about her left hand, too?"

The doctor stood up, mopping his brow with his handkerchief. His shirt, crushed to his chest by his suspenders, was drenched with sweat.

"I'm not cut out for this damned profession anymore, I'm too old. I need to do a nice calm autopsy, otherwise, I swear, I won't tell you a thing. I'm sick and tired of quick results after a hasty examination, I'm running the risk of telling you a bunch of nonsense that'll blow up in my face later, and I'll lose my reputation for infallibility."

Ricciardi shook his head.

"Well, that's something you don't have to worry about, you may not know it but everyone around here does: all you ever say is a bunch of nonsense. So a little bit more, a little bit less: go ahead and tell me some right now."

Modo smiled.

"That's what I adore about you: the way you buck up your colleagues. Well, now, here's what I'd say: pistol shot, fracture of both cranial bones, frontal and occipital, with full penetration of the brain. The bullet is right here, lodged in the backrest of the sofa. No burn marks, this shot wasn't fired point-blank, but I saw you examining the cushion, so you already figured that out. From the bleeding I can tell you that she was alive when she was shot. More than that I wouldn't venture to say without an autopsy, even under torture."

"Now just tell me about her left hand."

"The middle finger is dislocated, but there's no hematoma: it was done when she was already dead. And there's a small bruise on her ring finger, so that was when she was still alive. Maybe she died between one finger and the other. Ah, here's the ambulance from the morgue."

Ricciardi, hands in pockets, watched as the duchess left her palazzo for the last time. At least, her physical form. Behind him, her image was saying to him:

"The ring, the ring, you've taken the ring, the ring is missing."

VIII

Ricciardi insisted on leaving with Doctor Modo. That surprised Maione, who asked:

"Commissa', what's this, aren't you going to question the duke and the young master right away? If they were the only ones in the house, and they're still here, wouldn't it be best to hear what they have to say?"

His superior officer briefly shook his head, brushing the stray lock of hair from his forehead with his hand.

"No. First I need to know with some certainty what time the duchess was killed, and especially whether there are other findings from the autopsy. To question them now would only mean giving them advance warning. Anyway, you leave Camarda here, tell him to take note of who leaves the house. And to make sure that no one comes in, until ordered otherwise."

As they were leaving the palazzo, Sciarra and Sivo walked toward them, and Maione told them to make sure they could be reached and not to leave town, neither the two of them nor Sciarra's family, for any reason whatsoever. The doorman shrugged his shoulders in his enormous jacket and said:

"And where are we supposed to go? We're not going anywhere, Brigadie', you can be sure of that."

Maione conveyed the commissario's instructions to Camarda with a subtle hint of sadistic pleasure, because he found him munching on a large hunk of bread with fried zucchini. Leaving aside the stab of envy, his stomach noisily reminded him that lunchtime was long gone. Damn that fruit vendor and damn his belly.

They walked part of the way with the doctor; before he veered off toward the hospital, Modo was shaking his head.

"There's something fishy about this whole thing. What, you stick a cushion on my face, you push down on it so hard that my mouth leaves a mark, and you shoot me through it, and the whole time I obediently let you do it, without even lifting a finger? No, no: there's something fishy about it."

Maione agreed, as he huffed and puffed up the Via Diaz hill, sweat coming from his pores like water from a fountain.

"It seems strange to me too. And it also strikes me as odd that no one heard a thing; fine, there was a celebration going on, with all the noise, and the music, the shouting, whistling, and raspberries. But a gunshot is a gunshot, someone ought to have heard it at least indoors."

Ricciardi looked straight ahead, lost in thought, and, as usual, bareheaded. The few pedestrians they encountered stared at him and stepped aside in bafflement.

"Not necessarily. The bullet was fired into the cushion, and the real question is who was home at the time. Bruno, you need to let us have the results of the autopsy as soon as possible. I have a hunch that we're going to get some explanations from that."

Modo snorted theatrically.

"Well, that's a new one on me! Never once do you tell me: Doctor, take your time, there's no hurry. Enjoy your Sunday, get some rest, then tomorrow just do your job, however long it takes."

"All right, how about this: Doctor, at your leisure, let us have a nice clear report tomorrow morning, and no later."

The doctor stopped in his tracks and stared at Maione.

"Brigadie', seriously: let's join forces and kill him now. I want the pleasure of doing the autopsy myself. I'd even work Christmas Eve on that."

"No, Dotto', then what fun would it be to work on a Sunday without the commissario?"

Modo shook his head.

"Okay, I understand: everyone's conspiring against me. Anyway, I wasn't planning to make more than one visit to the whorehouse in Piazza Trieste and Trento, tonight. Just means that for once it'll be the whores who are crying."

Ricciardi waved goodbye with a quick flick of his hand.

"Crying tears of joy. You've just given me an idea: they might have murdered the duchess, if that meant being spared a visit from you. Well, until tomorrow morning, then."

Along the way, Maione informed Ricciardi of all that he'd found out by questioning the help about everyday life at the palazzo.

"The Sivo woman, Commissa', won't talk about the duke and duchess willingly. She's loyal, too many years living in that house. But it seemed to me that the key to it all is the young master; he must have had a motive for going to live all on his own in the attic, don't you think?"

"I agree: that's something we need to determine. And we also need to find out whether the duke is actually bedridden or whether, if he really needed to, he could make his way out to the anteroom."

"No, all three of them were very certain about that point, even Sciarra's wife, between one sob and the next. It's been years since the duke last walked, and in fact they're all expecting him to die any minute. But I have a piece of news for you: do you want to guess the name of the chaplain who comes to say mass at Palazzo Camparino? An old friend of ours: Don Pierino Fava, do you remember him?"

Ricciardi certainly remembered Don Pierino, the diminutive assistant pastor of the church of San Ferdinando, an opera enthusiast who had helped them to solve the murder of the tenor, Vezzi. An involuntary association made him think of Livia, the victim's beautiful widow, and he felt a surge of uneasiness and a twinge of pleasure.

"I remember him very well indeed; good, he'll be able to give us some useful information. We'll have to go call on him. And what do you have to say about the others?"

Maione mopped his face with his handkerchief for what seemed like the thousandth time.

"It's just not normal, this heat wave. Sciarra's only technically a doorman as far as I'm concerned, he strikes me as more of a Pulcinella with that enormous nose of his and that floppy outsized uniform. And then there's the voice, did you hear it? Still, he's not stupid and he can give us some information. The wife, on the other hand, what with housekeeping and children, and if you take into account the fact that she strikes me as pretty much of a dope, is not going to give us anything more than a confirmation where needed."

They'd reached police headquarters; the big street door with its shade gave at least the illusion of an oasis of cool.

"Anyway, you keep collecting information where you can find it, but be careful not to alarm anyone. You could talk to some of the people in the neighborhood. One thing you can count on is that nobody minds their own business, and that's certainly a family in the spotlight. What about that friend of yours, what's the name? The one who knows everything about everybody."

Maione's face took on a wary expression.

"What friend are you talking about, Commissa'?"

"What do you mean, what friend; or should I have called him your 'girlfriend'?"

A pained look appeared on the brigadier's face.

"Commissa', stop making fun. If you're talking about Bambinella, he's neither a friend nor a girlfriend, he's a questionable character and I don't have anything to do with him.

It's just that since, as you say, he knows everything about everyone, sometimes he can be useful, and that's all."

"And that's all I meant to say, don't you worry. He can tell us whether in certain circles anyone knows anything about that family, nothing more. See what you can find out. I'm going over to Caflisch to get something to eat, you want anything?"

Maione sighed and spread his arms.

"Not you too, Commissa'? No, thanks. I'm not hungry. This heat kills my appetite."

By the time Ricciardi got back to police headquarters the sun was already setting. Outside the door to his office he found Ponte, the deputy chief of police's doorman and clerk; a fidgety mannered little man, who couldn't manage to conceal the superstitious discomfort that the commissario stirred in him. This fear tended to translate into the unpleasant habit of darting his gaze in all directions without ever looking the person he was talking to in the eye, which annoyed Ricciardi no end.

"Commissario, *buona sera*. You were called this morning, I heard; for a murder, no?"

Looking at the door, the floor, and the ceiling.

"Ponte, you know perfectly where I was and why, there's no point in you pretending you're in the dark. I left word this morning and no one would have had any difficulty getting in contact with me all day long."

The clerk stared at the railing along the stairs.

"Of course, Commissa', you're quite right. I received a phone call from Dottor Garzo, who told me to let you know that he wants to talk to you first thing tomorrow."

Ricciardi made a face.

"Ah, exactly. A duchess is killed, and naturally gears turn at the highest level. You can tell Dottor Garzo that tomorrow morning I'll be at work, like always. And plenty of my colleagues will be at work, too, if he prefers to assign the investigation to one of them."

Ponte looked down the hallway with such intensity that Ricciardi wondered if he too could see the images of the dead cop and dead thief.

"No, what are you saying, Commissario, that would never even occur to the Dottore. He knows that there's no one like you in the place. He just wants to hear from you."

"And he'll hear from me. Have a good evening."

Ricciardi was climbing the steep street that led home; even after sunset the heat continued to lay siege to the city. Via Toledo on a Sunday night and in the summer took on a different appearance: the families emerged from their ground floor hovel apartments, the *bassi*, where the temperature spiked to intolerable peaks; in order to keep from dying of suffocation they took to the streets. The older residents sat on chairs they'd carried outside, the younger ones perched on wooden crates employed as benches, and they all chatted or played cards to kill time, until late at night. From open windows on the higher floors came dance music from the radio, along with the laughter of children and, here and there, a loud fight.

Ricciardi thought about how impossible it was in a setting like that to preserve one's right to privacy. And how, in that churning maelstrom of love, passion, wealth, and poverty, envy and jealousy sprang up like weeds—and with them, murder.

As he walked, he realized that wherever he passed he brought with him silence and discomfort, like a chilly gust of wind; he was the Other, an unfamiliar, unsettling figure, viewed as inherently dangerous.

He didn't really mind it, as he strolled uphill, bareheaded, hands in his pockets, the sound of footsteps echoing off the stone paving slabs; he wouldn't have wanted to feel part of all those emotions, which mingled with the thoughts of the dead whom he could glimpse here and there, wherever they'd been stabbed to death or sliced in two by the wheels of trolley cars or horse-drawn carriages. All that regretful yearning for life, the pain of letting the world go and the grief over a sudden death, wasn't really all that different from the passions of the living and their thousandfold busy little businesses.

Hunger, love; the desire to own things, the lust for power, falsehood, faithlessness. The murders to which Ricciardi was a daily witness were generally the product of all this. His mind drifted back to the duchess's repeated phrase:

"The ring, the ring, you've taken the ring, the ring is missing."

Who had she been speaking to? To her murderer, in all likelihood. But all too often he'd heard phrases that had been addressed to third parties, whether present or absent. Which ring? The one on her middle finger, torn off after her death? With her last breath, had she seen whoever it was that would later take it from her? Or was it the ring on her ring finger, with the bruise that served as evidence that the woman was still alive when it was taken from her?

Whether one or the other, the ring must have had some special meaning because no other valuables, and there were plenty available, had been taken. Something told Ricciardi that if he could find the ring, he'd find the murderer. Which meant it was a crime of passion, then. A crime of love.

Out of the corner of his eye, Ricciardi glimpsed a young woman leading a man by the hand through the door of a building. Love. His thoughts flew to Enrica. For more than a year she'd been nothing but a picture glimpsed through a window, nothing more or less than a painting by Vermeer, a piece of the normal life, so close at hand but so unattainable, that he'd always be denied. Seeing her embroider, wash dishes, the slow and precise gestures of her left-handed activities was a nightly spectacle that he'd never willingly give up, and he was glad to leave things as they were: she was safe from him and from the Deed, sheltered by the two panes of glass.

Then, that spring, while interviewing witnesses in the course of an investigation, he'd found her sitting across from him. And the distant picture, the faraway glimpse of normality, the painting by Vermeer suddenly became a flesh-and-blood human being, a woman with a scent, a skin, and a pair of eyes that he'd remember. He couldn't say whether it was better before: certainly, when Enrica was simply a name and a portrait of someone else's life, his loneliness had a different hue. Now, when he greeted her every night with a wave of the hand, and she responded to him with a slight tip of the head, he felt as if he were standing on the brink of cliff from which he might tumble at any moment.

But he certainly wouldn't live without it.

Today, moreover, his memory had played a trick on him: he'd remembered Livia. He almost smiled to himself: a whole lifetime spent bearing the cross of a nature that forced him into a life of solitude and contemplation. And then, in the same year, in fact, over the course of just a few months, he'd found himself confronted with emotions that he'd never expected to experience himself. Livia, too, had disturbed him in some fashion, unmistakably conveying to him that she wanted to get to know him better, for the man that he was.

He couldn't deny that for a lengthy, extended moment he had been torn: unlike Enrica, Livia had provoked in him a whirlwind of sensations from the very beginning, with her spicy perfume, her soft skin, her full lips, her feline gait, and when they had said goodbye, the hot and womanly tears that streaked her face in the rain.

As he climbed the stairs in his building, Ricciardi had three women in his heart and in his mind: one was closeby, one he believed, at least, was very far away, and one was dead.

IX

Today was a different awakening for you. After all these years, finally, a new awakening.

Not that anything has changed, to all appearances. You saw day dawning from your bed, as always; as always, the pillow beside you was untouched. You looked at that pillow, your heart crushed by the usual sorrow; as always, you were the first to get up, and you moved through the silence of an apartment that was so different from the way you like to remember it, when the children were little and they laughed and quarreled and ran, and your husband looked up at you and he smiled.

You make breakfast, a breakfast that someone may or may not eat. There are times when you put dishes and utensils away and throw away whole meals, untouched. You say nothing, you don't complain. You wouldn't even know how, you've never complained in your life.

Is it a crime to no longer have the strength to cry? To shout out your shame, your fatally wounded pride? Is is a crime to look away, to see your happiness slipping through your fingers like sand?

You believed it, when you swore that it was for always, on a luminous spring morning. It's been a hundred years since then. You can see pity in the eyes of your neighbors, your relatives, your friends. You know that along with that compassion there is also a certain derision, for your silence, for the way you bow your head and look away. Sweetness turns into cowardice. If I were in your place, they all say. You feel as if you can hear them.

The sun starts to filter through the kitchen window. The heat never subsided, all night long. You think of him. And you think that by now he's heard the news.

With slumped shoulders, facing the wall by the kitchen sink and waiting for your children to wake up, you laugh. Softly, you laugh.

Ricciardi looked around at Monday morning, on his way into police headquarters. In the summer, the beginning of the week seemed to be more of a day of regret, as if Sunday were a missed opportunity; as if people still needed an extra dollop of rest or enjoyment.

The commissario sensed it when he saw the barefoot, half-naked street urchins, their skin roasted by the hot sun, pouring out of the *vicoli* and chasing after the first, early morning trolley cars to hang on for the ride, the dangerous ride down to the sea on the Via Caracciolo. He sensed it when he saw that the earliest opening shops were still shut, the same shops that he normally found open for business on his morning walk; instead, now he saw only a few sleepy stock boys still wrestling open the heavy wooden shutters and setting out the display merchandise under the cover of the thick canvas awnings.

He sensed it when he saw the windows still closed, pilfering a little more sleep and shade from the sun, which was already high in the sky and scorching hot.

Ricciardi had another especially well developed faculty: his sense of smell. That rainless summer was therefore particularly painful for him. The odor of rot that wafted out of the sewers and gusted through the *vicoli* was nauseating. Everything that rotted in the hot sun and wasn't carted away made him gag as it permeated the street with its miasmas, befouling the air and making it impossible to breathe. Every day dozens of children and old people fell ill from poor hygiene, dying in their homes and at hospitals, to the utter indifference of the press and the radio. Ricciardi wondered how it could be that the newspapers conspired to whitewash that terrible situation, and instead chattered on in dulcet tones about the visits to the city of royal princes and transoceanic aviators. Everyone has their ghosts, he thought: it's just a matter of knowing how to ignore them.

When he got to the office he found Ponte waiting outside the door, bouncing on the balls of his feet as if he urgently needed to go to the bathroom. Unlike the usual state of affairs, for once the deputy chief of police was already in his office, and wanted to see him immediately. With a sigh, Ricciardi followed the clerk who continued to look everywhere except at the commissario's face.

Mario Capece was smoking on the balcony of the newspaper's offices. He always stayed later than all the others, after the frantic night's work that preceded the daily celebration as the paper's first edition rolled off the presses. He usually liked to watch the newsboys with their stacks of fresh newsprint on their shoulders, eager to shout the first headlines to a city that was still asleep. But today's headline was one he'd never have wanted to hear.

Mario Capece was crying. His colleagues watched him from behind, from inside the newsroom, unable to do anything to comfort him. When earlier that afternoon an exceedingly young copyboy had galloped into the newsroom, breathless and fearful to reveal his news, it was immediately obvious that something very serious had happened. From his office, Capece hadn't seen the boy arrive, and so the copyboy was first able to inform his deputy editor, a close old friend, fellow veteran of a thousand battles.

The man had taken upon himself the terrible assignment of breaking the news to Capece. The other journalists had seen him shut the door behind him, they'd waited through the moment of silence that ensued with bated breath, and then they'd heard their boss's despairing shout of extreme grief and sorrow.

The affair that Mario Capece, city editor of the *Roma*, was carrying on with Adriana Musso di Camparino was public knowledge; but what only a few close friends understood was the sheer power of the journalist's emotions. Emotions that had sabotaged an otherwise brilliant career, a career that had screeched to a halt just short of the editorship of the city's oldest newspaper; emotions that had exposed him to the ridicule and the pity of his adversaries, and that had isolated him, creating a vacuum around him. They had also chased away from him not only his wife but also his children, who were rigid and conservative as only the very young can sometimes be.

Capece had renounced everything for his love. In order to accommodate the whims of a beautiful and unstable woman, shallow and neurotic. A thousand times Arturo Dominici, Capece's deputy editor and his best friend, had tried to reason with him. And a thousand times he had run headlong into the virulence and power of an emotion that was as deep-rooted and incurable as a tumor.

It had fallen to Dominici to break the news to Mario, at the end of a day during which his friend had been more on edge and irritable than usual. He'd expected Capece to rush to the dead woman's side instantly, but instead he'd remained in his office until dawn.

On Saturday evening, Dominici hadn't seen Capece in the newsroom, and he'd only come in much later that night, and dead drunk to boot. The deputy city editor had attributed his friend and editor's pitable state to yet another fight: those fights were coming thick and fast these days. He'd helped him to stretch out on his office sofa and he'd reassured him. Once again he would take his place and supervise the production of that day's edition. Before falling asleep, slurring his words, Capece had said to him:

"It's over, it's over, Arturo. This time it's over for good."

Dominici hadn't believed him, of course. He'd heard the same phrase repeated a thousand times over the last three years. This time, however, his friend, gripping his arm, had pulled something out of his pocket and had showed it to him.

It was a ring.

Garzo was on his feet as he welcomed Ricciardi into his office, striding to the door to meet him. The commissario had learned to fear his superior officer's cordiality far more than his imperious tone of voice or his professional lack of discernment: from the two latter qualities he could defend himself with competence and wry irony, but the only way to combat his cordiality was try to reestablish a sense of distance and formality.

This time, however, he perceived a psychological state that he'd never glimpsed before in the deputy chief of police. He looked as if he hadn't slept all night: his tie was loosened, he had bags under his eyes, and his face was even covered with a shadow of whiskers.

It was a surprising thing: Angelo Garzo, a bureaucrat who had used image and personal relations as the engines of his career, never allowed himself to strike a pose or have an appearance that was anything less than formally impeccable. In those years, when every serious matter was referred to Rome, his remarkable diplomatic skills made him the most important man in the department. The chief of police turned constantly to Garzo for all contacts with the ministry and he, who didn't really know how to do anything else, was happy to oblige. Among his underlings, one particular statement of his had become famous. It had to do with the discovery of a guilty party through a chain of reasoning he had been unable to follow: shaking his neatly groomed head, he'd said that if you want to understand evildoers, you need to be able to think like them, and he, who was an upright person, would never be able to understand a murderer.

That Monday morning, however, it was a very different person who greeted Ricciardi. He pointed his underling to one of the two chairs across from his uncluttered desk, brusquely waved Ponte out of the office, and sat down in his turn on the same side of the desk as the commissario.

"I heard about the Camparino murder. It's a very grave matter, all our fates depend on this investigation. How are we doing?"

Ricciardi was baffled. He couldn't figure out what made this murder different from any other.

"She was killed in her home, probably with a gunshot between the eyes. I'm waiting for the autopsy results. Dr. Modo was in charge of that. If necessary, I'll go to the morgue later myself."

Garzo was wringing his hands.

"Did you talk to . . . did you question anyone at the Camparino residence?"

Ricciardi had no intention of giving his superior officer any more rope than necessary.

"For now, I've only talked to the help. That's three people. Later, we'll talk to the other residents of the palazzo, the family. And after that, suppliers and neighbors. According to procedure, in other words."

Garzo grabbed Ricciardi's arm.

"Right, exactly. Procedure. We're not going to follow procedure this time, Ricciardi. No, we've got to move carefully, very, very carefully."

Ricciardi managed to extract his hand from Garzo's grip with some difficulty, and he looked his superior officer right in his reddened eye.

"Dottore, forgive me but I don't understand; what do you mean, we're not going to follow procedure? Is there something I ought to know?"

Garzo leapt to his feet and starting pacing nervously around the room.

"Something you don't know? No. Actually, yes, probably there is. I always forget that you live a somewhat, shall we say, cloistered life, that you don't socialize. Well, then: Adriana Musso di Camparino is, or I should say, was, a very, very prominent woman in social terms. She led a life that was . . . how to put this . . . well, quite public. Such a lovely, wealthy woman attracted, necessarily—let me be clear, necessarily—gossip and chatter. And we must not listen to idle gossip, must we, Ricciardi? We are the police, and we must stick to the facts."

Ricciardi waited; it was obvious that Garzo wanted to say something, but that he lacked the courage.

"Well then, Dottore, wouldn't it be best if the person conducting the investigation were to be aware of this . . . chatter in advance, and if possible from an objective source? Instead of going around gathering gossip, in other words."

Garzo stopped his nervous pacing.

"Yes. Of course it would. Now then, Ricciardi, first of all you should be aware that as you proceed in this investigation you'll necessarily come into contact with . . . very particular sectors of society. Unusual ones, we might say. Where you won't be able to ask questions as easily as you might if you were interviewing, say, a trolley car conductor or a street sweeper. Prominent, powerful people."

Ricciardi leapt suddenly to his feet.

"Dottore, perhaps the best thing would be for you to assign this case to someone else. Cimmino, for example. I'd be happy to give him a report on the current state of progress, and if it comes to that, we haven't really learned very much yet."

Garzo seemed disoriented.

"What are you saying, Ricciardi? I wouldn't dream for a second of assigning this investigation to anyone else. You're the best investigator we have, and you and I both know that perfectly well."

"Thanks very much, Dottore. But it's also true that I'm not very diplomatic, unfortunately. And that I have another short-coming: I'm not very obsequious. I wouldn't want to disobey instructions, unintentionally, you understand."

Garzo took a step toward Ricciardi.

"It's out of the question, Ricciardi. It's vital that we find the guilty party as quickly as possible. Quickly, you understand? The fact is that a noblewoman, such a prominent personality, cannot simply be murdered in her home. Not in a safe city, a city like ours and all the other cities in Fascist Italy. The guilty party, surely a madman, a maniac, must be brought to justice."

"Well then, Dottore, what's the problem? We'll just pro-ceed with our investigation, as usual, and as usual, we'll do our best."

Garzo ran his hand through his hair.

"The duchess . . . now then, Ricciardi: the duchess of Musso di Camparino was having an affair. She'd been seeing a man for years. The matter was public knowledge, everyone knew about it."

Ricciardi remained on his feet, emphasizing the point that he still wasn't sure that he'd been assigned to the investigation.

"If it was public knowledge, shouldn't I know about it too?"

"The problem is just who the man was. It's Mario Capece, the chief news editor of the *Roma*. The newspaper, in case you've missed the point, that never misses an opportunity to nail us to the cross, even after the instructions to the press issued in 1928 by the Ministry of the Interior. Now do you get it?"

Ricciardi understood. In fact, this put Garzo into a situa-tion that was anything but comfortable. Either he investigated until he tracked down the guilty party, which inevitably meant treading on the toes of the most hostile press, or else he held back, running the risk of making a public admission of incompetence by failing to catch the culprit in such a sensational murder case. Garzo, and to some extent this did him honor, had chosen to track down the murderer. Or at least make the attempt.

"The relationship between the two of them wasn't the sunniest. The duchess was, let's say, a little . . . unstable. She liked parties, she liked to dance, she liked compliments. She liked to be courted. Fifty years ago Capece, and when he was well, the duke himself, would have been fighting duels every day at sunrise. These days, however, the only form of recourse was arguments and bitter, interminable public fighting."

"And if I may ask, how do you know this?"

Garzo didn't seem offended by the rude question.

"Everyone who happens to go to the theater knows it. The last fight took place on Saturday night, in fact, at the Salone Margherita."

"The last fight?"

Garzo seemed uncomfortable. On the one hand, he wanted to minimize, while on the other hand he didn't want to leave out any details that might prove to be important.

"I believe it was a matter of jealousy. Capece was accusing the duchess of . . . of looking at a young man, who was accompanying the Signora De Matteis, a lady who . . . well, that doesn't matter, let's not pursue that. In other words, they started dredging up old events, situations from out of the past. Then he slapped her. We all sat there openmouthed. Immediately after that, he grabbed her hand and yanked off the ring, shouting into her face . . ."

Ricciardi had leaned forward, interrupting Garzo with one hand.

"What's that, what's that? He took one of her rings? And what did he yell at her?"

Garzo was disoriented.

"I can't remember what he yelled at her. I think it was an insult, you know the word that people say to women when they're accusing them of being unfaithful. And he told her that she deserved neither his love nor the ring."

"And can you remember what hand he took the ring from? This is important."

Garzo mimed Capece's gesture, trying to reconstruct the duchess's position.

"From the left hand, I think. That's right, the left hand. Why, is it significant?"

Ricciardi had half-closed his eyes. He was reviewing the image of the dead woman, standing there, her hands at her sides.

The ring, the ring, you've taken the ring, the ring is missing.

"It might be, yes. It might be significant. Then what happened?"

"Then he stormed out, without a word to anyone. He even shoved my wife aside, complete boor that he is, and the poor thing was almost knocked to the floor. The duchess, on the other hand, went into the bathroom to redo her makeup and shortly thereafter she was back in her box, laughing and bantering with a couple of gentleman who had hastened to take Capece's place. That's just the way she was."

"And Capece wasn't seen again?"

Garzo furrowed his brow, doing his best to concentrate and remember.

"No, at least I didn't see him. But yesterday, at the Circolo dell'Unione, before anyone knew what had happened, the waiter told me that he had stayed there until later, drinking and ranting. Then he left."

Ricciardi tried to find out other details.

"Ranting about what? Also, what time did he leave?"

Garzo seemed to be stumped.

"The Circolo closes at midnight. And he was saying . . . he

was saying that there are women who don't deserve to go on living. But that doesn't mean a thing: people say all kinds of things, don't they, Ricciardi?"

The commissario looked his superior officer in the eye, without answering.

"In any case, Ricciardi, I'm telling you, or I should say, I'm asking you just this once not to step on people's toes just for the fun of it. The press is involved, and that may not be all. You're going to have to be careful when you question the family. The duke is very old and sick, he's on his deathbed: but he's still one of the wealthiest and most influential men in the city. And the duke's son, Ettore . . . is widely esteemed and respected, a man of culture, a philosopher."

It had become clear to Ricciardi that nothing useful was going to come of their conversation, only calls for caution.

"All right, Dottore; I'll keep in mind all this exceedingly useful information you've given me. And I'll keep you informed. Now I'm heading to the morgue; Doctor Modo promised me that he'll give me advance word on the autopsy findings. If you have no further orders, *buon giorno*."

And he left the room, plunging Garzo even further into his sense of insecurity.

X

Looking out from her balcony on the fourth floor of the Hotel du Vésuve, Livia was drinking in the view of the Via Partenope. Stretching out before her eyes, the smooth calm sea was taking in the splashing dives of hundreds of boys and girls from the rocks and from the walls of the castle, which had stood on the water's edge for countless centuries.

The day before, upon her arrival at the Chiaia station, she'd immediately felt the air ringing with the city's wholehearted welcome. She'd smiled when at least three men had offered her a lift—and one of them had said that he'd be glad to take her to the ends of the earth;—and she'd been indulgent with the urchins who immediately surrounded her clamoring for a penny, a piece of candy, or a cigarette. She recalled a discussion in a Roman drawing room, a few weeks back, when an arrogant businessman had said how sick and tired he was of these Neapolitan *scugnizzi* who waited, in swarms, for arriving tourists at the port and the train station; they begged, the man had said, and they slipped their little hands in anywhere, eager to pilfer and steal. She'd broken in, informing him that the true underlying cause of this behavior was the state of poverty and neediness for which the city's most powerful citizens were ultimately responsible, and that in any case children always brightened her spirits; far more than certain dull conversationalists whom it had been her misfortune to meet in the city of Rome, for instance. She smiled as she recalled the icy silence that had settled over the room; no one there had the nerve to gainsay a woman who, as they all knew well, was a close friend of the Duce's wife and the Duce's daughter.

She had hired one of the distinctive red public automobiles, a three-seater with a yellow strip, and told the driver that she wanted to take a spin around the city before going to the hotel. She wanted to regain familiarity with the streets and the piazzas that she remembered swept by winter winds, places that she had experienced at such a sad time in her life. Now she saw sunlight and cheerfulness, strolling vendors shouting their wares, spontaneous would-be singers and smiling women, lovely shop windows and little children playing with rag-balls in improvised fields, darting among and around automobiles and trolley cars. It was a crazy, laughing city, and she liked it.

She couldn't say how much weight the fact that this was Ricciardi's city had on her opinion; in any case, she suspected that her memory of the commissario played an important part. She'd decided to let this first day go by, so that she could explore the battlefield before unleashing her first attack. She considered what dress she'd wear, what pert daring little hat.

She smiled at the sea and the sky.

Maione had made the rounds of the merchants of Santa Maria La Nova, in accordance with Ricciardi's instructions. It hadn't been easy: not because there was any reluctance or hesitation on their part, but rather because the Musso di Camparino family actually had no direct interactions with the quarter in which it lived.

The duke was held in the highest regard for his humane generosity toward the organizations that assisted the needy, but he'd been bedridden for over a year by a grave pulmonary disease and everyone expected him to die any day now.

Young master Ettore, who was about thirty, practically speaking lived on the terrace, surrounded by the plants that he cultivated with such passion. He wrote articles for newspapers and journals about philosophy, and was a celebrated scholar on the subject. It was said that he sometimes went out at night, but no one ever seemed to see him.

The duchess, on the other hand, was everywhere. There wasn't a party, a gathering, or a social event that didn't count her among its inner circle. Lovely and elegant, she put on a display of wealth and opulence on every occasion. She was the duke's second wife, and had been for ten years now: he married her a year and a half after the death of his first wife, to whom Adriana had ministered as her nurse. Maione detected disapproval from the sausage-maker he was talking to, given the fact that they hadn't even waited for the end of the second year of mourning.

Regarding the household help, the quarter was a goldmine of information. Concetta Sivo was a tranquil lady who was widely respected, a careful frugal shopper and a skillful manager of her household. She had no relatives in the city, and every couple of months or so she went back to the village where her elderly aunt and her cousins still lived. When they talked about the Sciarras, everyone smiled, amused by his comic turns, her utter simplicity, and the four children's lively voracity, constantly fighting over the last bite of food or visiting the local shops begging for something to eat.

In other words, these were people who did their work conscientiously, but easy enough to trick if some ill-intentioned individual wished to get into the palazzo. Moreover, the other night the neighborhood festa had been particularly crowded and noisy, and had ended with a burst of especially deafening fireworks that had illuminated the piazza and left everyone's ears ringing. Maione concluded that no one would have heard cannonfire, much less a gunshot muffled by a cushion.

Nothing especially interesting, in other words; except that every one of those businessmen had offered him something to eat, and he—with death in his heart and especially in his stomach—had been forced to turn down the offer in every case. Sadly shaking his head, he decided to move forward the timing of the visit he had planned to pay on Bambinella: if there was something worth knowing, he'd know it.

The knight of commerce, Cavaliere Giulio Colombo, saw his wife and started worrying. It was hardly an uncommon event for his energetic spouse to come in to inspect the shop; what worried him was the grim expression he'd glimpsed on her face through the plateglass window.

The family's chief source of income was the handsome hat shop at the corner of the Via Toledo and Piazza Trieste and Trento, near the church of San Ferdinando. In the thirty years they'd been in business, they'd developed a loyal clientele, to whom the Cavalier and the three salesclerks provided meticulous and personal service. One of those salesclerks was the husband of the youngest daughter, a capable young man and a very hard worker; the only headache he gave his father-in-law, a longtime liberal, was his enthusiastic support of the Fascist Party, which Colombo considered to be uncritical and therefore verging on fanaticism.

He was in fact discussing the increasingly common nighttime raids of the enforcement squads that, hiding behind the Fascist flag, committed acts of common brutality, when he saw his wife arriving. Signora Maria had a strong personality, even if she was capable of being a sweet helpmate and a perfect mother: problems arose only when the two roles conflicted, and this was one of those occasions. Cavaliere Giulio immediately guessed, even before the bell on the front door had stopped ringing, what the purpose of her visit was. It was about their daughter, Enrica; and her marriage.

Not that there was any marriage in immediate sight, in fact, to tell the truth, that was exactly the problem: that there was no marriage on the horizon. Maria strode to the cash register, an enormous piece of glistening metal machinery that was the pride of the store and behind which her husband had tried to conceal himself.

"Can I speak to you, alone, if you please?"

Uh-oh. This meant things were serious.

"Certainly. Marco, you stay at the cash register. I'm going in back."

Like all the city's haberdasheries and tailor shops, there was a room in the back where the various items could be adjusted for a better fit. Just then, it was empty because the two employees were on their lunch break.

Maria came right to the point.

"What do you intend to do for Enrica?"

This was a discussion they'd had more than once. The father was very fond of his firstborn daughter, who shared his smiling, orderly character; he didn't mind keeping her at home for as long as he could. His wife, who had noted this impulse, missed no opportunity to point out to him and especially to Enrica that, at twenty-four, she had amply reached the age when she ought to be thinking about starting a life of her own; all the more so, considering that these were hard times and business wasn't good enough to let them take care of the needs of a large family, actually two families, since the other daughter, with her husband and infant son, was still living with them. If only she were willing to meet some nice young men, instead of insulting every new suitor who ventured to show a little interest.

The night before, when she had lanched into her usual jeremiad, her husband had cut her off with a gesture of annoyance, begging her just to let him listen to the radio for once. Then and there, Maria had said nothing, but the way she glared at him promised nothing good: and in fact here she comes now, thought Giulio, more determined and combative than ever.

"You don't understand what a serious matter this is. Your daughter is an old maid, and she's starting to look like she's going to be an old maid for the rest of her life. For now, she has us, but we're not going to live forever; one day, when we're dead and gone, what will Enrica do, go and live in an old people's home, without a child to care for her?"

There was no stopping her once she got on her hobbyhorse, and Giulio knew it all too well. Might as well try to be conciliatory.

"But what do you think I can do about it? Should I grab her, put makeup on her, dress her up, and put her out on the street? If she doesn't want to go out, what can I do about it?"

Maria had been waiting for those exact words.

"If she doesn't want to meet anyone, then it's up to us to bring someone into the house. Here's what I've decided to do."

Maione had met Bambinella a year and a half ago, when he'd been hauled into police headquarters along with four other streetwalkers.

There were a great many prostitutes in business for themselves, and they were openly competing with the city's officially sanctioned bordellos, with relative impunity; but there was no violating the basic principle that the city had to present at least an apparently clean façade; moreover, the madams of the officially licensed brothels, who were required to pay taxes on their business, often complained to the city officials who frequented their houses of ill repute. From time to time, therefore, the mobile squad would make citywide raids, making a clean sweep of the streetwalkers pitching their wares to passersby, especially in the streets of the city center.

That night Maione, who was on duty, found himself with a complicated situation on his hands: the other girls were waiting patiently for their inevitable release; but the youngest of them all was writhing and fighting and, unexpectedly, bit the hand of a policeman, who in turn slapped her violently in the face. At that point she began to shout and the timbre of her voice unequivocally revealed her true nature. Maione intervened, separating the young man from the other girls, but in the long hours over which he held him in the cell, he was unable to obtain the basic elements of his identity, first and last names, date and place of birth; what did surface however was a complex personality—that of a young man who had learned to accept the fact that he was profoundly different from other young men without, however, resigning himself to hide the fact. Quite the contrary in fact: he felt like a woman and it was as a woman that he wanted to earn a living. The same way that other poor and desperate women were often forced to eke out their existence.

In the months that followed, the brigadier frequently encountered Bambinella, who seemed to have a gift for always being in the midst of social circles where murders ripened and were committed. A strange relationship of reciprocal esteem, if not friendship, developed between the two men, who could not have been any more different. Moreover, and above all, Bambinella had a remarkable network of acquaintances and contacts, and therefore a bottomless wealth of information, which he made available to the brigadier, and to the brigadier alone, without ever actually becoming an informer. It was all gossip with a foundation of fact that more often than not proved to be enormously helpful in this or that investigation. In exchange the mobile squad had unwritten orders to ignore the presence of Bambinella among the prostitutes who plied their trade on the outlying border of the Spanish Quarter, along the Via Toledo. One hand washes the other, as the old saying goes.

Bambinella lived in a ratty attic apartment at the end of a *vicolo*, not far from Corso Vittorio Emanuele. From his window he could look out on a bit of countryside next to the

Vomero hill and, on the other side, a slice of distant blue sea. Maione, as hardly needs to be stated, got there in a puddle of sweat, after a long uphill climb and a hundred or so stairs, hungry as a wolf.

And, as hardly needs to be stated, Bambinella was having something to eat.

XI

Everything has to be normal. Everything has to be the way that it is every day.

You've cleaned and tidied the apartment, let it never be said that the children have been neglected or that there's a spot of dust on the credenza. Let no one say that the curtains are stained, or that the linen is less than spotless.

Now you've gone to do the shopping for the day's meals. You bring home a wrapped package of macaroni, the bread, the tomatoes. You have a fine lunch to make, and then a nice dinner. And tomorrow another lunch, and another dinner. And on and on it goes, because he'll be coming home, and he'll sit down across the table, and he'll smile at you. It'll all be just the way it used to be, once again. Just the way it was.

It's hot, and you walk along under the ferocious sun, loaded down with groceries. Your head starts to spin slightly, and no one offers to help.

You go on smiling just the same.

"Why Brigadie', what an enormous pleasure. Come right in, make yourself comfortable, sit on the pouf, here, next to me. Do you mind if I go on eating? Today of all days I'm dying of hunger, even with this heat. Care for some?"

Maione felt the room spinning around him, and let himself flop down onto the large damasked cushion.

"Oh my goodness, Brigadie', don't you feel well? You're

white as a sheet! Come over here, and I'll give you a little sugar water!"

Maione weakly waved his hand in front of his face.

"No, no, don't worry, it's just the heat. But what are you eating, if I may ask?"

"Oh, I just made a bowl of pasta, I know I ought to think about my figure but, I told you before, today for some reason I'm just starving. Maybe it's because I had a hunch you'd be coming by, a big handsome man like you, and I thought I'd better get something to eat to keep my strength up."

"Oh, I've told you a thousand times, there's a line I forbid you from crossing, can't you get that through your head? You know that I don't even fool around with . . . with women *like* you, much less with *you*! Now look what you're making me say . . . so come to the point, why is it that you were expecting me? Who told you that I might be coming by?"

Bambinella coquettishly tightened the silk kimono against his breast and put one hand over her mouth to stifle a giggle.

"No one told me. But everyone in the city knows that yesterday the duchess of Camparino was murdered, and a girlfriend of mine who works as a maid in the building across the street told me that you and your commissario were there; why on earth were the two of you working on a Sunday?"

Maione, partially reclining on the large cushion, was fanning himself with his cap.

"What, do I have to explain my schedule to you? Not on your life: in this city not a leaf turns without everybody knowing the details. How can you do a job like mine if you're working in the middle of a bazaar? In any case, yes, I'm here to ask you if you can give me any information about this duchess. In the quarter where she lived, nobody seems to know a thing, though of course everybody actually knows everything."

Bambinella was toying with the pasta left over in the bowl, while Maione looked on hungrily.

"Eh, Brigadie', the duchess . . . That duchess has a story that for lots of us was like a fairy tale, the fairy tales they tell little children. Only, as you've seen, it's not a fairy tale with a happy ending."

"What do you mean? A fairy tale, how?"

"The duchess wasn't born into money. She was a soldier's daughter, and her father was killed in the war. But she was beautiful, very beautiful indeed. I knew a guy who lost his head over her, a silk merchant, if I remember right. But she had other things in mind, she wanted to be independent, she didn't want to have to say thank you to anyone. And so she decided to become a nurse."

Maione was doing his best to control Bambinella's tendency to wander off topic.

"Yes, but when did she get married to the duke?"

"That's what I'm telling you about, if you'll only have the patience to listen . . . So, the first duchess was quite the matron, a respectable member of the best society. Very religious, she spent all her time in church, helping the poor, in other words, the classic high society matron. Then she got sick, a nasty disease, you know that, no? The kind that starts with a bout of dizziness, a fainting spell . . . Are you all right, Brigadie'? I don't know if I like your looks today . . ."

Maione feigned a kick from the pouf where he was sitting.

"Hey, don't be a clown, I told you! I'm not sick, I'm healthy as a horse! Go on."

"Eh, and such a lovely personality you have! So, to care for the duchess they hired Nurse Adriana, as lovely as sunshine and bursting with health. The sickness went on and on, and finally, to make that long story short, the duchess passed away. And the nurse hopped into the bed, in place of the sick woman."

"When did this happen?"

Bambinella raised enameled nails to the tip of his nose.

"Let's see, now . . . ten years ago or so."

"And how did the marriage turn out?"

Bambinella shrugged.

"And how do marriages usually turn out, Brigadie'? Fine at first, then worse and worse, and then, at the end, a disaster. Though I have to admit that when people marry for money, things usually go a little better, because at least both parties tend to mind their own business. Still, the poor duchess, God rest her soul, didn't really know how to calculate her own best interests. And when the duke, who's a very old man, fell sick himself, she didn't shut herself up in the palazzo pretending to grieve."

Maione listened attentively.

"What do you mean, she didn't shut herself up in the palazzo?"

Bambinella snickered again.

"Brigadie', there are times when you make me feel sorry for you. You live in a city like this one, you do the job you do, and still you don't know the basic things that everyone else knows. That's why I was put here, so that I can explain things to you. Between you and your handsome mute commissario who never laughs, you're both a little cut off from the real world."

Maione snorted in annoyance.

"What are you talking about, cut off from the real world? Someone has to keep their eyes on the serious matters, and not spend their lives gossiping about who's climbing into whose bed. Now, go on, tell me."

"It's very simple: Adriana meets a young man just like her, cheerful, intelligent, and ambitious. They fall in love. It's against his best interests, because it damages his career, and it's against her best interests, because she's no longer invited to the better salons and drawing rooms. Still, they fall in love and for love, they tell everyone to go to hell. This is the part of the story I like best."

The brigadier finally felt he was getting to the heart of the matter.

"And just who is he, this Prince Charming?"

"Prince Charming would be Mario Capece, Brigadie'. The journalist who runs the *Roma*. The one who, apparently, in the end, killed the duchess."

I'll never see you again.

That's the only thought in my mind, I can't think of anything else.

Do you remember, the very first time? We were introduced, at the theater. They were talking but I never heard a word. I was lost in your eyes, in that smile of yours. I could feel the passion swelling inside me, the passion that's never subsided.

I'll never see you again. It seems impossible.

Your face in my hands. The scent of your skin. You taught me that it's possible to get drunk without a drop of wine, as the song lyrics go. It all seemed wasted, the time I spent without you. Even my children were so much wasted time. Work was wasted time. Any price I might have to pay was a trifle, for an hour with you.

I'll never see you again.

Your laughter, a thousand silvery corals on marble, the sound of life itself. I can't believe it, I'll never hear you laugh again. You drove me crazy, you made me sick with love. The purest happiness in the most completely impure embrace.

And the fury, the red fury of seeing you smile at another man, watching as you sneak a glance at him. I can't believe that the last time my hand touched you, it was to hurt you. I can't believe it.

And I can't believe that I'll never see you again.

A moment's silence followed Bambinella's statement; from the window, along with the baking heat of early afternoon came the sound of crickets and occasional birdsong. Maione knew his informant's tendency to exaggerate and over-drama-tize, but he was still impressed.

"What do you mean, 'apparently killed her'? How do you know that Capece murdered the duchess?"

Bambinella shook her head, opening her heavily mascaraed eyes wide.

"No, Brigadie', don't try to put words in my mouth that I never said. I don't know who murdered the duchess. In fact, I have to tell you that I hope it wasn't Capece. I'm very fond, you know, of love stories, but I don't like murder stories one bit, on the other hand."

"So what? We're not in a theater, where you have to like how the story ends. Did Capece murder his lover or not?"

"How would I know, Brigadie'? All I can tell you is that everyone's convinced that it really was him. The fact is that Donna Adriana was one of those women who loved to drive men out of their minds, and she knew how to do it. If you ask me, she really was in love with Capece, but even so she was always a bit of a slut. And Saturday night at the Salone Margherita the thing happened, and it happened bad."

Maione was having a hell of a time keeping the conversation on subjects that he wanted to know about.

"What thing happened Saturday night? Bambine', I beg of you: it's hot out, my head is spinning, and I'm dying of hunger here, I can't eat and I can't tell you why. Don't you get started too, now. Tell me what you want to tell me, and don't waste my time."

"Oooh, Brigadie', are you on a diet? But why, you're so charming the way you are, a man with girth and presence?"

The brigadier's ferocious glare was more than sufficient to rein Bambinella in.

"All right, all right. I'll tell you what happened. But let me make it clear that the reason I know these things is that a girlfriend of mine is a housekeeper at the Salone Margherita, actually to tell the truth, I hear that they're going to promote her to the wardrobe deparment . . . eh, Brigadie', don't lose your temper, what a bear you are! Well, at any rate, at intermission everyone was standing around drinking, smoking, and gossiping because that's one of the reasons people even go to the theater. Just like that, Capece starts yelling at the duchess, saying that she had no right, that it was always the same thing with her, that he wouldn't put up with it a second longer."

"Why, what had the duchess done?"

Bambinella spread his arms wide.

"Who can say? No doubt, she'd said hello to someone, or she'd smiled at someone else. She often did. In any case, he was shouting and she was laughing. Just like that, my girlfriend told me that she threw her head back and was laughing loudly, ha ha ha, ha ha ha, as if he was a comedy skit. And that's when he did the thing with the ring."

"What do you mean, the thing with the ring?"

"He grabbed her hand and, shouting into her face that she didn't deserve to have it, and that he never wanted to see her again, he yanked a ring off her finger."

Maione wanted to know more.

"What ring? What ring are you talking about?"

Once again, Bambinella shrugged.

"What would I know about it? So she told him: 'Go ahead and take it, the miserable ring. Why don't you give it back to that ghost of a wife of yours.'"

"Why, is Capece a widower?"

"No, he's no widower. It's just that I've heard that Capece's stopped thinking about his wife entirely and has been ignoring her for years; I hear that she's all hearth and home and church, the complete opposite of the duchess."

"And then?"

"And then, in front of everyone, he gave her an open-handed slap that knocked her head right around. A couple of men stepped forward, it's a disgrace to see a man hit a woman in public. But she gestured to them to stop, dried the blood dripping out of her mouth, straightened her hair, and turned and went back into the theater."

"And what did Capece do?"

"He left; but first he shouted something."

Maione leaned in toward Bambinella, aware of his own hesitation.

"What did Capece shout?"

"He shouted: I'll kill you with my own hands."

XII

This is the worst time of the day. The time when the sun shows no more respect for those who can't seek shelter, when the sun is at its most merciless. It is I who must help you all, and I move into the shade those of you that I can, the geraniums, the begonias. The hedges, the jasmines, bougainvilleas, and ivies; all I can do is watch you as you consume your reserves, the water that I gave you this morning. You have to stay there. In your place. Everyone in their place.

And what's my place? Here, with you. In this empty palazzo, empty room after empty room, silence upon silence. A palazzo filled with ghosts. He too is a ghost. My father. I don't remember him like this, gasping and wheezing in a bed, fighting a losing battle. I remember him big and strong, laughing happily with Mamma. Mamma. Mamma. What an enchanted word, a word that I utter not with my mouth, but with my heart a thousand times a day.

Mamma, you know. You know that the most important thing is love. It's love that gives you the place you occupy. You always used to say that to me, that love was your true home, your true country. But you never explained what to do, if that love is somehow wrong.

Now she's dead. Dead, Mamma. Just like you. Just like my father, even if he's still there, gasping. And maybe just like me, and my mistaken love.

I open the drawer in the secretary desk, the concealed spring-operated drawer. I take out the ring. Your ring, Mamma.

I clean it again, to make sure that there's no trace of her filthy blood. That it's just the way it used to be.

When it was on your finger. Mamma.

Ricciardi was thinking how paradoxical it was that the places where the Deed gave him the fewest visions should be hospitals and cemeteries. But then again, it made perfect sense: it was passions and strong emotions that generated violent deaths, not pain; and what inhabited those places was primarily pain.

He'd decided to wait for the results of the autopsy at the entrance to the mortuary, at the rear of the building. The hospital was ashamed of death, and so it did its best to hide it. Death represented a failure, a defeat.

Groups of people in tears, faces ashen with weariness and suffering. Women dressed in black held up by grim-faced boys, turned into grown men in the space of a few hours when confronted with loss. Parents, sons and daughters, wives, husbands. Regrets, words left unspoken. Memories.

Ricciardi stood to one side, unable to avoid being a witness to more pain and grief. He couldn't have said which was worse, the dull repetition of the departed's last emotion or the abyss into which the survivors were plunged.

The mortuary door swung open and Doctor Modo emerged, drying his hands on the hem of his stained labcoat.

"Well, look who's come to bring his sunny smile into this place of suffering. Ciao, Ricciardi: welcome to our little theater. Were you so eager to see me again that you couldn't resist or do you think that the atmosphere of the morgue suits you better than the one at police headquarters?"

"Sooner or later someone's going to notice that the atmosphere of police headquarters suits you better than the hospital does. And I'll have to come get you, and I'll throw away the key after I do. How did it go, are you done with the duchess?"

Modo smiled broadly.

"Oh, we had a long talk, your client and I. And she gave me lots and lots of information, but it's all very, very confidential. I'm only authorized to release it if provided with a lavish dinner, your treat."

Ricciardi shook his head.

"At last. Concealing evidence. I knew that would be the charge that would finally allow me to put you away where the sun doesn't shine. And considering this heat, I'm even doing you a favor. Fine, fine, but we'll have to meet at the trattoria near police headquarters; I'm waiting for Maione, who has some information of his own. Which he's giving me free of charge."

Maione hadn't managed to pry any other interesting information out of Bambinella; in particular, he'd tried to find out something else about the other residents of the palazzo and their habits, but as far as he could tell there was nothing more that his informant could add to what he'd already told him.

He'd only detected an instant of hesitation when it came to the duke's son, Ettore; Bambinella knew that the man stayed out very late practically every night, and that sometimes he slept somewhere else, though she had no idea where he might go. Maione had decided that, since the man was a scholar, the circles he frequented were unlikely to have anything in common with Bambinella.

In the terrible afternoon heat, hungrier than ever, Maione decided to go see Ricciardi and apprise him of the results of his investigations. He found the commissario in his office, waiting for him.

They traded accounts of their day: the commissario shared with the brigadier his impressions of the conversation with Garzo; Maione informed Ricciardi of the information he'd gathered in the neighborhood around Palazzo Camparino and from Bambinella. Ricciardi sat there, thoughtfully, fingers knit in front of his mouth.

"So everyone thinks it was Capece who did it. Sometimes, the most obvious solution also happens to be the right one: after all, life isn't a novel. We'll have to question him."

"Yes, Commissa', but we'll have to move cautiously. You heard what that ignorant boor Garzo said, no? We'll wind up putting him on the alert and then he'll reach out to someone in high places and the next thing you know they'll put a gag order on us."

"You're quite right. We'll move carefully, at least as carefully as we normally would. Tomorrow we'll go to the palazzo and talk to the two surviving dukes, and we'll see what they have to tell us. Among other things, from what you tell me, there seems to have been bad blood between husband and wife, stepmother and stepson."

Maione scratched his head with the handkerchief.

"Did you get anything from Doctor Modo? I checked the shell against the models that we have in our archives, and it's just as you expected: a Beretta 7.65 from the war, not the old model but the pistol they issued to officers toward the end, in '17; there are still thousands of them in circulation. Nothing unusual about it. I sent two policemen to canvas the room from top to bottom, nothing else emerged. The murderer only fired that one shot."

Ricciardi nodded agreement.

"That extortionist Modo said that he'll report on the autopsy only if I buy him dinner. Why don't you come along, it's the trattoria near here, at Santa Brigida; that way you can hear too."

Maione turned paler still.

"No, Dotto', I'm not hungry. If anything, you can tell me about it tomorrow."

"No, I insist: four ears are better than two. And after all, when have you ever had a problem with eating twice? I don't want to stay out late tonight either. Let's hear what Modo has to say and then we'll go home."

Maione resigned himself.

"All right, at your orders. But I'm not going to eat anything. I'll just watch you have dinner, then I'll eat at home."

Enrica sensed something strange. Her mother had returned from her walk and seemed excited: she'd brought a bouquet of flowers and had told the housekeeper to get out the fine silverware and polish it. She'd tried to find out the reason for such lavish care for the dining room table on an ordinary day of the week and in response had received nothing more than a nervous giggle and a shrug.

When Maria was like that, there was no point in insisting, as Enrica knew all too well; but she could sense a strange uneasiness. At a certain point she saw the woman who normally came to do her mother's hair enter the apartment; at that point she asked whether there was some special occasion that she knew nothing about, and she was told that the woman was there for her.

Her eyes opened wide, and before she could say anything in response, she was told:

"And put on your best dress. We're having guests for dinner tonight."

Along the short stretch of road from police headquarters to Via Santa Brigida, where they had an appointment to meet Doctor Modo, Maione and Ricciardi encountered only a few living souls and one dead one. The living ones were boisterous young boys on their way back from the beach, their clothing wrapped in dripping bundles, barefoot and wet-haired, who were filling the air with loud laughter and rude bantering. The dead man, whom only Ricciardi could see, of course, was dissolving slowly in the massive heat with his heavy jacket, dating back to the end of winter.

He was a construction worker who'd fallen off the roof of a palazzo, where he'd been repairing a rain gutter. With a back curved right round like an umbrella handle and with blood gushing from his mouth, he kept saying:

"It'll hold me, the cornice will hold me."

Famous last words, thought Ricciardi, as he did every time he passed by him, averting his gaze. Maione misinterpreted his superior officer's expression.

"What is it, Commissa', do you have a headache, too? My head's been spinning like a top for the past few days."

Ricciardi replied:

"In fact, you've been looking a little peaked, for a few days now. Are you feeling all right?"

"Sure, sure, I'm feeling fine, but I'm eating less. And in this heat . . ."

"I understand, and right you are to do so. But I'm just as hungry as ever, hot or cold. And Modo, as you can see, feels the same way. There he is, waiting for us."

The doctor was already sitting at one of the small outdoor tables on the sidewalk, beneath the awning that provided shade from the last rays of the setting sun.

"Oh, here comes my dinner now. My dear Brigadier, are you joining us tonight? That must mean the coffee'll be your treat: I wouldn't want to do you wrong."

Maione smiled.

"*Buona sera*, Dotto'. Sorry, I'm sitting this one out, strictly a spectator. I'll listen to you talk and watch you eat. No one said anything about paying."

Ricciardi took a seat; to the proprietor hovering nearby he pointed to the bowl of baked pasta that towered in front of Modo.

"The same for me, if you please. Now then, Bruno; can you

talk to me about the duchess or would that ruin your appetite?"

Modo chewed with his mouth full. He shook his head.

"There's nothing on earth that could ruin my appetite. On the Carso front, I ate under a hail of Austrian shells: it's a simple matter of survival. So let's talk about your client: a very lovely woman, who was in excellent shape despite her age, which I'd place at roughly forty or so. Am I right?"

"Forty-two, to be exact. She was born in 1889, on January 15th."

"She had the body of a young girl, believe me. From what they tell me, she was a woman who drove men crazy. All right then, first let's talk about the bullet. You saw it, someone shot her through the cushion: there are fragments of cloth and even feathers in her brain, along the trajectory that ends in the sofa's backrest. Fracture of the frontal bone, occipital bone, etc. And there's no doubt that her heart was still beating, when she was shot."

Ricciardi leaned forward, having caught the careful phrasing.

"What do you mean, her heart was still beating?"

Modo snickered, his mouth still full.

"How nice, to have an attentive audience. What I mean to say is that clinically speaking, the lovely duchess was still alive. But only clinically."

"Which means? What are you saying, clinically?"

"Well then: your murderer, perhaps to keep her from screaming, had pressed a cushion good and hard over her mouth and nose. So the Signora was already dying of suffocation. Practically speaking, she was in her death throes when she was shot."

Maione was impressed.

"Excuse me, Dotto', and just how can you tell? I don't know, from the lungs, the throat . . ."

Modo shook his head.

"No, no, Brigadie', nothing that internal. You can see from the face. The red patches around the mouth and neck, for instance. And certain little spots on the inside of the eyelids, which are known as 'petechiae.' Those are veins and capillaries that rupture as the victim struggles to breathe. It's a typical mark of suffocation."

It occurred to Ricciardi that the image of the duchess, which kept uttering its phrase about the ring, had a nice round bullet hole in its forehead, so that when she was shot, she must have still been alive. He asked:

"But if she was suffocated, how could it be that she was still clinically alive when the murderer shot her?"

Modo shrugged, without breaking pace as he ingurgitated the baked macaroni.

"Evidently, the murderer wanted to make sure he'd done the job. You can't always be sure, when you kill someone, that what you've done is really irreversible. Perhaps he thought he'd been recognized. Or as long as he was at it, he wanted to make sure the gun worked. In any case, they had quite a struggle."

Maione was again surprised; struggling to tear his eyes away from the spaghetti sauce that the doctor was mopping off his bowl with a chunk of bread, he said:

"What are you saying, Dotto'? She looked like she was just sleeping, the duchess."

Modo, who had wiped his bowl completely clean, leaned back in his chair with a broad smile.

"You weren't expecting that, were you? The duchess was rearranged, nice and comfortable, so that the bullet hole in her forehead lined up. The autopsy was quite informative, this time. In any case, it all must have happened in quick succession. The woman died between midnight and two in the morning, on the night between Saturday and Sunday. There's no question about that."

*

You shouldn't have laughed. If you hadn't laughed, I wouldn't have done it. I loved you, desperately. I'd never have hurt you.

You never understood my pain, my despair. Perhaps I never possessed you; but I always felt that you belonged to me, since the very first time I met you. And I'll never see anything as beautiful as your smile, your face cradled in my hands; I'll never feel anything as marvelous as you, breathing in my arms.

I wish I could explain to you how horrible it was to see you catch another man's eye, trigger his smile. To feel you turning your charm elsewhere to chain one man to you, and then another, and another still. Without respect, without any consideration for me. But I would have put up with anything, as long as I could keep you close to me. Because I loved you.

But you laughed. You laughed right in my face. And I couldn't take it.

Ricciardi asked:

"Well then, what else have you discovered?"

Modo raised his hand, counting on his fingers.

"One: two broken ribs, not from trauma but from pressure. Someone placed a curved object on her chest, possibly to hold her still. A knee, for instance. Or something else, who can say? Two: four broken fingernails, on both hands. And no trace of skin, which means that she tried to grab a fully dressed body or something else, again, who can say? Three: her left hand, truly in very strange condition. The ring finger with a nice deep cut, bleeding: evidently, someone tore a ring off. Middle finger, sprained, without hematoma. Someone pulled on her finger after she was dead, perhaps trying to take another ring. Or perhaps . . ."

Ricciardi concluded, sarcastically:

". . . something else, who knows what. So what else do you

have in store for us? I can see from your face that you still have a surprise."

Modo smiled like a little boy.

"Your client, my dear sad Ricciardi, had a tear on the inside of her left cheek. Someone had beaten her, before killing her."

XIII

Standing in front of the mirror and knotting his tie, Giulio Colombo was definitely angry. And to make matters worse, he couldn't really be angry with anyone other than himself.

Upon his return home that evening, when his Enrica, as always, had come to take his hat, his cane, and the usual kiss on her forehead, he hadn't had the courage to look her in the eye. The whole way home he'd done his best to talk himself into believing that what he'd done had actually been for his daughter's own good, but instead he couldn't shake the deeply unpleasant sensation that he'd played a nasty trick on her.

This is the way matters stood: that morning, when his wife had confronted him with grim determination, setting forth the urgent necessity of doing something to protect Enrica from a terrible fate of loneliness and poverty, even though he knew the woman was exaggerating, he'd lacked the strength to push back, and he'd allowed her to talk him into it.

Just a short distance from his shop there was another large establishment, which sold fabrics; the manager of the place was an old friend of his, Luciano Fiore, who worked with his wife Rosanna. The couple, decidedly well-to-do, had an only son, Sebastiano, who at age twenty-eight was still a bachelor. This was due to the fact that to his parents, and especially to his mother, every girl out there seemed inadequate in terms of beauty, health, or property. Actually, Giulio suspected that none of the girls were interested in the young man, who was fatuous and superficial, and who lived far too well at his parents' expense to have any interest in starting a family of his own. He had confided his suspicions to his wife, who had roundly accused him of lacking the courage to face up to the matter. And so he had given in, and had gone over to Fiore's store to invite him to dinner, with wife and son, that very night. His friend's wife had appropriated the situation and had informed him of her enthusiastic approval: actually, she had long thought just how adroit a solution it would be, and was already dreaming of a single, immense shop specializing in hats and fabrics, and run by her son.

Giulio found Rosanna Fiore to be deeply unlikable, and felt the same way about her son, whom he had only met once or twice. Poor Luciano, he thought, was the constant victim of his wife's personality. Then it occurred to him that he himself might be in the same situation, and that thought only further blackened his already dark mood. It was hot out, very hot, and the idea of putting on jacket and tie even at night, even at home, certainly did nothing to improve the situation.

Once again he asked himself why he'd allowed himself to be talked into organizing this ambush for his poor sweet Enrica.

Maione was walking uphill, following the *vicolo* that led him home. It had been a long, difficult day, made worse by the terrible heat that persisted, even now, in the dark. He was thinking about what Bambinella had told him about Capece, and about how love leads to passion, and passion to rage, and rage to bloodshed. What Modo had said, concerning the fact that the duchess had been beaten before dying, fit in neatly with the account of what had happened at the theater.

In a certain sense, even the clumsy effort to arrange the duchess as if she were sleeping was an act of posthumous respect; the brigadier had gotten used to accepting the contradictions implicit in crimes of passion, where the murderers first killed without pity and then performed acts of tenderness toward their victims.

As he was mulling over these thoughts, he heard his name being called, and his heart suddenly raced; he remembered all too well that deep, musical voice. He replied: "*Buona sera* to you, Filomena. How are you?"

The woman was standing at the entrance to the little alley known as Vicolo del Fico, beneath a votive shrine with an ancient image of the Madonna painted on the wall.

"I'm just as the Madonna wishes me to be, Brigadie'. You see, I'm in charge of the flowers and candles; every so often I light one myself, and say a prayer for the well-being of the people who are dear to me. I include you in their number: I haven't forgotten the help that you gave me."

She underlined those words with a brief caress of the scarred side of her face, which was turned to the shadows. The other profile, faintly illuminated by the streetlamp, was as Maione remembered it: heartbreakingly beautiful.

"Don't think twice, Filomena; after all, it's my duty to help people. And with you it was a pleasure, as you know. In fact, I only wish I could've done more. Your son Gaetano, how's he doing?"

"Fine, thanks. He's no longer an apprentice, the master mason has hired him, he says he's good at what he does. He took the place of Rituccia's father, do you remember her? That little girl who lived nearby, now she lives with us."

Maione remembered her perfectly: a serious little girl, with a sorrowful, unsettling look in her eyes. One of those encounters that punctuated the events in which he had been embroiled a few months earlier; when, one fine spring morning, he found himself stanching the bloody wound that had forever altered that woman's face. In a single dizzying instant, the brigadier relived the new and profound emotions that spending time with Filomena had stirred in him.

"Would you care to stay for dinner? I could make you something cool, maybe macaroni with tomato and basil. As I recall, you liked that dish, or am I mistaken?"

Maione could hear his stomach rumble, like distant thunder.

"No, thanks, Filome', I'm having some digestive problems; I'm going to just skip dinner, tonight."

In the partial darkness, the woman stepped closer, scrutinizing his face.

"Are you all right, Raffae'? You strike me as pale, hollowed out. And you've lost weight. Don't you worry me now, you know that I care about you."

Maione couldn't have hoped for a more flattering compliment. He'd lost weight. As if someone had told him he'd grown wings and a halo.

"Don't be ridiculous, no, no, it's just that I've had a long day, a very long day. Maybe I'm just a little tired."

Filomena was eyeing him with concern, her head tilted over on her shoulder. She was beautiful. Without warning, she reached out her hand and caressed Maione's face. The hand felt light and cool as a breeze to him. He barely touched the visor of his cap, then turned and fled, feeling like a coward the way he did every time he saw her.

Rosa Vaglio was one of those women of bygone times who expressed her love by making food. And since she'd been born dirt poor, the greater the love, she thought, the more the food, condiments added. And since she loved Luigi Alfredo Ricciardi more than anything else on earth, she cooked for him a succession of terrible dishes that would have easily killed a full grown bull, if that bull had ventured to eat her eggplant parmigiana.

The first time she had seen him, he was covered with blood, cradled in the midwife's hands, with his beautiful green eyes still shut. She'd held him in her arms even before his poor mamma, the sweet Baroness Marta, who had died so many years ago. And she had watched him at play a thousand times, while she knit or washed clothing with one eye out to make sure he was in no danger, silent and reckless as he always was.

She had sat up, watching over his restless sleep, wondering what terrible things he might be dreaming when she saw him jerk and murmur in his sleep. She'd kissed his forehead a thousand times, trying to detect the slightest warmth of fever that she was infallibly able to discern. When his mother died, and even before that, she had become the inflexible administrator of the family's substantial assets, which Ricciardi ignored entirely; it was she who maintained the correspondence, in her unlovely, oversized handwriting, with the overseers and share-croppers: she never overlooked a cent, and she set everything by so that it would be fully accounted for when Luigi Alfredo finally woke up from his obsession with being a policeman and made up his mind to take his rightful place as the Baron of Malomonte, and started a family of his own.

This matter of the family was Tata Rosa's one great obsession and regret. Her simple mind had few bedrock certainties, and one of those was that without children, no life could be considered complete. She had devoted her own life to Ricciardi, and he had repaid her with more worries and concerns than ten children could have given her, with his stubborn solitude; what she could not accept was the idea that he was willing to let his family's name die out. All too often, even though she was aware that she was becoming obsessive and intrusive, she had tried to push him to socialize more, to get to know girls, and all she got in return was a shrug and a pat on the cheek. She'd even wondered whether her boy was one of those who just didn't like girls: but her heart told her that that wasn't the case, his only problem was that he was not yet ready. He was waiting for the right moment.

And now, after all these years, as Rosa set a mound of baked macaroni, spiced up with every condiment imaginable, before him, she finally thought that the time had come. She had noticed some time ago that, when he looked out his bedroom window at the young woman who lived across the way, Ricciardi had begun to wave a hasty greeting with one hand. Of course, he had no idea that she could look through a crack in his doorjamb to see what was happening in his bedroom; for that matter, how else could she be sure that he was all right, when he shut himself in at night?

And the girl, she had seen from her own window, responded with a slight nod of her head. The ice was beginning to melt. As far as that went, in this heat wave the ice had never really had a chance, thought Rosa. And she smiled.

As usual, Ricciardi had first begun to smell the odor of Rosa's cooking from at least two hundred yards away. He was well aware that he had a highly developed sense of smell, but still he wondered how it could be that the entire neighborhood failed to rise in open mutiny against the toxic fumes that filled the air, fumes that clearly originated in his *tata*'s kitchen. Still, he had to admit that the smells that came from his apartment were no worse than the varieties of rot that wafted out of the surrounding *vicoli*. In other words, there was just no getting away from it.

Along the way home from his meeting with Modo, he had continued to mull over what the doctor had told him. There was no mistaking the fact that the duchess knew her murderer: the padlock hadn't been forced, the keys were in their place in the drawer, nothing had been broken among the countless items in the anteroom. Still, there had been a struggle, and it was demonstrated by the marks on the victim's body; as well as the cushion pressed down on her face, forcefully, clearly to make sure that the duchess was unable to scream. Perhaps Maione was right: before heading home, he had said that in his opinion it was the murderer himself who had arranged the dead body, out of respect, out of love.

Out of love. How many strange, absurd things he had seen people do out of love. And how treacherous, he thought as he ate under Rosa's vigilant gaze, this sentiment could be as it made its way into the folds of one's thoughts, infecting one's soul. He had struggled and continued to struggle, but he couldn't seem to keep himself from thinking with growing anxiety about his innocent nightly appointment, and the slight wave of greeting that he exchanged with his across-the-street neighbor. He couldn't have said whether it was worse or better than before, as he watched her embroider from hiding, just to drink in her normality, like some healthful herbal tea.

He knew nothing about love. But if he were ever to talk about it, he would've said that it was important to protect the object of one's affections from evil, even if the evil happens to be in the person in love. Especially if the evil happens to be in the person in love. And so in his case, if love was what he felt for Enrica, then it was incumbent upon him to keep her safely distant from his curse, from the savage and terrible pain that he carried within him.

That was why he continued to stay far away from her, why he never looked for an opportunity to meet her, to be able to talk to her, look her in the eye, hold her hand. That's the way it had been for over a year, until fate finally put them face to face. And now that pure, sweet emotion, experienced from a safe distance, had been tainted with the scent of flesh. For twenty-three hours a day, Ricciardi wished that the previous situation of checkmate could be reinstated; unsatisfying though it certainly might have been, it was at least reassuring.

But for an hour a day, for *that* hour, on the other hand, he'd have gladly flown the twenty-five feet that separated them to embrace her and kiss her a thousand times. And now that hour had arrived.

With his heart in his throat, after closing his bedroom door, Ricciardi went over to the window.

Enrica was distraught with rage and despair. A trap had been laid for her, without even asking her views or opinions. She'd tried all night long to catch her father's eye, but he'd taken great care to look anywhere but at his daughter's face. As for her mother, of course, she was perfectly at her ease in her role as the lady of the house, never stopping once as she regaled her guests with Enrica's domestic gifts.

She had found her father's two friends intolerable, a badly matched couple in which the wife was an unctuous, bullying harridan while the husband was a miserable wretch without qualities, practically a mute. As for the son, he was the main reason for her rage. An unpleasant, ignorant, uninteresting man; he knew how to talk—and never stopped for an instant—about nothing but clothing, automobiles, and high society, topics that could not have been any further from her interest.

It had been her mother, of that much she was sure. She had decided to go on the offensive, after whining for years about how urgent it was to find her a fiancé. She had become increasingly insistent, but Enrica never thought that she would stoop so low: to bring a man home, and without even asking! Her upbringing and her social standing kept her from being openly rude, but no one could force her to be pleasant. And so she had remained silent throughout the meal, for once served in grand gala in the drawing room; the hours went by slowly, with the incessant chitchat of that prettified dandy in her ears, and she was forced to tolerate her mother's continual invitations to take part in the conversation and the harridan's compliments, why, what a lovely young woman, what lovely hands, what a lovely smile. She was nauseated.

And now she was also desperate, because it was already ten o'clock and the guests showed no signs of leaving. And she wouldn't be at the window to see the only man she wanted to listen to, if only he would say something to her.

Ricciardi had spent half an hour watching the darkened kitchen window, waiting in vain. The sense of disappointment had grown within him, along with some slight concern for Enrica's well-being; he'd been certain that she would never miss their appointment except for some serious reason, some disaster, and it pained him not to know.

Just as he was about to give up and go to bed, he glimpsed out of the corner of his eye a gleam of light from the corner of the apartment building across the way: another room in the Colombo home had its lights turned on. There was a part of him that recoiled at the thought that he wanted to see who was there and what was going on, intruding into another family's life like the lowest and most common gossip: but the other part of him easily won the battle.

Justifying his actions with the thought that he was only trying to ensure that Enrica was well and safe, he rapidly calculated just which window in his apartment would offer the best view of the illuminated room, and to his horror he realized that would be his *tata*'s bedroom.

Rosa was just about to go to bed, having completed her rosary with the invocations of the proper saints. She had a nightcap on her head, her hair gathered inside it, a long nightshirt, buttoned from neck to feet, and she was pulling up the bedclothes when she heard someone knocking at her bedroom door.

"Who is it?" she called out, absurdly.

"It's me, who did you think it was? No one lives here but you and me," said Ricciardi.

"What's the matter, don't you feel well?"

"Yes, I feel fine, don't worry. I just want to see something from your window. Can I come in?"

"Of course, be my guest."

And Rosa saw Ricciardi open the door; she saw him give her a guilty look; she saw him go over to the window, muttering something about having seen some suspicious activity in the street; she saw him stand for several long seconds with both hands gripping the windowsill, holding his breath; she saw him brace himself against the wall with one hand, as if he were about to faint; she heard him moan softly; she saw him turn, pale as death, biting his lip; and last of all, she saw him leave the room, shutting the door behind him, after saying, "It was nothing, nothing at all, I must have been mistaken. *Buona notte.*"

At that point Rosa got out of bed, slowly pushing the covers aside, and in her turn went over to the window; there she saw a certain young woman sitting primly on a sofa, as stiff as if she'd swallowed a broom, with a smiling well-dressed young man whispering into her ear.

At first, she was worried. But then she decided that the ice tends to melt faster if you light a nice hot fire underneath it.

And with a smile, she went back to bed.

XIV

The following morning, anyone crossing paths with Maione and Ricciardi, who were on their way to Palazzo Camparino to question the two dukes, would have failed to notice any substantial changes in the expressions of either one: the commissario, dark and silent; the brigadier, sweaty and angry. Actually, though, both their moods had deteriorated considerably.

Maione had had a nightmare. There was Lucia who was giving immense bowls of macaroni with ragu to the damned fruit vendor Ciruzzo, laughing and telling him that he needed to put some flesh on his bones, that he was far too skinny. Behind the closed door, but he could see her perfectly as you can only in dreams, Filomena was weeping, begging him to eat what she'd cooked for him and him alone; it was impossible to see what was in the bowl, but he could smell a celestial aroma. Maione, who the night before had put on a heroic show of a lack of appetite and had eaten only two peaches, in his dream continued to decline the offer, and sat there, suffering, watching the detested Di Stasio as he enjoyed his meal.

The nightmare had worsened both the brigadier's hunger and his anger, and the next morning once again he'd tried to don his summer uniform, but without success; so now he was walking up the Via Medina apparently in the same black mood as the day before, but in reality, he was furious.

The dominant emotion in Ricciardi, on the other hand, was

bafflement. He found himself in the presence of an entirely new emotion, and he had no idea how to deal with it.

Unlike Maione, he'd had no nightmares, but that was only because he hadn't slept a wink all night long. The image of a smiling Enrica, with a stranger whispering sweet nothings in her ear, was tormenting him. The part of him that had insisted on keeping his distance, well aware of just how impossible it would be to have a normal relationship, now piped up loudly, reiterating its reasoning; but the commissario suspected and feared that it was too late in any case, and that thought terrified him in some way.

He contemplated with genuine fascination the emotion that had surged through him, its reverberations echoing in his chest all night long. A real, physical malaise: not mental, the way he'd always imagined it, the thousands of times that he'd heard dead people talk about it, whether they'd been murdered for love or had killed themselves for love. In reality, it was a stabbing pain behind his stomach, in some unspecified spot under his lungs, and it affected both his breathing and his intestines. A violent and enduring pain that, if you tried to think about anything else, would immediately snap your attention back and keep your thoughts from wandering.

The sheer irrationality of the sensation made it impossible for him to examine the problem the way he was accustomed to doing with his work. He kept repeating to himself: if you've always known you couldn't approach Enrica, that you had to protect her from your pain and your absurd nature, how dare you suffer like a dog now, just because you've seen her with another man? What sense is there to this suffering of yours?

It makes no sense at all, he answered himself. All the same, the stabbing pain behind his stomach, somewhere beneath his lungs, remained just as intense.

Neither of the two men, as they struggled with their own malaise, had noticed the state of mind of the other; the policemen who had watched them as they left headquarters had, though, and they had exchanged knowing winks: this was no day to tangle with them.

Along the way, Ricciardi once again encountered the man who'd been beaten to death, launching his invective against those who had killed him:

"Buffoonish clowns, you're nothing but four buffoonish clowns. Four to one, for shame, for shame, you buffoonish clowns."

The commissario just grew darker and grimmer. He thought to himself: you could have lived a normal life, had a wife and children. You could have eaten and drank, laughed and played. You could have sat on a sofa, at night, whispering sweet words to a girl. And instead, you got yourself beaten to death in exchange for the satisfaction of talking smart to some idiot with a billy club. The usual damned waste.

The palazzo's front door was half-closed, as was customary when in mourning. On the closed door panel a sign read:

FOR THE DEATH OF THE SIGNORA DUCHESSA
ADRIANA MUSSO DI CAMPARINO.

Sciarra, the doorman, was sweeping in the courtyard, doing his best to stay in the shade where however it was already perfectly clean. With every stroke of the broom, he had to pull up the sleeves of his shirt, which kept slipping down and covering his hands. Near him, the same two children they had encountered on their last visit were eating two enormous pieces of bread and cheese. As soon as the man saw Ricciardi and Maione, he came toward them with that pouncing gait of his.

"Commissario, Brigadier, good day to you. How can I be of service?"

Maione wasted no time on rote courtesy, in part because he

was clearly irritated at the sight of the children stuffing themselves hand over fist.

"I only need you to take us in. We're here to talk with the duke and his son."

Ricciardi broke in:

"First I want to take a look at the duchess's room, though. Isn't the housekeeper here?"

"Of course she is, Commissa', I'll call her for you immediately."

"One more thing, Sciarra. Where were you, the other night, when the murder happened?"

The doorman spread his arms, letting the sleeves trail below.

"Where do you think I was? Upstairs, at home, keeping an eye on these two devils."

The older of the two spoke, while still noisily chewing his food.

"So unless Papà comes and feeds us, we refuse to go to bed. We only eat when Papà's there!"

Maione made a face.

"Then Papà must always be there, because every time I see you, you're eating."

"What can you do about it, Brigadie'? These two are wolves, they're not human children. I don't know where they got it, not from my side. Wait for me here, I'll go and get Concetta."

Here they come now. I can see them both clearly, the big bulky brigadier in uniform and the other one, the skinny one: the commissario. I asked Concetta and she told me what they asked her yesterday.

I was amazed: I thought that they'd want to talk to us immediately, me and the old corpse. But instead they just left. Maybe they wanted to let us steam for a while, bubble in our broth. But I didn't simmer and wilt, even if it's hellishly hot. I stayed here, good as gold, tending my plants, here on the terrace. Without altering a gesture, without uttering a word I wouldn't have said normally.

Not because of their suspicions, not because of that. But because I refused to allow yesterday and today to be different days, in any way, shape, or form. Nothing's happened. Has something happened, after all, when a sewer rat dies down in the filthy alleys, in the *vicoli*? Has something happened if a rabid bitch is stoned to death by a band of street urchins? No. Nothing's happened. Life goes on, the same as before, with everyone in their place. The bigger the picture, the less the details count. And here, really, nothing's happened at all.

Though, actually, I wouldn't say that absolutely nothing's happened. After all, I have the ring back.

Concetta materialized at the top of the stairs in silence; this woman, Maione thought, had the ability to appear and disappear without anyone seeing her. Even as big and tall as she was.

"Gentlemen, a good day to you. I'm at your service."

Ricciardi looked at her as if he'd just awoken from a nap.

"And a good day to you. We're here to speak with the duke and his son, but first I'd like to take a look at the duchess's bedroom. Could you take us to see it?"

"Certainly, Commissario; it's still just as the duchess left it, as you know she never even got a chance to retire for the night. Come right this way."

They passed through the anteroom. Ricciardi immediately saw the image of Adriana di Camparino in front of him; staring right at him with her dead eyes she repeated:

"The ring, the ring, you've taken the ring, the ring is missing."

And we'll see if we can't find it, he thought to himself.

They followed the Sivo woman as she moved soundlessly, through a long series of rooms. There was a scent of cleanliness and everything was in perfect order, but the general impression was of a place devoid of life. They strode through an endless succession of drawing rooms, each of them wallpapered and upholstered in a different color. They also passed through a chapel, dominated by an altar with a reliquary that seemed quite ancient. Concetta stopped and genuflected, rapidly crossing herself; Maione took off his cap and bowed his head, while Ricciardi paused to take in a wheeled gurney. The house-keeper, following his gaze, said:

"It's for the duke, when the priest comes to say mass."

Immediately after that, she ushered them into a large bed-room, at the center of which stood a double canopy bed, draped with mosquito netting. Here the prevailing hue was rose, from the silk wall coverings to the oversized cushions, the upholstery of the sofa, and the two armchairs in one corner. The French doors led out onto a balcony overlooking the piazza.

Paintings and photographs celebrated the duchess's beauty, portraying her in every pose imaginable: at the wheel of a sports car, in an evening gown, dressed as a bride. The painting that took pride of place on the wall facing the bed depicted her, lovely and half-nude, covered with a sheet that she held over her breasts with one hand. The woman had been well aware of how beautiful she was and had made full use of the fact.

Ricciardi thought about death, about how the woman had appeared before his eyes. When she was alive, as he could see from the pictures in the bedroom, she'd always been keenly aware of her appearance: carefully made-up, her hair done in a permanent, her clothing pressed. In the other picture, available exclusively to him, aside from the bullet hole in her forehead, she had rouge smeared over her face from the cushion, as if on a painter's palette, her fine silk dress rumpled and creased, one stocking half off. The final violation. Death makes a mess.

The odor that pervaded the room was the same scent that he'd noticed under the smell of cordite in the anteroom: a floral essence, on the heavy side. The choice, thought the commissario, reflected the duchess's true nature, wealthy but hardly the product of a refined upbringing. When it comes to clothing, you can always ask your girlfriends and the owners of the boutiques for advice, but perfume is far too personal of a choice.

The arrangement of the objects suggested that the woman must have gone out in a hurry, leaving her dressing table in disarray and her armoire half-open. As if reading his thoughts, Concetta, who was standing in the doorway, whispered:

"She always left things higgledy-piggledy, the duchess. For all she cared, after all we were there to tidy up after her. But now, I can't say why, it gives me a strange feeling to enter this room. Not in the anteroom, even though there's still blood on the sofa, and it won't come out. But here, I get that strange feeling."

Ricciardi made a sign to Maione, who opened the drawers of the nightstand. In the first drawer, atop the linen and underwear in plain sight, sat a bundle of letters tied together with a blue ribbon. The brigadier hefted them with one hand, after rifling through them quickly.

"They're all signed 'yours, Mario.' She certainly didn't seem to be particularly afraid that anyone might see them, eh, the Signora?"

Concetta didn't seem surprised. She shrugged.

"And who would have seen them? The duke and the young master have never set foot in here. I don't look at that sort of thing and Mariuccia doesn't know how to read. She could have tacked them up on the walls and it wouldn't have changed a thing."

Ricciardi sensed the disapproval more in the words than in the tone of voice. It struck him as sarcasm, not resentment. Of course, you could never be certain.

"Aside from the duke and his son, and the duchess of course, who else came into this room?"

Concetta shot an eloquent glance at the letters still in Maione's hand, and then she said:

"How would I know, Commissa'? I go to bed early at night, I already told you. And the Signora had the padlock keys."

We get it, thought Ricciardi. "Yours, Mario" had access to the bedroom, as well as the heart, of the lovely duchess.

"All right. Don't touch anything in here, leave it exactly as it is, until you hear otherwise from us. Now announce us to the duke."

After a sleepless night, dominated by the thought of Ricciardi who had waited in vain for her to appear at the window, Enrica arose the next morning grim and determined. If her sweet disposition and her upbringing had both conspired to keep her from being openly rude to her guests the night before, now she had made up her mind to have it out with her parents. She would not only tell them that Sebastiano did not interest her in the slightest, but she would also forbid them, from that day forward, to plot behind her back again, even if they thought they were doing it for her own good. Guessing at her intentions, however, her mother had left the apartment at dawn, telling the housemaid that she was going to pay a call on a cloistered aunt, a nun; her father, moreover, had left for the shop at least an hour earlier than his usual time of departure.

All right then, thought Enrica. Then I'll come see you, my dear Papà; I'm really interested to see what you have to say for yourself.

Nonetheless, she tended to her household duties, and it was only after she'd washed up, done the grocery shopping, and given instructions for lunch that she changed her clothes, put on her hat, and set out for the shop on the Via Toledo.

XV

The bedroom where Matteo Musso, duke of Camparino, was losing his final battle was immersed in shadow. You could smell the aromas of disinfectant and putrefaction, lye and stale urine, medicine and dust. Ricciardi recognized the stench of death.

Once their eyes became accustomed to the dark, the two policemen distinguished a silhouette in the bed, the source of the rhythmic gasping they'd heard when they entered. It would seem that the duke was asleep. Suddenly, however, a raucous voice said: "Conce', open the shutters just a little. Let me see who's come to call on me."

The woman moved soundlessly in the darkness, demonstrating that she had a perfect knowledge of the arrangement of furniture and objects, and opened the window just a crack. A shaft of light entered the room, illuminating Ricciardi and Maione like a spotlight in the night.

"Your grace. My name is Ricciardi and I'm a Commissario of Public Safety. This is Brigadier Maione, with me. First of all, my condolences for your loss."

The vague shadow had taken on some outlines. On the pillow lay a skull, hollowed out cheeks and eyes, a shiny bald cranium; an exceedingly skinny neck sank under the sheets, from which protruded a parchment-like arm. The hand looked like the talons of some bird of prey, the yellowish fingers wiggled slowly.

"Forget about that. A stranger has died here, what should I

care about it? Be seated. Conce', make the Commissario and the Brigadier comfortable."

His voice sounded like the rasping of a metal file on sandpaper. It sent shivers down your back. The heat in the bedroom was tremendous.

"Please, don't go to any trouble, Signora, *grazie*. We'll only be here a short while, just a few questions, if you have no objection, your grace."

Once again the hand waved softly, as if giving permission. Maione decided that over time, the duke had gotten used to expressing himself in this fashion, with gestures, to save his breath. Ricciardi went on:

"When was the last time you saw the duchess?"

There were a few moments of silence. Just when the commissario was starting to think that the duke must have fallen asleep, the scratchy voice said:

"Have you ever spoken to a dead person before, Commissario?"

This time it was Ricciardi's turn to be left breathless. Just like that, point blank, that question. As if the duke had possessed, from his deathbed of pain, the faculty of peering through the darkness and into his soul.

"What do you mean by that?"

The tone of voice was harsher than he meant it to be, but the duke hardly seemed to notice.

"You can see with your own eyes exactly what I mean. I'm a dead man, Commissa'. Not today, not tomorrow, or whenever they carry me out of here. I died when my wife passed away. Not this one, of course. My wife, my real wife."

With some effort, Ricciardi had resumed breathing normally. A metaphor. It had been nothing but a metaphor.

"Why do you say that, your grace? And if I may venture to ask, what does it have to do with my question?"

"It has a great deal to do with it, Commissario. A man dies

at the very moment that his life no longer means anything to anyone else. And the last person I had any meaning for was Carmen. I died when she died."

Ricciardi didn't know what to say, so he just waited.

"Right now, you're talking to a dead man. It's a novel experience, isn't it?"

You have no idea, thought Ricciardi. The duke went on:

"A dead man doesn't deserve affection or care. He's just there to be exploited for his possessions, for his money. Every so often, maybe, you might bring him a flower. The woman you're talking about, Commissario, the last time she came into this room was at Easter. She came in laughing, she threw open the windows and let in a gust of cold air. She looked at me and she started laughing again; if you ask me, she was drunk. She said, it's Easter Sunday, Christ is risen, why don't you get up, too? She put a bunch of flowers into a vase, on that dresser, and then she left. Who knows who even gave her those flowers. I couldn't tell you when the time before that was."

The effort that it took the man to go on talking must have been enormous. His sentences were fragmentary, and he had to catch his breath every third or fourth word. Maione felt an urge to leave: the heat, the stench, and the discomfort he felt as he listened to the duke were becoming intolerable. But Ricciardi seemed willing to go on asking questions.

"How long ago were you married?"

The implicit meaning of the question was clear to Maione, and also to the duke: there was such a vast age difference, how could he have thought it would turn out any other way? The old man cackled, until a violent burst of coughing interrupted his laughter. Concetta hastened over to the bed with a handkerchief and dabbed at his mouth.

"She was young and I was already old. You see, Commissario, what cruel tricks old age plays on us. A glance, a word, a smile: and suddenly you feel interesting again. I knew it, I always knew that what Adriana wanted was the title, and the money. And I took her in all the same. Because she was beautiful and young. I gave her what she wanted, and I took what she had. As long as I could, as long as I was capable of it. It was an exchange, nothing more than an exchange."

In a way, the chilly nature of the reasoning horrified Ricciardi more than the broken, gasping voice.

"There's no such thing as love, Commissario. Love is an illusion. There's only self-interest, everyone wants something that someone else has. If you think that love is wanting someone else's well-being, you're lying to yourself."

Ricciardi half-closed his eyes, and he saw a young woman sitting on a sofa, listening to a man's promises. He should have let her go, if what he really felt was love, but instead he felt like he was dying. The stabbing pain behind his stomach returned for a brief instant.

"What about hatred, Duke? What does hatred make you do? When the illusion of love vanishes, what's left?"

Maione scuffed the floor with his foot. Concetta stood like a statue in the shadows.

"Hatred is a thought, Commissario. An impulse, perhaps even a desire. Someone who's busy dying hour after hour, someone who never leaves his bed and depends on the kindness of those who come to assist him, cannot afford the luxury of hatred. Because it's a luxury too."

Ricciardi considered what the duke had just said. He couldn't imagine that shell of a man murdering the duchess; but still the duke was clear-minded, he could have issued orders and given instructions. Out of the corner of his eye he studied Concetta, who didn't even seem to be breathing.

"You have a son, isn't that right?"

The question fell into silence. It seemed to Ricciardi that even the rattling of the duke's dying lungs had changed its tone. After a few moments the man replied.

"Yes, I have a son. His name is Ettore."

No affection, no emotion. A simple stark statement. Ricciardi waited, but the duke didn't seem to have any intention of adding anything; when he did speak it was to say:

"I hope you'll forgive me, now, Commissario; I'm very tired. I'll be glad to see you again whenever you like, but right now Madame Death wants my sleep."

"Of course, your grace; pardon me. Just one more thing: did your wife wear a . . . special ring, as far as you know? Something of particular value, I don't know, a rare stone perhaps?"

The duke coughed again, and it took him a while to gather his breath and his strength for a response.

"My wife, my real wife, my Carmen had a ring. It was my family's ring, with our coat of arms; the ring that all the duchesses of Camparino wore. I took it off her dead hand, but I wish I'd never done it, I've regretted it every instant of my life since then; and I gave it to her, to Adriana. As if she were worthy of wearing it. When you're finished with the . . . with her, give it back to us. To my son. It's the only part of her I wish I had back."

Ricciardi decided that this was hardly the moment to inform the duke that the ring had already been taken from the interloping gold digger; and for now the brief description of the object was all he needed. He said goodbye and left the room, and a relieved Maione followed him out.

Livia walked out of the elevator in the hotel lobby; instantly, she was surrounded by a porter, a coachman, and a bellboy who, until a few seconds earlier, had been snoozing in the late-morning heat. Two men reading the paper as they sipped their coffee looked up and both whistled softly and admiringly.

The woman was stunningly beautiful: she'd spent more than two hours trying on, over and over, just some of the countless dresses that she'd brought with her; in the end she'd selected a little light gray dress in a fine material, with a black handbag and black shoes. The hat, set at a coquettish angle on her short, dark brown hair, had a tiny black veil, her one concession to her state of mourning. If it had been entirely up to her, she'd have dispensed with that as well, but she didn't know what Ricciardi thought about it and so she'd decided to keep at least a marker of her loss, which was more social than it was emotional. She wore black gloves on her hands, in fishnet, just like her stockings.

Elegance was one of Livia's distinguishing characteristics, like her feline movements and the spicy aroma of her perfume. As always, her entrance into any room immediately captured the attention of one and all, and never let it go.

The two men had risen and, with allusive smiles, come over; they clearly belonged to the elite, discreet army of gigolos that brightened the holidays of solitary female tourists, especially foreign ones. Livia smiled and gestured with one hand to the only member of the group whose services interested her: the coachman.

The man, hat in hands, bowed and inquired: "Where can I take you, Signo'?"

With a smile, Livia told him. Her offensive had finally begun.

XVI

After they left the bedroom, Ricciardi asked Concetta to go and see whether the duke's son was available to see them; they waited in the anteroom, in the company of the ghostly image of the duchess, which kept repeating its denunciation of the disappearance of the ring.

Ricciardi thought in silence, his hands in his pockets, looking out the window down into the palazzo courtyard. The building's height kept much of the courtyard in shadow, including the luxuriant bed of multicolored hydrangeas. The commissario wondered whether the murderer had hidden in one of the many nooks and crannies, or if he had entered with the duchess, upon her return home.

Part of his thoughts, though, went to the words the duke had spoken, words that made him ponder himself and his life. A man dies at the very moment that his life no longer means anything to anyone else; those words had gouged a hole into his chest. He thought of Rosa, of the excessively maternal care she lavished on him; he thought of Maione, of the rough and only partial confidences they exchanged, now and again; he thought of Doctor Modo, and the cutting irony and refined mockery that characterized their relationship, as well as the occasional beers they drank together; he thought of his mother, her silent love, her weary smile.

Am I alive? he wondered. And if not, when did I die? Looking out the window, he saw Sciarra below him, busily raking dead leaves out of the flower bed. Not far away from him, the two children were quarreling, the older girl hiding something under her dress; probably something to eat. The little man whose sleeves were too long would turn around every so often and pretend to chase them, then he'd return to his work with a broad smile on his face. Well, no doubt about it, Sciarra was still alive. The woman standing behind him, however, whose immense grief at departing from her earthly existence he could feel against the back of his head, was not.

He thought irrationally of Enrica, of just who the man whispering into her ear with a smile might have been. Whoever he was, he wasn't like him: he wasn't condemned to solitude. He felt a stabbing pain in his stomach: this sensation too was starting to become familiar to him.

Soundlessly, Concetta came to summon them. The young master could receive them now.

Just once, for a change, you devote yourself to yourself for a bit. You've washed your hair in the large washbasin of the porcelain bath accessories. You rinse your hair with the pitcher, using water that you heated in the big cook pot in the kitchen: it's something you haven't done in ages. Now you're brushing it out, sitting in front of the mirror; again, something you've almost forgotten how to do. Lazily, you also wonder whether it's worth the trouble of curling it with a permanent, instead of pulling it up into a bun on the back of your head, the way you always do: your hair's not ugly after all, once it's washed and loosened. It's not dull anymore. There's a new glistening light to it.

There's a different expression in your eyes, as well; you wonder what it could be. What could be new about them. Perhaps it's just the hint of a smile.

Perhaps you want to be ready when the time comes.

The staircase was cool due to the thickness of the palazzo's outer walls. As they climbed, Maione, who was still panting and sweating, directed a question to Concetta's vast back:

"But with all the empty rooms in the building, why on earth did the young master choose to go live on the top floor?"

Concetta replied without raising her voice, as if she were in a church.

"The young master moved upstairs after his mother's death, ten years ago. He loves plants, he keeps them on the terrace; so he wants to be close to them. Also, it's comfortable for him, he has two large rooms."

Ricciardi broke in to ask:

"Is there no direct access, from his apartment to the second story? Is it absolutely necessary to take the stairs?"

"Yes, you absolutely have to take the stairs."

They'd reached a landing, with a small wooden door. Maione asked:

"And who lives there?"

Before Concetta had time to answer, the wooden door swung open and a boy looked out. His resemblance to Mariuccia, the housemaid, was unmistakable. In one hand he held a book, in the other, a chunk of bread and tomato.

Glaring venomously at the snack, Maione answered his own question.

"Why did I even ask? The Sciarra family. You must be the eldest, no?"

The boy, intimidated by the uniform, nodded his head yes. He resembled his mother so distinctly that Maione practically expected him to start sobbing at any moment.

"Yessir, Vincenzo Sciarra, at your service. I'm going to the after-school tutoring session."

"Well, then get going. But don't your jaws get tired, chewing all the time like that? Go on, don't just stand there."

The boy took off, while Ricciardi looked at the brigadier and shook his head.

"This fasting you're doing isn't good for you: you're becoming intractable."

Gosh, thought Maione. By those standards, the commissario's been on a fast since the day he was born.

They'd now come to a large ornamentally carved door, a few steps higher up.

Concetta, who had gone in to announce their arrival in the meanwhile, came back out.

"If you please, go right on in. It's the door at the far end of the first room. I'll wait for you downstairs."

They walked through a large messy room, a cross between a drawing room and a library. There was an imposing desk piled high with books, both open and closed, with sheets of paper scattered across it, covered with a close, slanted script; one wall was covered, floor to ceiling, with a bookcase made of dark wood, overflowing with books; there were two armchairs, and between them a small table on which sat a trumpet gramophone, while on the floor lay several 78 RPM disks. On another low table sat a bottle of liquor, with a few dirty glasses.

The impression was of a place where one or more persons lived every minute of the day, working, relaxing, and resting; and where someone who might tidy up was only rarely admitted. Light and an intense scent of flowers came in through a set of French doors, half open, along with the sound of someone whistling.

Ricciardi and Maione exchanged a glance and then headed toward the half-open door. The brigadier called out, asking leave to come in:

"*È permesso?*"

The whistling stopped and a low, musical voice said: "*Prego*, come right ahead. I'm out here, on the terrace."

The setting was somewhat surprising. The light of the sun, at its zenith at that time of the day, was filtered through plants of every kind: the only thing missing was trees, even though some of the climbing vines had trunks of considerable size. Ricciardi was no botanist but he had grown up in the country, in regular contact with fields, orchards, and gardens, and he understood the attention and the immense love required to create that only apparently wild tangle of plants. Whoever cared for that open-air greenhouse had to devote a great deal of time to its cultivation, along with considerable enthusiasm.

From one corner a young man of pleasing appearance, about thirty, came toward them. He wore a white shirt with the sleeves rolled up onto his forearms; he was slender, with a dark complexion, and a hooked nose and a thin mustache. His black hair, parted in the middle, was wavy and neatly brushed. With a frank and open smile, he extended his hand.

"A pleasure. I'm Ettore Musso."

"The pleasure is all ours, Signor Duca. I'm Brigadier Maione from Naples police headquarters, and this is my commanding officer, Commissario Ricciardi. Our sincerest condolences for your loss."

The man looked at him vaguely, as if he hadn't quite understood what Maione had just said. Then he burst out laughing.

"That's rich! No, forgive me, gentlemen, but that's truly rich. For my loss, did you say? Condolences?"

Maione stared at Ricciardi, nonplussed. The commissario, on the other hand, was looking at Ettore; his expression hadn't altered. When he'd finished laughing, the man went on:

"Excuse me. I really am unforgivable. Please, make yourselves comfortable. Would you like something to drink? Or to eat, perhaps?"

He sat down on a wrought-iron chair, which stood with two other chairs like it around a small tile-top table. At the center of the table was a carafe of coffee and a dish of sweet rolls and a bowl of marmalade. With an apologetic air he added:

"I'm breakfasting late. I'm afraid I was up until very late last night; I've only just woken up. Now what can I do for you?"

The two policemen sat down. The man's manner was certainly charming and the setting was pleasant. The plants, recently watered, provided shade and humidity, making it pleasantly cool. The corner with the table was free of buzzing insects, which could however be heard everywhere else on the terrace. Guessing what Ricciardi was thinking, Ettore said:

"Bravo, Commissario. So you noticed, eh? If you don't want insects around you, you need only choose wisely when it comes to picking the plants you put near you. You must above all avoid flowers: they're lovely to look at from a distance, too, and the scent will reach you just the same."

While he was speaking he'd taken a roll, spread marmalade on it, and now he was nibbling at it eagerly. Maione felt his instinctive liking for Ettore melt away.

Ricciardi finally spoke:

"May I ask you to explain why you laughed, Duke? I failed to grasp what was funny about what the brigadier said. That may just be because I don't have much of a sense of humor."

Ettore stopped, then he laughed again, scattering bits of bread all over the table.

"No, forgive me again. The reason is quite simple: the death of my . . . of my father's wife is perhaps the best piece of news I've received in the last several years. And so it struck me as ridiculous to have you offer your condolences, that's all."

Ricciardi looked him hard in the eyes. He wanted to be very sure of what he was taking in.

"And why is that? News of a death, and a violent death at that, the death of a woman who was still young. How can that come as good news, Duke?"

Ettore waved his hand in front of his face, as if shooing away something unnecessary.

"I beg you, Commissario, please. Just call me Ettore, or

Musso; but let's dispense with titles. They couldn't be any further from the way I think and feel, believe me. How can it come as good news, you ask? Nothing could be simpler: I hated that woman. I hated her with all my heart and all my soul. Didn't they tell you that?"

A moment of awkward silence ensued, a moment that Ettore spent continuing imperturbably to eat and gracefully sip his coffee. To Maione and Ricciardi it seemed unbelievable that, on the day after a murder committed in his home, Ettore should candidly confess that he'd hated the victim. The man must have an ironclad alibi, they both concluded.

Ricciardi said:

"May I ask where you were on the night between Saturday and Sunday, between midnight and two in the morning?"

There was another moment of rapt silence. Ettore dabbed at his mouth with a napkin and got to his feet, stretching lazily. He walked over to an opening in the hedge through which it was possible to see the piazza; there was no one but a small knot of children playing, indifferent to the heat and the bright sunshine.

"This, as I'm sure you would tell me, is a strange city. Clamped between the sea, the hills, and the mountain, it continues to grow on top of itself. The *vicoli* get narrower, the buildings grow taller. Everyone on top of everyone else, more and more, just to keep from being pushed any further away. And so we're all in constant contact, without respite. No one has any time to themselves. And why did I hate her, you may ask me? The answer is simple. Because she had nothing in common with me, with that weakling of a father of mine, and above all, with my mother, whose memory she besmirched with her mere presence. That's why."

His tone of voice remained unchanged, still just as cheerful and conversational as before. It was as if he were chatting about the weather or his plants.

"She slipped into this house through deceit, and through deceit she cast a spell on my father, and with the same deceit she won herself friends and lovers. She took our name and donned it like a dress, with utter indifference for those who, centuries before her, bore it proudly. That is why I've stopped using it. She cast shame on us all, with her continuous and unconcealed adultery, going so far as to bring her lover, a married man with children, under the roof of this home."

The silence that followed was broken by the cries of the children below and the seagulls that pinwheeled lazily through the sky overhead. Ricciardi mused that, whoever Adriana Musso di Camparino might once have been, she was now a badly restitched piece of old clothing lying on a slab in the morgue. And all that remained of her was an image made of mist that no one could see but him, an image that went on endlessly repeating a senseless phrase and bleeding from a bullet hole in its forehead. He said again:

"Where were you, sir, on Saturday night?"

Ettore went on as if he hadn't even heard him:

"As you can imagine, anyone would have hated her in my place. To keep from having to see her, I moved all the way up here. And from up here I look out on this city and its populace, and I admire my plants. And I learn a great deal. These are meaningful times, Commissario. Times that will forever be remembered. Destiny is about to make itself felt, and everyone can see that: you need only read, look around you, listen to the radio. Those children down there, you can see them: they don't know it. But there will come a man who will lead them toward the sun, who will make them the masters of history. They live like little animals, the way their fathers and mothers did, incapable of understanding even whether they're alive or dead. But they must stay in their place. All that matters is that each and every one stays in their place. That everyone does their part. In the world of tomorrow there is no place for deceit; and therefore there is no place for women like my father's un-dearly departed wife."

Maione sweated in silence, under his cap. He was thinking that people were simply no longer ashamed to say certain things, even in the presence of two strangers. And that the fact that they were in uniform, or at least that he was, must make people like Musso assume that they too were fanatical supporters of the Fascist regime. He was also thinking that all that nonsensical chatter must be an attempt to shift attention away from the commissario's question, though he was certainly not about to let himself be distracted.

"Sir, I asked you a question. I'd like you to answer it."

Ettore turned his back on the view and looked Ricciardi in the face. Now he was no longer smiling.

"I didn't kill her, I'm sorry to say, if that's what you're asking. I should have, and I could have done it a thousand times over the past ten years. And God only knows how much I'd have wanted to. But I didn't kill her. Maybe out of fear, or perhaps out of courage. I couldn't say. And when she died, if she died during the night between Saturday and Sunday, I wasn't home. I returned home at dawn, and I came directly up here."

Maione seemed to have dropped off into sleep, as he always did when he was at the peak of his concentration. He asked:

"Forgive me, but I have a question: do you own a pistol? Or, as far as you know, does your father own one? In other words, are there weapons in the house?"

"No. No firearms, in this house. If I'm remembering rightly, there must be a saber somewhere, my father was an officer. But no pistols."

Silence followed Ettore's words. Even the insects stopped their buzzing for an instant.

"And where were you, that night?"

The man held the transparent gaze of Ricciardi's eyes.

"That, Commissario, is none of your business. If you have

nothing else to ask me, I'd like to go back to my plants. *Buon giorno.*"

As they went back out through the study, Ricciardi noticed a large, yellowing photograph, hand-colored, framed, and hanging in the place of honor over the desk. An elderly woman with a proud gaze, a hooked nose just like Ettore's, and the same line of the mouth. In her hands, crossed beneath her bosom, she held a rosary.

On her left ring finger a golden ring could be seen, with a heraldic crest.

XVII

Looking through the plateglass window, Giulio Colombo saw Enrica arrive, and noticed how she resembled her mother: in just two days he'd been subjected to two assaults on his tranquility, and for two different reasons.

It seemed harder for him to face his daughter, because he felt guilty about what he'd done to her; the evening had hardly been a success, precisely because of the girl's stubborn refusal to join in the conversation. In fact she'd spent nearly the entire dinner grimly looking out the window, despite her mother's best efforts to draw her out by praising her domestic and cultural gifts. As far as that goes, he himself hadn't been particularly impressed with the Fiores' son, a fairly superficial young man who had bored him stiff with a lengthy disquisition on the latest automobile models: there was no topic on earth that attracted him less, as he was a diehard proponent of the belief that those horrible noisy contraptions were irreparably ruining his city.

Nor did the situation improve after dinner, when they all went to sit in the drawing room: while the mother took command of the conversation, gossiping relentlessly about the entire city and in particular about the talk of the town, the murder of the duchess of Camparino, the son sat down practically on top of Enrica, and whispered in her ear incessantly; an unseemly approach, especially considering it was the first time they'd met. Giulio had given signs of annoyance, but one angry glare from his wife was enough to stop him cold, and so he sat there obediently, pretending not to notice what was happening. Poor Enrica had scooted over as far as she could, closer and closer to the armrest, pursued implacably by Sebastiano. A genuine nightmare. Once the three guests had left, Giulio had heaved a sigh of relief and then braced himself for the inevitable argument, but Enrica had immediately withdrawn into her bedroom without even wishing him goodnight. That was the first time he could ever remember that happening: his daughter's goodnight kiss was a consolation he sorely hated to miss.

And here she came now. Her expression, usually so sweet, was grim and set. Giulio wondered whether there was a reason that everyone had it in for him. He sighed and prepared for the clash.

Ricciardi and Maione, on their way back from Palazzo Camparino, were still in bad moods; but at least their work was distracting them from their personal problems. The interviews with the duke and his son, instead of clearing up any details of the case, had only stirred new doubts. Maione seemed especially baffled.

"Commissa', what do you think of this? The duke certainly isn't strong enough to break a couple of anyone's ribs, he might not even be capable of getting out of bed. Still, I don't know if you noticed, the housekeeper obeys him like a lapdog, and she's plenty strong."

Ricciardi walked, lost in thought.

"Yes, that's true; and there's another thing: the Sivo woman, who kept us company close to the duke the whole time, stopped at the door with Ettore, she didn't even come in. And the room struck me as remarkably messy, while the rest of the palazzo is clean and tidy. I'd like to understand the relationship between the two of them."

"I'd like to understand what relationship there is between

the father and the son, Commissa'. The fact that the son doesn't want to be called 'Duke,' for example, seems important to me. And then the father, when you asked him, said, 'Yes, I have a son,' full stop. It seems curious to me."

"That's true, you're right: that's an odd thing too. No doubt about it: a nice case of family togetherness. All of them held together by hate."

Maione continued to be baffled.

"But why, after ten years, would either the duke or his son have wanted to kill the duchess? By then, the situation was what it was, everyone was minding their own business. The duchess had her journalist, Ettore was cultivating his plants, and the duke was dying in his bed."

Ricciardi had seen too much in his time to believe in stable situations.

"Why, haven't you ever seen things change all of a sudden? A situation that you always tolerated, and one day without warning you can't take it anymore. A word, a chance phrase. Maybe even the heat. Or an object, a piece of jewelry; and you lose your temper, you grab a gun, and you shoot.

"And then you recover your senses, you wake up from the madness, and you try to put things back the way they were, taking advantage of the fact that you know the house and you can make it all nice and orderly the way it was. Of course that's happened to me, Commissa'. As for the piece of jewelry, you're thinking of the duchess's hand, aren't you? I remember exactly what Doctor Modo told us: dislocated finger, abrasion on the other finger of the same hand. And I noticed that you asked the duke about the ring. I meant to tell you that the portrait in the young master's den was wearing a ring: if you ask me, that was the first duchess, God rest her soul, she had the same nose as her son. And that's the ring that's disappeared."

Ricciardi ventured a half smile.

"You don't miss a thing, do you? Even in this heat, and as

hungry as you are. The only thing that strikes me as strange is the silence. If there was a struggle, as it would seem from the contusions on the body, then there must have been an argument, and in fact the killer put the cushion on her face to keep her from screaming. How could it be that no one heard a thing, inside the palazzo or out? It was nighttime."

Maione smiled and shook his head.

"Commissa', you're underestimating the neighborhood festas, it's obvious that you're not from Naples. We common folk have nothing but those festas, when it comes to having fun: we sing, we dance, and we misbehave until dawn. Believe me, you can't hear a thing for a mile around, at least. And the festa in the Santa Maria La Nova neighborhood is especially famous. There's the bonfire of old wood and a sort of tarantella contest: if you stop dancing you lose. The local girls spend months and months on their dancing dresses. You have to trust me on this, they could have sung the entire third act of *La Traviata* in the duchess's anteroom and nobody would have heard a thing, not even from the room next door."

Ricciardi wasn't so sure.

"Well, fine, maybe nobody could hear. But getting into and out of the palazzo is no simple matter, and the festa was going on right outside the front door. Can you imagine that no one noticed a thing? I don't believe that the murderer dressed up as a tarantella dancer. I can't figure it out, there are certain details that make me think of a well-planned murder and there are others that point to an impulsive fight."

Maione, mopping his brow, shrugged his shoulders.

"It's not necessarily so, Commissa'. If the murderer was moving quickly, he could get in and out without any trouble. No question, Sciarra's children were eating, as usual, handfuls of *semenzelle* in the middle of the festa, and the front door was wide open; or else, and this is a possibility worth considering, the murderer actually came in with the duchess. We haven't even talked to 'Yours, Mario,' yet, have we? Capece was at home here, from what we've heard."

"You're right. Until we've talked to Capece we can't say a thing. Late this afternoon we'll go to the *Roma* and talk to him, journalists work at night, right now we wouldn't find a soul. As for me, I'm going to go eat a *sfogliatella* at Gambrinus. What are you going to do, go on playing the fakir? Make sure you don't wind up like the famous donkey: just as he'd almost learned how to go without eating, he up and died."

Maione sighed.

"Sure, sure, Commissa', make fun all you like. The way things are going, the less I eat the more I sweat, and the tighter my jacket fits me. One of these mornings, I'm going to lose my patience and lock myself into a trattoria, and nobody's going to stop me then. You go ahead, take your time; I'll wait for you back at headquarters, I'm going to go assign those lazy bums a few jobs to do. I'll see you later."

Livia had asked the carriage driver to leave her at the Largo della Carità: she wanted to take a stroll and take in the city.

Even the brief ride in the open carriage had been exciting, she'd pulled up her veil and the breeze on her face, with the smell of salt water and flowers, had been an unexpected, priceless pleasure. It was very hot, but it didn't bother her: she'd waited too long for this morning to let minor considerations such as the weather ruin it for her. Before long, unless unforeseen developments intervened, she'd be looking at the reason she'd come back to this city.

She'd calculated her timing carefully: she wished to run no risks. She'd make sure she got to Gambrinus ahead of the usual time when, as she remembered perfectly, Ricciardi came in to eat his quick and solitary meal. This time, she thought to herself, even if he wasn't expecting it, he'd have company. The street was just as she'd remembered it, broad and crowded. A number of dark, ragged children clustered around her, begging for coins. Laughing, she reached into her clutch bag and grabbed a little small change; then she flung it far away, the coins landing in a tinkling cascade, glinting in the sunlight; like a school of fish chasing a chunk of bread, the *scugnizzi* leapt at the coins with a collective shout.

Along the way the woman, striking and elegant as she was, attracted the attention of at least four men, who whistled after her and tossed off admiring comments. She was accustomed to attracting attention, but the explicit approach, so typical of the Neapolitans, amused her. And she also liked the sober elegance of the women that she saw on the street, even those who were less well-to-do but still strove to present a pleasing appearance. Not all of them, of course.

In particular, when she was already quite close to Piazza Trieste and Trento, and Gambrinus, she crossed paths with a tall young woman wearing tortoiseshell glasses; the young woman was walking briskly and she crossed the street ahead of her; she noticed that she had a natural elegance and a nice body: she could guess it from her long legs. Nonetheless, Livia decided, she wasn't making the most of what she possessed. She'd undermined her best qualities with an antiquated dress, an old woman's hairdo, and especially with a grim expression that didn't suit her at all. Idly, she guessed that the young woman had some reason to be irritated.

Not Livia: she felt perfectly happy, and at peace with the world. She smiled at the sunlight and walked toward the Gambrinus and its café tables.

XVIII

Enrica had just stepped into her father's shop, and she greeted the salesclerks and her brother-in-law; because there were a few clients choosing among various styles of hats, she prepared to wait for Giulio to have a chance to talk. She loved him very much and she was truly sorry to have to ask him for an explanation of what had happened, but she had no doubt that it was necessary. She couldn't allow her tendency to avoid conflict to be mistaken for a blank check that meant her parents could decide her life on her behalf.

Her inborn discretion made it imposible for her to confide in her parents that she was already attracted to a man, much less a complete stranger; not to mention the fact that, finally, she had a regular date with his glance after more than a year of being aware that there was someone at the window across the way, every night.

It was out of the question even to think of talking about it with her mother, who was notoriously obstinate; she'd only intensify her efforts to drag her daughter out of that romantic fantasy that was bound to lead nowhere. She could just hear her now, going on and on about turning twenty-five and heading for a future of poverty and loneliness. She didn't care what others thought, not even her parents: she'd wait for him, if it took a hundred years.

Because there was one thing she knew with absolute certainty: for Luigi Alfredo Ricciardi there was no one on earth but her. He only needed to realize it, and make up his mind to speak.

Just as she was waiting for her father to be done talking to a fat matron who couldn't make up her mind which imitation cloth fruit to put on her hat, the bell on the door rang, announcing Sebastiano Fiore's entrance into the shop.

Ricciardi arrived at Gambrinus in a noticeably worse mood than he'd been in a few minutes earlier, when he parted ways with Maione, who was heading back to police headquarters. There was a good reason.

He had just been covering the last part of the way, where the Via Toledo runs into the Piazza Trieste and Trento, when the man responsible for his sleepless night stepped out of the front door of one of the shops. Truth be told, he was only one of Ricciardi's preoccupations, and at that moment not even the foremost: but he was still one of the most significant. To make a long story short, bidding his unseen mother goodbye, and therefore looking into the shop as he stepped out of it, the self-same young man Ricciardi had seen whispering into Enrica's ear the night before turned and crashed right into him.

He was tall, much taller than he'd seemed from a distance, and heavy, as well; the impact almost knocked Ricciardi over. He glanced fleetingly into Ricciardi's face with a few hasty words of apology, and he found himself staring into a pair of eyes that scrutinized him coldly, without expression. He apologized again, somewhat worried this time, and moved away, stepping through the front door of the store next door.

The stabbing pain right behind Ricciardi's stomach returned instantly, savage and excruciating. To Ricciardi the man appeared devastatingly handsome, athletic and well dressed. His eye, professionally trained to pick up even hidden details, noticed the silk shirt, the two-tone shoes with the perforated toe caps, the gold tie clip, and the wafting cologne. Neither did the gardenia in the buttonhole nor the straw hat escape the commissario's notice, and he would have been able to draw up a complete description of the individual without any effort.

The most immediate effect of that encounter, which should perhaps have been described as a clash, was the distinct sensation of his own devastating inadequacy; Ricciardi understood that in the eyes of any healthy woman that man would be a hundred times prefereable to him. For the first time he took in his own external appearance, and saw himself for the skinny, drab, poorly dressed individual that he was: hatless, shoes dusty from long walks, an old skinny tie without a tie clip.

And he felt only irritation with himself, for having thought of that man as a rival in love. He hadn't the slightest intention of even entering the competition, especially because he realized that his unlikely victory would only bring pain and sorrow to the woman who became his companion in life: a portion of his curse. And so, he thought again, so much the better. Better for everyone if Enrica found a handsome, well-mannered, well-to-do gentleman, who would certainly make her happy.

The thought of course brought him no comfort: when Ricciardi walked into the cool shade of Gambrinus he was a man on the brink of despair.

The Livia who was waiting, sitting at a carefully chosen table, was a woman filled with hope. She hoped, first and foremost, that Ricciardi would arrive, and that he wouldn't be late, because the pressure of her aspiring squires was becoming oppressive. When she'd decided to smoke a cigarette to kill some time, five little hovering flames had immediately been lit before her, like votive candles in front of a sacred image; there was one contender in particular, dressed entirely in white, who was staring at her with clear intention, convinced that he was irresistible. At that point, she, who had certainly been in a similar situation many times before, started staring right back at him, until he got to his feet and came over, asking her:

"May I sit down?"

Whereupon she promptly responded:

"Absolutely not."

The man was flummoxed. It was hardly a common occurrence to see such a beautiful woman sitting alone in a public place, and the opportunity seemed too delectable; for that matter, it was unthinkable to ruin his reputation as a womanizer, built up over so many years of honorable activity, by retreating immediately. And so he decided to persist:

"Signora, you're much too beautiful to be sitting alone. I can't stand by while that happens. So I'm going to sit down no matter what you say, and if someone has to leave, it will eventually have to be you."

Livia looked toward the door: at that exact moment she saw Ricciardi come in.

With a luminous smile on her face, and without ever taking her eyes off the commissario, she said:

"I wouldn't recommend you try that: the person I was waiting for has just arrived."

Sebastiano Fiore walked into the Colombo family shop, straightening his tie, still a little unsettled by the odd look that the stranger had given him; what on earth can that be about, he thought, I barely grazed him. Thanks to his mental inclination never to focus too long on a single thought, he immediately regained the frank and jovial smile he'd been sporting until just a few seconds earlier.

At first he'd put up some resistance when his mother had ordered him to come to dinner at the Colombos'; he'd planned a night out with his friends at Scoglio di Frisio, the famous restaurant. But when Mamma got something into her head it was best not to resist with too much determination, otherwise the economic retaliations she was capable of unleashing could create serious problems, especially now that he was losing at cards and he'd piled up some debts that were even bigger than usual. And so, he'd decided, let's go ahead and sacrifice a night out on the altar of sheer necessity.

Then, to his surprise, the evening with the Colombos had produced an unexpected and quite agreeable piece of news: the girl that he was being introduced to proved to be anything but unpleasant, with an attractive—if somewhat infrequent—smile and a long pair of legs. No doubt, she dressed like a fifty-year-old and wasn't quite as smitten with him as she ought to have been: but this might yet prove to be beneficial to his plans. In fact, Sebastiano had a very precise strategy in mind: he meant to go on living comfortably on his wealthy parents' backs, without changing his social rounds and routines in the slightest.

In order to pull that off, however, he'd have to go along with his mother's ambitions, at least formally; and what better way than to get engaged with a girl like the Signorina Colombo, who was discreet, quiet, and anything but intrusive? His mother would be pleased, and she'd resume his allowance, in fact, she'd increase it, because getting engaged meant spending money on gifts, flowers, and so on and so forth; the theory of merging the two businesses was a very appealing one; and most important of all, the future operation of the business could be delegated to the bride, and he could go on living the way he always had: without working.

For that reason, the minute he saw the nondescript girl arrive at her father's shop, he'd immediately combed his hair and started off after her, intending to seize this opportunity to invite her out for a cup of coffee.

At Gambrinus, of course.

Ricciardi had changed his habits, though only by a little. For the past month, he'd stopped sitting at the inside table that faced the plateglass window overlooking the Via Chiaia and instead sat outside, under the awning.

The reason for the change had nothing to do with the arrival of the brutal summer heat: it had just happened that, exactly a month ago, in fact, a husband whose wife was cheating on him had decided to take justice into his own hands by murdering his wife's lover with a bullet to the head. At the moment of his premature demise, the unfortunate victim, a young lawyer, had been sitting with a newspaper in his hands and a cup of coffee on the table in front of him, right next to the table where Ricciardi usually sat to consume his rapid daily lunch. The commissario hadn't been present when the horrible scene unfolded, but that did nothing to interfere with his clear and unmistakable view of the lawyer, who went on reading his newspaper, with half his face reduced to a pulpy mess of blood and bone fragments, and repeating:

"Now how long is it going to take her to get free of that stupid chump and come join me?"

But instead of her getting rid of him, once and for all, now it was the allegedly stupid chump who was sitting in a dark jail cell somewhere, mulling over such issues as faithfulness and vendetta.

Since the sight wasn't particularly appetizing, Ricciardi had decided to migrate to an outdoor table which, for a habitudinarian like him, had not been a pleasant experience. But that day, the tables on the sidewalk were all taken and he was forced to venture back inside. He hoped that he wouldn't be forced to share a table with the dead man: he didn't want company at all, much less the company of such a monotonous conversationalist.

As soon as he stepped through the door he caught a whiff of perfume. His sensory memory was faster than his conscious one, so he glimpsed the lithe figure, the limpid eyes, and the catlike stride even before he thought of Livia, immersed in that exotic spicy scent. He looked around and there she was, smiling, sitting in the corner opposite the dead man but like him, waiting for someone to arrive. Standing next to her was a man in a white suit, one hand resting on the back of a chair, in a friendly pose.

Ricciardi took in the situation at a glance: the man's stance and attitude immediately suggested an idea of unwanted intrusiveness; Livia in contrast was looking in his direction, with a radiant smile on her face, in an implicit call for aid. On impulse, he headed straight for the table and, before he could get a word out, he once again heard Livia's voice, just as harmonious and musical as he remembered it:

"There, you see: the person I was waiting for. I'm here for him, and only for him."

The walk to Gambrinus with Sebastiano was surreal: Enrica had gone to the shop in the first place to tell her father in no uncertain terms that she never wanted to see the young man again, and now she was going with him for a cup of coffee, like a pair of lovebirds on their first date.

When Sebastiano had come in, with the paltry excuse that he needed change for a large bill, she'd been left aghast. When he invited her to the café, she'd launched Giulio a pleading look, but he'd given his permission with a fatherly smile, in part to stave off the inevitable quarrel with his daughter; and now here she was walking the short length of sun-drenched street in the least desirable company imaginable. Moreover, she'd been unable to refuse the man's arm, which he'd offered with that stupid smile of his the minute they stepped out of the store.

She was furious with herself, for having lacked the courage to simply refuse the invitation or at least the promptness of mind to invent a serviceable excuse; furious with her father, for allowing that idiot to dare to take such liberties; with her mother for having woven the web in which she now found herself tangled; and with Ricciardi, for taking so long to make his intentions known.

She just hoped that she didn't run into anyone she knew.

XIX

L ivia and Ricciardi sat looking at each other, in intense
   silence. The woman could not have received a more
   definitive answer to her doubts about what she would
feel at the sight of him: she experienced the familiar but almost
forgotten hollow pit in her stomach, her heart had begun to
race, and she could sense that her face was red with pleasure
and embarrassment. The man in white had withdrawn, foiled,
once he saw that the unmistakable electric charge between the
two of them firmly precluded any chance for a rival.

The commissario was tangling with a distinctly new sensation, and he decided that he had encountered a greater variety
of strange new emotions in the past two days than in all the rest
of his life. To see Livia there, so far from where he'd assumed
she was, and even more beautiful than he remembered her, had
made a deep impression on him. He didn't know what to say.
As in a trance, he'd sat down at her table and now he was
watching her as she smiled at him, as if they'd only been apart
for a moment. The last time they'd looked each other in the
eye, a rough wind was tossing the waves off the Via Caracciolo,
blowing her hair and streaking her face, along with tears of
grief and frustration. Going against his own deepest instincts,
perhaps, Ricciardi had said farewell to her, certain that he'd
never see her again. He felt sure deep down that, even though
he was probably going to live the rest of his life alone, if there
was a place in his heart, that place belonged to Enrica.

But now he had to admit that he was happy to see her, smiling and beautiful as she was; but he was also vaguely worried, because of the twinge of danger and instability that the woman had always radiated.

"What are you doing here?"

Livia's smile didn't once fade as she looked deep into those wonderful green eyes that had stirred her so powerfully all those months ago. She was searching for a spark of pleasure, a modicum of cordiality on his part: but she saw nothing. Not yet, anyway. But she had no intention of giving up easily.

"I could tell you that I'm here to do some sightseeing: this city of yours is famous around the world, isn't it? I could tell you that I've come to make peace with a place that brings to mind sad, painful situations. Instead, I've decided to tell it straight: I've come to see you. To see you again."

The grand piano in the lobby was playing a song about an ungrateful heart and the dead man on the other side of the room kept asking when his lover would get there. The waiter, recognizing Ricciardi, had brought a *sfogliatella* and a coffee to the table without his even ordering it. Ricciardi know how to interrogate suspects and arrest criminals, he knew how to interpret the dying words of ravaged corpses; but he didn't have the slightest idea of how to respond to Livia. It suddenly dawned on him that his mouth was hanging open and he snapped it shut with a faint pop. He said, in a much brusquer tone than he intended:

"You could have asked first, maybe written a letter. Why are you so sure that I wanted to see you again?"

Livia laughed, as if Ricciardi had just made a joke.

"Let's just say that it never even occurred to me. That I choose to believe that you'd feel some inclination. Or that at least you'd be courteous enough to welcome me with a smile."

The commissario felt as if he'd been slapped in the face, even if Livia's gentle voice and her smile couldn't conceivably suggest any ill will on her part.

"Forgive me; of course I'm happy to see you. I was just wondering why you'd make such an . . . unusual choice of location for your holidays, that's all. Can I order you something?"

"At last, a little bit of normal conversation. One of your magnificent Neapolitan espressos, *grazie*."

Ricciardi turned around to look for the waiter, his glance darting around the room. He saw at least four men shooting him envious looks, including the man dressed all in white. He saw the curious looks of three married women, trying to catalogue this unfamiliar couple. He saw the lawyer's corpse looking toward the entrance with his one remaining eye, incessantly asking himself when a certain stupid chump would let his woman come join him.

And he saw Sebastiano whispering into Enrica's ear, and he saw Enrica looking in his direction, her eyes welling over with tears.

She would have preferred to drink her espresso standing at the counter, to cut short the torture of Sebastiano's inane company. She'd decided to head straight home afterwards and put off the conversation with her father. She felt she lacked the necessary strength. But her suitor had insisted they sit down inside for a few minutes, and he'd even stopped to ask the pianist to play his favorite song. She'd followed in his wake obediently, scheming all the while to come up with a plan that would let her leave as soon as possible. And then she'd found herself looking at Ricciardi.

At first she thought that her own mind must have somehow materialized her dream, so closely did her thoughts match what she was looking at; but the woman who was smiling at the man she loved was not her.

She allowed herself to be led to the table, and she sat down on the chair that he pulled out for her, never taking her eyes off the woman before her: Ricciardi was looking at the woman, and had his back turned toward Enrica. To Enrica's eyes, Livia's makeup was overdone and garish, she was dressed eccentrically, and the way she smiled certainly couldn't be described as refined; in a word she was cheap and showy, undoubtedly something of a tramp. She was forced to admit that her facial features were comely enough and that her body, as far as she could see, was presentable; but those gloves and her fishnet stockings, the little hat with the veil turned up, that dark red lipstick on her mouth . . .

She had an urge to go over and slap her face, especially because of the sheer vulgarity of the way the woman was staring at Ricciardi, so intent and rapt, without the slightest awareness of her surroundings. How dare she: did she think she'd capture him with that gaze? Didn't she know that the man had a gentle, sensitive soul, that he was capable of watching a girl embroider night after night for more than a year, without daring to speak a word?

She pricked up her ears to try to hear what they were talking about, but they were too far away; what she managed to intuit was that her accent wasn't Neapolitan, and that it might be from the north. She should have guessed it: northern Italian women were famous for their reckless, libertine ways.

Then she noticed that he was talking to her in his turn, and when Ricciardi turned around to summon the waiter, she burst into tears.

It seemed to Ricciardi that he'd suddenly become the center of the universe: Livia was looking at him and smiling; Enrica was looking at him and crying; the dead lawyer was looking at him and talking to him; other men and women who were sitting in the café were looking at him and murmuring; the waiter, who had hastened over, was looking at him and asking him what he'd like. The only one paying him no attention whatsoever was Enrica's young companion, intently whispering to her as usual, and he was absurdly grateful for the fact. He wasn't a bit comfortable in this sort of situation.

He wished he could get up and run outside, or else go over to Enrica to tell her that things weren't the way they looked; but, he thought in an instant, what could he possibly say to a woman who might very well be experiencing the happy beginnings of what looked to be—there was no mistaking the fact by now—a genuine and full-fledged engagement? And the last thing he wanted to do was hurt Livia; he'd already been far too abrupt with her. In the meanwhile, he'd allowed his mind to wander, and he'd completely missed whatever it was that the woman had just said to him.

"I beg your pardon, could you say that again?"

"I asked you if you were on vacation too, or whether you're still working."

"No, no, I'm working. I don't take vacations . . . that is, I don't often go on vacation. We're working on a case just now, a woman, a murder. In fact, to tell the truth, I'm running late, there's someone I should be questioning, today in fact."

Livia had no intention of letting herself be shaken off so easily, after all this time.

"But you still haven't touched this, what do you call it?— *sfogliatella*—and your coffee. Eat up first, and then I'll let you go. Though not until we've decided when and where we're going to meet again. I told you, I'm here for you, and this time I'm not going to let you get away, leaving me standing in the pouring rain."

"Well, there's little danger of that: as you can see, it hasn't rained here in months. All right, I'll eat; but then I have to go."

The back of his neck was tingling with Enrica's gaze and the pain of the dead lawyer: he couldn't have said which of the two made him uneasier. But there was one thing he did know: the thought that she was with him meant that the pain behind his stomach simply wouldn't let up. He wanted to leave, immediately.

He gulped down the *sfogliatella* in a few bites and swallowed the espresso all at once, scalding his mouth and throat. In the meanwhile, Livia updated him on an intricate program that involved visits to museums and monuments and days at the beach:

". . . and of course, I intend to be taken to dinner by you, or to the theater if you prefer. Otherwise, I won't give you any peace, and you know it: even if I have to come snatch you up directly in police headquarters."

Just as she uttered the magic word—police—an angel materialized next to Ricciardi's chair; a big stout angel, drenched in sweat, wearing a winter uniform jacket.

"Commissa', forgive me, but I expected you back and so I just thought I'd come and meet you partway, on the off chance that something had happened. But, am I wrong or is this Signora Vezzi? What a nice surprise, Signora. What are you doing down in these parts?"

Ricciardi could have hugged Maione for his timeliness. He hurriedly stood up.

"Yes, Maione, thanks for coming to get me. We need to get going. The Signora is here on holidays, and we happened to run into each other. But now we'll have to say our farewells to her."

Livia had stood up in her turn, and she smiled at the brigadier. Standing up, lithe and elegant, she was prettier still.

"Yes, Brigadier. I'm taking a holiday here, and I've decided I'm in no hurry to leave. We'll certainly have other occasions to meet."

She'd spoken in a loud voice, extending her hand to Maione who clumsily bowed over it and kissed it. With dazzling rapidity, as if it were part of the same motion of getting to her feet, she turned toward Ricciardi and kissed him on the cheek. "Well then, we'll see you soon," she said. And she left, followed by the eyes of everyone in the place.

She had kissed him. That vulgar wench had kissed him, and she'd done it right in front of her. What's worse, he'd let her kiss him: and yet, he'd seen her, she was sure of it, their eyes had met.

She'd left the house to defend her dream, ready to fight with her father for the first time in her life, and now that very same dream had crumbled before her eyes. Sebastiano, unaware of what was going on around him, went on chattering fatuously about horse races and parties: Enrica hadn't listened to a word he'd said.

Ricciardi, pale as death, had turned in her direction and was looking at her. His eyes were eloquent with an immense sorrow, as if he were looking out the window of a departing train, never to return. He lifted his hand to his cheek, brushing it. He shook his head ever so slightly, as if he couldn't believe what had just happened, or as if he were simply denying it.

Enrica stood up: she absolutely had to maintain her decorum. She felt like she was dying. The piano was still playing the same tune it had been when they'd walked in, only two minutes ago, but it seemed like an eternity. She turned to Sebastiano and said, in a firm voice:

"I have a headache. I need to get some fresh air. Take me for a walk outside, *caro*."

And she, in her turn, left on the man's arm, without a glance in Ricciardi's direction.

XX

Maione was escorting Ricciardi back to police headquarters; it was still too early to go to the offices of the *Roma* to interview Capece, plus Garzo wanted to see the commissario before they talked to the journalist.

As they walked, the brigadier for once wasn't thinking about the heat or his hunger, terrible though they both might be: he'd been happy to meet the tenor's widow, who had already shown some interest in Ricciardi the last time; he remembered that he'd even taken the liberty, with some awkwardness and embarrassment, of recommending that Ricciardi open up a little bit and spend some time with the woman, who struck him as not only quite beautiful but also a decent person. He also remembered that Ricciardi hadn't seemed entirely indifferent to her charms. Nothing had come of it and in the end she'd left.

All the same, he'd detected odd emotions in the air, at Gambrinus, as if the commissario were struggling with a difficult situation, almost as if he'd been caught red-handed. He wondered why, given the solitary life that he led. Perhaps he himself had been the cause of the awkwardness; perhaps the commissario would have preferred not to be seen on such a personal occasion. And so he'd chosen to make no comment about his meeting with the Signora.

When they got back to the office they found Ponte as always, anxiously awaiting them at the door so that he could accompany them to see Garzo. The man was pouncing back and forth in the throes of his usual anxiety and, as soon as he saw them, he started toward them.

"Commissario, Brigadier, *buona sera*. Dottor Garzo is waiting to see you, both of you; he says to come by his office before you go out again."

Maione spoke as if the other man weren't even there:

"Let's go see him immediately, Commissa'. Otherwise I'm liable to beat this guy silly."

They followed Ponte to Garzo's office, where the deputy chief of police was waiting for them at his desk.

"Well, well, I know that you're going to head over to the newspaper, now."

The unceremonious start to the meeting was a clear indication of the deputy police chief's concerns.

"Yessir, Dottore. This morning we were at Palazzo Camparino, and we spoke . . ."

". . . with the duke and with his son, I heard. And I also heard that, as is unfortunately all too often the case, you were intrusive and rude. Now you tell me, Ricciardi, do I always have to tell you the same things? And every blessed time, do I have to get telephone calls from prominent people, complaining about your lack of respect?"

Garzo punctuated his tirade by pounding his fist on the top of his desk: he was irate, and he wanted the fact to be known. But the only one who jumped at the sound of it was Ponte, who had been standing in the doorway. There was a moment of silence, in which Maione glanced over at Ricciardi, his eyebrows knit and a look on his face that promised nothing good: he seemed ready, at a gesture from the commissario, to lunge at the deputy chief of police's throat. Ricciardi spoke, and his voice was little more than a whisper.

"I'm going to repeat something that I've already told you, sir, since it would appear that you failed to understand it the first time: you are free to assign this damned investigation to whoever you please. But if it's my investigation, then stick-ing your nose into my business. If we fail to catch the guilty party, you can certainly do whatever you think best. But in the meanwhile, you are not to question any of my decisions. None of them."

It had been little more than a hiss, but the effect was that of a gunshot in a church. Ponte pulled his head down between his shoulders, as if he'd heard an explosion. Maione went on look-ing at Garzo with the same irritated expression. The deputy chief of police stood frozen, as if Ricciardi had suddenly slapped him in the face. As for the commissario, he hadn't even taken his hands out of his pockets; his stray lock of hair dan-gled over his forehead, his eyes were focused on his superior officer's face, and he never blinked an eye.

After what seemed like an endless lapse of time, Garzo took a deep breath:

"I'm not saying that . . . unquestionably, you know what you're doing. All the same, I believe that it's my prerogative to expect you, when you interact with . . . certain individuals, to show a minimum of . . . well, damn it: you report to me, and I have to deal with the reckless nonsense you pull. I have every right, and it's my duty, to ask you to take care how you oper-ate! The duke, as I've told you before, is a very sick man; but his son is healthy as a horse, and he frequents . . . he has very highly placed friends. Very. And the press . . . the press is still powerful, even after the most recent directives."

This wasn't a day on which Ricciardi was likely to feel pity for Garzo. Too many things had happened.

"I don't care in the slightest about the power of the press. If the duchess turns out to have been murdered by the editor-in-chief of the paper, I'll bring him to you in leg irons. It's up to you to decide what to do about it. That's my duty. It's what I'm expected to do, and it's what I'll do. May I go now?"

Garzo had a large red patch on his neck, directly above his

tie, as he always did when two equal and opposite forces left him powerless: in the case in question, on the one hand he'd have happily relieved Ricciardi of the investigation and started a nice fat disciplinary proceeding against him; but on the other hand the chief of police was pushing him to come up with a rapid solution of the Camparino murder—all of Naples was talking about nothing else. It was the second of these pressures that prevailed, of course: the one that was most important to the advancement of his career. Still, he wasn't going to miss the satisfaction of one parting dart.

"You can hardly expect awareness of social sensitivities from someone who has no life of his own. Do as you see best: but I swear, if you don't solve this case, you'll rue the words you've said here today. You'll rue them bitterly."

And he waved his hand in the air, as if he were shooing a fly away. Maione took a step forward: perhaps he had finally found someone on whom he could vent his irritation over his hunger, the heat, and the fruit vendor. Ricciardi laid a hand on his arm, and the two men left the room. Ponte softly shut the door.

Usually, Lucia enjoyed ironing: it felt as if she were caressing her loved ones, exploring the pleats and folds of their clothing and at the same time thinking of the expressions and the movements of her children and her husband. But now it really was too hot; the white hot coal enclosed in the iron sent scalding waves of heat up her sweat-drenched arm. She sighed, and sprinkled water from a small basin onto one of Raffaele's shirts. She checked the stitching of a button right on a line with his belly and shook her head: she'd have to reinforce it. He's still got a little too much belly, but it'll slowly subside.

She smiled as she thought of him; after all the years they'd spent together she still liked him just as much, perhaps even more. Wiping her brow, she wondered how it had ever been possible, even in the horrible grief of those years, to forget how much she loved him and how her very life depended on her man. She felt a stab of pain at the thought that she could have lost him, by neglecting him as she had; just imagine how many other women would have been glad to take him, handsome and good-hearted as he was.

She caressed the shirt, and with one hand she smoothed out a last wrinkle underneath the collar. I'm the wife, she thought to herself. You can look, but don't touch.

Or I'll claw your eyes out.

He became aware of someone knocking insistently at the door. He'd fallen asleep at his desk, his face resting on his arm, the half-empty bottle of liquor in front of his eyes. He tried to remember, as he reemerged from the mists of sleep; and he remembered.

Memory swept over him like a wave, renewing the incandescent pain that he'd managed to stifle by getting drunk. He was alone, in his office at the newspaper. He heard the noises from the newsroom, the typesetting of fresh news, tomorrow's paper going through its birth throes; but it wasn't the way it usually felt, those sounds gave him no comfort. Nothing would ever give him comfort again. Because Mario Capece had forever lost everything that mattered to him, the love of his life. And the worst thing about it was that he'd lost her through a fault of his own.

The unknown hand continued to pound on the door, close to the jamb, and the noise was making his head explode. He shouted:

"Come in, damn it!"

Whoever it was tried the handle, and then he remembered that he'd locked the door. He got up and went to unlock it, with a stabbing wave of pain to his forehead. Better to die, he thought. An artery bursts, and goodbye sorrow. Maybe what the priests always told us is true, and I'll be able to see you again someday, my love.

Standing at the door was Arturo Dominici, his deputy editor; worry was stamped clearly on his face.

"Mario, are you all right? Everyone's been looking for you. Did you sleep here again last night?"

Capece gestured in annoyance.

"Yes, yes. I haven't been anywhere else. What do you want. What's happening now?"

The man spoke in a low voice, shooting furtive glances over his shoulder.

"There are two . . . the police are here, the mobile squad. One's in uniform, the other one's in civilian clothes. They're looking for you."

Mario smiled wearily.

"At last. They took their sweet time, almost two days. Show them in."

"Do you want me to be present too? As a witness, you know."

Capece looked at his friend intensely: he deeply appreciated the offer, knowing as he did that Dominici too assumed that he was guilty of Adriana's murder.

"No, Arturo. That's not necessary. If I need you I'll call you. *Grazie*."

Ricciardi and Maione walked into the office just as Capece was throwing open the window. The room was hot as an oven and it reeked of stale air and liquor; it was like being in a bar. They introduced themselves and when Capece pointed them to two chairs, they sat down. Maione asked the journalist his name and age and other basic details, and he supplied them with a voice that was only slightly slurred and with eyes half-closed from the pain of his migraine.

Capece wasn't tall, but his frank and extroverted expression gave him an imposing air. His professional skills were highly esteemed, and the fact that he didn't pander to the powerful, that he criticized or praised openly and as he saw fit, had won him the admiration of many, but also the hatred of the fanatical supporters of the regime. His weak point had been his affair with Adriana, a weapon that the fanatics had used to hinder the career that he would certainly have enjoyed otherwise.

The man that Ricciardi and Maione had before them, however, was a different person from the one that Mario Capece had been until just a short while ago. His three-day growth of whiskers, his loosened tie, his shirt half-untucked, his single buttoned suspender, and his waistcoat dangling open were so many signals of the state of prostration into which the journalist had slipped. Still, he looked at them mockingly and said:

"Well then, you must be Commissario Ricciardi. The solitary hawk at police headquarters, the man who doesn't want career advancement. The implacable hunter of murderers. I've been following your work, did you know that? Your progress is interesting. Your superior officers are afraid of you, and so are those who report to you. They say you bring bad luck."

Maione was about to repond but Ricciardi held up his hand.

"Interesting information. But as luck would have it, we're not here to talk about me today, but about you, Capece. And in particular about the death of a woman whom, from what I've heard, you knew very well. Is that right?"

Capece shot to his feet like a spring suddenly released, his bleary eyes red with rage.

"The death of a woman, you say. A woman I knew well. Careful, Ricciardi: never use that tone of voice again. Never again. That woman has . . . had a name, and her name was Adriana Musso, duchess of Camparino. And I didn't know her: I loved her. Not that I'd expect you, a dreary little policeman who lives alone, to understand. But I loved her."

Maione had no intention of tolerating that tone, no matter what Ricciardi said. He leapt to his feet and, towering over Capece, leaned toward him, placing both hands flat on the desktop.

"Listen up, Capece: you try talking to the commissario like that one more time, and dead woman or no dead woman, I'll smack you so hard that you'll get over your drunk in the blink of an eye. You respect us and we'll respect you. Otherwise, we can go have this little chat at police headquarters, and your children will wake up to find that their father's in prison. Do you hear what I'm saying?"

Capece and Maione stared at each other for a good thirty seconds, face to face. Ricciardi watched the journalist as the two men faced off, wondering whether this reaction was a product of his personality or simply a state of despair. He opted for the first factor, but with some reservations.

At last the man sat down, and the brigadier sat down after him. Unexpectedly, he smiled.

"So you do you have blood in your veins, after all! And you don't find your courage only when you outnumber your opponent. Fine, then, let's respect each other. And I'll answer your question: yes, I knew her. And I didn't kill her. Even though it's my fault that she's dead, and I'll never be able to forgive myself for the fact."

Ricciardi tried to delve deeper: "What do you mean, it's your fault?"

Capece smiled a bitter smile, staring into the void.

"You must already know that on Saturday night we had a fight, at the Salone Margherita. I have no doubts that you were informed, because that incompetent Garzo, the deputy chief of police and your boss, was there, and I'll never forget his face and his foolish stunned expression. It was a typical lovers' skirmish. But, idiot that I am, I stormed out of the place and I let her go home alone, or else accompanied by who knows who.

That's just the way she was, you know: instinctive. And someone killed her."

While he was speaking he'd started weeping, without even realizing it. Tears rolled down his cheeks, in a silent incessant stream, like some hemorrhage of unbroken grief. Maione, who'd been pleased to hear that open reference to Garzo's incompetence, handed him a handkerchief.

Ricciardi resumed:

"And you, where did you go?"

"I went drinking. First at the Circolo dell'Unione, then in one cantina and then in another, and finally to the train station where there was the one last bar in the city that was still open. I was alone, I imagine you want to know that. No one can confirm it. Nor do I care whether or not you believe it."

XXI

Ll alone in your kitchen, you wait. You know that he might never come back home. You've factored that into the equation.

You've known ever since you saw him slap her face, ever since you saw him storm out the door, alone. You know where he went, and what he did. And you know that, logically, he'll be the first one they'll think of.

The cookpot bubbles away. It's hot, so very hot. On your forehead, on your lip, beads of sweat form that you mop away with your handkerchief, before they can drip down to ruin your hair or your makeup.

You've dressed the way you usually do, you want him to find you neat and clean, if he happens to return. If by some chance they let him go. And if they decide not to, then he brought it on himself, then he asked for it. It was only natural that this is how it ended, you always knew it.

And that's why you're sitting and waiting now. Not that this is the first time; so many other nights you've pretended to sleep, your ears uselessly alert for the sound of a key turning in the lock, the sound of a door opening. So many times you've prayed for hours on end, hoping for him to come home. But this time it's different.

Because, whether or not he comes back, today is a new day.

Ricciardi broke the silence that had followed the last statement.

"What were you fighting about?"

Capece smiled.

"I told you. It was a lovers' skirmish. Jealousy. Do you know what jealousy is, Commissario? No, I imagine that you don't. You're a famous loner, aren't you? No wife, no girlfriend. No friends, I believe. Yes, yes, you told me before: we aren't here to talk about you. Jealousy, I was saying. The green-eyed monster that mocks the meat it feeds on, as the English poet put it. That poet we soon won't be allowed to read anymore. It's true, Commissario: jealousy is a monster. But it isn't true that those who suffer from it create it, no, that's not true. Adriana was beautiful, incredibly beautiful. The photographs that you might have seen of her don't do her justice, and neither do the unfortunate remains that you recovered. I don't want to know what you've done with her, don't tell me what it was like. I've heard about a gunshot, that much I know. And I'd just as soon know nothing more."

The commissario had no intention of dropping the matter amidst the journalist's literary lucubrations.

"And what exactly was the reason for this, I believe you called it, skirmish?"

Capece hesitated, then he said:

"There was a guy, a young man, who was squiring some old hag to the theater. He was a gigolo, a kept man. Or for all I know he was her grandson, I can't say and I don't care. He kept staring and staring at Adriana while I pretended to watch the show. But I never really looked away for a second; I was watching him, and I was watching her. When she noticed him she started returning his glances. Once, twice, a third time. And smiling: you can't imagine how lovely she was when she smiled, Commissario. She knew it, that she was beautiful; and she enjoyed playing with men, the way a cat toys with a mouse, using her beauty like a claw."

His tone of voice changed, as he thought back to the situation that night in the theater. A muscle in his jaw twitched uncontrollably, his right hand kept clenching into a fist. A man like this, thought Maione, would be capable of anything. Ricciardi said:

"Then what did you do?"

"What did I do? I put up with it for as long as I was able. And then I exploded, then I couldn't take it anymore. Jealousy is a vicious beast, Commissario. It stabs you right behind your stomach, clamps you like a vise. It's a physical sensation, and it won't let up."

It looked to Maione as if Ricciardi had suddenly turned pale; the commissario brushed his hand over his jacket, right on a line with his solar plexus. Perhaps he'd eaten something that disagreed with him. Capece went on:

"But I could never have done anything to hurt her. It's absurd to say it, I know that: I could have throttled her with my bare hands, and yet I would never have hurt her. I don't see how you can believe me, but that's the way it is."

The commissario wanted something more. He wanted to know about the ring; he could hear the voice of the dead duchess as if she were sitting inside his head:

The ring, the ring, you've taken the ring, the ring is missing.

So he asked:

"And then what happened?"

"And then we started quarreling. I asked her to explain her behavior, and she laughed in my face. She ridiculed me, in front of that callow young man, in front of the whole room. The more she laughed, the more I saw red. And then I hit her, I slapped her in the face. Like this," and he imitated the way he'd hit the woman. "She stopped laughing, she looked at me with hatred. And I grabbed the ring, and I turned and left."

"What ring?"

Capece put his hands in his pockets, in a moment of confusion. Then he pulled a golden ring with a small diamond out of a fob pocket in his vest and set it on the table.

"It's a small thing, of no real monetary value. But it was a token of our love, a miserable trinket I gave her when . . . when we first met, on a certain occasion. I told her that she didn't deserve to have it, and I yanked it away from her. I think I hurt her when I did."

Ricciardi hadn't once stopped staring Capece in the face the whole time. More than his words, he was trying to understand his emotions, which veered sharply between hatred and love.

"What do you know about how she was killed? You talked about her being shot in the head, and this is public knowledge. You must know other details, from the line of work you're in. Who do you think could have done it?"

Capece fell silent, staring into the empty air. Then he started to talk again, in little more than a murmur.

"When I first started, this was a different profession. Very different, more than the two of you would ever be willing to believe. You could tell stories, you could provide commentary. A journalist would pursue an investigation and he was allowed to talk about it, sometimes we even cooperated with you policemen. Then the decision was made that the world was clean, that there were no more murders. It was decided at a drawing table, while completely ignoring reality. A telegraphic circular letter came in, one of the ones we call *veline*, at the beginning of 1926, and no one paid it any mind. I remember how we laughed in the newsroom, we laughed until the tears came; the orders had come down to 'demobilize the crime reporters.' As if it were possible to sit down at a telegraph machine and, by tapping away with your forefinger, eliminate darkness from the human soul. Then, three years ago, on September 26, 1928, the prefect called us into his office. All of us, editors-in-chief, bureau chiefs: and he said that from that day forward the *velina* of 1926 would have to be followed to the letter. I remember his exact words: with special reference to the reporting of suicides, crimes of passion, rapes and abductions, and so on, because they can have an unhealthy effect on the spirits of the mentally weak or weakend. Can you imagine? Everything that happens all around us, the things you see from dawn till dusk, must no longer exist as far as the press is concerned."

Ricciardi didn't understand what this had to do with Adriana's murder.

"And so?"

Capece stared at him with reddened eyes, as if he were a particularly stupid student.

"And so? And so this was no longer the job I'd set out to do. If all I can write about is the party of the Baroness Thus and Such or the visit of the royal prince and princess, if I have to talk about this ship being launched or a formation of seaplanes crossing the Atlantic, then that's not my profession anymore. But I don't know how to do anything else, so I kept it up, though my heart wasn't in it. Then I met Adriana and life regained its color. This is to explain why we can no longer explore and investigate, discover how it is that John Doe killed Richard Roe. And this time, believe me, I thank God that's how it is. Already, I'm struggling with the guilt of letting her go home alone, and slapping her in the face before she left."

He looked at his open hand, as if he were seeing it for the first time.

"Can you imagine? The last time this hand touched her, it was to slap her face."

And he began crying, sobbing. Maione and Ricciardi exchanged a glance; each, without knowing anything about what the other was feeling, saw in Capece's sobs the emotions that he was feeling so deeply at that moment.

Once he had recovered, Ricciardi asked in a gentle tone of

voice: "Forgive me, Capece. But you understand perfectly well that I have to ask you this. Do you own a revolver?"

Capece looked up and stared defiantly at Ricciardi:

"First you're going to have to arrest me, Ricciardi. If I'm a suspect, first you're going to have to arrest me. I'm not going to answer your questions, this one or any of the others. Take care, I know all about your methods. I still have weapons, you know; not the ones you're thinking of. I can still take you apart, one piece at a time, with a single article. Now, get out of here. I want to drink, and I want to sleep."

Ricciardi and Maione were walking slowly, hunched under the burden of their thoughts. Capece's interrogation had touched them deeply. The brigadier finally broke the silence:

"Commissa', I don't know. I feel sorry for this man, it pains me to see him, but I have to tell you honestly that he strikes me as the kind of guy who could lose his mind from all this grief. I've seen other men like this, heads of families, fathers, respectable people, but sensitive, far too sensitive. For better and for worse."

"It's true, all too true. He's a good man, no doubt about it. But he's also a person who could do something rash, because he feels he's been humiliated or else because he thinks he's losing something. And in the end he challenged us, but it was only out of despair."

Maione ran a finger under his collar, trying to get a little cool air.

"Well, whatever the case, they're not letting us work under ideal conditions, eh, Commissa'? That idiot Garzo threatening us, now Capece here threatening us, the young master with his plants on the terrace threatening us. But we can't threaten anyone: if we do, we'll wind up in a world of trouble."

Ricciardi nodded.

"True, but we'll go on doing our best to get our work done. Do me a favor: make the rounds of the cantinas and dives, find out if anyone remembers seeing Capece getting drunk. Maybe he passed out someplace, someone saw him, and we'll strike him off our list. Otherwise, we'll get a warrant and go search his office and his home to see if by any chance he happens to own a Beretta 7.65."

"Yessir, Commissa'. It's just that in the cantinas and dives, people drink but they also eat, and lately, whenever I go someplace people are eating, it gets on my nerves. Anyway, the young master gardener strikes me as quite a lunatic too. Maybe he's got a nice Beretta tucked away somewhere. Or not?"

Ricciardi shot Maione a rapid glance.

"You, with this food obsession of yours, sooner or later you're liable to kill someone. And then I'd wind up having to put you in prison."

Maione laughed bitterly.

"And I'd eat more in prison than I do at my house, these days, Commissa'. Even if you put me on bread and water!"

"As far as the young master is concerned, you're perfectly right, and don't think that Garzo can bark loud enough to throw a scare into me. We've got to do some digging, and the first thing I want to find out is whether on the night in question the young master was at home, or whether he might have come in just a few minutes after his stepmother. The festivities were underway outside, as we know, so if they quarreled it's entirely possible that no one heard them. All right, we'll learn more tomorrow. For now, let's go home, because it's late and it's still just as hot as ever. I'm not even hungry."

Maione spread his arms.

"Lucky you, Commissa'. The heat makes me even hungrier. *Buona notte*, then, and I'll see you tomorrow."

XXII

Sitting in an armchair and knitting, Rosa watched Ricciardi eat. Or really: she watched him play with his food, pushing it around the plate with his fork.

This truly was an unusual turn of events; even in his darkest hours, he'd never lost the ravenous appetite that was a crucial element of his personality. It wasn't like he savored his food: he bolted it fast, one mouthful after another, his forehead creased by a single deep wrinkle of concentration, as if he were intent on completing some challenging task. But when he was done, the plate was wiped clean.

Not this time. The sheer rarity of the situation upset his *tata*, and in fact she hadn't even reacted with her usual daisy chain of criticisms and complaints to the effect that, if he insisted on eating street food, he was bound to ruin his digestion once and for all. He was ashen, preoccupied, and even more silent than was customary for him. She'd asked him whether he was having troubles in the office, and he'd vaguely nodded his head; nothing more.

Rosa decided that whatever it was, it must have something to with the conversation that the Signorina Colombo had had with her suitor in the drawing room across the way. And she couldn't understand why a man like Ricciardi wouldn't finally take action, seizing the initiative and establishing some direct contact with the girl. He had everything he needed to make him a presentable prospect: he was young, he had money, he was educated. To her eyes, he was also stunningly handsome.

As she went on knitting, she shot him occasional glances over the top of her eyeglasses, and heaved a sigh; happiness is a rare bird, and it lands only rarely, and then where it wills. Rosa remembered Ricciardi's mother; she'd been very fond of the woman, and was at her side till the day she died. She too, like her son, was silent, with a vague, incomprehensible sense of suffering that served as a kind of basso continuo to her otherwise gentle character. She too, like her son, had long spells, times when she absentmindedly looked into the distance. At times like that, no one could say where she was wandering in her mind; she too, like her son, had everything she needed to be happy, and yet she was not.

Ricciardi got up from the dinner table; he understood that Rosa was worried about him, but he couldn't bring himself to pretend that everything was all right. Not tonight. He feared the moment when he'd have to look out his window; he was attracted and repelled by the illuminated rectangle on the far side of the *vicolo*, where the healthy customary life of a family had always gone on, the life that gave him so much peace. After all, what could be healthier, what could be more customary, he thought with bitter irony, than a woman and a man being introduced, getting engaged, and getting married, and a new family coming into being?

I'm the one who isn't normal, he thought; I can't forget that. I'm the one who's persecuted by the dead, the dead who incessantly tell me about their pain, who infect my soul and my life. I'm the one who can't dream of a woman and a family, much less think of having children.

And so he asked himself for the thousandth time, why does this hurt you so much? Why won't this knot in your stomach unravel, why such despair? You're not consistent, that's your problem. And you're cursed, just as your mother told you twenty-five years ago.

He closed the bedroom door behind him and walked over to the window with his eyes shut tight. He heaved a deep sigh and opened them, only to see the shutters in the Colombos' kitchen pulled to. Over there, on his left, the aggravating glow of the drawing room lights.

Enrica had gone back to her father's shop wearing a mask of steely indifference. In her heart, fury was taking the place of sorrow; irrational though it was, she felt betrayed, as if she'd caught Ricciardi red-handed. And she felt like more of an idiot than ever before: why on earth would she expect a man like him, handsome, upper-class, young, and attractive, not to see other women? For all she knew, this woman was his fiancée and, since she lived up north, as her accent suggested, the two of them saw each other only rarely. In spite of herself, she had to admit that she, the other woman, was captivating, if you liked that sort of thing. Too flashy for her tastes, but charming. Even the insipid Sebastiano, on their way out of the café, had been unable to keep from darting the woman an admiring glance.

It might be true that every night he came to his window and watched her embroider; but after all, what did that really mean? The stupid pastime of a man with a girlfriend far away. She'd even kissed him goodbye. The very thought made her stomach lurch violently. How strange, she mused: jealousy is a physical sensation. So different from the elegiacal descriptions of sentimental suffering given by poets and novelists; it's a genuine form of pain. Like a case of gastritis.

She hadn't said a word to her father, who'd been visibly relieved; instead she'd agreed when Sebastiano had asked if he could come see her at her home, after dinner. After all, why shouldn't she? It would take her mind off things, and anything would be better than sitting by the window stitching, looking out at the darkness in the window across the way. That other woman was in town, and he'd certainly be going out tonight.

On her way home, she thought of the days ahead of her, without the evening to look forward to. And the nights without dreams. She felt her wet cheeks, and realized those were tears.

Ricciardi went into the dining room but didn't twist the light switch on the wall. In the darkness he walked over to the radio and turned a dial. The music of an orchestra filled the room. The yellow glare of the front panel illuminated the outlines of the sofa and the two armchairs; he sat in the one from which it was possible to see a corner of the window across the way, which was illuminated. He tried to picture to himself, as he always did when he was listening to the radio, the room from which the music was coming: the people who were playing the instruments and the faces of the dancers, each man staring raptly into the eyes of his female partner, the way they twirled on a shiny marble floor. In the picture in his mind, there were no dead people, no translucent, suffering figures repeating obtuse, meaningless phrases; there was only life, in his thoughts. Just as there was only life in the drawing room of the Colombo family, where every now and then he'd see the mother or the father walk past, smiling or involved in an animated discussion about something. He didn't see Enrica, and he imagined her sitting somewhere, she too staring raptly into the eyes of the young man he'd bumped into that morning.

Now there was a man singing on the radio. It was a song from a couple of years ago; the tune was familiar, a tango, but he'd never paid any attention to the words. The man sang, in a slight falsetto:

"No, it's not that I am jealous,
It's just that those other fellas
Smile at you and blow you kisses:
How I want you as my missus!

Dare I ask, on bended knee
If you'll plight your troth to me!
No it isn't jealousy, I'm just a bit too zealousy!
Never fear: it's not the green-eyed monster!"

That tore it: he'd had enough. He stood up brusquely from the armchair, switched off the radio, and went to get his jacket. He needed some fresh air.

Two hours later he was still walking. The streets were deserted, save for the occasional hurrying figure slipping furtively into some half-empty doorway. The city never stopped its dealings, day or night, in the heat and in the cold.

Every so often, some corpse or other appeared before Ricciardi's eyes, faintly illuminated by the passion of its death; a delegation that never failed him. He considered that at least he could always count on their company. How ironic: the loneliest man who ever lived can never hope to be entirely alone.

A woman was standing in the doorway of a *basso*, with a yellowish foam oozing out of her mouth and running down the front of her black dress. Who knows what she swallowed, Ricciardi thought. As he walked past her, he heard her say:

"You told me that I was the prettiest one. Then why are you with her?"

Right, he asked himself. Why? And who'll give you an answer now, in the darkness of night? You'll be forgotten, or perhaps you'd already been forgotten, even before you decided to end your life. Wouldn't it have been better, really, to go on living, so that you could have forgotten him, that liar?

Brokenhearted suicides made up the bulk of them. The misery and the shame, certainly; but above all this damned illusion, as the Duke of Camparino had put it, that makes you think you can't survive without her for even a day. And so you put an end to your sufferings, amid even more atrocious torment: a leap into the void, a noose, an open gas valve, or else poison, like the woman he'd just encountered.

He was reminded of a man who dangled from a butcher's meat hook, which he'd carefully positioned right below his chin, and then kicked away the chair on which he was standing. He remembered the excrement that had gushed from his twitching sphincter, the blood that had streamed out of him, drop by drop. It had taken him hours to die: without a shout, a plea for help, a second's reconsideration. He'd stood there looking at him for a long time when he was assigned to inspect the scene: he listened to his last words, addressed to a certain Carmela:

"What a nice white dress you're wearing today, Carme'."

His sister, in tears, had told him that the man's fiancée had left him to marry another. The very day of the wedding, he'd gone to the church with a gift in his hands. And then he did what he did.

Ricciardi hadn't understood, and he still failed to understand. But now, in the heat of the night, amidst the mutterings of the dead and the sound of his footsteps echoing on the cobblestones, the stabbing pain that clamped his stomach began to give him at least some slight idea. You learn something new every day, he mused.

He turned the corner and found himself in a little piazzetta. From a building with a closed street door came a faint sound of music, either a radio or a small combo. Without quite knowing why, he stopped in the shadows, just as the door cracked open, letting out a shaft of light and a figure dressed in black.

Ricciardi looked closer, because the movement of the person who had just emerged struck him as familiar. He heard a nervous giggle. The music had suddenly become a little louder, as if the door behind which it was being played had been left open. He saw an arm reaching out the door, as if to catch and halt the person who was leaving.

"Don't go. Not yet."

Not much more than a whisper. He'd been able to distinguish the words only because there was no other noise.

The figure that had walked out the door turned around, and the face was illuminated by the glare of light from within. Ricciardi felt certain that his impression—that he had seen that person somewhere before—was correct. But he had never seen the other person, the person who leaned out the door and, taking the brightly lit face tenderly in one hand, placed a long, leisurely kiss, a kiss that was sweetly requited.

It was not so much the scene that made an impression on Ricciardi, nor the fact that he'd understood who the person was who'd been the object of such powerful and requited passion. It was neither the hour nor the music nor the laughter that came from inside, unmistakable evidence of a party that would no doubt continue for many hours to come.

What left him standing there openmouthed, at the street corner, was the clothing worn by the person who had given the kiss.

XXIII

Don Pierino Fava, the assistant pastor of the church of San Ferdinando a Chiaia, emerged from the confessional. This time, he had almost half an hour until it was time to say mass.

He devoted his early mornings to hearing confession: he knew what time he'd begin but he could never predict when he'd be finished. Sometimes he waited in the darkness and the silence for dozens of minutes at a time, praying for someone to open the grate and recite the formula: Father, forgive me for I have sinned. There were other times, however, when upon his arrival at six in the morning, he'd already find a number of his flock waiting, sitting on the benches beside the dark wooden booth that was covered by a heavy curtain. They were waiting to cleanse their consciences.

Running his hands over his tunic, buttoned from neck to feet, to smooth out the creases, Don Pierino remembered the beginning of his priesthood in Santa Maria Capua Vetere, the town near Caserta where he was born. With his open nature, in love at once with God and all creation, he took his vocation seriously and cheerfully, the way he did everything in his life. The quarter where his parish was located had taken him under its wing: diminutive, olive-complected, and cunning, he'd become *'o munaciello*, a reference to *munacielli*, the mischievous ghosts of legend. In reality, though, he was a born helper: unfailingly at the side of those who had need of aid, and there were plenty of people who fit that description. San Ferdinando in fact had both aristocratic streets inhabited by the elite and, bordering them, a bona fide ghetto, where the police were afraid to venture.

Constant contact between these two sharply contrasting social worlds led to thorny situations, to bullying, violence, and rape. An atmosphere of malaise seethed under the surface, as if a rebellion might break out from one day to the next. The poor, the misfits facing the daily challenge of obtaining food and fighting off the terrible diseases that infested the *vicoli*, seemed increasingly unwilling to simply stay in their places, to look on passively at the opulence and squandering of their wealthy neighbors. And there was a proliferation of thefts, robberies, and purse snatchings.

As far as he was able, Don Pierino counseled against violence which, besides being immoral, tended to deprive families of their fathers, either because they had been arrested or because they'd been killed; in such cases he took care above all to comfort the children, bringing them food and clothing. He allocated a portion of the parish's offerings to make those purchases, taking advantage of the elderly parish priest's lack of attention, and made his own contributions out of the extra money he earned tutoring the children of the aristocrats and businessmen of Via Toledo and going to say mass in homes where invalids lived who could not come to church.

The only, so to speak, *profane* passion that Don Pierino allowed himself was the opera. With the aid of a member of his parish, a doorman in charge of a rear entrance, he was sometimes able to slip into the San Carlo Opera House for rehearsals or even for actual performances. These were moments of pure delight for him, in which he felt as close as one could be to God and to the masterpieces of His creation. He'd met Commissario Ricciardi during his investigation of the now notorious Vezzi case, the murder of the world's greatest tenor, which, sadly, had taken place in his presence.

Those tragic events returned to his mind that morning, when he thought he saw the Commissario's silhouette appear from the darkness of the church. At first he assumed that his mind was playing tricks on him, because the two men had had no occasion to meet again since that case. With a twinge of sorrow, he had realized at the time that Ricciardi was not a religious man; and this struck him as odd, because he sensed that the policeman was endowed with a profound sense of spirituality. He seemed to live behind a barrier of grief and pain, to which he was a constant witness; and it was as if this prevented him from even interacting with his fellow human beings, at least any more than was strictly necessary.

The shadow had moved from the far end of the nave and was coming toward him. The air was filled with the continual murmuring of the old women, who were reciting their orations beneath the main altar. When the dark figure had drawn close enough, Don Pierino realized that it was none other than the man he'd just been thinking about.

"Commissario Ricciardi, what a pleasant surprise! I'm happy to see you here; if you only knew how many times I've thought of you, in the past few months!"

He was smiling, standing on tiptoe and shaking both of the commissario's hands in his. He seemed like a child who had just received a gift.

"I'm happy to see you, too, Father, believe me," Ricciardi replied. And it was the truth. The priest had been very helpful to him in the Vezzi investigation, and on that occasion they'd established a relationship of trust, if not friendship: they were too far apart, in terms of values and experiences, to have all that much in common.

"Forgive me if I haven't come to see you before this," he said to the priest when they had reached the sacristy; "daily life is the enemy of even the best intentions, as you must know well. How are you? Still the opera lover?"

Don Pierino hadn't stopped smiling.

"I'm a man of steadfast passions. But am I misremembering or did someone promise me that we'd go to the opera together sometime? The new season is beginning before long."

Ricciardi admitted:

"You're quite right, Father. I won't break my promise, you'll see: a commitment is a commitment. But could you spare me just a few minutes right now? I need a little information that you may be able to give me."

The little priest pulled a large pocket watch out of his tunic and examined the dial.

"Yes, Commissario. We have almost half an hour before I need to get ready for mass. You're always quite the early riser, which is a commendable virtue. Go ahead and ask."

Ricciardi, who hadn't slept a wink, was ashen, with dark circles under his eyes. Don Pierino had noticed, but something about the commissario's expression told him not to delve into it.

"Did I interrupt anything? I wouldn't want to cause you any trouble."

The priest smiled with a hint of sadness.

"There's nothing worse, you know, Commissario, than confessions. It's a cleansing process, and you have to take the burdens of others onto your own shoulders and carry it away."

Ricciardi thought how very similar that was to the work that he did, when he found himself in the presence of a dead person. Only he couldn't cleanse away a thing. Don Pierino went on:

"At first I didn't mind it: that's just what I was thinking about when I saw you. I felt as if I was sharing something, helping my flock and providing a little comfort. But that's not how it is. Sin provides no comfort. It's a wound, and it leaves behind it a scar and a weakness: it will be committed again, over and over."

"Well then, Father, what good does it do to clean up?"

Don Pierino shook his head.

"No good at all, perhaps. And perhaps all the good in the world. It's important that they come on their own two feet, to bring their imperfection to God. And it's never the way you might expect, you know, Commissario; there are harmless looking little old ladies who do terrible things, and well known, feared gangsters who confess to little baby sins. That's what hidden scars are like. Everyone has their own."

As had often happened whenever he talked to the priest, Ricciardi was somehow entranced. This man's faith was practical, social, and active. None of the empty words he remembered from the Jesuits he'd studied with as a boy, with their otherworldly doctrine. All the same, time was passing, and that long night had left its marks.

"Father, I don't want to take too much of your time. You say mass, I'm told, in the home of the Duke of Camparino."

Don Pierino's dark and expressive face contracted in a pained expression.

"Yes, the poor duchess. A terrible thing. So you're looking into the case. I wouldn't have thought so."

Ricciardi was surprised.

"Why not?"

The assistant pastor shrugged his shoulders and spread his arms wide.

"It's an influential family. And you don't have a reputation for being particularly diplomatic, you know."

The commissario shook his head.

"I never knew that I was so famous; yesterday a journalist, and today you. No, I'm really not very diplomatic, Father. What interests me is the truth: and you, with the work you do, know very well that the truth isn't diplomatic."

"The walks of life where I spend my time, Commissario, are where you find the people who need comforting. And often those are places where the police are well known and feared.

But no one says anything bad about you. They say that you're quiet, and mysterious, too; there are a few superstitious souls, and I'll tell you this with a smile, who say that you bring bad luck, and that you're friends with the devil. But the poor say that an innocent man never suffers at your hands. Tell me, if I may ask; what do you want to know?"

"Whatever you can tell me, Father. Relations between the two dukes and the duchess, for instance. The household help. Or the duchess's friends."

A sad expression appeared on Don Pierino's face.

"Commissario, why would you insult me like this? Do you think somehow that it's my job to gather gossip? I go to bring spiritual comfort to a very sick man, who's too sick even to kneel and pray. I'm certainly not going to pay any attention to who they welcome into their home, or what they say to each other."

Ricciardi shook his head vehemently.

"No, no, Father: don't even think such a thing. I know what kind of a person you are. But something terrible happened in that house, and the same thing could happen again. Murder, to borrow your own words, is a scar that often tears open again, and it's my job to keep that from happening. I'm not asking you for gossip, which is of no more interest to me than it is to you. I just wanted your impressions."

The priest smiled, reassured.

"There's not much I can tell you, I arrive and I say mass, then I leave. The housekeeper, Signora Concetta, is so silent and discreet that sometimes she frightens me, the way she appears suddenly. You've seen Sciarra, the doorman, yourself: he's a funny little man who spends his time watering the hydrangeas and playing with his children: I've never seen children eat so much in my life. You never hear or see his wife. No, I'd say that the scar you're looking isn't to be found among the palazzo's servants."

"What about the duke?"

"The duke made a mistake. He was a widower, he had a difficult son on his hands, one whom he never spent much time with. He thought that he could regain his youth by taking up with a younger woman, but then he fell sick. He gradually lost interest in the things of this world, formal considerations, social conventions. He's a good man, you know, Commissario. He's not afraid of death; to him it only means an end to his pain and a chance to be reunited with his first wife, whom he loved very much."

But the commissario remembered the words of scorn that the old man had uttered concerning his second wife.

"But he clearly felt some resentment toward the duchess. I noticed it when we questioned him."

"That's only human, I think. The duke is dying, he's bedridden. The duchess was . . . a free woman, who allowed life to sweep her away, and who chased after it the way a leaf chases after a mountain stream. She wasn't wicked, she was just lively, like certain children chasing after a rag-ball. I didn't see her much; I doubt she was very religious. Her husband wouldn't forgive her for losing all interest in his home and his family, perhaps. I couldn't say, he'd never talked to me about it."

Ricciardi thought it over.

"What about the son? How did he get along with his stepmother? On this topic everyone's evasive but him, and he says it, loud and clear: he hated her."

Don Pierino shrugged his shoulders.

"Ettore is no ordinary young man. He's very well read, and he's deeply religious. But he's also a young man with very strict principles. He never forgave his father for his second marriage: he broke off all relations with him, I don't think they've spoken in years. The duchess was the exact opposite of his poor mamma, and the memory of his mother is very important and immediate to him. I think his attitude is really quite normal.

But I don't think he's capable of violence; let me say it again, he's very religious."

"What kind of life does he lead, Father? Who does he frequent? Why hasn't he married?"

Don Pierino smiled again, after hesitating briefly.

"Everyone has their own personality and their own friendships, no, Commissario? And neither you nor I are married, it strikes me. We've followed our own paths, and neither of those paths led to a wife or children. And neither, it seems to me, did Ettore's. But that doesn't mean we're not children of God. That doesn't mean we don't have our parts to play."

Ricciardi sat for several long seconds, looking at the assistant pastor's seraphic expression, and following the thread of his thoughts. In the end, he said:

"All right, Father. I thank you for your help. There'll be a funeral, eventually; will you be officiating?"

"Yes, Commissario. I'm the closest thing that family has to a spiritual father, I believe."

"Then we'll see you at the palazzo. I believe that Brigadier Maione and I will both be attending."

XXIV

It hadn't gone according to her rosiest hopes, but it hadn't gone all that badly either. While she was finishing her makeup in front of the mirror, in her room at the Hotel du Vésuve, flooded with sunlight and the bracing smell of salt water, Livia was thinking back on Ricciardi, the day after her meeting with him at Gambrinus.

He was exactly the way she had remembered, as she'd thought about him a thousand times, over the last few months. Dark, smoldering, mysterious. Those eyes that stared without intent, green as the wintry sea, chilly and transparent as glass; he made no attempt to be likable or attractive. And instead he *was* attractive, terribly so; Livia found him wonderfully different from any other man she'd ever known, any man who'd ever courted her. He could be surly, no doubt about it, and he seemed remote: and yet her sensibilities allowed her to detect, behind the appearance of those somewhat brusque manners, the kindness and gentleness that would make the woman who succeeded in drawing them out of him a very happy woman indeed.

As she ran the lipstick brush over her lips, Livia thought about Ricciardi's hands: those fine, tense hands that he usually concealed in his pockets. And she thought about what it would be like to feel them sliding over her body, at first hesitant and then increasingly confident.

She tilted her head slightly to one side and tried out her most seductive smile: the mirror reflected the face of a woman in the prime of her loveliness, her large dark eyes melting and captivating, her lips parted to reveal gleaming white teeth, a coquettish dimple on her chin. She decided that she would pick up Ricciardi at police headquarters that very night, when his shift ended. She'd ignore any objections he might raise: and she'd absolutely forbid him to have his say.

After all, she was Livia Lucani: no man alive, however mysterious and reserved he might be, could resist her charms.

Maione stuck his head into Ricciardi's office.

"Commissa', *buon giorno*. It's hotter today than it was yesterday, impossible as that seems. Shall I bring you a cup of freshly made ersatz coffee?"

Ricciardi shook his head.

"Heaven forbid, the day's already looking bad enough, let's not make things even worse. Why don't you come in and sit down, instead: let's try to figure out where we are with things."

Maione let himself drop into one of the chairs in front of the desk. The office was shrouded in shadow; to protect against the morning sun, Ricciardi had, as usual, left his shutters half shut. The noises of the city as it awakened rose from the street below. The sound of a ship's horn as it set sail split the air.

"Lucky them, that they're going somewhere, eh, Commissa'? There are times when I feel like leaving myself. New places and new faces. I wonder if it would be better or worse."

"What would you expect? I doubt it would really be any different. People are the same wherever you go. The same passions, the same crimes. Today we're going to the duchess's funeral."

Maione was surprised.

"Why on earth would you want to go, Commissa'? We never attend the funerals: all that curiosity, all that mistrust; after all, we're policemen."

Ricciardi was resting his elbows on the desk, knitting his fingers together in front of his mouth.

"I know; but usually we avoid going to keep from causing the family problems. Here I doubt the family cares very much. I'm interested in seeing who's there and who isn't, and I want to see the faces of those who are attending."

Maione tried to figure out who the commissario's suspicions were focusing on.

"Who are you thinking of? If you ask me, given what we know right now, the suspects are Capece and the young master, Ettore Musso. And that's a problem because they're exactly the people that that idiot Garzo says we're supposed to leave alone."

Ricciardi nodded in agreement.

"That's right. Ettore makes no mystery of how much he hated the duchess, and everyone who's been willing to talk to us confirmed that. Even Don Pierino, whom I went to see early this morning, admitted that relations weren't good, and you know that if he says it, that something wasn't right, it must have been unmistakable."

"Still, Commissa', I'm not ready to discount the duke entirely as a suspect, perhaps with a little assistance from the housekeeper. If you ask me, she has all the strength needed, and it also strikes me that anything the duke tells her to do, she does. And the duke didn't seem to cherish her all that much, his wife."

Ricciardi responded, pensively:

"That's also true. Then there's the whole question of Capece, who, unless you're able to track down some elements of evidence, has no alibi, just like the young master. Listen, let's split up the tasks; that'll save us some time: Ettore to me, Capece to you. Aside from making the rounds of the taverns, gather some information on the family, the life he leads, where he lives, and so on. We don't have a lot of time, and we'll need to be discreet, otherwise Garzo will weigh in and stop us from doing anything."

Maione smiled.

"Commissa', forgive me if I venture to say, but you don't have to tell me to be discreet. After all, sometimes you ask people questions that are like a slap in the face. And with a tone, moreover . . . Just promise me that if you do decide to talk to the journalist, the duke, and the young master, at least wait for me, so we can go together: that way at least I can act as witness."

"A witness? Who'd ever listen to you: you're false as a three-lira coin. Come on now, let's get moving. Let's not keep the duchess waiting."

You know, I remember, Mamma. I remember it, when we were together: when we laughed, when we talked. When I could even choose who to talk to. When my father would sit beside me and help me to study. I remember when he'd hold my hand with a pen in it, dipping it into the ink; I even remember the pages and pages of upright strokes, the smell of the paper.

I remember, Mamma. I remember walking holding hands with you both, you on one side and him on the other, in the Villa Nazionale; you greeted the people you met with a smile, sometimes he'd even doff his hat. You were beautiful, Mamma. I wonder if you remember it, too, how pretty you were when you smiled.

Then you were gone, you from one side, him from the other. I looked away, perhaps, because I didn't even notice; but then at a certain point you were both gone. When is it, Mamma, that a child is no longer a child? When he's tall and strong, and can make his own decisions? Or when he knows how to help, or has a job and children of his own?

You know, if you ask me, Mamma, you're a grown-up when you can finally see the way things are. And if you see the way things are, then you have to intervene, you have to solve the problem.

Or at least try to.

When Ricciardi and Maione turned the corner of Piazza Santa Maria La Nova, they found themselves in the presence of the customary trappings of a high-society funeral. The hearse had already arrived, a horse-drawn carriage, and it was a spectacle in itself. Eight horses in all, harnessed two-by-two, black, tall, and formidable. They were foaming at the mouth from the weight they were pulling and the great heat; on each horse's head, a high plume, black like the harnesses. Specially trained, the magnificent beasts made absolutely no noise: they neither scraped their hooves, neighed, nor blew. Behind them, the hearse itself, a complex Baroque construction of inlaid wood and stucco and gleaming glass. One last journey in grand style, before the admiring eyes of one and all. Only the passenger would fail to appreciate the show.

The piazza was immersed in an unnatural silence. A motley crowd was massed around the palazzi and the church; only around the hearse was there an empty space, as if the people were fearful of being contaminated by death in its purest and most popular image. The coachman, with his long black tailcoat and his likewise-black top hat, was standing waiting with the whip in one hand, next to the rear wheel which towered over his head. Further along, vainly seeking a patch of shadow, the eight musicians who would walk before the funeral procession playing solemn marches stood smoking and complaining about the heat; the sun flashed golden off the instruments that lay on the ground.

The arrival of the two policemen caused an immediate wave of murmuring, like the sound of the wind springing up in a forest. Behind the friends, the authorities, and all those who wanted at all costs to be standing at the side of that influential family in this grim moment, there were hundreds of simple onlookers: the murder had made an enormous impression, even though the press, in accordance with instructions received, had devoted little space to it, with none-too-veiled references to the possibility of a banal robbery gone horribly wrong. The duchess's life, which she'd lived without any false modesty, did not allow for privacy even in death.

They were waiting for the coffin to be carried out of the palazzo. At the duke's request the religious service had been performed by Don Pierino in the family chapel, where the corpse had been transported from the morgue at dawn of that day. Everyone, therefore, would have a chance to give one last farewell in the short distance from the front door to the hearse, and then during the procession to Poggioreale Cemetery.

The large church in the piazza however still demanded attention, with the mournful sound of its death knells ringing out regularly.

Ricciardi looked around. In the front row, he recognized the prefect and the chief of police with their wives, surrounded by the other municipal authorities. Sitting near them, a step behind but strategically visible, was Garzo. The eyes of the two men locked for a brief instant, and in that time Ricciardi managed to detect a mute disapproval for his inopportune presence. The commissario held the man's gaze without even hinting at a greeting.

Around the hearse, leaning against the walls of the palazzo, and even up against the gate of the nearby church, stood a vast number of flowered funeral wreaths; the black ribbons adorning them bore the names of families who wished to pay homage.

Maione, who as always seemed to be half asleep, was focusing on the contrasting attitudes of the various groups that made up the crowd. Those who were in tears, sincerely heartbroken, young, and well-dressed must have been the companions of the duchess's riotous nightlife, the gilded youth of Neapolitan high society. There weren't many of them. Grim-faced and uneasy, dressed in black and with expressionless faces, on the other hand, were those there to pay their respects to the elderly duke and to his family, and they were for the most part prominent officeholders and members of the city's highest nobility. Behind them stood the inevitable crowd of rubberneckers, drawn by the dead woman's reputation as a libertine and by the horrible manner of her death.

The brigadier looked for Capece but couldn't see him, neither in the front row, which was certainly understandable, nor in the crowd at large. Maybe he just couldn't bring himself to come: that was something he could understand.

From the open half of the front door emerged Don Pierino, dressed in his funeral vestments, with two altar boys beside him. Behind him came the coffin, in ornately carved dark wood, carried on the shoulders of four pallbearers. The priest blessed the bier which was placed, with some visible effort, in the carriage. The heat that came beating down from the noonday sun was intolerable.

In a wheelchair, the duke was pushed across the threshold of his home, and he looked like another corpse. His unnatural pallor, the horrifyingly skinny neck, which lay enfolded in the collar of his shirt, the equally sticklike limbs, and his blank expression spoke of death even more than the hearse, the horses, and the coffin could. The black suit, matched by the tie and shoes last worn some time before his illness, gave some idea of what his physique must once have been and how it had been laid waste by illness.

The wheelchair was pushed by Concetta, as imposing and silent as ever, her face impassive. One step behind her came the Sciarras, she in tears with her handkerchief crushed to her mouth and he serious-faced, his eyes sorrowful over his enormous nose; his oversized hat and jacket making of him a pathetic figure in a tragic setting. A line of important personages formed immediately to shake the duke's hand and speak a few brief words of condolence to him. The impression that Ricciardi and Maione gathered was that everyone, both because of the heat and because of the prevailing atmosphere, was eager to leave as soon as possible.

A few minutes later something happened which was destined to be the talk of the town for months to come: Ettore appeared in the doorway, dressed in a white suit, with a walking stick and a red tie. His straw hat, likewise bright white in color, shaded a perfectly clean-shaven face, with a broad smile beneath his narrow mustache. He wore absolutely no sign of mourning, neither a black band on his arm nor a black pin on his lapel, where instead he sported a splendid gardenia. After addressing a cordial greeting to the prefect, who was just then paying his respects to the duke, he strolled off whistling cheerfully.

If someone had thrown a bomb into the middle of the piazza, the effect could not have been more explosive. A loud buzz ran through the crowd. It startled Don Pierino who was raptly praying over the coffin; the priest whirled around in confusion, and when he saw Ettore strolling off jauntily, an expression of intense sadness appeared on his expressive face. There was even a brief burst of laughter from the back of the crowd, followed by an indignant call for respect from a few of the onlookers.

Ricciardi, who was watching from a vantage point not far from the front door, caught a rapid exchange of glances between Concetta and Mariuccia, as if the two women had just seen clear confirmation of something they'd already discussed.

The procession, which would accompany the duchess on her final journey on this earth, formed up. Concetta firmly interrupted the line of people greeting the duke and accompanied him back into the palazzo. The man's expression hadn't changed the whole time: Ricciardi decided that he must be exhausted. Behind the hearse, walking with Don Pierino and his two altar boys, were the Sciarras, man and wife, and an eld-erly couple, the duchess's distant cousins; after them came the local authorities and the crowd. When the door of the hearse was closed, the coachman climbed up on the seat and snapped his whip. The orchestra began playing Chopin's funeral march and the horses set off, matching their step to the cadence of the music.

Ricciardi and Maione split up and mingled in the crowd, a few feet behind the front row. They eavesdropped on the comments people made under their breath, comments that for the most part referred to the Camparino family, the performance that Ettore had just delivered, the poor duke and how long he still had to live. There was no shortage of moral judgments concerning the duchess, who was always viewed unfavorably in comparison with the duke's first wife.

And Ricciardi realized that there were a great many people wondering where Mario Capece might be and what he might be doing. And whether and when he'd have the unmitigated gall to make an appearance.

XXV

I'll walk with you, my love. I'll go the whole distance, every step of the way. I'll stay close to you for as long as I can, for the fleeting instants that remain to me.

I'll stay with you because as far as I'm concerned, you never died, and you never will. Because my hands, my body can't go on living a minute longer if you're gone. I'll carry you in my soul, because I gave that soul to you, and it remains your home. No one can take you away, not the horses, not the horrible music, not the fake grief on the faces of those who claim the right to follow you even closer than I can.

What do they know about your smile, the words you say, the sound of your breathing when we're alone together? What do they know about my grief and the weight that I feel in my chest?

That's why I'm here, hidden in the midst of the crowd so that no one will recognize me; so that no one will feel the need to come over to me and tell me that this isn't my place.

Instead, this *is* my place: as close as possible to you.

And if someone tried to send me away from here, I'd kill them with my bare hands.

The funeral procession was scheduled to travel up the first half of Corso Umberto and then disband at Piazza Nicola Amore: in the local vocabulary of Neapolitan place names, the Rettifilo all the way to the Quattro Palazzi; not a short distance, especially in that baking heat. With every martial step of that team of eight horses, the crowd dwindled as it became clear that by now, with the main protagonists no longer present, the performance would offer no further titillation.

As the procession passed, the shops that were still open shut their doors, and the women crossed themselves while the men lifted their hands to their hats, in a military-style salute. Perhaps the duchess actually inspired more sincere pity in the strangers following her bier, Ricciardi mused, than in those who were there as a mere formality. Among the many people who stood lining the street to salute the procession as it passed by, the commissario noted one of his old acquaintances, a man who had been beaten to death and who invariably muttered, the words leaving his mouth along with a mist of blood and a spray of shattered teeth:

"Buffoonish clowns, you're nothing but four buffoonish clowns. Four to one, for shame, for shame, you buffoonish clowns."

Ricciardi, without turning to look, appreciated the lugubrious irony of the phrase applied to the funeral. So many to one, it's true. And it's equally true that for the most part the many are buffoonish clowns, he thought, looking thirty feet or so ahead of him at the balding back of the deputy chief of police Garzo's head.

When they reached the piazza and Don Pierino imparted his final benediction, there were no more than fifty or so onlookers.

It was just then that Maione, before heading off downhill toward the harbor, recognized Capece's silhouette, his face covered by dark glasses and a downturned hat brim. He recognized him from his posture more than his facial features: his shoulders hunched and his legs slightly stiffened by the terrible psychic suffering of the past few days. He signaled to Ricciardi, who nodded back and set off after him: he was interested to see where he'd go.

You follow him, and you do your best to ensure that he won't see you. It's not a problem for you, you've become quite the expert in going unnoticed; for so long, you've simply erased yourself out of your own thoughts. Your oblivion has given you this one last gift: it's made you invisible.

You carefully selected a dark, nondescript dress, a hat that's out of fashion, your shapeless old shoes. You blended into the crowd. You recognized him just before you saw him, you can still sense him with your flesh, you have no need for eyes or ears when it comes to him.

You watched him for a long time, from a distance. You saw the pain in the small, unimportant gestures. No one could understand and in fact, no one did: only you understood. You smiled as you realized that, in that piazza crowded with people, there were really only three people: him, you, and her. As always, the way you've been accustomed to having it, for years now. You followed him as he walked, under the implacable sun, without stopping, without staggering. She takes a step, he takes a step. You take a step. And of course, no one saw you. No one recognized you. It was just the three of you.

But for her, it was the last time. You smile again, under your hat, while the heat makes the walls of the distant palazzi shimmer.

After all, you owed him that much.

Ricciardi stepped closer to Don Pierino.

"Father, I just wanted to say hello. I imagine this was no ordinary funeral for you."

The little priest was sweating copiously beneath his tunic and his vestments. He had a deeply sad expression on his face, uncustomary for him.

"As you know, Commissario, a funeral is always painful, it's a natural thing. It's the very commemoration of pain and sorrow, of abandonment, of absence. It's my job to console, to make it clear in a dark moment that the separation is only temporary. There's no death, there's no absence. We'll all meet again, in a better world. You may not believe it, Commissario, but it's possible to see the dead again."

Ricciardi grimaced.

"And who says that I don't believe it, Father? No one knows better than I do that the dead don't vanish, that they leave a visible trace of their sorrow and pain. It's to provide solace for that grief that we exist. We, and the law."

Don Pierino shook his head.

"There's another justice that cancels grief, Commissario. And it's not of this world. In any case, this time I felt practically useless. Certainly, I saw a sister of mine down the road that leads to a more beautiful home. But all around me I sensed neither love nor grief. Not enough, at least. And no one was offering comfort, except for the good-hearted Mariuccia Sciarra who suffers the grief of simple souls, which vanishes as quickly as it came."

This was exactly the aspect that Ricciardi wanted to explore in greater depth.

"And yet, Father, it seems strange to me. The duchess was certainly not well loved; but from what I heard she wasn't a bad person either, not the sort of person who had done so much evil that she'd have no one close to her. Not even in the midst of all these people."

The priest was still wearing the same sad expression.

"Sometimes we do evil without even knowing it. It's one of the devil's cleverest tricks, Commissario: it surprises me that you, who deal with it on a daily basis, wouldn't know that. He mixes evil in with good, pain in with love. And he conceals it, he makes it indistinguishable. And so, if you love without regard for anything, you can cause pain to someone else; by laughing you can make someone cry. Think about it, Commissario. I wonder if the solution to your doubts lies in this fact."

After saying these words, Don Pierino climbed onto the seat of the hearse and set off for Poggioreale. This last part of the journey was for him alone.

I followed you. I waited for you to go out, I knew you thought I was with my friends. But I lurked in a doorway and I waited.

I've learned to recognize the tone of what you say even when you don't speak, you know that, Mamma? The expression of your eyes, the movement of a hand. The rooms you go into, the rooms you avoid. You learn over time. Then we think about the same things, even if we don't talk about them: and when we think about the same things, we think the same way.

This morning I knew that you meant to go out and I even knew where you were going to go. I understood it from the creaking of your dresser door, the armoire that you never open, the one with your old dresses. I heard you climb up on the chair to get something from your hat rack. I even heard you sing under your breath, when you thought I was still asleep. And I was right.

Step by step, on the far sidewalk, hiding behind other people: but I could have just walked ahead of you, certain as I was where you'd be going. I got there: all those people. I almost lost you. But he was there too, I saw him even before I saw you. And I found a place to wait, at the far end of the room, I watched the two of you, close and yet so distant. I followed you both, step by step, again, without losing sight of you once, each of you with your grief, each of you with your absence. And me, with mine.

We were all walking together. But each of us was walking behind a different funeral procession, Mamma.

Each of us mourning a different death.

Maione had followed Capece through the *vicoli*, and it

quickly became clear to him that the man was wandering without a destination.

Every so often the journalist would stop, pull out a handkerchief, and mop his face; sweat and tears, thought the brigadier. At a certain point he saw him slip into a cantina that sold wine. He waited for him for half an hour, and when it became clear that he wouldn't be coming out in any condition to do anything dangerous to himself or anyone else, he left.

The duchess's funeral had been a truly saddening experience for Maione. It reminded him of his own Luca's funeral, which he could still remember through the mists of the horrifying pain that he'd felt then and still felt now. Fewer people had attended, perhaps, and he certainly couldn't afford eight horses or a band playing the funeral march: but he was certain of one thing—the love that he'd felt surrounding him, from his family, his colleagues, and the entire quarter. He thought back to the interview with the duke, the gasping voice, the terrible heat, the suffocating odor of death in the room; but he also remembered the man's words, which had struck home to his soul. A man dies when his life no longer means anything to anyone else. Maione's simple soul had continued to reflect on this phrase, uttered by a man who was about to depart this world in utter silence. He'd decided that if this principle was true, then so was its opposite; in that case his Luca—whose off-kilter laugh he heard every day of his life, whose cap, tipped back on the back of his head at a rakish and decidedly non-regulation angle, he could see vanishing around every corner, whose expression he recognized every day on the faces of the boy's mother, brothers, and sisters—had never really died at all.

Two hours later, as he left the sixth tavern, Maione finally decided that this investigative tactic wouldn't lead to anything for a number of reasons. He couldn't hope to overcome the mistrust that the proprietors felt toward the police, since every one of them had something to hide or at least something to be ashamed of; the customers that came in every night were too numerous and unpredictable for them to remember someone who, in all likelihood, was also not particularly interested in chatting; and last of all, the ones who were willing to talk to him still felt they had more in common with a man wanted by the law than they did with a policeman, and they tailored their answers accordingly. Conclusion: he'd sweated like a pig, he'd salivated gallons at the sight of all kinds of delicious food, and he'd come up with nothing.

Maione mopped his brow with his oversized handkerchief, loosened his tie, and made a decision: the time had come to go see Bambinella again.

XXVI

From the kitchen, Maria Colombo watched her daughter in the dining room, tutoring three little boys; two of them were the children of a well-to-do lumber wholesaler, and they were twins; the third, tiny and dark-skinned, with bright dancing eyes, was the concierge's grandson.

Enrica often talked to her about how extremely intelligent this third little boy had proven to be, how he often did his work twice as fast as the twins, even though he was two years younger. While Enrica received a regular and sizable salary from the children of the lumber wholesaler, from the concierge's family she received nothing but plentiful smiles and boundless gratitude.

Whenever Maria pointed it out to her, Enrica would reply that you don't live on bread alone. There, that was exactly what drove Maria crazy about Enrica: her absolute lack of any common sense. On the subject of marriage, too, which they'd discussed endlessly, that was always at the root of their disagreement: practical common sense. Could it be, Maria wondered, that she was the only person in the family who recognized that time was passing, that youth makes way for old age and that it wouldn't be long before a fresh face would no longer do Enrica any good? Or did she think that she could just wait indefinitely for her Habsburg prince to ride in on his white steed, to turn her into a queen?

Most important of all, her daughter wasn't such a beauty that she'd capture a man at the first glance: Maria, who was her mother, had the courage to admit it herself. And so she'd finally taken charge of the situation, and she'd forced her husband to invite the Fiores to dinner.

For a whole day she'd waited for Enrica's inevitable reaction: she knew that behind her sweet and tranquil nature there was a stubborn soul, anything but compliant, and that it certainly would be no easy matter to persuade her to accept this imposition. But it was for her own good, so she'd be able to respond, blow for blow, even at the cost of alienating the girl's affections for a week or two; then Enrica would understand and even thank her.

That's what a mamma's for.

For the second time in three days, Maione knocked at Bambinella's door.

"Brigadie', what do you think, can I start to consider you one of my suitors? Next time you come, though, why don't you bring, oh, I don't know, a flower, a box of pastries, just anything. I'll take you to meet mamma and we'll iron out the details."

Maione was still panting from the climb, and he was drenched with sweat.

"You've got one thing right, I don't have the breath to breathe, much less to tell you to go straight to you-know-where. I'm a bad man to joke around with, you know that? Better cut it out, or one of these days I'll come calling on you one last time, and the next thing you know you'll be sitting in a cell and I'll be throwing away the key!"

Bambinella flirtatiously raised one hand in front of her mouth and she giggled girlishly.

"Madonna, do you know how much I like a fiery man? All right then, Brigadie', don't work yourself up into a rage: it just means that I'll wait patiently, I know that sooner or later you'll make up your mind. The important thing is that you remember: for you it's always free of charge."

Maione hauled back to throw a slap that Bambinella dodged with a dainty motion. Both of them burst out laughing.

"So the truth is, Bambine', that this story of the duchess is deep and complicated. Not so much the facts themselves; it's that we can't operate freely."

Bambinella, who, as usual, was wearing her silk kimono, walked toward the table where she'd been sitting before Maione arrived.

"I understand, Brigadie'. You've got the press, the nobility, and the authorities to deal with. All of them are people you can't exactly throw into a cell without thinking twice, like you can with girls like me. It's less of a headache when they murder poor people, for you cops, eh?"

Maione raised his voice.

"No, it's not less of a headache. How dare you say such a thing? Why, do you think that Brigadier Raffaele Maione pays less attention to what happens to poor people? Listen, for saying something like that, I won't just throw you in jail, I'm liable to kick your ass down the stairs!"

Bambinella laughed openly. When she laughed, her womanly affectations and imitations vanished, and she sounded very much like a horse.

"Brigadie', how little it takes to piss you off! I know, I know: you and your commissario, the handsome one who carries a hex, you treat poor people and rich people just the same. That's why we respect you. After all, what do you think—if I really thought that, would I be helping you?"

When Bambinella sat back down, Maione noticed that she had an enormous dish of fried anchovies on the table in front of her.

"What is this, a conspiracy? Everyone seems to be eating here, at every hour of the day or night! You must have agreed on this behind my back, all of you: the minute you see me coming you start eating something? Since when do people sit down to eat at three in the afternoon, if I might ask?"

With her mouth full, Bambinella replied:

"No, Brigadie', it's just that at lunchtime I wasn't hungry, so I had only a little hard biscuit and tomatoes—*fresella con pomodori*. Then Gigino came by, the fishmonger down below who, every so often . . . okay, you get it, but truth be told, the man has a wife who is truly revolting. In other words, the man has no money, but he breaks my heart, and so this is how he settles his accounts, a few anchovies, a sea bream or two. The anchovies are nice and fresh, if I didn't cook them right away in this heat, I'd have had to throw them out. But try some, try some, there must be five pounds here, I can't possibly eat it all myself. Hold on, I'll get another plate and a fork."

Maione let himself drop heavily onto the ramshackle sofa and waggled his forefinger.

"No, no, forget about it. I made a promise and now I can't break it. But listen here, now: I want you to tell me everything you know about Mario Capece and his family."

Bambinella's mascaraed eyes opened wide in a sincere display of astonishment.

"Oh, so now he's the guilty party? My girlfriend who works at the Salone Margherita told me all about it . . ."

Maione raised his hand:

"No, hold up just a minute: that's not what I said. In fact, I have my doubts that it was him at all, even though he can't give us an alibi. The thing is, we have to check him out carefully so that we can rule him out as a suspect. So, spare me your personal opinions and just tell me what you know. And swallow first, because if you talk with a mouthful of anchovies, you'll be even more revolting than usual."

"*Grazie*, Brigadie', you're always such an exquisite gentleman. It's always a pleasure to talk to you, a girl feels appreciated for what she is. Now then, Capece: all I know I told you the other day. Capece wasn't someone you saw in the usual social circles, before he struck up this affair with the duchess.

He was a journalist, and he was even a good one. Then, five or six years ago, he started seeing her and he became a public figure. Still, I never heard anything about him that didn't concern the duchess. That is, if people mentioned him, they always mentioned her in the same breath."

"And just how long had this relationship been going on?"

Bambinella took a second to answer, busy as she was chewing her mouthful of fried anchovies.

"Five, maybe six years. Forever. In their way, among the, so to speak, non-regulation relationships, they were an old couple; you know it, Brigadie', men switch lovers more often than they do wives. Not the two of them: they'd really been together for some time."

The policeman wanted to know something more about the man's life when he wasn't with the duchess.

"For instance, his wife, his children? Had he moved out or was he still living with them? And his family, I don't know, his parents?"

Bambinella shrugged her shoulders and joined her greasy hands together, palms flat.

"What can I tell you, Brigadie', I don't really know. Certainly, he slept with the duchess more nights than not, I think. The two of them, what with going to the theater, the movie house, and out to dinner in fancy restaurants, were out on the street until dawn, then he had a job after all, and I don't think that left much time in the day."

Maione felt downcast, a victim of the heat and the heap of fried anchovies that Bambinella was methodically shoveling down.

"Then how on earth can I find out something more?"

After a moment of silence, spent chewing while lost in thought, Bambinella's face lit up.

"Maybe I can help you out, but it's not recent information. A girlfriend of mine—honest, and a hard worker—used to keep house for the Capece family. Then she had a piece of blind luck, she met a guy from the Pendino quarter who ran a shipping service, a couple of horses and two or three wagons, he'd bring the goods in from Mugnano . . . okay, okay, I understand, Brigadie', but try to be a little patient: I have to tell stories my way, otherwise I lose the thread. So, as I was saying, what with one thing and another, this girlfriend of mine, Gilda's her name, now she's had this brilliant career and she's in a brothel at La Torretta, she's making money hand over fist. Now everyone calls her Juliette. I don't remember how long ago it was that she kept house for the Capeces, but she can certainly tell you something."

Maione shook his head in admiration.

"Certainly, Bambine', there are times when you seem like a spider at the center of her web: even if you don't know something, you always know someone who does. Would you take me right away to see this . . . Signorina, what's her name, Gilda Juliette; and let's see if she can tell us something about Capece."

Ricciardi knew very well where he needed to go in order to start understanding something more about the murder of the Duchess Musso di Camparino. He needed to head home. To be exact, he needed to reconstruct the senseless route he'd taken the night before, in search of the sleep he'd never found.

As he climbed the Via Toledo, gasping under the whiplash of the hot sun, doing his best to stay in the shade of the palazzi, he reflected on the dance of emotions around the duchess and her death. A woman who had turned her beauty into a tool, an instrument with which to climb the social ladder, to amuse herself, to charm others. And then she'd become that beauty's slave, a prisoner of the passions that her own beauty ignited, and which she no longer knew how to extinguish.

Love is one thing, but passion is quite another, Ricciardi thought. This is the real difference. My feelings for Enrica, for example. I want her welfare and happiness, and if the young man can make her happy, then I ought to be happy too. Perhaps that is love. Then, there is passion, this stabbing pain in the belly, this vise grip that seizes your stomach. The picture of Enrica's eyes filled with tears, the emptiness in his heart, this anxiety on his flesh. The inability to sleep, the street by night, a sense of regret, even though he had nothing to regret.

It is passion that leads to murder, he mused. Perhaps in all these years I've attributed faults to love that it does not deserve. I wonder how you can eliminate a passion; probably by replacing it with another passion. His mind, in defiance of his attempt at self-control, leapt to Livia; her smiling face, the dimple in her chin, the scent of spices. And the long legs, sheathed in fishnet stockings, her feline stride.

And especially, the fleeting kiss that she'd planted on his cheek as she left, as if it were the most natural thing in the world. Then and there, caught as he was in the tempest of emotions prompted by the sight of Enrica, he'd felt embarrassed, practically annoyed. But now, as he walked under the arch of Port'Alba and turned into Via Costantinopoli, he thought back to the pressure of her lips and the whisper of her breath. As always, he'd been too brusque, and he regretted it.

It wouldn't make any sense to go in search of her; but if he ever did see her again, he promised to give her the pleasure of his company, at least once. She wasn't like Enrica: Livia was a strong, independent woman, he couldn't hurt her. A relationship without a future, he decided, but possibly one with a present.

As he drew near to his destination, he forced himself to regain his focus and concentrate on what he'd come to do. Love or passion, he thought.

Let's see what kind of animal we're dealing with.

XXVII

Walking through the city streets with Bambinella wasn't the greatest, as far as Maione was concerned; the incredibly piercing voice and the dozens of friends the man had, which required affectionate billing and cooing and lengthy, nerve-racking pauses on the cobblestones, exacerberated the effect made by the dubious appearance, the garish colors, and the heavy makeup.

Moreover, it could hardly be healthy for the transvestite to display publicly his close contacts with the police, albeit with no one other than the brigadier; the world of the *vicoli* frowned on these contacts, even on the part of those who had nothing to do with the darker dealings of the underworld, but might simply be aware of them. By common agreement, then, they made an appointment to meet directly in La Torretta, the poor quarter close to the waterfront, at Mergellina. That was the location of the brothel where Gilda worked, the Capeces' former maid who'd enjoyed such brilliant career advancement.

Maione was the first to arrive. He'd stopped at a fruit and vegetable shop, where he devoured two plums and an apricot; it actually seemed to make him hungrier. He'd insisted on paying, despite the proprietor's protestations: no, he had it in for the entire professional category of grocers now—an extension of his antipathy toward the notorious Ciruzzo, the skinny and intrusive fruit and vegetable vendor.

The fact that he'd arrived early only worsened his already bad mood. The brothel, in fact, was located on a cross street of the broad Viale Principessa Elena; hardly a main thoroughfare, in other words. He found a place to wait in the shade of a tree, thirty feet or so away from the entrance with a brass plaque, on which was engraved: "Casa di Madame Yvonne." There was quite a coming and going, and every soldier, sailor, or office clerk who went in or came out shot him a look somewhere between the scornful and the concerned: what was a uniformed brigadier of the Neapolitan police department doing there loitering in the shade of a tree? Was he noting down the identity of everyone who frequented the house, or was he laying the groundwork for a raid? Or was he simply working up the nerve to go in himself?

Finally Bambinella showed up, swinging her hips on her stiletto heels, wrapped in a tight-fitting red-flowered dress.

"Forgive me, Brigadie', but I had to stop twice to get something to drink, it's so hot you wouldn't believe it."

Maione wanted to speed things up.

"Sure, sure, that's fine. But let's go in, all we need now is for your girlfriend to be busy, and the two of us to be seen sitting together in the waiting room."

The entrance to the brothel was through a small wooden door and up a steep staircase. At the top of the stairs, they were greeted by an old woman with a broom and a bucket in her hands, cleaning an already spotless landing.

"Never once do they let you clean in peace; never a moment of calm and quiet, day and night," she grumbled ungraciously, stepping aside to let them pass. Maione thought better of telling her he was there on official police business, but he shot her a hostile glare that she returned in full.

At the end of a hallway wallpapered in red silk there was a large room with sofas and chairs lining the walls, dominated at the center by a large wooden dais and desk. Behind it sat a middle-aged woman whose hair was dyed a red not found in nature and whose face was so made-up that it would have been impossible to recognize her when she woke up in the morning. As soon as she saw Maione and Bambinella walk in, she got out of her chair and strode toward them with a grim, furrowed brow.

"*Buona sera*, Brigadier. Excuse me, but I should inform you that in my house, only my own young ladies are allowed to work. If you're here for a threesome, I can certainly let you choose two of my misses, but I absolutely cannot allow you to bring . . ."

Maione broke in brusquely, stemming her flow of words:

"No, Signora, forgive me but you seem to have misunderstood. I'm not here to enjoy myself, I'm here strictly on police duty."

The woman put on a worried face and took a step back.

"I don't know what you're talking about. My operation is in strict compliance from every point of view: taxes, health certificates. The receipt book for all the services rendered and paid is available for your inspection, just say the word . . ."

Maione started to lose his temper.

"Enough, Signora, be still: who asked you anything? I'm just here to talk with a signorina who I understand works here, according to what the signore—" pointing to Bambinella, who quickly corrected him: "Signorina . . ."

The woman gave Bambinella a disgusted glare, and then turned back to Maione.

"Why, are you suggesting that one of my young ladies has broken the law? I can guarantee the utmost supervision under my roof, but once they're outside of my control, responsibility for their actions . . ."

The brigadier seriously considered leaving a five-fingered handprint on the thick layer of greasepaint that covered the madam's face.

"Signora, no one's done anything wrong here. Unless I decide that you're trying to interfere with a police investigation, and if I do, then I'll wrap you up, along with all your young ladies and that bad-mannered concierge sweeping out on the landing, and slap you behind bars for a while."

His tone was abrupt; the woman lowered her head as if he'd just slapped her on the back of the head.

"At your orders, Brigadie'," she said obediently.

Ricciardi had found the street door, though not without some difficulty. Nocturnal landmarks are provided by the lamplighter; in the light of day everything looks different. He stepped into the courtyard and the welcome shade, and noticed a doorman's booth close to the main entrance. The doorman himself was walking toward him, a tall and powerful-looking young man, asking him in a peevish voice what he might be looking for. Ricciardi identified himself:

"I need some information. Who lives in this building?"

The young man looked him up and down. From inside came the sound of scales being practiced on a piano, frequently breaking off for mistakes. The answer was slow in coming; the two men looked each other in the eye. Finally, the doorman said:

"Why, who are you looking for?"

Ricciardi understood that he needed to eliminate this stumbling block promptly.

"Listen: if you want to answer my questions, we can get this over with and I'll stop bothering you. If you want to play games, then I'll come back on official business and we'll take you someplace where I can make you talk whether you want to or not. That's up to you."

There weren't many citizens out there likely to resist Ricciardi's will when he hissed his determination eye-to-eye, with unwavering intensity. And the doorman certainly wasn't one of them. He blinked once and replied:

"At your orders, Commissa'. Ask away."

The policeman was duly informed that this apartment

building, not far from the Conservatory, was occupied by two families with small children, an elderly retired widower, and several female music students from a small town in the southern region of Lucania.

"They're the ones you can hear practicing," the man pointed out.

On the second story were the offices of a shipping line, which were closed at that time of year.

"As far as you know," Ricciardi inquired, "was there a party last night? Did someone have a reception, with music and guests, that might have gone on until quite late? With prominent guests?"

The doorman shrugged.

"I couldn't say, Commissario. I don't live here, and when I lock up at night I go straight home, I have little kids myself. Still, if you tell me that there was a party here until late, I would have thought someone would complain this morning. That seems odd to me."

Ricciardi was starting to think that his exhaustion, the night before, had played a trick on him; or perhaps he might have misremembered the building. Just as he was about to thank the man and go looking for another similar front entrance, the man said:

"Unless . . . sometimes they stay late, on the top floor. Still, music would strike me as odd."

"Why, who lives on the top floor?"

Instinctively lowering his voice and looking up, the doorman murmured:

"The Fascist Party's on the top floor. Fascist Party headquarters."

Maione and Bambinella followed the expansive derriere of Annunziata Caputo, alias Madame Yvonne, up another steep flight of stairs; then they walked down a narrow corridor, with closed doors up and down both sides, at the end of which was a small room with a large window from which, if you craned your neck, you could glimpse the sea. The air was cool and clean and slightly briny, and in the distance you could hear the cries of children playing and seagulls swooping.

In the middle of the room there was a table, around which sat a few young women, laughing, smoking, and chatting. Some of them were bare-breasted, most of them were seeking a little cool air near the window. When the brigadier walked in, even though he was accompanied by the *maîtresse*, there were little squeals of fear; the girls covered themselves as best they could and retreated to the far end of the room. But Madame spoke to them in a reassuring voice:

"Don't worry, young ladies, the brigadier isn't here to arrest anyone. He just wants to talk to . . ."

Maione interrupted her in a weary voice:

"Let me guess, Signora: that's Juliette right there, no?"

Seated on a sofa against the wall, off to one side, a half-naked young blonde was hungrily consuming a large chunk of bread dripping with tomato sauce.

"Brigadie', please forgive me, but this morning we literally had a parade through here. A freighter came in, and there were more than three hundred sailors who haven't seen dry land for a year. Genoans, Portuguese, Russians: a veritable Babylonia! I haven't managed to get a bite to eat all day, now I have a moment to recover. I hear that it's the same in every bordello in Naples."

Bambinella listened raptly to her friend, as if she were describing a safari in equatorial Africa, and darted proud glances at Maione from time to time.

"No, don't think twice, in fact I hope you don't mind that we showed up at this time of day without calling ahead. The brigadier, here, just wants to ask you a couple of questions, you answer freely, and don't worry: I can vouch for him."

Maione snorted in annoyance, shooting rapid, suffering glances at the uneaten chunks of bread and tomato still littering the table.

"Eh, so it's come to this: I need a recommendation from Bambinella! Now then, Signorina: what's your name?"

The girl proved to be amiable and intelligent. Her name was Gilda, just as Bambinella had said, and she came from the Rione del Vasto, a neighborhood behind the train station. The fifth-eldest of nine children, she'd gone to work as a housemaid at age sixteen because her family could no longer afford to feed her. Now that she was twenty-two, she earned enough in her current line of work to maintain her four younger siblings and her mother. Their father had vanished, three years earlier, and had never been heard from again. "Either he's dead or he shipped out," she said, her jaws working industriously all the while, and without a hint of regret.

When she decided to become a housemaid, she'd been hired immediately by the Capece family, whose income was climbing along with the brilliant newspaper career of the head of the family. Gilda described a time that was not so much wealthy as hopeful, a household full of penny-pinching as well as laughter. "But it wasn't weird," she said, "because the signora helped me with the housekeeping and I helped her with the children."

The Capece family had two children: Andrea and Giovanna; Andrea, the boy, was the elder of the two. When Gilda decided to quit after the first year, Andrea had been twelve and Giovanna was seven.

"So now," Maione calculated, "they're sixteen and eleven."

"Yes," said Gilda. "And he's become a handsome young man. I wonder if I'll find him on top of me in here, some of these days."

Gilda knew what Andrea looked like now because every so often, up until a couple of years ago, she'd gone by to say hello to the Capece family; she had fond memories of her time there.

"But then I didn't want to go back. The last time was just too weird," she said again.

Maione didn't understand.

"What do you mean, too weird?"

Gilda seemed to shudder at the memory, despite the heat.

"It was like going to pay a call on a family of dead people, Brigadie'. Everything was different."

"How, everything was different how? What do you mean?"

The girl hesitated before answering. Bambinella, who was sitting beside her and holding her hand, squeezed it quickly to encourage her. She looked over at her friend and went on:

"The family I remembered was poor but they were happy. They treated me like a daughter; we were always lauging together. The signora would sit down next to me and teach me everything, how to cook, how to sew. She used to say that later on, once I'd found a husband and started a family of my own, I'd know how to do it all. Then I . . . well, my life went the way it did. I don't regret a thing, eh. But I expected that Signora Sofia, the wife, would dress me down, that she'd tell me I'd done wrong."

"So what happened?"

"Instead, when I went to see them, she sat me down in the drawing room, like a grand lady. I felt uncomfortable, I wanted to go sit in the kitchen. But she insisted, she said, come sit in here. You made the right decision, I'm the one who chose the wrong life. And the apartment . . ."

Maione was sensitive to every detail.

"The apartment? What had happened to the apartment?"

The girl tossed her yellow-tinted head of hair.

"No, no, nothing had really happened. It was all the same. But still it seemed . . . dead, everything was dead. The little girl sitting at the table, studying, white as a sheet, she barely said hello to me. The boy, Andrea, gave me a big strong hug, and then he left the room, right away, as if he was ashamed or something. But the signora talked and talked to me, I thought she'd never stop."

"And what did she talk about?"

"She talked about the old days, about when I lived there with them. She talked about her husband, as if he was dead though, as if he was a memory from long ago. Without hatred. She didn't say anything to me about it, but maybe she knew that I'd heard all about the affair with the duchess. Everyone's heard about it. And her, too, Brigadie': her eyes were empty. As if they'd taken her heart out of her, her stomach, her brain, everything inside her. And that's why I said, before, that it seemed weird to me. And that I don't ever want to go back there."

A long silence followed. Bambinella was stroking her girlfriend's hand, as if she were consoling her for some loss. While Gilda was telling her story, she'd never altered her tone of voice; but now she wore an expression of profound sadness. The splotches of tomato sauce around her mouth made her look like a little girl playing at being a grown-up.

After a pause, Maione asked:

"Now listen to me carefully, Gilda: do you remember by any chance whether there was a pistol in the apartment? Think as hard as you can and try to remember: this is important to us."

The girl was about to answer the question, then she stopped. She looked at Bambinella, and then at the brigadier, and said:

"The master of the house served in the war, he was an officer. His pistol is locked up in the desk drawer, one time he showed it to me to throw a scare into me, and he had a good laugh at my expense, too. But he keeps it locked up, and he has the only key."

XXVIII

When Ricciardi and Maione met up again at headquarters, night had already fallen. The brigadier brought back the information he'd gathered from his round of bars and dives, from Bambinella, and from Gilda, the maid-turned-prostitute.

For his part, Ricciardi was evasive, skimming over the results of his personal investigation; it wasn't that he didn't want to share his information, but he thought that the trail he was following might prove to be dangerous—even just knowing about it—and he preferred to leave Maione in the dark. At least for now.

Every piece of information that they'd gathered on Capece and Musso seemed to strengthen the impression of guilt for both of them. And, paradoxically, the stronger the impression became that each of them was the murderer, the less there seemed to be any solid evidence proving it. It was a real stumper.

Just as they were trying to determine their new investigative strategies, they heard a nervous tapping at the door of Ricciardi's office. Maione gave him a knowing look:

"If you ask me, it's that snake, Ponte. He's the only one who'll knock on the door the same way he talks and the way he looks you in the face: all hesitant, without conviction. Listen to him: he's practically scratching like a dog."

Ricciardi sighed and called out: "*Avanti!*"

It was Ponte, of course, sweatier and more nervous than before.

"Commissario, *buona sera*. I'm here to ask you to come straight up to Dottor Garzo's office. He said right away, immediately, in other words. Please, come with me."

After such a grueling day, the last thing that Ricciardi felt like was resisting the little man's darting, evasive gaze; moreover, even if he couldn't say so to Maione, he was curious to hear what new objections the deputy chief of police had to make. And so he caught both the brigadier and Ponte by surprise when he stood up and said, agreeably:

"Did he say right away? Then we'll come right away."

They found the deputy chief of police pacing back and forth in his office, like a lion in a cage; his collar was unbuttoned, his tie was loosened, his jacket was draped over a hanger, and his vest swung open. On his desk, normally so immaculate, with only a few neatly stacked files, were scattered sheets of notepaper with transcriptions of official transcribed phone messages, various documents, and broken pencils. As soon as he saw Ricciardi and Maione come in, he started to berate them:

"I warned you two! You can't say I didn't warn you! It's exactly what I expected to happen, and now it's happened. Now what do we do, Ricciardi? What now? Tell me what you plan to do now, why don't you?"

Ricciardi didn't blink. He stood there, hands in his pockets, his lock of hair hanging over his forehead, a half-smile playing over his lips. Garzo stood seething, waiting for an answer. Maione and Ponte, behind Ricciardi, were both wondering what the commissario would say now. Ricciardi shrugged briefly and said:

"If you don't tell me what's happened, I don't very well see what I can tell you."

This time Garzo had no intention of allowing himself to be lulled by Ricciardi's tone of voice.

"The publisher of the *Roma* called. And do you know who

he called? He called me! Not the chief of police, as he ought to have done. The bastard called me directly, knowing full well who's in charge of day-to-day operations."

"And are you in charge of day-to-day operations?"

Garzo was too upset to catch the ironic tone of voice.

"And do you know what he said? He said that it's his intention to run an article lambasting the intolerable methods being used by the police. That the police, without any solid evidence, and let me repeat that, without any solid evidence, are actually conducting newsroom raids. Now do you understand? An article in the newspaper! And it's all your fault, you and your trusty sidekick here!"

He'd finished up with a flourish, pointing a finger at Maione and panting. He was truly beside himself. Ricciardi replied in the same tone of voice as before, as if he were asking him whether he'd like a cup of espresso.

"I'm glad you asked us to come upstairs, Dottore. If I'd known that you were still in your office at this hour, a highly unusual state of affairs, I'd have already come to talk to you. I need to request an authorization."

Garzo blinked furiously, as if he'd just woken up from a particularly bad dream.

"Authorization? What authorization?"

"Authorization to search the residence of Mario Capece, chief news editor of the daily newspaper, the *Roma*, and question the members of his family."

Mamma santa, thought Maione. This guy's gonna have a heart attack any second now. And in fact Garzo seemed to be struggling to stand upright. He paled visibly, took a couple of steps backward, felt around behind him with one hand until he found the arm of his chair, and let himself flop down into it, with a dull thump. His mouth gaped silently until he was finally able to take in a mouthful of air and he exhaled. At last he said, in a faint voice:

"What, Capece? Haven't you heard a word I said to you? What I just told you is—"

"I know exactly what you just told me. The fact is that today's investigations have revealed a number of important elements. We now have good cause to believe that the Duchess of Camparino had just recently begun having an affair. A different one."

Garzo was having difficulty catching his breath.

"Another affair? With who?"

Ricciardi showed no pity.

"I'm not yet ready to tell you the name, Dottore. But this person holds one of the highest offices in the city administration."

Garzo felt as if he'd just been shot. One of the highest offices? Which one? Faces swam past his mind's eye: the prefect, an older man who commanded an immense and loyal following in Rome; the high commissioner, who'd been appointed directly by the Duce; and the chief of police, who was waiting eagerly for him to make a false step so he could rid himself of a formidable rival.

Ricciardi and Maione almost felt as if they could hear the cogs grinding away in the deputy police chief's brain as it feverishly processed this new information. A catastrophe. He could see a catastrophe looming. Once he felt sure that his superior officer had taken in the scope and dimension of the problem, Ricciardi continued:

"And so, unless we can move quickly to exclude Capece from the short list of potential suspects or else, an equally practicable alternative, charge him with the murder beyond any reasonable doubt, then we'll inevitably be forced to reveal that it was his jealousy over this new affair of the duchess's that drove him to make that jealous scene the other night. And we'd have to reveal the name of . . . the other man."

Garzo shot to his feet, as if someone had just jabbed him in the derriere with a hatpin.

"No! Never! This must never happen, Ricciardi. You

understand that, don't you? We'd be playing into their hands, giving them a chance to strip me of the . . . strip us of the necessary investigative independence. What do you plan to do, to prevent such a development?"

Ricciardi shrugged his shoulders once again, keeping his hands in his pockets. His tone of voice became even vaguer than before.

"Hmmm, I don't really know. Maybe, if we could find the weapon used in the murder, we could just arrest Capece without bringing up the matter at all. It's not in his interest, either; from what we're able to determine, he had a fair number of reasons to be jealous, so why would he want to make a number of powerful enemies before going to trial? And if we don't find the weapon, we could start looking elsewhere once we're done: perhaps the murderer was someone else."

Garzo pondered the implications of what Ricciardi had just told him for a minute. In the end, he saw the light. A slow, broadening smile spread across his face like a river reaching the ocean. Still, a large bright red patch remained on his neck.

"Yes. Yes, yes. Yes. That's fine, Ricciardi, you'll have your authorization. Do as you suggest. But for the love of all that's holy, make sure that no one hears about the . . . the other thing. No one. Ever. Tomorrow morning, you'll have the document on your desk first thing. And one more thing . . . *Grazie*."

As they left Garzo's office, Maione was beside himself with excitement.

"Commissa', this time you practically laid that poor sap out flat. But what's all this talk about another affair? I gather you invented it out of whole cloth, but what was the purpose? It won't take even a fool like Garzo more than a day or two to figure out that there's no third party."

Ricciardi shot a quick glance behind him to make sure that there was no one eavesdropping. With people like Ponte, you could never be sure.

"I had no alternative: I had to raise the stakes. Otherwise he'd bind us and gag us, and then we wouldn't have been able to move an inch. Instead, I feel pretty confident that with either Ettore or Capece something's really about to come to the surface. The information you uncovered today, about the pistol at the Capece home, is the only concrete thing we've come up with, and we absolutely have to go. I'll say it again, this was the only possible way."

Maione took off his cap and scratched his head.

"Then what can I tell you, Commissa'? You've done the right thing. And may the Lord Almighty set our feet on the right path."

Sofia Capece was chopping onions and thinking about animals. About herbivorous animals, to be exact.

She was thinking that even the gentlest animals, the ones at the end of the food chain, the most non-aggressive animals, the ones without claws or fangs, could still become violent and dangerous. They turned vicious if they saw their young endangered. And it was the females, the ones charged with the preservation of the species, who were responsible for the birth and protection of the young, and who had to make up for the shortcomings of the males, the males that were out hunting or on some other foolish pursuit, leaving lairs and caverns unguarded.

She was determined to defend her home and her young. She could not allow a mistake made by their father to dangerously undermine their future. This was her duty, as the Duce himself had said more than once.

As she made dinner for her children and her husband, who probably wouldn't come home that night, either, Sofia smiled as she considered the fact that in the end the deadliest of all animals is the female of the species. The male kills, struggles, and bellows. The female defends. Because, while the male may be strong, the female is cunning.

*

Enrica was chopping onions and thinking how stupid she'd been.

Perhaps her mother had a point when she said that a woman's mission is to find a husband and have children. That there was no point in waiting for the love of your life, bcause what really matters most is to have a home of your own and the safety of a strong presence at your side. Perhaps Sebastiano, in all his obtuse fatuousness, devoid of mystery and allure though he might be, would have provided that presence, and might never have failed her: a solid shopkeeper on the Via Toledo, which was what her father had always been, after all.

And yet Enrica couldn't see that her father and Sebastiano Fiore had anything in common: her father was a dreamer, he had progressive, liberal political ideas, generous impulses, and a deep-rooted sense of honor; the other man thought only of frivolous things, and didn't strike her as much of a worker, for that matter.

But what alternatives did she have? Instinctively, she looked toward the dark window on the opposite side of the *vicolo*. A lonely, enigmatic man, with a hard, dangerous job, feared by everyone and perhaps hated too. Probably dating a woman who looked like she'd just stepped down from the silver screen, where she was playing a gangster's moll.

No, her mother was certainly right: better to just stick with Sebastiano, and think no more about it.

She dried her tears with her sleeve. Damned onions, she thought.

As she chopped onions, Lucia Maione was weeping and smiling. The tears were for the acrid odor that came from the plate, where she kept piling up fine slices; the smile was for her husband.

She'd noticed that now he was being far more attentive to

the way he ate, just as she'd asked him to do. She was sure that he'd understood how important it was to her, to keep him in good health for at least another fifty years. She couldn't live without him, she'd finally understood it. In those years, those long years in which she'd been the high priestess of her grief and sorrow, she'd run the risk of losing him entirely: now she saw him for what he was, a handsome, imposing, captivating man; his honesty, his rectitude would keep him from having an affair on the side. If he ever fell in love with another woman, he'd leave her. And she couldn't have blamed him: after all, she'd really abandoned him.

But now she was determined to take care of her man. She wouldn't let anyone take him away from her, not even God Almighty. She added the onions to the vegetable soup she'd made, without meat or pasta, and set the pot on the flame.

Rosa took the pot off the fire. The policeman who had come to tell her that Ricciardi would not be home for dinner that night had just left, raising his fingers to the visor of his cap in a sign of respect.

So where was he going to eat dinner? And what would he eat? Certainly something that was going to make his stomachache even worse. Did he think she hadn't noticed, that for the past three days he'd constantly been putting his hand on his tummy? She shook her head in concern. By now she'd concluded that Luigi Alfredo's real problem was Signorina Colombo, the daughter of the haberdasher who lived in the building across the way.

That morning the wife of the butcher that both families frequented had come to fix Rosa's hair. She'd told her all about how, the very same day that Ricciardi had begun acting so strangely, she'd been summoned urgently to do Enrica's hair, in preparation for a visitor that she would be seeing later that day.

The mother had told the hairdresser that she'd arranged a

dinner without her daughter's knowledge, and that she was very worried about the girl because at age twenty-five she still wasn't engaged. The woman had been very accurate, reporting to Rosa word for word.

Shaking her head, she wondered how she could tell her young man that the time to move was now, that he needed to take charge of his life. That life cannot be lived looking out the window.

Wearily, she picked up an onion and started chopping it for tomorrow night's dinner.

XXIX

When Ricciardi closed his office door behind him, it was already practically dark. In the half-light of the hallway, he could clearly make out the images of the dead cop and thief, luminescent with curdled suffering.

"*Maria, Maria, oh, the pain,*" the policeman was saying. Exactly, thought Ricciardi. The pain.

He was so tired. As he walked down the steps of police headquarters, in his mind the details of the Camparino murder were floating disconnected and devoid of meaning, like asteroids hurtling through the night sky. The ring taken, he thought, reminded by the voice of the dead man who had just spoken to him. And the traces of gritty dirt on the carpet, the broken ribs, the padlock that hadn't been forced. The keys in the drawer, the broken fingernails. Details, each of them with a weight of its own: but that only worked if placed into a framework whose principal figure was fully understood.

Ricciardi was frequently sardonic when people told him about the detective movies or yellow-jacketed mystery novels that had come into fashion over the past few years. In the plots of those books and films, everything always fit perfectly, and the detective found only clues that led unerringly to the guilty party.

He didn't like the movies and he rarely read novels: he didn't like pretending when it came to murders. He thought there was already plenty of crime out there, without any need to invent more of it. And anyway, reality was quite a different matter: false leads were indistinguishable from real leads, at least until you could get a better idea of the larger picture.

Lost in these thoughts, he jumped when he heard the officer on duty at the main entrance call to him:

"Commissario, *buona sera*. There's a lady here to see you."

He stepped aside, to let Livia come ahead.

As he looked at her, Ricciardi realized that even though he'd only met her recently, she was always more beautiful than he remembered her. She was wearing a silk blouse with broad horizontal stripes and a skirt that sat snug on her hips, slightly flared just below the knees. On her head, with her hair cut short to leave her long neck visible, she wore a cloche hat at a rakish angle. Her long legs, sheathed in transparent stockings with a black stripe up the back, slipped into a pair of high-heeled shoes. Her generous décolleté was adorned by an amber necklace, and it inevitably attracted men's eyes. Her tapered hands wore black, elbow-length gloves.

She gave the policeman a dazzling smile, and the man was clearly charmed.

"*Grazie*, officer. It's been a pleasure to wait with you."

The policeman snapped a smart salute, though he was apparently still unable to close his mouth. Ricciardi gave him a nasty look, but couldn't bring himself to upbraid him. Instead, he addressed Livia:

"Good evening, Signora. To what do I owe the pleasure of your visit? Do you have some information for us?"

The woman quickly guessed that the commissario was ill at ease in the presence of a subordinate, and picked up the lifeline he had thrown her.

"Yes, Commissario. I'm here to report to you on . . . on the matter in question. It'll take some time, though. I don't think we'll be finished soon."

Ricciardi nodded, stone-faced, then he turned to the officer: "Capezzuto, send someone to my apartment; have them say that I won't be home early, and I'll get something to eat on my own. Don't forget, now."

The policeman snapped his mouth shut loudly and said: "Yessir, Commissa', don't give it a second thought. I'll send someone immediately."

As soon as they were out the front door and around the corner, Livia burst out laughing as she slipped her arm through Ricciardi's.

"Did you see that? Wasn't I subtle? That means I could be a policewoman, doesn't it?"

The commissario looked at her face; she truly was splendid. Her smile illuminated her features, underlined by a light and skillfully applied makeup; but it wasn't just that. It was the light that he saw in her eyes whenever she looked at him. Ricciardi remembered the first time they'd met, when her husband had been murdered: her gaze was dimmed with suffering and regret. It was a gaze that he knew well, that he glimpsed regularly in the living and the dead: the gaze of sorrow. Then it had started to change, especially toward him. The veil had slowly slipped away from her eyes and now she looked like a young girl who'd just gotten what she'd always wanted.

"So why have you decided to show up here? How did you know that you'd still find me in the office at this time of night?"

She laughed again.

"But I know that you always work until late! Don't you remember telling me that yourself? But to make sure I didn't miss you, I came at seven o'clock."

Ricciardi was sincerely astonished.

"At seven? But it's past nine now! What did you do, that whole time?"

"I read a three-week-old copy of *La Domenica del Corriere* from cover to cover, twice; it was the only thing you have in the guard's waiting room beside depositions, crime reports, and registers. And I chatted with your sentry for a while: but I was doing most of the talking, actually, because he didn't seem able to get out a sentence without tripping all over himself."

"I can well imagine; you're certainly not the kind of individual that poor Capezzuto deals with on a daily basis. In any case, I'll repeat the question: what are you doing here?"

Livia was still smiling, as they walked arm-in-arm. Her good nature and her beauty attracted the stares of the passersby they encountered.

"If you want to be rude, by all means, go right ahead: this is a magical night, have you noticed all the stars? I have no intention of letting you put me in a bad mood. I've decided to kidnap you, for one evening. Since I know you'll never come to see me on your own two feet, I came to you. And I want to take you to a nice place, I want to drink something sparkling, I want to look at you, and I want you to look at me. I want to laugh, and I want you to laugh with me. You might as well resign yourself to it."

Ricciardi looked up. It was true: there were thousands of stars in the sky. And it was a pleasant night, with a warm wind that carried away some of the muggy air. Why not? he said to himself; after all, you told yourself you ought to be less of an oaf with her, the next time you saw her, if you ever did. His mind shot to Enrica, straight as an arrow. And like an arrow, it ricocheted off the whispering young man, and fell to earth at his feet.

"All right, I'll go along with your demands, but under duress. We can't stay out late, though: tomorrow I have a long—"

". . . and difficult day, so it's no different from any of the others. Don't worry, I'll distract you from your top-secret investigations for no longer than two hours. Just enough time to go get some dinner."

So they went to eat at a restaurant just outside the Galleria, popular with singers after the opera at the Teatro San Carlo. It was a remarkable thing that Ricciardi, who lived in Naples and worked not far from there, had never heard of the place while Livia, who lived four hundred miles away, was welcomed as an old friend by the restaurant's proprietress.

"I sang a few times in Naples, you know," she explained, once she'd extracted herself from the woman's hug.

It was a strange evening, for Ricciardi. All of the men in the place, whether accompanied by women or not, stared at Livia. The commissario felt waves of envy wash over him, and, all things considered, the sensation wasn't unpleasant; there was someone wishing they were in *his* shoes, for a change.

They ate fish freshly caught from the Gulf of Naples; the proprietress, who was also the chef, told them about the fisherman who went out every night just to supply her restaurant, and the challenge of adapting her various recipes to suit whatever the catch of the day happened to be—and it was never the same. She asked Livia who Ricciardi might be and what work he did, as if he weren't sitting right there; Livia replied that he was a professional musician in a symphony orchestra, and he was grateful to her. He even tried to imagine, as that beautiful woman regaled him with stories from her own career, what it would be like if it were actually true: if he'd played, say, the violin or the double bass. If he'd led a normal life, where the challenge was to make it to the end of each month, wearing shoes that might be falling apart, but still without the constant flood of grief and without a dead man talking to him at every street corner.

He didn't contribute much to the conversation: his stories weren't the kind you could tell over dinner. But he never thought he'd feel so completely at ease. Livia's lovely musical laughter was intoxicating, even more than the chilled white wine that accompanied the fish.

Two *posteggiatori* came in, the charming singing musicians

who provided atmosphere in restaurants of this kind: a guitar and a mandolin, strummed and plucked with virtuosity by skilled fingers. The songs, the true voice of Naples, reawakened sleeping souls and brought age-old emotions back to the surface. The proprietress of the restaurant prodded Livia to sing, and she held out as long as she could, laughing lightly. Finally, she gave in and, looking into Ricciardi's pale green eyes with her dark, luminous eyes, she sang the first verse of *'O sole mio*. Her accent was anything but Neapolitan, and it was a song meant to be sung by a man: still, her contralto voice was as warm as, if not warmer than, the salt air wafting up from the sea, and when she was done the whole room burst into thunderous applause.

When they left the restaurant, it was past midnight. The late hour, the long day, the wine, and the new feelings had all gone to Ricciardi's head, and he looked back at himself, as if from some window. He couldn't seem to shake a bad feeling that he was somehow doing Enrica wrong; but in some other way Livia was soothing the pain he felt in his stomach. If that's the way it's got to go, then let it, he thought vaguely.

As for her, she was happier than she'd been in many years. Pulling Ricciardi out of his shell was like mining for diamonds, difficult but very gratifying. And in his eyes—not always, but occasionally—she'd seen the gleam of a new light. She knew he liked her, but she could also sense an obstacle of some sort, something that kept him from opening up completely. She'd cleverly persuaded him to tell her his life story, all about his family: she'd confirmed that there was no other woman, at least not one who formed part of his life, institutionally speaking; but her intuition told her that there was another woman in her smoldering dark commissario's heart.

That's no big problem, she thought to herself. If she got in, she can also get out. All I have to do is find a way to open the door and take her place.

Ricciardi was walking her back to the hotel; she was leaning on his arm, enjoing the darkness that enveloped the Piazza del Plebiscito, the columns and the statues of bygone kings, with only the sound of her shoes on the broad stone slabs. She'd read the inscription on the entrance to the church, and Ricciardi was explaining that it was the vow made by a king of Naples to put an end to an outbreak of the plague, when in the little alley leading into the piazza, a few shadows emerged from the overall darkness.

At first Ricciardi, who was looking at the inscription and translating it, didn't notice a thing; he sensed Livia's hand squeezing his upper arm, and he turned around in time to see four menacing figures surrounding them. He couldn't see their faces; it was too dark for that. But the commissario's attention was caught by their dark, rumpled suits, by the heavy boots they were wearing, and especially by the clubs in their hands.

Livia let a moan escape her lips and one of the men told her to keep quiet, with a rough insult. Ricciardi turned to face him, staring at him fearlessly. The man took a step forward and slapped him, once, hard, in the face. As he was raising his hand to hit him again and the other three were bearing in, Ricciardi spoke, in a firm voice, as if he were reciting a poem:

"*Buffoonish clowns, you're nothing but four buffoonish clowns. Four to one, for shame, for shame, you buffoonish clowns.*"

One of the four men heaved a deep sigh, as if he'd just been punched in the stomach. They stepped back, exchanging glances. One man let his club fall to the ground, turned, and took to his heels. Two others followed him almost immediately. The last man, the one who had slapped him, said:

"You be careful, Ricciardi. You be careful where you wander late at night, and the questions you ask. Because if you're not careful, next time it won't be clubs. It'll be knives."

Then he, too, turned and ran.

XXX

Contrary to his own expectations, Ricciardi slept like a rock; perhaps because he needed to catch up on sleep from the night before. He'd dreamed, that much he knew, but he couldn't remember much about it: something muddled involving shoes. Probably the boots of the four unknown men, he was thinking the following morning, back in his office.

What had happened explained a great many things, while raising plenty of other questions. He'd decided not to mention it to anyone, not even to Maione; first he wanted to test the various connections, understand more clearly just what had triggered the attack. He was sorry for Livia, who had found herself caught in the middle of a highly unusual situation; he felt sure that she considered his life even stranger and more difficult than it really was, and this, for some reason, rubbed him the wrong way.

He hadn't been afraid, not even when that man had slapped him, because he knew they'd only been sent to scare him; but Livia's presence had made him weak. He'd felt responsible for her safety, he'd shielded her with his body, but he couldn't help thinking what he would have felt if it had been Enrica with him. He'd walked her back to her hotel in silence; he didn't know what to say. She'd never let go of his arm, squeezing it gently, as if giving him support rather than being supported herself. When they said goodnight she'd kissed him, brushing her lips against his; he hadn't responded to the kiss but neither had he warded it off.

Looking out his window at the city that still hadn't entirely woken up that morning, he decided that love is a liquid. Like water, only denser, a fluid similar to oil, which fills every space until it takes on the shape of its container, filling in all the odd shapes, contaminating everything. And the worst kind, the strongest kind, is the love that flows through the darkness, accustomed to overcoming every obstacle, the love that knows neither patience nor rest. I saw it last night, he thought. And the love that flows in the night, the love that hides, never forgives those witnesses who have glimpsed its path.

Maione appeared in the door, an early riser just like him.

"*Buon giorno*, Commissa'. How are we doing, this morning?"

"As always. And there are others who were at work even earlier than me, today. Look what I found waiting for me, on my desk: it's a search warrant for the Capece apartment, and authorization to question his family."

Maione rubbed his hands.

"Oh, and at last they let us work the way we ought to. Also because, the way things stand now, Capece is the prime suspect, wouldn't you say, Commissa'?"

Ricciardi continued to stand looking out the window, his hands in his pockets. The faint hot breeze blowing in from outside gently tossed the shock of hair that hung over his forehead.

"Hmmm, I don't know, you can never be sure. There are still a few things that aren't clear yet."

"You're thinking about the young master, eh, Commissa'? Still, Capece, do me a favor: there's the pistol, and he owns one; there's the alibi, and he lacks one; there's the motive, and he has one; there's the eyewitness testimony in his favor, of which he has none. You'll concede the point: it all fits together?"

The commissario gestured vaguely with one hand.

"That's what scares me the most, when it all fits together. He loved the duchess, no? On this point we agree. And he truly seemed on the brink of despair when we talked to him. And he came to the funeral: if you ask me, a murderer wouldn't normally run that risk. It could have been him, I'm not saying it couldn't. But it's still not a certainty. Let's go and see for ourselves."

"Yessir. Shall we go immediately?"

"No. We'll go later. I have something to do first, an errand of my own. You wait for me here, I'll be back in an hour or so."

Maione nodded. But he was concerned.

Livia hadn't slept a wink. It wasn't so much the fear, which surprised her because she'd had every reason to be afraid: what had really put a chill in her heart was the fear of losing him.

Strange, for a woman whose husband had been murdered, she mused; and yet she never remembered feeling that same stab of pain in her heart except once, years before, when the doctor, standing by the cradle in which her baby lay, had shaken his head hopelessly. Who was this man? she asked herself. What had he done to her, that he mattered so much even though there was nothing between them?

By the light of dawn, on the balcony of her hotel room, she realized that she was crying. For no good reason.

Ricciardi arrived at Palazzo Camparino just as the church bell was chiming nine. Sciarra came to meet him with a broom in hand, followed by his son, who was sniveling.

"Commissa', *buon giorno*. At your orders."

Ricciardi nodded toward the child who was yanking on his father's sleeve, making it even longer than it already was.

"And why is this little one crying?"

Sciarra grimaced in a comic leer, beneath his gigantic nose.

"Well, why do *you* think? As usual, Commissa': he's hungry, and he wants me to feed him. What can I do about it, if he can never get enough?"

The child objected between sobs:

"No, Papà, that's Lisetta who always eats my snack, and you never say a thing to her."

His father glared at him disgustedly.

"You're the spitting image of your mother: you're always crying. *Piangi e mangi*—when you're not crying you're eating. But tell me, Commissa': what can I do for you? Do you want to talk to Donna Concetta? I'll call her for you right away."

"No, don't call anyone. I want to talk to you first."

Sciarra turned pale and gulped.

"What do you mean, you want to talk to me? I already told you everything I know, I even talked to your Brigadier Marrone, too . . ."

Ricciardi struggled not to laugh in his face.

"Maione is his name. And I have a few other questions to ask you. Where can we sit and talk?"

The little man hesitated, looked around, and said: "Make yourself comfortable in my little place, in the booth by the front door. I'll go get another chair and send this scourge of God to his mother, so they can have a nice long cry together, and they'll both be happy."

He came back a couple minutes later, staggering under the weight of a chair he'd found in the kitchen. His hat, turned around backwards, had even fallen down around his eyes.

"Ask away, Commissa'," he sighed as he took a seat.

Ricciardi waited for the man to adjust his uniform, pulling up the sleeves and turning his hat around, before he spoke.

"All right, then, Sciarra: let's talk about young master Ettore. I need to know as much as possible about where he goes and his routines. What he does and what he doesn't do."

Sciarra spread his arms.

"I don't know much about him, Commissa'. He spends his days on his terrace, all on his own . . ."

Ricciardi interrupted the litany decisively, raising one hand.

"Let's get one thing clear: I will take you in and I will lock you up, for obstructing an investigation. So fast it will make your head spin. I don't believe that you're a doorman and yet you don't know a thing. I know for sure that you come and go, that you venture out frequently into the world. So don't talk nonsense, and most important of all, don't waste my time."

Sciarra folded over as if he were under a hail of fists and boots.

"Commissa', understand me: I have to work here, I can't lose this position. You can't even imagine how much my children eat, where would I turn, where could I take them with me?"

"And if you want to keep your place here, then it's in your best interests to tell me what I want to know."

The little man heaved a deep sigh.

"Fine, if that's what you want, that's what you'll get. To tell the truth, I see little enough of him, he spends the whole day on his own, out on the terrace. He takes care of his plants, he waters them himself. He doesn't want any help: one time my son, the eldest, looked in his door because he thought he'd heard him crying, and he rudely kicked him out, in fact my poor boy tumbled headlong all the way down the stairs . . . He told him that he needs to stay in his place, that he should never dare to look into his apartment. That's the way the young master is: sometimes he'll give you a smile and a wink, or he'll give candy to the children. Other times, you'd think he'd just killed someone, he'll glare at you with pure hatred, so that the children go sobbing to hide under their mother's skirts."

Ricciardi wanted to know more.

"Aside from his moods, I want to know where he goes late at night, when he leaves."

Sciarra stared at him, wide-eyed. Ricciardi could distinctly see the beads of sweat forming on his enormous nose.

"But I don't know that! I can tell you that sometimes . . .

that he goes out often, at night, yes, that's true. While I'm watering his hydrangeas, he gives me certain lectures, he says that flowers ought to be watered in the morning, at dawn, or in the late afternoon, but I'm already up at six, and in the evening if I'm not there the children don't eat and I go to bed late . . ."

"He goes out, you say. Where does he go?"

"I don't know that, like I told you. One thing's for certain, he doesn't come and tell me about it. And he sure doesn't tell his father; in fact, he never even goes to see him at all. One time he said to Donna Concetta: if the old man dies at night, don't come looking for me. And for that matter, the duke doesn't want to see his son either. He doesn't give him a thought; he says that the boy is dead, just like the first duchess."

Ricciardi had no intention of following the doorman's ramblings.

"By any chance, did you ever see anyone come to pick him up? Or did he ever come home with anyone?"

Sciarra furrowed his brow with the effort of remembering.

"One night, this last winter, it was raining hard. I'd closed the front door, and no one had the keys but the duchess and the young master. That night someone started pounding on the door, fists and boots, and I woke up and opened the door. There was a car outside, with someone in it, waiting. And a chauffeur who told me to go at once to summon the young master. I went upstairs, and the door was open. I called once, twice. He came out, with a face on him . . . it looked to me like he'd been crying. He didn't say a word to me, he just went out, climbed into the car, and drove off into the rain. But I couldn't see who was inside, Commissa', I swear to you."

Ricciardi nodded, as if that was exactly what he'd been expecting.

"Can you describe the car? Was it marked in any way, I don't know, official insignia?"

Sciarra looked away.

"No. I don't remember, but I don't think so. But the car was black, in any case. Big and black."

After a moment's thought, Ricciardi asked another question: "One last thing, Sciarra. The padlock. Are you sure that no one had the keys but the two of them?"

The little man looked the commissario in the face again.

"Yes, Commissa'. The duchess, to lock up at night, when she came in; and the young master has an extra set, in case he needs to come in late, for whatever reason. And in the morning, it looked as if the duchess had opened the padlock: it was fastened and hanging next to the chain."

Ricciardi stood up.

"Fine. Now take me up to talk to young master Ettore again."

XXXI

Concetta walked into the duke's bedroom, as if she were walking on air. She waited for her eyes to become accustomed to the dark, listening attentively for any variation in the deep wheezing rattle that came from the bed. She was sure that she hadn't made a sound, not even the faintest rustle. She waited. A pigeon cooed on the windowsill. Out of the sound of the death rattle surfaced a raspy voice, as if the dying man were talking in his sleep:

"He's back, isn't he? The commissario, the young one. The one with the pale green eyes."

In the darkness, Concetta nodded, her fingers knitted together in her lap, looking straight ahead. He couldn't have seen her, he couldn't have heard her. But he knew she was there, and how long she'd been there; she'd long ago ceased to be astonished at the old man's abilities.

"It'll all come out. We can't prevent it."

Concetta considered the matter. Then she said: "Not necessarily. He's always been so careful."

The duke said nothing for several long seconds. His cough shook his chest; his hand scrabbled around on the nightstand, cluttered with phials and ampules of medicine, and snatched up a filthy handkerchief, which he pressed to his mouth; after which he looked at it with his rheumy eyes.

"Blood. But how long is it going to take, the damned sickness? How long will it take to carry me off?"

Concetta tried to steer him away from that thought.

"What should we do? How can we protect him?"

After another fit of coughing, the duke replied:

"There's nothing we can do. Not now. It'll have to go the way it goes; after all, better this than . . . complete ruin."

Concetta bowed her head and left the room.

At the door of Ettore's apartment, Sciarra and Ricciardi found Concetta waiting for them, still and silent as a statue. As soon as he saw her, Sciarra shot a begging glance at the commissario and, at his nod, took to his heels with unmistakable relief.

The woman said: "Please wait here," and started in to announce the new arrivals. Ricciardi stopped her, firmly, with one hand on her forearm.

"*Grazie*, Signora, there's no need. I know the way."

And he walked past her, striding into the apartment.

Ettore, in shirtsleeves and wearing a gardener's apron, was squatting down next to a vase, clipping away. From the gramophone came symphonic music which he hummed along to, frowning. He looked up when he sensed a presence and found Ricciardi standing in front of him, just as an unusually frantic Concetta arrived on the scene. He turned and spoke to her:

"Damn it. Can't a man be left in peace in his own home, now? What the devil's come over you, don't you even know how to do your job anymore?"

The woman gasped, openmouthed, as if she'd been punched in the stomach, her face red with shame. Ricciardi felt it was his duty to weigh in:

"No, in fact, she tried to stop me. But I wouldn't let her come to warn you."

Ettore had gotten to his feet. He'd reacquired his self-control, and now he was smiling sardonically.

"If I may ask, where did you get this haughtiness of yours? You've got nerve, Commissario. I thought it the first time I saw you."

"Nerve? Why, does it take nerve to question a suspect? Or maybe there's something else I should be worried about? What else should I be afraid of?"

Ettore continued to smile, but his eyes were shooting flames.

"Can we speak openly, Commissario? I think so, otherwise you wouldn't have come alone. I know people who can send you into internal exile before nightfall. Or who can arrange for you to be transferred to Sicily, Calabria, or the Veneto. People who can send you to a dark little office somewhere to fill out forms eight hours a day for the next thirty years. Do you know that?"

Ricciardi hadn't blinked.

"That's fine, Dottore. That's how you want me to address you, isn't it? You reject your name and title, but not the privileges that go with them. If you choose to threaten me like this, it must mean that you feel threatened. What is it that's threatening you, in that case? Can your highly placed friends protect you from murder charges, too?"

Ettore laughed with gusto, his head thrown back, hands on his hips.

"You're just fabulous, with your dunderheaded stubbornness. I didn't kill that bitch. I already told you that. I should have, but not now; ten years ago, I should have killed her. It wasn't worth the trouble anymore."

"And yet, the spectacle you put on the day of the funeral had the air of a public statement of some kind. And you never miss an opportunity to vent all your hatred for her. Why would you do that, other than to point suspicion away from you? And this refusal to say where you were, the other night; is your secret so unspeakable that you'd prefer to risk standing trial for murder?"

Ettore was caught off guard. His expression shifted, from sunny to serious, almost grief-stricken. His mouth twitched, as if he were about to speak, once, then twice. Then he looked Ricciardi in the eye.

"A murder trial? Prison? Those are mere trifles. I'd rather die than tell you where I was. And not because I'm hiding something about myself, let me make that point very clearly. It's that . . . there are other people. I can't, and I don't want to make choices for these other people, that's all. And so I won't tell you where I was that night. Not now, not ever."

Ricciardi shook his head.

"I don't think you understand. We don't have any other suspects who admit so openly that they hated the duchess. Whoever might come under suspicion, whoever we might accuse of the murder, would be sure to defend themselves by pointing at you."

Ettore shrugged.

"And I'll defend myself too, using the weapons that I possess. You have no idea of who that woman was. You can really have no idea. It could have been anyone, starting from her chief lover, or any of the hundred other lovers that she certainly took. She must have driven the journalist crazy; she played with him the way a cat toys with a mouse. That's what she did with the old man, until she finally destroyed him."

"But you won't tell me where you were, or what you were doing. You force me to investigate, you understand that. I'm not the kind of person you can throw a scare into. Nothing can scare me."

Ettore seemed baffled.

"I don't know what you're talking about. Go ahead and investigate, if you think you must. For my part, I can only defend . . . the choices of the people who were with me. My own choices—I have no need to defend them. And don't worry: I won't use my name and my title. Neither for good nor for evil."

Maione didn't ask Ricciardi where he'd gone, all alone. Very simply, he assumed that if the commissario had wanted to, he would have told him about it. He only hoped that the man wasn't getting himself into trouble: they were dealing with dangerous people on this case. He felt as if he were walking across a minefield.

"Commissa', we're ready. How shall we travel, when we go to call on the Capeces, by car? The address is above the Parco Margherita, in the Rione Amedeo. It's quite a distance, in this heat."

Ricciardi shook his head.

"No, *grazie*. I'd like to go on living for another three, maybe four years. I don't drive, and if you drive the car we'll be coming back pulled by the duchess's eight horses. No, but I would like you to call the newspaper and alert Capece. It wouldn't be right for us to show up at his apartment without letting him know. And if you ask me, it's better for us to see him where he lives. We'll be able to understand a little more about him."

Maione, who considered himself to be a first-rate driver, looked hurt.

"Commissa', you just don't want to let go of this idea you have about the way I drive. Sure, we might have hit a lamppost once or twice, but that doesn't mean that a person doesn't know how to drive. All the same, if that's how you want it, that's how it will be. Shall I make the call?"

The brigadier knew that Ricciardi didn't like to talk on the telephone. The commissario felt as if he wasn't reading the other person's thoughts if he couldn't look them in the face; and it had always given him an unpleasant impression, that soulless, black, Bakelite contraption that talked.

"Yes, go ahead. And one more thing: go change your clothes. I don't want to knock at the door of perfectly respectable people, who are no doubt already having a hard time keeping up appearances with their neighbors, in uniform as if we were there to arrest some perpetrator."

Lucia looked out the window at her husband, as he walked down the *vicolo* toward Via Toledo, dressed in civilian clothing. She was worried: he'd come home at an unusual hour, in a bad mood, and then he'd gone to change, washing up hurriedly in the kitchen sink, practically without a word to her. And it was clearly Lucia he had it in for; in fact, he'd tenderly caressed the children when they ran to greet him.

She asked him why on earth he was home at this hour. He'd told her, without looking her in the eye, that he had to do some plainclothes work and he needed his dark brown suit: had it been pressed? Of course it had been pressed, she'd replied, stung by the insinuation. And you'll find a clean shirt in the drawer, scented of lavender, fresh and sweet-smelling. As if I'd leave your things in a mess.

He hadn't said a word; just went to get changed. He came out of the bedroom looking fancy, with a faraway look in his eye. She asked him if he wanted something to eat, seeing how it was past lunchtime, maybe a little of the fruit that she'd bought from Ciruzzo that very morning. He'd given her a cold hard stare and then, with a chilly, "No, *grazie*," he'd said goodbye with a brusque peck on the cheek and headed back out.

Lucia was bewildered, lost. Raffaele changing his clothes in the middle of the day, Raffaele coming home to wash up, pat his face with cologne, and go back out in civilian attire, and especially Raffaele refusing an offer of food. She felt a stabbing pain behind her stomach and placed her hand on her abdomen: indigestion, she decided.

But she was wrong.

Ricciardi walked along next to a well-dressed, silent Maione. He'd even tried asking him whether something had happened to him, but the brigadier's expression made it easy to guess that he was in no mood for conversation. Actually, everything was conspiring to spoil the large policeman's mood:

the heat, the stubborn insistence of his superior officer that they walk to where they were going, the dark brown jacket that he could barely button in spite of his nutritional sacrifices, and the picture, which he couldn't get out of his mind, of his wife going to buy fruit from the cursed, albeit award-winning purveyors of fruits and vegetables, Ciruzzo Di Stasio and Sons. Homicidal impulses alternated with the certainty of an imminent fainting spell, due variously to the heat or the hunger, or a combination of the two. He felt something like a contraction behind his stomach and, as he walked, he raised his hand to his sternum. There, he thought, the onset of a myocardial infarction.

But he was wrong.

For his part, Ricciardi was thinking. Capece and his pistol on the one hand, Ettore and his stonewalling on the other. And the possibility of an armed burglary gone wrong, or of a third man who had not yet made his public entrance onto the stage of the duchess's life: just who, for instance, had seen her home, that night? Witnesses had seen her leave the theater alone, but there was no reason not to think that she might have met someone afterwards: the dizzy chaos of the festa would have concealed unusual visitors from sight, in all likelihood.

Serving as a backdrop to these thoughts, Livia surfaced intermittently in the commissario's mind, staring round-eyed at the four buffoonish clowns as they tried to attack Ricciardi; Enrica surfaced too, sitting at Gambrinus, her eyes filled with tears. His mind instantly raced to the debonair smile of the young man with her, and as it did, he felt a stab of discomfort in his stomach. Maybe I just need something to eat, he thought.

But he was wrong.

XXXII

Now, it was true that Maione was a bad driver, and it was also true that Ricciardi, presented with a choice between driving and walking, always preferred the latter solution; but for that particular route, between police headquarters and the Rione Amedeo, there was another reason, as well.

Some ten days earlier, right on the Via Dei Mille, an automobile had swerved out of control and hit a lamppost head on; it wasn't going all that fast, but the windshield had shattered and killed the small family that was out showing off its brand new car: husband, wife, and a little boy, riding in his mamma's arms.

Ricciardi had read about it in the newspaper, and had taken great care to avoid passing by the scene of the crash, knowing full well that the Deed would be sure to treat him to a very unpleasant moment. Now he had no choice, but it was one thing to walk through on the sidewalk, quite another to experience it aboard a bouncing, jolting vehicle propelled by Maione's hysterical foot on the gas pedal. Walking would be the lesser of two evils.

Walking along under the pitiless hot sun, he braced for the vision the way a boxer prepares for his adversary's punch. He knew that, however much he steeled himself, it would still catch him by surprise. And in fact the first time he looked up, he was greeted by the sight of man, woman, and child sitting in midair, where there had once been an upholstered bench seat, just a yard away from a steel lamppost that was still bent from the impact.

Without stopping, casting a sidelong glance, Ricciardi saw that the man had been run through by the steering column, as was almost always the case in accidents of this kind; his crushed and perforated thorax was a dark crater in the middle of an elegant cream-colored jacket, his face was startled, with staring eyes and open mouth, and from the mouth ran a couple of streams of blood from the punctured lungs. The phrase that the dead man kept uttering showed that he knew what was about to happen:

"*Madonna, the brakes, the brakes, we're going headfirst into the wall.*"

Not the wall, Ricciardi thought. Before the wall, the post. Everything in its proper order.

The wife and the son, in contrast, were blithely unaware. That's a small mercy. Ricciardi noticed that the woman's head was almost severed; perhaps it was detached entirely from her neck once the woman was already dead. But in that moment, as he looked at her, the head was still joined to the body by a slender strip of flesh on the left side, cut cleanly through by the metal frame of the windshield: the entire neck, including the spinal cord. Above the horror of the artery spraying useless blood like a fountain, the face exhibited a grotesquely complacent smile:

"*You're dying, you're all dying of envy for our nice new car.*"

Look who bought it in the end, thought Ricciardi grimly. And he couldn't help but take a quick look at the little boy, three years old, perhaps; no more. He'd been run through by a large shard of thick windshield glass; Ricciardi saw that the shard of glass had pierced his chest, first pinning him to his mother, and then the two of them to the bench seat.

As he listened, the commissario discovered where the family had been heading on its outing, so sadly cut short.

"*Gelato at the Villa Nazionale, Papà promised me, a nice cup of gelato.*"

All this pointless pain, thought Ricciardi as he unconsciously heaved a long sigh. Maione interrupted his grim silence to say:

"Eh, I know, it's hot out, Commissa'. Don't you think it would have been smarter to take the car?"

They could tell from a good distance which building it was, because Capece was pacing back and forth in front of the entrance, smoking nervously. When he spotted them he hurried in their direction.

"Ricciardi, Brigadier. I owe you my thanks; not everyone in your position would have shown me this consideration, to let me know so that I could be here. I appreciate it deeply. My children and my wife have nothing to do with this whole matter. They've already had to suffer too much, through my own fault. And now this added humiliation, having the police in their home . . . no offense meant, let me make that clear: still, as you must understand, it isn't easy."

Ricciardi nodded, gesticulating brusquely with one hand as if to shoo away a fly.

"Don't mention it. When we can, we always do our best to avoid certain situations; especially when there are innocent people involved. Shall we go upstairs?"

Capece led the way, showing them through an atrium that ended in a broad staircase. The building had clearly seen better days, but it was still a very presentable place. The journalist's family lived on the third story; when they reached the apartment door, the man twisted the handle of the doorbell. Ricciardi and Maione exchanged a rapid glance, since they'd both guessed that Capece had waited for the two of them to arrive before going upstairs to his own home.

The door was opened by a girl who looked to be about ten

years old, and who closely resembled her father; she looked at him in happy surprise and threw her arms around his neck with a joyful cry. Capece was embarrassed but also visibly moved, and he picked the little girl up and hugged her close with glistening eyes. Maione and Ricciardi hung back, to keep from intruding on that wonderful moment of closeness. The brigadier couldn't help wondering how long it had been since the father and daughter had last seen each other.

In the end, without setting down his daughter, who still had both arms wrapped tightly around his neck, Capece gestured for the two policemen to enter the apartment.

"Prego, Signori, go right on in. Giogiò, darling, these two gentlemen are . . . friends of Papà. Now you be a good girl, get down, and introduce yourself."

The little girl, once again with her feet on the floor, smoothed her skirt with a very feminine gesture, and curtseyed impeccably.

"*Buon giorno*, Signori and friends of Papà. My name is Giovanna Capece and I'm eleven years old."

Ricciardi gave her a half-smile. Maione doffed his cap and said, with a bow:

"*Buon giorno* to you, Signorina Giovanna Capece, eleven years of age. I am Raffaele and the gentleman, here, is Signor Ricciardi."

The little girl considered introductions to have been satisfactorily completed. She smiled and said: "I'll go call my mamma."

But she was already there, behind her, standing in the doorway. She was a good-looking woman, perhaps just a shade nondescript, thought Ricciardi. Not tall, dressed in dark clothing, Capece's wife didn't catch the eye, thought she certainly had no evident shortcomings. Chestnut hair, fair-skinned, she had large lovely eyes and a sweet expression. Her face—and both Maione and Ricciardi noticed it—bore the signs of prolonged suffering, with deep wrinkles under her eyes and around her mouth.

Just then, however, the woman's gaze seemed to be illuminated from within. She was staring at her husband, with the hint of a smile and an expression of unconditional devotion that verged on the shameless.

In fact, Capece was clearly uncomfortable, and looked away from the woman. He addressed the two policemen, without even bothering to say hello to her.

"This is my wife Sofia. These gentlemen are Commissario Ricciardi and Brigadier Maione. They're here to . . . to ask a few questions."

Almost a minute went by, during which the woman never took her eyes off her husband, while he looked at Ricciardi and Maione looked at the floor. For his part, the commissario continued to observe Sofia's ecstatic expression, thinking just how nice it must be to have a wife who looked at you like that; and also how powerful the passion must be that a gaze like that communicated. In the end, the woman seemed to awaken from her trance, and stroking her daughter's hair, said to the girl:

"Darling, go play in your room now. Then I'll come join you."

The girl curtseyed again and left. As he watched her run off, Ricciardi asked:

"Is she your only child?"

Sofia answered before her husband could speak, with a proud smile: "Giovanna also has an older brother, Andrea. He's out studying, right now, even if he's still on summer vacation. A smart and conscientious young man, just like his father. He'll be back soon."

The three glanced at each other with a certain awkward discomfort, even though there didn't seem to be a speck of irony in the woman's words; indeed, she went on smiling at her husband, as if this were the most normal situation in the world. Once again, Ricciardi wondered how long it had been since the man and woman had seen each other and why the wife failed to display any bitterness toward her husband. For his part,

Capece seemed unwilling to emerge from his dull grief: in his face and on his clothing, filthy and rumpled, he still bore the marks of sleepless nights and too much wine.

"If you please, Ricciardi. Come this way, have a seat in the drawing room."

The apartment, at least the rooms they walked past, was tidy and clean: everything in its place, the scent of lavender, wallpaper and curtains without tears, rips, or wrinkles. Yet it was lifeless.

It seemed like a diligently executed performance, more than a home where a family lived.

They sat in the drawing room. Sofia seemed completely unruffled; and yet her husband had just introduced their two guests as policemen, and she couldn't be unaware of what had happened, and the fact that the whole city was talking about it. Ricciardi tried to read the woman's attitude, as she sat beside her husband on a sofa.

"Signora, forgive the intrusion. As you may have heard, sadly, a horrible thing has happened. The unfortunate death of . . ."

"The Duchess of Camparino, of course, I know. No one's talking about anything else these days. And I also know that the lady was an acquaintance of my husband, who was helping her to write her memoirs. That was why the two of them were spending so much time together: for work. These are hard times, you know, Commissario: a man who wants to make sure his family lacks for nothing must often work more than one job. And my husband, who's talented and smart, is a very hard worker. And he's a wonderful father and husband."

Sofia's rant ended in an awkward silence. Maione was raptly staring at the porcelain figurine of a peasant girl, as if it had been doing the talking. Capece was staring intently at his wife, with a mixed expression of horror and compassion. Ricciardi nodded.

"I see. All the same, since your husband was one of the last people to see her alive, we must ascertain whether he is aware of anything that may be useful to our work. Could you tell me where you and your family were, on the night between last Saturday and Sunday?"

Sofia at first seemed confused, and then she burst out laughing.

"Where else could we have been? Here, of course. Like always. The children were in their bedrooms and my husband and I were in ours. Sleeping. Why, where were you that night?"

Ricciardi and Maione exchanged a surprised glance. Capece went on staring at his wife, without any change in his expression; in the meanwhile, she had placed a hand on his leg, as if to keep him there. As if she were afraid he might fly away any minute.

The Commissario went on in the same tone of voice.

"And yet that's not what your husband says, Signora. Your husband states that he was up and about all night long, making his way through the various taverns down near the port. Are you sure of what you just told us?"

Sofia furrowed her brow in irritation.

"How dare you question my statement? My husband must be confused. I assure you that all four of us stayed home that night, and no one went out. I keep the key under my pillow at night, and I'd certainly have noticed if anyone had taken it, don't you think? I confirm every word of what I said, and it's up to you to prove otherwise."

Well, thought Maione, the Signora was right about that. It's up to us to prove otherwise.

Just as Ricciardi was about to respond, Andrea, the Capeces' oldest child, came in. He was a tall young man, with his mother's complexion and hair color, and at sixteen he looked older than his age. His hair was plastered to his forehead with sweat and he carried a few books bound with a leather strap under his arm. His face was a kaleidoscope of emotions: his cheerful expression was quickly replaced by a look of concern at the sight of strangers in the place, and then chilly hostility when he saw his father. For his part, Capece looked at him with tenderness and started to get up and greet him, but Sofia intensified the pressure on his leg to make sure he remained seated.

"Commissario, this is Andrea, and as I told you, he'd gone out to study. Andrea, Commissario Ricciardi and Brigadier Maione are here to ask a few questions. For some reason, they're convinced that on Saturday night your father was away from home, instead of here, asleep, like all of us. Can you tell him, too, that that's simply ridiculous?"

Maione admired the woman's speed and cunning; she had just informed her son of the situation and spoon-fed him the proper response, as well. Ricciardi hadn't stopped staring at the woman, after a fleeting glance at the boy.

Andrea, on the other hand, was looking at his father, with an expression of absolute and unmistakable contempt. A palpable sense of tension had just descended over the drawing room.

"Mamma, I was sleeping. You know how it is, I'm a heavy sleeper: I don't know who's in the apartment and who isn't. But if you say he was here, then he must have been here. I would have to guess that a woman knows if she's sleeping alone or not. Do you need anything else from me? If not, I'm going to go wash up."

Ricciardi was well aware of how useless the testimony of a minor would be; still, he had the impression that the son's unmistakable resentment toward his father was the weakest link in the chain that the Capece family was coiling around its own safety and serenity.

"How long has it been since you last saw your father?"

The question dropped into the silence like a firecracker. The boy, who had already stepped across the threshold, froze and slowly turned back to look at Ricciardi. The mother tried to break in, but the commissario halted her with one raised hand.

"Commissario, I'm on vacation, I get up late. This morning, when I got up, my father had already left. And yesterday, when I went to sleep, he hadn't come in yet. You know, he works at the newspaper; so he doesn't get in until late. Now, if you don't mind?"

And he turned and left the room.

XXXIII

Why did you do it? Why, Mamma? This was our chance to get rid of him, to make him pay. To free our faces once and for all of his slaps and the misery that he heaped on us, we who were once his family.

No one could have whispered behind our backs anymore; no more shame; no more slander. We could finally have walked with our heads held high, because everyone would have understood that we are the victims.

But instead you chose to save him. I don't understand why. It would have been simple justice if they'd finally hauled him off and tossed him into the place he deserved, so he could reflect on all he'd done. Reflect on the crime he committed.

He didn't deserve our help. He doesn't deserve a thing. But you still love him, even after everything you had to put up with.

I don't understand.

In spite of himself, Ricciardi was impressed with the ambiguous nature of the boy's answer. Like mother, like son, he thought. Maione, on the other hand, was watching Capece, his expression; the journalist's animated face was reflecting contrasting emotions: mortification, sense of guilt, humiliation. But also a certain fierce pride, the last-ditch defense of a powerful feeling that had outlived its object. Once or twice, he'd opened his mouth as if to say something, but then he'd stopped. In some way, it seemed that his wife's hand, intimately resting on his thigh, was dominating his will.

The commissario started talking again.

"Capece, I'm going to have to ask you a question again that I already asked you once at the newspaper. I warn you that the document I have in my pocket authorizes me to search this apartment, but I believe that you'll agree with me that it would be best for everyone if that could be avoided. Searching a home is a violation of a family's privacy; we don't want to do it, and I assure you that you wouldn't enjoy having it done. We're only looking for one thing, so I'll ask you: do you possess weapons, in this apartment?"

Maione was watching Sofia's hand, which lay motionless. Capece seemed to come back to earth from the mists of some recollection, his gaze became sharper, more present. After a long hesitation, he said:

"Commissario, I fought in the war. I was an officer. War is a horrible thing, nothing but pain and grief: but I was a young man and I believed in it, in this fatherland that has now become an excuse for every sort of abuse. To remind myself how useless a thing war is, I kept my pistol. But I keep it under lock and key, in my desk drawer, unloaded and without bullets. There are no other weapons in the apartment."

Ricciardi nodded.

"All right. Let's take a look at this relic."

Capece stood up and led the way. His wife followed behind him, tranquil, with a half-smile on her lips as if she was about to show her guests a nice drawing her daughter had done. They reached the study through a single door that separated it from the drawing room. Capece reached up onto a bookshelf, felt his way along it, and found a key; he went around behind the desk and opened the long central drawer under the desk-top. He pulled open a metal box without a lock and opened it.

He looked up, his face white, eyes round with astonishment.

"It's gone! The pistol's vanished!"

Ricciardi turned to look at Sofia and he saw on her face the same surprise as on her husband's. If the two of them were playacting, they were very good. Husband and wife stared at each other: they were clearly aghast. Capece said:

"But who could have taken it?"

The woman had lifted a hand to her mouth and was shaking her head very slightly, as if she wanted to deny an unmistakable fact.

"Why . . . I don't know. We hadn't seen it in years. We've had four or five different maids over the years. You can sell a pistol, can't you? They might very well have stolen it, and we'd have never noticed. I can give you the first and last names of all the maids . . . I never touched it, and neither did my husband! And in any case, as my husband told you, it wasn't loaded. You can't possibly think . . . that's absurd!"

Maione and Ricciardi looked at one another, then they focused their attention on the Capeces, who were now clearly in the throes of fear. The commissario said:

"All right. We're leaving for now. But you need to think hard and try to find that revolver, and keep in touch with us about any and all developments in your search."

Capece shot them his assent in a glance, his brow furrowed by the thousand thoughts that were taking shape. His wife had lost all her confidence and was casting sidelong looks at the journalist. The disappearance of the pistol seemed to have sown doubts in her mind that her role as public defender might have been, at the very least, overhasty.

As they were leaving, as if it were an afterthought, Ricciardi turned and said to the man:

"Ah, Capece, I'd like to ask you a courtesy: the ring, you know the one. The one from the Salone Margherita. Make sure we can have access to it, it's a part of the investigation."

And, glimpsing a flash in Sofia's eyes as he went, he said goodbye and left.

Ricciardi would have preferred to skip going by the scene of the car crash a second time, but he couldn't suggest a pointless detour to Maione; in part because now the air was even more scalding hot than before, if that was possible. So he had to listen again to the dissonant chorus of the dead family, with the child anticipating an ice cream he'd never enjoy.

He tried to distract himself by thinking back to the Capece family: certain looks, certain equilibriums, certain tensions that might have escaped him just a month ago, now struck him as obvious; but they altered the picture that he'd been building up until then. Maione, who had not stopped mopping his brow with his handkerchief, broke the silence:

"Commissa', what do you think of all this playacting about the pistol? Everyone looking at everyone else all surprised: 'Oh, Jesus, whatever happened to our little toy? It was here until just a few years ago, we all remember clearly, but one of those horrible maids must have stolen and sold it off on the black market'?"

Ricciardi, however, wasn't certain.

"Wouldn't it have been simpler just to say that there was no pistol? We wouldn't have found it in our search and that would have been the end of it. No, I don't think so. What I think, instead, is that they hadn't coordinated their stories. Husband and wife glared at each other indignantly, each of them convinced that the other got rid of it. The family is defending Capece, at least, that's what I think."

Maione was trying to stick to the shade to limit the damage inflicted by the intense heat. Two large patches of sweat were rapidly spreading under the sleeves of his light-colored jacket.

"The fact remains, Commissa', that the pistol didn't emerge and Capece has no alibi: because we know that the Signora is talking nonsense when she says that her husband slept with her on Saturday night. He hasn't slept with his wife in years, take it from Raffaele Maione. And after all, he told us himself, no?,

262 · MAURIZIO DE GIOVANNI

that he made the rounds of the dives and taverns, after going to the theater."

"That's true; but now it's up to us to prove that. If Signora Capece will testify to that effect and her husband decides to accept her help, then we're back at square one. We have to follow all the leads, the clock is ticking. You go home now and get back in uniform, because I don't even recognize you dressed like that. I'll see you back at headquarters."

"And what are you going to do, Commissa'?"

"I need to go and check something out. See you later."

You watch him leaning out over the balcony railing, smoking. The way he used to do, a hundred years ago, when you were still a family. Every so often, back then, he'd go out on the balcony, and you'd wonder where he was wandering in his thoughts, what ideals and what thoughts he was chasing. He's a man, you used to think. He needs his little moments of solitude.

Then solitude ended up being yours. Days and nights spent wondering where he was, and what he was doing. And fearing the answers.

He didn't say a word, after the two policemen left. You'd prepared all your answers, you were ready to give him another chance; you thought that the fact that you'd defended him, that you'd stood by his side, would strip the veil away from his eyes, the enchanted veil that that witch put on him with a spell, years ago. That he still had a family, after all. A wife. You thought that he'd have reacted by embracing you, in tears, thanking you for what you'd done. Maybe even scolding you for the risk you'd run by helping him. Instead he just went out onto the balcony, turning his back on you without even looking you in the eye. You don't mind, it's just the way he reacts.

That's not why you did it: not to earn his gratitude, much less his pity. You did it because you still love him, because he's the only man you've ever had in your life, the father of your children. Because you couldn't afford to lose him, just because he'd made a silly mistake.

Even if the mistake in question was a murder.

After leaving Maione, Ricciardi walked toward police headquarters: only once he was certain that the brigadier could no longer see him did he change direction and head for Largo della Carità.

He couldn't have pinpointed his reasons for wanting to keep his friend separate from that part of the investigation. Perhaps, he thought, because it was based more on feelings than on concrete facts; or else because of the danger, or else the situations that it might precipitate. Or else because, after the attempted attack on him and Livia, it had now become a personal question.

The thought of Livia brought the memory of the evening he'd spent with her back into his mind, the evening prior to the incident with the four gorillas. He'd enjoyed it, there was no denying the fact. He'd felt, if only for a few hours, free of the burden of solitude that the Deed had placed so squarely upon him. The woman was beautiful, amusing, and intelligent; the pleasure of her company and the unmistakable envy and admiration that washed over him in waves—both from men and women—had also coddled his ego. He wasn't in love with her: he understood that from a simple comparison between the memory of those moments and the despairing, heartbreaking emotions that he felt in his chest when he thought about Enrica. But maybe that's the secret, he thought: perhaps, to be happy, it's important to limit one's degree of emotional involvement.

He felt like an emotional apprentice. At his age, when most men have already had wives, children, and countless clandestine or frankly commercial sexual encounters, all he knew about love was the snips of monologues spouted by the various cadavers that he'd met. As he was walking in the shaft of light from the setting sun, he thought to himself that love is an infected root that seeks out the best way to survive: a fatal illness with an incredibly long course that causes addiction, making the victim prefer suffering to well-being, grief to tranquility, uncertainty to stability. He thought by free association of the image of the dead woman and her two rings, the ring that had once belonged to the first duchess and the other one, now in the journalist's possession: two lovers' troths, forcefully torn from the victim's fingers, one when she was still alive and one when she was already dead.

Even the place where he was going, and the nocturnal image that he'd glimpsed there, was evidence of the fact. And it seemed indicative to him that he'd witnessed that scene while he was out wandering around aimlessly, in the throes of incoherent depression after glimpsing Enrica and the man he assumed was her new boyfriend. Love was a mirage that, even in the best of cases, only offered scraps of itself, stolen in the still watches of the night.

Like the passionate kiss that he'd witnessed in the doorway before which he was now standing.

Her lips clamped tight as she stood in front of the mirror and buttoned her dress to the neck, Rosa was getting ready to leave at a time of day that was unusual for her. It was a hot day, and she would certainly have been happier to stay at home than to be out and about: but for once she felt it was her duty.

She couldn't stand to see Ricciardi suffering. He'd never had a very cheerful appearance, and she'd never once heard him laugh, at least not since he became an adult; he was silent and shy, but at any time of the day or night, she knew, or thought she knew, how he felt and what his mood was. For the past few days, though, her boy, the boy she had promised to protect, a solemn oath sworn to his mother on her deathbed, was suffering terribly. He never ate, he'd go out in the middle of the night and come home just before dawn, he'd sit there at night and listen to the radio in the dark for hours: and all this began the night he'd rushed breathless into her room to peer across the *vicolo* at the window across the way.

Once she was done with the row of buttons and had firmly fixed her hat in place with two hatpins, Rosa went over to the little window in the broom closet, at the end of the hallway; from there she could just get a narrow glimpse into a small bedroom in the Colombos' apartment, specifically the room where the oldest daughter slept. She could just make out the headboard of the bed, with a wooden cross hanging on the wall, the nightstand with a water glass and two books, and the pillow upon which the girl's head rested, facedown. From the movement of her shoulders, clearly visible from a distance of fifteen feet, Rosa saw evidence of what she'd expected: Enrica Colombo was crying.

She nodded with satisfaction and did what all the women in that quarter did whenever they needed to gather some information: she went to the hairdresser.

XXXIV

The street door was open and the doorman, who had pointed out the Fascist Party offices to him, wasn't there. Ricciardi decided that anyone could go in: after all, it was just an association of citizens.

In fact the four flights of stairs that led up to the top floor were bustling with people, men climbing and descending the steps, in pairs or small groups, chatting and laughing. Ricciardi sensed the usual arrogant excitement, the noisy, slightly forced cheerfulness of the largely male assemblies. On the landing there was a double door, both panels swung wide open, and through it could be seen a large atrium filled with people; their clothing was varied, ranging from the sober elegance of light-colored suits and bowties to mortar-spattered workers' smocks and overalls. Through the gap of a door swinging ajar, he glimpsed a man polishing a rifle, singing a love song in dialect.

At first no one paid any attention to Ricciardi, and he was forced to walk around a knot of four men, braying with laughter at a dirty joke; as soon as he walked into the room, however, a man with a ferocious expression came up to him and asked him roughly who he was and what he wanted. Silence fell immediately, even though the man hadn't spoken in an especially loud voice.

Ricciardi clearly sensed the wave of hostility that washed over him from everyone in the room, but he didn't take his eyes off the face of his questioner: he looked at him fixedly for a long time, until the man finally lowered his eyes. There was a burst of nervous coughing from somewhere out on the landing. In a firm, low voice, he said:

"I'm Commissario Ricciardi, from police headquarters. But I imagine you already know that."

From a small knot of men at the far end of the room a man broke away; Ricciardi recognized him immediately: it was the guy who had threatened him the night before.

"So what? You are who you are, but you're still not welcome here so you'd better get out. Just because things went your way once doesn't mean they will again. Take my advice, leave on your own two feet while you can still walk, it's good advice."

The atmosphere had turned grim and tense: silence was absolute, you couldn't even hear anyone breathing. On the far side of the room the man with the rifle had stopped singing and now he was standing up menacingly from his stool, striding to the doorway with his gun leveled. Everyone was looking at Ricciardi, who hadn't shifted his gaze away from the man who'd first asked him who he was. He now slowly turned toward his old nocturnal acquaintance and stared at him, expressionless, his eyes empty and transparent; the *squadrista* stepped back almost imperceptibly and jutted his chin, arms akimbo, hands on hips, in an unconscious imitation of the one figure that made him feel confident.

"Thanks for the advice," said Ricciardi. "I'll leave when I've been given the information I need."

"Maybe you didn't understand: you need to get out of here right away, otherwise we'll see you out in our own way, which will even spare you the trouble of taking the stairs."

The threat was accompanied by a nod of the head toward the window. A single nervous laugh was heard, and was immediately stifled; the mocking smile on the man's face faded. Ricciardi acted as if he hadn't heard a word.

"I'm here to talk to Ettore Musso di Camparino."

The other man took a step back, as if he'd just been slapped; a confused muttering arose from all the little knots of men. Many of them exchanged what looked like frightened glances.

The man recovered and took a step forward, lips tight, eyes wide, angry. He laid a hand on Ricciardi's arm: both of the commissario's hands were still in his pockets:

"Now that's enough! I told you that you need to beat it, and . . ."

From behind the group of men, which had formed a menacing circle around the two of them, came a calm voice:

"Mastrogiacomo, cool down. That's enough now."

The little crowd parted as if a lion tamer had just snapped his whip. Standing in a doorway, through which a desk piled high with papers could be seen, was a thin, smartly dressed man who looked to be around forty. The *squadrista* took his hand off Ricciardi's arm as if it was red-hot, and suddenly looked very confused.

"Yessir. But, forgive me, Dotto', I thought that . . ."

The man at the door looked at Ricciardi with curiosity. He gestured vaguely in Mastrogiacomo's direction, and the man fell suddenly silent. Without taking his eyes off the commissario, he said:

"Bring two coffees to my office, please. *Prego*, Commissario: come this way."

And Ricciardi followed him into his room.

The large-bloomed rose is very beautiful: a solitary flower that only blooms in pairs. It requires a great deal of care. I have to make sure it's exposed to constant humidity, because it's very delicate; if it's too dry, it won't bloom properly. There's nothing sadder than finding crumpled, heat-scorched leaves and petals on the ground.

Flowers are sensuous. The color and texture seem to be that of flesh, velvety, iridescent. And the care you devote to them should be the same as if you were caring for the flesh of a loved one: devout, impassioned. You must maintain the silent spell of love, sprinkling the flowers with drops of water, watching as they pearl up on the convex shapes of the petals, like beads of sweat on your lips after making love.

Last night I dreamed that I'd been locked up. Without me here to care for them, all the flowers shed their petals and the plants withered and died, only to be replaced by rapacious wild weeds. If they ever did cart me off, no one would tend to you, my exquisite roses; or to the begonias, or the oleanders. It's quite sufficient to see the cold and indifferent care that is bestowed on the hydrangeas, down in the courtyard, in spite of all the instructions I constantly give that dull-witted doorman with his oversized schnozzola and his tribe of children. What useless people.

All care would be lost, every last shred of honor pertaining to this house, if they were to take me away. You, too, Mamma, in the hereafter, would suffer, I'm sure of it. And yet I wouldn't say a word. I wouldn't try to defend myself.

Because love, Mamma, comes before anything else. And if I had to defend anything at all, I'd defend my love.

My first, great love.

The man led Ricciardi into his office and shut the door. The room was shrouded in shadows, the shutters on the windows were pulled to and partially closed; the furnishings were limited to a desk and two chairs. The walls were covered with shelving that rose all the way to the ceiling, piled high with fat files marked with letters and numbers. Facing the door he'd just walked through, the commissario saw another closed door, emblazoned with a portrait of a helmeted Mussolini.

His host sat down and pointed Ricciardi to the other chair. He stared at him intently, with his small, expressionless blue eyes. After a minute he spoke:

"Now then: Luigi Alfredo Ricciardi, commissario with the mobile squad for the past three years or so. Born in Fortino, province of Salerno, thirty-one years ago. Orphaned of both father and mother. You're an odd duck, did you know that? Filthy rich, acres and acres worked by tenant farmers, with a vast income. And yet you work for pennies, really, and you show no signs of seeking advancement in your career. An interesting man, I'd say."

In his turn, Ricciardi leveled his gaze at the man speaking to him, without so much as blinking. The man's accent was northern, possibly Ligurian or Piedmontese; his voice was chilly and remote, like a scientist delivering a lecture.

"You know who I am. I'm impressed, and even flattered by all this attention. Would it be too much for me to ask you to tell me who you are?"

"My name is Pivani, Achille Pivani. I'm . . . let's just say that I'm a Party official, a temporary guest in this lovely city of yours."

He fell silent again, as he drummed his fingers lightly on his desktop. He sat straight-backed, his shoulders not touching the back of the chair. A muscle twitched on his temple, as if he were chewing without moving his jaw. After a short while, he asked Ricciardi:

"May I ask what you're doing here?"

The commissario smirked.

"What's this? You know everything about me and yet you don't know what I just asked your oversized trained ape?"

Pivani shook his head.

"I know, I know. I owe you an apology, even if, believe me, I had nothing to do with it. Mastrogiacomo . . . some of our militants are eager to please me, in a sense. And so they take certain initiatives, in keeping with their nature. They're like a bunch of mischievous children, street urchins, really."

Buffoonish clowns, thought Ricciardi.

"No, Pivani. They're not street urchins: they're criminals. With blood on their hands. It doesn't matter what happened to me last night, but what they're doing every day, and they're becoming bolder and bolder. And they get this boldness from you and those like you. You're their accomplices, and you know it. If not actually the masterminds behind them."

The commissario's tirade, even though it was hissed in something close to a whisper, had been violent and unexpected. Pivani blinked. He seemed to think it over, then he admitted:

"You have a point; I've even told them at the highest level that these men can become a problem. You must understand that even an elevated and noble idea like Fascism can become, in the hands of some ordinary idiot, a weapon to settle old personal grudges. It's already happened elsewhere, and it's starting to happen here, too. But that's not our intent, please believe me. When we find out about something, we take care of it ourselves."

Ricciardi had no intention of showing any sympathy.

"Then you know that your man Mastrogiacomo, or whatever his name is, and his friends, murdered that unemployed man in Via Emanuele Filiberto. Don't ask me how I know, but I do know. Even though I have no evidence, or even a criminal complaint."

Pivani leaned forward, eyes narrowed.

"Are you certain of it? Absolutely certain?"

Ricciardi nodded. The man picked up a pen, dipped it in the inkwell, and wrote something on a sheet of paper.

"I'll take care of this, Commissario. I'm not here to shed blood."

"Then why are you here? Aside from bringing order and civilization, of course."

Pivani gave no sign of having caught the irony.

"My . . . organization is assigned to identify the enemies of the Party. You should think of me, of us, as . . . colleagues, in a certain sense. Except, we're less fortunate than you. We can't work in the light of day, the way you do."

Ricciardi snorted.

"I don't believe I'm going to let you make this comparison, Pivani. How should I address you, by the way? Do you have a rank, do you hold some office?"

The man smiled, affably.

"My rank and my office would be incomprehensible to you. Pivani is enough. In any case, it's my job to know everything about everyone: I was sent here for that purpose. I'm a sort of . . . let's say, a kind of inspector, that's good enough. Fascism in Naples hasn't been in good hands; you may remember the accident in which Padovani died, a comrade from the earliest times, a man who marched on Rome at the Duce's side in 1922. Certain values, certain aspects of the Party have changed. I'm here precisely to see whether this . . . change has been incorporated."

Ricciardi remembered all too well the tragedy in the Via Generale Orsini; it had been five years ago. He'd been one of the first to arrive on the scene of the catastrophe; the balcony from which the high-ranking member of the Fascist party was greeting the crowd celebrating his birthday had collapsed, killing nine and seriously injuring thirty or so. Many aspects of what Pivani called an "accident" had never been cleared up. The scene that greeted the commissario's eyes when he arrived was hellish: his ears picked up both the screams of the injured and the lamentations of the dead who had suddenly been snatched from the world of the living. He shuddered, remembering that rumors flew around the city that Padovani's cult of personality had begun to become an annoyance to the Duce. Very strange, that accident. And providential for the Party, as well. Pivani was still talking:

"It's always been a problem, the excess of zeal. And also the cult of personality, the Duce aside, obviously; you understand clearly that the party base is made up of the masses, mediocre and incapable of thinking for themselves. It's in cases like this one, where four useless idiots decide they want to do something to please their bosses, that violence erupts. They need to be guided, supervised every hour of the day. But those who conspire in the shadows are a problem too, and must be stopped. And that's where we come in."

We, meaning OVRA, thought Ricciardi, the legendary Fascist secret police, whose existence the regime stubbornly refused to acknowledge. All the terror and violence that this whispered name inspired, bound up in this inoffensive little man.

"I don't care what you do. Nor do I care what you find out, rummaging around in the dark as you do. What I do care about is what Ettore Musso di Camparino was doing here, the other night. And where he goes when he goes out, and what he does. What I care about is who murdered his stepmother, the duchess, and why they killed her so pitilessly. And I want to know whether it was him."

In the ensuing silence he heard someone knock at the door; Pivani called loudly to come in, and Mastrogiacomo stepped forward with a tray on which sat two steaming cups. He set it down on the desk, and just as he was about to turn and leave, Pivani, who hadn't once looked away from Ricciardi's face, as if he were hypnotized, addressed him:

"Mastrogiacomo, when the commissario leaves, later, make sure that he's not bothered by so much as a stray breeze. Then come to see me with your three colleagues, you know very well the ones I mean. We need to talk about a trip you're going to take. You'll be departing immediately. A long trip: pack your bags."

The man heaved a deep sigh, and just as he was about to say something in response, Pivani turned his head and looked in his direction. That was enough. He walked toward the door, retreating with his head held low; when he reached the threshold he straightened and clicked his heels, delivering a straight-armed salute, and then left the room, closing the door behind him.

XXXV

After waiting for what seemed to him like a sufficiently long time, Andrea Capece entered the room that the two policemen had recently vacated to leave the apartment. He found his mother sitting on the small sofa, her hands in her lap, looking out through the open French doors onto the balcony where his father was leaning over the railing and smoking a cigarette. The sight gave him an unpleasant feeling, like he was experiencing a scene out of the past, and so he was. As a child, he had spent hours listening to the spreading silence separating his parents.

This time, however, he felt a strong sense of repulsion: for his father, who had once again shown himself to be ungrateful and indifferent, but also for his mother, who was obviously not yet fed up after all the years of humiliations to which she had been subjected, directly and indirectly, by that man. He thought how everyone is born either hammer or anvil: and the anvils are happy to be pounded, because it's in their nature.

He walked over to her and speaking in a hushed voice, for who knows what reason, told her that he'd be going out for half an hour or so, to give a notebook to a friend. The woman nodded without turning around to glance at him; she continued to stare at the mute back of that stranger smoking and staring out from their balcony. Andrea left the room with a sense of relief, as if he just been forced to witness something horrifying against his will.

He walked out the front door without haste; he took a

quick look around, but in the brutal afternoon heat, there was no one in sight, except for a beggar who was probably sleeping off a drunk in the shade of a tree across the street. He walked a few yards, and then slipped through a small wooden door leading down into a cellar. The stench of damp rot washed over him, but he paid it no mind; he walked over to the wall, removed a book, and put in his hand to pull out something wrapped in newspaper. He unwrapped it.

Mamma, he thought, I don't know why you protected him from the police. After all the things he's done, after what he did to you. But then I don't even know why I tried to help.

Gripping his father's pistol in one hand and placing his forefinger on the trigger, Andrea decided for the hundredth time that love was a fatal illness, and that he for one would never fall in love. Not for all the gold in world.

After Mastrogiacomo slunk, mortified, out of the room, Pivani dipped his pen in the inkwell again, and drew a line across the note he'd made earlier, with the nitpicking care of an accountant. Ricciardi, slumped in the chair, hands in his pockets, went on staring at him, waiting for the answer to his question: what had Ettore Musso di Camparino been doing there, and where was he the night his stepmother was murdered?

Pivani looked back at him, calmly.

"Dottor Musso is a respected authority in his field; did you know that, Commissario? A political philosopher, one of the most respected in the country. Behind that shy and sensitive exterior he conceals a penetrating mind, and he has admirers at the highest level in the national government. On a confidential basis, he writes many of the speeches that the Duce himself delivers before the Italian parliament and to the most eminent cultural organizations."

Ricciardi seemed rather unimpressed.

north, but she'd never betray my secret: it would mean losing
money and social position. There's hunger up north, too,
Commissario, did you know that? Plenty of hunger. People
still take ships to America, out of Genoa. The party demands
you have a wife, if you want to advance your career. Children?
Well, if God doesn't send them to you, you can hardly go out
and buy them, can you? I had never . . . I'd never done anything. When I was a kid, in boarding school, there was an older
boy. He wanted to hurt me, but instead he helped me understand who I was. And I kept it to myself. That is, until I met
Ettore."

Ricciardi listened. And as he listened he recognized the
movements of the diseased root, the sneaking love that knew
how to make its way down the least obvious pathways, infil-
trating, first, dreams and only later the flesh. He thought about
Enrica, and he wondered, absurdly, if he'd ever watch her
embroider again.

"Of course, we didn't say anything. But believe me, Commissario, when I tell you that in that very instant, the moment
our eyes met for the first time, we recognized one another. If
you only knew how many times we thought back to that
moment; if I live to be a hundred, it will still be the most
important instant of my life. How many times I reached out to
him; how many times we both tried to strangle this damned
feeling. We talked all night about nonsense, one conversation
with our mouths, quite another with our souls, with our hearts.
We walked for hours, and it was brutally cold out; I come from
the north, and I've never felt such cold weather as I experienced here. Then, outside his front door, just as day was dawning, we said goodnight. And then, on an impulse, without even
knowing how or why, I kissed him. He locked himself up in his
apartment, and he refused to see me again. Even though I've
always avoided all public occasions, I never missed a party, a
theatrical performance, a dance recital, or a symphony—all in

the hopes of running into him; and I never saw him once. Then, one night, when it was pouring down rain, I found him standing right in front of this desk, where you're sitting now, streaming wet like a stray dog, his eyes glistening with fever, his lips trembling. He was magnificently handsome, and he was in a state of despair."

Pivani fell silent. Large teardrops were rolling down his cheeks, but his voice remained calm, as if he were dictating a report. When he resumed, he looked up fiercely at Ricciardi.

"To answer your question, then, I can tell you that Ettore Musso di Camparino, on the night between the 22nd and the 23rd, was here, with me. Making love with me. And then sobbing, despairing, along with me. Wondering what would become of the two of us, because in the world that the two of us were helping to create, there was no place for people like us. And there never will be."

XXXVI

What emerged was a story of furtive encounters and letters burnt after being read, stolen kisses and hidden tears. It was strange for Ricciardi, too, accustomed as he was to receiving confessions and peering down into the desperate abyss of loneliness, to hear someone talk about love in that atmosphere choked with files looming high in the semi-darkness, with the odors of tobacco smoke and ink and dust mingling in the air, and with the relentless heat.

The love that Achille told him about was hopeless, and it had no future; a love that was above all a threat, a love that never saw the light of day. In spite of everything, however, it refused to die, obstinately outliving every rational attempt to put an end to it. A hundred times they'd left each other, promising never to meet again, and a hundred and one times they'd sought each other out again, with the feverish urgency of need and the creeping sensation of a new defeat. Pivani relived that pain, twisting his hands, staring into the dark, his voice firm, little more than a whisper.

He couldn't rule out the possibility that someone at party headquarters might suspect something about the excessively close friendship between a member of the Fascist hierarchy and the young philosopher: but fear of the secret police was too great for anyone to voice their suspicions. The proscription lists, prison, and the chance of being forbidden all employment all lurked menacingly in the offing; it was so much easier to go along with the situation, so most of them simply did their best to comply with the demands of that dangerous little man from the north, with all his mysterious power, frequently called on the phone by the party's most prominent figures in Rome—figures to whom he often gave terse, irrevocable orders. And so while Ettore, a few days earlier, was telling Achille about being questioned by Ricciardi and how worried he was, Mastrogiacomo had memorized the name—Ricciardi—as he was taking coffee to Pivani's office; then, when the doorman reported to him that the commissario had been asking questions about who might be visiting the party headquarters at night, he'd taken it upon himself to intervene, determined to win merit in the eyes of his superior officer.

Ettore deeply hated his stepmother, Pivani made clear; but an act of violence like that wasn't part of his nature. He was a man of letters, gentle, sensitive, a man who loved flowers and possessed no weapons. The picture that emerged from Achille's description, as well as the alibi that he himself was providing, let Musso off the hook and left a great many obscure points in the duchess's murder.

"I understand, Pivani. And I realize all the implications of your story, both public and private. Still, I have to warn you that, unless we're able to identify a guilty party in this murder, it may be that you will be subpoenaed to testify, and you'll be expected to repeat what you've told me here today; otherwise it will be easy for anyone, especially after Musso's little scene at the funeral, to target him for the murder. You realize that, right?"

Continuing to stare into the empty air, Pivani smiled sadly.

"And what would you do in my position, Ricciardi? Would you just hang back and watch him being sent to prison, suffering the shame of seeing his venerable family name dragged through the mud, like some ordinary brute, some untutored criminal? And just to save my own hide, to boot? No; I'd gladly come testify. Perhaps it would even be a form of liberation, after all the sleepless nights staring at the ceiling, after the thousands of fears that the story might get out and ruin our miserable existences. I am—we are—in your hands, Commissario. Our only chance is that you find the murderer."

Ricciardi got up from his chair.

"No easy matter, I assure you. The duchess was a prominent woman, as you know. I'm being strongly pressured to move quickly; otherwise they'll take the investigation out of my hands, and it will be my duty to hand over everything I've found to my successor."

Pivani had put on a pair of reading glasses and was opening a file that lay before him on his desk.

"I can't give you any classified information; or at least, nothing that you can use openly. The organization I work for, as you know, officially doesn't exist; what do you call an open secret, you Neapolitans? Pulcinella's secret, is that it? All the same, I can tell you something that might prove useful. Among the people we have under surveillance is a certain Mario Capece, the journalist who was the duchess's lover. He isn't dangerous, but he never misses an opportunity to scatter to the four winds his opinion that the regime has silenced the press."

Ricciardi nodded.

"Sure, he told us the same thing; but that doesn't strike me as open dissidence. It's more like nostalgia for the past, as far as I can tell."

Pivani smiled, looking over his eyeglasses at Ricciardi.

"You always try to defend people, eh, Ricciardi? It seems to me that you, too, are much more kindhearted than you'd like people to believe. I know that Capece is no seditionist. But people are reluctant to mind their own business and no one ever misses an opportunity to make a favorable impression on us. So we received a number of reports and we were obliged to put him under a soft surveillance. We aren't having him followed, so I can't tell you whether or not he was at the Musso di Camparino home the night of the murder; but he wasn't at the newspaper, there we have a . . . we can say that with confidence, in other words. But what I can tell you, and it certainly might be a useful piece of information, is that his son, Andrea, a sixteen-year-old boy, did something peculiar. Here it is, let me read it to you: 'The above-named Andrea Capece, sixteen years of age, late at night on Tuesday, August 25th, emerged from his home carrying a package wrapped in newspaper; he walked down the *vicolo* next to the residence in question, entered a ground floor storage area in the building at number 104, and came out again six minutes later, only to return to his home.' Since the one under surveillance is the father, and we have no desire to alert him to our interest, we decided not to institute a more in-depth investigation: in other words, we didn't go to see what was in the package. But if I were you, I'd keep an eye on him, on that boy. After all, even a child can pull a trigger."

Ricciardi stood up. The interview was over; he said farewell with a nod of the head and walked to the door. Ricciardi already had his hand on the handle when Pivani spoke again:

"One last thing, Ricciardi. Tonight, I've been talking to myself, here in my office. Just musing aloud, nothing more. Maybe I saw a ghost, and I just started talking. Aside from that willingness to testify that I promised you if it should happen to come, God forbid, to a trial, none of the information that I've given you must ever have a source: otherwise, I won't be able to do anything on your behalf. Nor will I want to. Is that clear?"

Ricciardi nodded. But Pivani still wasn't done.

"And as long as I'm chatting with this ghost, I want to give him one other little tidbit of advice. I know that you're fond of Dr. Bruno Modo, the medical examiner. You're right, he's a decent man, one who's willing to treat someone in need, even if that someone can't pay for his services. So if you want to help him out, tell him to be careful what he says in public; especially when he's had a glass or two too much to drink. It really would be a pity if something bad were to happen to him."

When he got back to police headquarters, everyone had left for the night, except for a very worried Maione, sitting on the bench outside his office door and fanning himself with his cap. As soon as he saw Ricciardi arrive, he leapt to his feet.

"Commissa', what on earth happened to you? All this time! I sent Camarda to see if you were at Palazzo Camparino, I went back myself to the Capece home to see if you'd forgotten to ask them something. I even called your place, to see if by any chance you'd turned up there. By the way, Signora Rosa is waiting up for you, she says that she made you pasta and squash for dinner."

Ricciardi grimaced and put his hand on his stomach.

"You just had to tell me that, didn't you, to make me lose any desire to go home at the end of a long day? When Rosa makes squash, it takes me two days to digest it. You're right, though, I forgot that you'd be here waiting for me; and I hadn't noticed how late it had gotten. Come into my office, I'll tell you the news."

He rapidly brought the brigadier up to date on the information that was pertinent to the investigation. He told him nothing about the illicit relationship, nor did he even mention Pivani's name, both because the less his friend knew about it, the less danger he was in, and because he wouldn't have known how to reveal to him—out of shame and respect—the depth of that relationship and the suffering that accompanied it. He told him that he had been to the Fascist Party headquarters where, by chance, two nights earlier he had seen Ettore go in, and that he'd learned that the duke's son was collaborating on a number of secret operations now underway, and that he had been told that Ettore was in those offices the night of the murder, as well.

Maione listened openmouthed; when Ricciardi was done he blurted out:

"Excuse me, Commissa', but what were you doing in the middle of the street two nights ago, when you saw the young master going to visit the Fascists? And why didn't you tell me about it, why didn't you have me come with you? They're very dangerous people to deal with. And who did you speak with, at Fascist headquarters? Those people take care of their own, it's obvious that they gave him an alibi: it's like asking a water vendor if the water is cool!"

Ricciardi raised both hands.

"Oh, oh, don't jump on me! First of all, I didn't think I'd be able to talk to anyone, I just swung by there to get it out of the way while you were going to get changed. And the other night, it was so hot out that I couldn't get any sleep, and that's why I was out walking. When I went by tonight, they finally let me speak with an important figure there, and it struck me that he didn't even like Ettore very much, and I think he told me the truth. We'd have to check it out, let that be clear. But it would explain why Ettore wouldn't tell us where he was. In any case, it's late now, we'll talk it over tomorrow. You go home and get yourself something to eat, you must be starving by now."

Maione put on the expression of a suffering man:

"Commissa', you can't begin to imagine just how hungry I am. All right, good night. But do me a favor: the next time you think you might be going someplace dangerous, would you be so good as to let me know?"

In the drawing room, after dinner, Enrica did her best to avoid looking at Sebastiano as he was about to sip his coffee. From the very first evening he'd come to her home, she'd noticed a horrible thing: the man held the handle of the porcelain demitasse with two fingers, extending his pinky—that in itself struck her as intolerable—and then he pursed his lips as if he were about to kiss the rim of the cup, another equally ridiculous act, and finally he inhaled his coffee with a loud sucking noise. She could have strangled him.

What would everyone think if they knew that Enrica, the fragile, delicate, shy young woman whom they all loved for her gentle nature, was actually considering first-degree murder? The thought made her smile and the clueless Sebastiano interrupted Operation Espresso to respond with a loving glance. Conceited fool, thought Enrica, and smiled again. And to keep her mind off the sucking sound that was about to fill the room again, she recalled the conversation that she'd had that afternoon with the hairdresser, and all the questions that the woman had asked about Enrica's supposed engagement, a piece of news that she'd denied categorically. That same hairdresser, she mused, also did the hair of Luigi Alfredo's housekeeper; how nice it would be, if the woman's curiosity had been prodded by him: that would mean that he was still interested in her, that the damned woman from the north was nothing more than a friend, and that she still had a prayer of a hope.

She shut her eyes, bracing herself for Sebastiano's horrible sucking sound: she decided that there was no way that she could spend her life waiting, every time he drank a cup of espresso, to hear the gurgling of the unfortunate liquid as it flowed from the lovely demitasse down into the grotto of his gaping maw.

She was certain that when Luigi Alfredo drank a cup of coffee, he made no noise at all. And that he kept his pinky finger unextended, like a real man.

Lucia went to meet Raffaele the minute she heard the key turn in the lock. She'd sent the children to bed when she realized that he'd be home late, and she'd kept his dinner warm: a bowl of vegetable soup. He let himself drop into the chair, dripping with sweat from the long uphill climb from police headquarters and the stairs up to the top floor. She peered into his face with genuine concern: he seemed tense and nervous to her. She wondered what he had on his mind. Or who.

Instead, her husband looked at his soup bowl, sifting the vegetables with his spoon. After a while he asked her how she'd spent her day. She told him that she'd gone to do her grocery shopping and then she'd spent the afternoon cleaning and shelling the vegetables that she'd used to make that soup. By the way: Ciruzzo, the fruit and vegetable vendor, sent his regards.

He looked up at her as if he'd received an electric shock. He dropped his spoon into the soup and stood up, saying:

"This soup is revolting. Sometimes I think I ought to do like the commissario does and eat out more often. I've lost my appetite, I'm going to bed. *Buona notte.*"

Astonished and humiliated, Lucia watched him leave the room, wondering what on earth she had done wrong.

Ricciardi had hardly eaten a bite. He'd pushed the pasta around in the bowl for ten minutes or so, his mind clearly chasing after faraway thoughts. Rosa had watched him, standing at the threshold of the kitchen door, the whole time.

When he stood up from dinner, giving her a sidelong glance and bracing himself for the usual furious scolding, she astonished him by clearing the table in silence. To his astonishment, there was not so much as a single pointed comment on his lack of consideration for a weary old woman who had worked all day to put delicious food on the table for him when he got home.

Actually, his aged housekeeper was much less worried than she had been for the past few days; the hairdresser had come back to her, in accordance with her instructions. After all, the woman was eager to collect the second half of the tip that she'd been promised, and she came bearing good news. Excellent news, in fact: the young Colombo woman wasn't engaged and, even better, had no intention of getting engaged. It was her parents, worried about the girl's age, who were pushing her to get to know the son of the proprietors of the shop next door to theirs; they were hoping that sooner or later love might bloom, spontaneously.

The danger was still clear and present, thought Rosa as she washed the dishes; but there was at least at little hope.

Ricciardi had retired to his bedroom, resolute that he wouldn't look out his window, even by chance: he didn't want to suffer the disappointment of once more seeing the shutters across the way closed. Of course, his determination faltered, and he sat in the dark watching the little corner of the Colombos' drawing room that could be glimpsed from his bedroom window. He saw the infamous young man, by now comfortably ensconced on the sofa, drinking an espresso; indignantly, he wondered whether the man ever planned to go home, if indeed he had a home. Across from him sat Enrica, hair neatly gathered in a bun, eyeglasses, hands in her lap. She was smiling at him, or at least that's how it looked to Ricciardi.

Until recently, and every night for many months before that, he'd seen the figure of a woman who had hanged herself on the floor above Enrica's apartment. Every night, as he looked at the sweet image of Enrica embroidering, he'd had to behold the chilling contrast with this body dangling lazily from a rope tied around the hook holding up the chandelier. Rosa had told him that the woman was a newlywed who'd discovered the truth about her unfaithful husband; when she'd furiously confronted him, he'd beaten her and then abandoned her.

Ricciardi had seen, all too clearly, the neck stretched out by the dislocation of the vertebrae, the blackish tongue, cut halfway through by the final spasm of the jaws, dangling out of her mouth, the bulging eyes, protruding from the sockets; the large stain of urine and feces released by the sphincter onto the white wedding gown, which she'd insisted on wearing for this last macabre dance with death. The woman had repeated to Ricciardi, every night, her invective against the woman who had stolen away her husband. Against the other woman, and not against the man who had betrayed her:

"You damned whore, you took my love and my life."

She again came to mind now, nearly three months after she'd slowly dissolved into the night, leaving behind only an aura of sadness at first, and then, finally, nothing. She came to mind as he watched Enrica smile at her man and then look away, perhaps thinking of the future they might have together, their children and, someday, their grandchildren: the future that his fundamental nature, however, made impossible for him.

He felt the now familiar stab of pain in his stomach and a powerful surge of nausea. He thought of the hanged woman and himself, two fates not really as far apart as one might think. And the new pain, the dull and selfish suffering that now had a name he couldn't even bring himself to utter.

The summer night was busy with the buzz of people talking in the street, sitting in front of the doors to their ground-floor *bassi*, to escape the heat. Somewhere a piano was playing, and he could hear singing, but he couldn't make out the words. The music was heartbreaking, perfectly suited to Ricciardi's sorrow. He looked at the man drinking coffee in Enrica's home, unsuspecting, all smiles: and for the first time, he hated someone with every fiber of his being. He hated that man because the place he was sitting belonged to him, just as the woman that he was smiling at belonged to him; that life, and that normal world, those dreams and that future all belonged to him, too.

He coldly contemplated that hatred, as if it were a strange

animal he'd never laid eyes on. A disease that could prove fatal. A disease that could make you kill.

Suddenly, in the heat of the night, surrounded by the sound of faraway music, Ricciardi understood who had killed Adriana Musso di Camparino. And why.

XXXVII

Capece felt the stabbing pain of jealousy as he dreamt of the young man who'd smiled at Adriana at the theater, and he woke up with a jerk. He looked around and for a long moment had no idea where he was: odd, considering he was in his own home.

My home, he thought bitterly. This isn't my home. This isn't my place. Everyone has a place of their own, he thought, the kind of thoughts you have when you first wake up, lazily, hovering between your last dream and the reality that filters in a little at a time: and this isn't mine. My place is close to Adriana, close to my love: if she's no longer part of this world, then I no longer have a place where I belong.

The night before he'd stayed out on the balcony for hours, until his wife figured out that he didn't want to talk to her and retreated into her bedroom. Then he'd stretched out on the sofa and had fallen asleep, overcome by the rapid succession of events and the traumas of the past few days, plummeting into an unrestful, agitated slumber. He couldn't remember what dreams he'd had except for the one right before awakening, the glance that he'd intercepted between his lover and her young admirer at the theater, the glance that had unleashed the last, furious fight. As dawn crept into the bedroom with its promise of another day of oppressive heat, Capece experienced for the thousandth time a stabbing pain in his stomach, a surge of blood to his head, and an uncontrollable wave of fury. A blind will to wreak havoc, to destroy and kill.

In the dim light, he looked at his hand. And he started to weep, silently.

As the first rays of sunshine extended across the piazza across from city hall and through the glass panes of his windows, flooding the office with bright light, Ricciardi was already sitting at his desk. He'd hardly slept a wink, with the crashing waves of conflicting emotions inside and the new understanding he'd gained of the Camparino murder; and so he'd risen from his bed while it was still pitch black out and had made his way to the empty police headquarters building, with the cop at the front entrance snoring away—he hadn't even seen him go in; there was no one about but the two dead men on the stairs, engaged in their perennial portrayal of grief, greeting him as always; but he paid them no mind.

He was waiting for Maione, so that they could agree on a strategy. They couldn't get this wrong: one reckless move would prevent him from obtaining the evidence they needed. The brigadier, too, was an early riser, though perhaps not to the same degree as his superior officer, and Ricciardi would have enough time to give him the instructions he had in mind.

He whiled away the time by catching up with the paperwork he'd been neglecting for the past few days; he was raptly compiling a report when he heard a knock at the door. At last, he thought. He called out:

"*Avanti*, come in!"

The door opened just a crack and to his immense surprise, Ricciardi found himself gazing admiringly upon Livia, even more seductive than usual, smiling at him from the threshold and holding up a brown paper package.

"Good morning. I'm here to bring breakfast to a certain Commissario Ricciardi, who I'm told is the most charming man at police headquarters. Would you be able to point me to his office, by any chance?"

She wore a light jacket that was reminiscent of a sailor's blouse, dark blue with white cuffs; the skirt echoed the same motif, rode tight around her hips, and hung knee-length, revealing the white-silk stockings that sheathed her legs. Her blouse, open at the neck, revealed the woman's magnificent décolleté; her cunning little cloche hat partly concealed her short hairdo that framed her lightly made-up face, which, at that moment, was illuminated by a stunning smile.

Ricciardi, who'd sat there breathless for a moment, got to his feet and waved her in. After he recovered, he said:

"What are you doing here, and at this hour of the morning? Aren't you on vacation?"

Livia laughed, sat down in the chair facing the desk, and started to open the package.

"Vacation? Believe me, when you're dealing with someone like you, and you're trying to make friends, there's no time for leisure. You're a man who needs to be chased, because if I sit down and wait for you to come to me, there's a considerable risk I'll just get old and unsightly. I don't have much time left to me, you know.".

Ricciardi wasn't accustomed to this sort of gallant fencing, and he was clearly out of his element.

"It's just that it doesn't strike me as quite right, that you should come here to police headquarters. It's not a very nice place, for a lady. There are criminals and policemen, and I couldn't say which of the two is worse. And after all, it seems to me that it will be a long, long time before you become ugl . . . an old woman, I meant to say."

Livia opened her eyes wide and raised one hand to her throat, feigning scandalized surprise:

"But what do these ears of mine hear? Is it possible that Commissario Ricciardi, the least gallant man in all of Southern Italy, has practically just paid a compliment? Surely that cannot be: no doubt I haven't yet awakened and I'm merely dreaming."

Ricciardi shook his head and smiled in spite of himself.

"Well, all right then: anyway, you always do whatever you please. And about the other night: you can't say that I didn't warn you, that being around a man like me can be a dangerous thing. Anyway, they were just four hotheads who . . ."

Livia stopped him, by putting one hand on his. The contact, warm and seething, was anything but disagreeable to Ricciardi. Looking him right in the eye, she said:

"You don't have to say a thing. I'm a grown woman, and what I want or don't want to do, I decide for myself. And don't think for a second that it's any different where I come from: these days, the criminals are commiting their crimes under a flag. Don't worry about me at all. If anything, I'm worried about you. If you like, I can make a call to Rome and speak with . . . let's just say that I know people who are, ah, quite influential. I can arrange to have you left alone, now and for good. You need only say the word."

Ricciardi replied firmly:

"Don't even think of it. Aside from the fact that I have nothing to fear, I can take care of myself very nicely, thanks. I've already taken my own countermeasures; nothing else is going to happen."

Livia sighed, reassured.

"Then I have nothing else to worry about, just keeping your stomach full; look here what I've brought you: four puff pastries, *sfogliatelle* the way you like them, piping hot. The little shop on the corner, what's the name again? Ah, that's right, Pintauro. It's even open at this time of the morning, did you know that? And I wasn't even the first customer of the day, from what the cashier told me, along with a stream of compliments. Here, have one."

Maione stuck his head in the door just as Livia was handing a steaming hot, odorous pastry to Ricciardi, who was standing right next to her. His eyes widened as he stared at Livia, the puff pastry, Ricciardi, and again the puff pastry. Then he snorted and extended his arms.

"No, really, this is verging on harassment! In this city everyone seems to be eating from dawn to dusk, the minute I show up! When on earth have you ever eaten anything, Commissa', in this office at this time of the morning? And you, too, Signo', forgive me, but do you really think it's right to send the aroma of *sfogliatelle* wafting down the staircase and into the courtyard? I thought I was having hallucinations, I was sure of it! Don't take this the wrong way, but we're here to work, you know!"

Livia looked over at Ricciardi, still holding the *sfogliatella* in midair, caught off guard by the brigadier's furious outburst. The commissario shrugged his shoulders.

"Ah, Maione, at last you're here. No, the signora here just happened to be passing by and dropped in to say hello. In fact, here's what she'd just got through saying: 'When will Brigadier Maione be coming in, I brought a *sfogliatella* for him too?' And I'd just told her that you should already have come in by now."

Maione looked at Livia's hand and the *sfogliatella* as if he were about to lunge and tear them both off in a single ravenous bite.

"No, *grazie*, Signora, I couldn't think of eating at this time of the morning. My stomach wakes up long after I do, if you want to know the truth. And forgive me for what I just said, but in this heat I don't sleep well and I'm always on edge. Did you have any orders, Commissa'?"

Ricciardi had walked around the desk and taken a seat at his usual place.

"Stay just another moment or two, Raffae'; it might be that the Signora Livia, here, can lend a hand. Come in, and take a seat, please."

Maione sat down next to Livia, who was looking at Ricciardi, clearly electrified at the idea of being made privy to his thoughts. The harder she found it to tune in to that mysterious man, the more irresistibly she was attracted to him.

"All right, Livia, listen carefully. Imagine that you're head over heels in love with a man. And you think that he's yours, all yours, for all time. Then, all of a sudden, you witness something, a glance, a word: something that makes you think you could lose him, see him leave with another woman. What would you feel, what would you do?"

Maione looked curiously at Ricciardi. He immediately guessed that he wanted to reconstruct the situation Capece had been in at the theater. It wasn't a bad idea, he thought, to ask Livia: what they needed was a person from that milieu, that world of luxury where hunger was unknown, to understand how the journalist might have reacted in the face of the prospect of losing the woman he loved.

For her part, Livia felt her heart racing: at last, Ricciardi was speaking of love. Admittedly, this was hardly the ideal place for it: she might have hoped for a candlelit dinner, in a restaurant down by the water, for example. What's more, they were in the presence of a witness, that hairy brigadier with his peculiarities. All the same, he was talking about love, and perhaps he'd chosen that setting because it made him feel safer, less vulnerable. She smiled at him.

"I'd be willing to fight with every weapon at my disposal, for him. I'd fight with my whole being: I'd never declare a truce—never."

Ricciardi looked her in the eye.

"That is, if you had the time to think it over, of course. But then and there? If you realized that all that stood between you and happiness, between you and love, in other words, was another person? And if it occurred to you that, if you could only get rid of that person, you'd have your love back and no one could ever take him away again?"

There was a moment's silence. Maione was trying to imagine Capece that night, at the Salone Margherita, in the very instant that he slapped the duchess in front of everyone and then tore the ring from her finger. That scene spoke eloquently of a loss of control and a new determination: a new desperation.

For her part, Livia decided that Ricciardi wanted to understand what she was made of: whether her aristocratic and modern appearance concealed the strength and spontaneity of a woman of the south, the kind of women he was accustomed to. She didn't want to disappoint him, but as far as that went she knew that she had a fiery and passionate nature: and so she had no difficulty being sincere. She lowered her voice and narrowed her eyes slightly as she said:

"I imagine that I'd be capable of doing anything, for the man that I loved. Anything. Even the worst things imaginable. Even murder."

The word fell between then and made a tremendous noise. They sat there in silence, weighing Livia's phrase from differing points of view. After a few seconds, Ricciardi spoke to the brigadier:

"Maione, I'm going to have to ask you to go get changed, one more time. I need you to go someplace in civilian attire, and when you come back here I'll tell you where. To pick up a package."

Maione stood up, made a slight bow to Livia, and left the room. Ricciardi spoke to the woman:

"Thank you, Livia. You've helped me a great deal, you can't imagine how much. But now I have to go: I have urgent business to attend to, some very important things to take care of."

The woman sighed as she got to her feet.

"I get it, you're sending me away: as usual, for that matter. But don't think for a moment that I'm a woman who gives up easily. And it's not something that happens often, that I want to get to know someone better. So, once again, resign yourself to it: I'm not easy to get rid of."

Having said that, she left. Through the open door, Ricciardi caught sight of a lawyer who, craning his neck to see her better, tripped and fell in a cascade of files and documents.

XXXVIII

S ofia Capece decided that her husband would have to resign himself to it: she wasn't going to be easy to get rid of.

She'd gotten out of bed repeatedly during the night, to go watch him sleeping on the sofa in the drawing room. It wasn't like having him in her bed again, but she was a woman who knew how to wait: she'd already waited so long, she certainly wasn't frightened at the idea of the few days that still separated her from a return to normal life. Because that was one thing Sofia was sure of: it was only a matter of time.

Mario had been sleeping fitfully: she'd heard him murmur, toss and turn, and sigh. At a certain point, she'd even had the impression that he was weeping. To her way of thinking, this was a good sign: it meant that deep inside he was conflicted, that a battle was being fought within him, and that she, Sofia, was sure to emerge victorious. As far as that went, the other woman was dead. She no longer existed.

Truth be told, this was not the solution that she would have hoped for: all too often she'd dreamed that her husband, recovering from the spell under which he'd labored for so long, would return home on his own two feet, contrite, begging forgiveness for the wrong he had done her. In her imagination, she saw herself as accommodating, sweet and gentle as ever, happy to take him back into her home and her bed, to offer him that domestic warmth that he might have forgotten by now, a warmth he was surely beginning to miss, as reluctant as he might be to admit it. She was still, in spite of everything, his wife. She'd sworn before God that she'd love him and honor him for the rest of her days.

She smiled as she fluffed the cushion and placed it back on the sofa. Mario had left the apartment before dawn, she'd heard his footsteps on the stairs and then out on the street. But he'd be back, she could tell. And after all, where else would he go? This was his home, this was his family. Her son came over to her to give her a kiss and say goodbye, he was going to school for the summer preparatory course; he was a boy any father would be proud of, and Sofia decided that the boy resembled his father more every day. Just one more reason for the man to return home. She told him not to stay out too late, because his father might be home in time for lunch.

Because she had turned to go back to the kitchen, she failed to glimpse the grimace on Andrea's face. It was probably just as well, because the sight of all that hatred would only have frightened her.

Maione had found himself a place in the shadow of a doorway, right across from where the commissario had told him to go. The heat truly was infernal: inside, in the atrium, there wasn't a breath of air, while outside the sunlight was intolerable; so the brigadier, in civilian attire as his superior officer had ordered, had positioned himself right in front of the palazzo's street door. He was starting to suspect, however, that this location might be the worst possible combination of the shortcomings of the two others. He was fanning himself with his cap, occasionally wiping his forehead with his handkerchief, and every few minutes or so pulling out his pocket watch only to discover that time was passing exceptionally slowly; the heat was slowing him down too, he thought.

Just a few yards away stood an ice cream cart; evidently the vendor had decided that rather than taking up a position in the nearby Villa Nazionale, where competition was particularly fierce, he'd do well to try it here: before long, the street would be thronged with children, most of them belonging to well-to-do families; therefore, they had money in their pockets and they were very, very hungry.

Not that Maione was any less hungry than they were; at least a dozen times he'd reached into his pocket for his coin purse and the ten-cent price of a lovely ice cream cone, cool and delicious, which he knew he'd gobble down in an instant. Still, even if he was dressed in civilian garb, he was there to work and he needed to resist all distractions. What's more, every time he felt the pangs of hunger and thought about eating, a picture of the fruit and vegetable vendor Ciruzzo appeared before his eyes, thin as a needle, smiling broadly, and he could hear the voice of that idiot Lucia, remarking on what good shape he was in, even though he was the same age as Maione. What does that matter? he thought. You have the constitution you're born with. And after all, with my weight, I can always sit on him and crush him. He smiled at the thought.

He checked the time again: it wouldn't be long, he thought. He'd walked a long way, but he didn't mind: he felt like a man of action; sitting in drawing rooms questioning people wasn't something he wanted to do. He'd gone to a place near the Capece home, right where the commissario had told him: a small door in a blind alley, a dead-end *vicolo*, leading down into a dank, filthy cellar. He'd looked for a brick slightly out of place in the wall, finding it by touch, lighting matches in the darkness: he'd gotten his hands dirty, and then he'd rinsed them at a little spigot, splashing some water on his face as well. It had taken him some time, but he did find something, just as Ricciardi had said he would. He'd asked the commissario how he knew where it would be and he'd dodged the question; Maione suspected this had been another tidbit he'd picked up on his stroll through Fascist headquarters. And in fact, he was now waiting for a possible murderer to show up, and if nothing else, a person guilty of concealing evidence; under his sweaty arm he was holding a package wrapped in newspaper, containing a Beretta 7.65 pistol that in all likelihood had killed Duchess Adriana Musso di Camparino.

Ricciardi looked up from the form he was filling out and checked the clock: it was almost time. The early afternoon sun was beating down relentlessly and pedestrians were few and far between. From his office window came the screams of seagulls and, every so often, ship horns from the nearby harbor.

He thought that setting sail for somewhere else wouldn't be bad at all. Any ship would do, perhaps a freighter, with a distant destination. And a new life, new landscapes, new circumstances. And yet, he mused, a man like him had nowhere to flee. The dead speak the same language everywhere, dully repeating their last thoughts; and they would certainly befoul the air he breathed no matter where he went. He could run away from everything and everyone, but not from himself: that was his curse. Through the doorway, left open in hopes of a crossdraft, he could glimpse the dead thief. *I won't go back, I won't go back in there*, he repeated, like always. From the scorched bullet hole in his temple oozed blood and brains. You're going to persecute me forever, thought Ricciardi. Forever.

He sighed as he got to his feet; he had to go join Maione and his guest.

Rosa removed her hatpins and took off her hat, overheated but contented. She wasn't accustomed to being outside in the heat of the afternoon, especially during the month of August, but circumstances had demanded it.

She remembered that when the young master was just a little boy, back in the village, there was a group of hooligans his age who used to torment him; nothing dangerous, of course: they'd laugh when he went by, they'd lure him with offers of games and then abandon him, all alone, in the dark or out in the open countryside. Luigi Alfredo hated it, even if he never talked about it; she could only guess at his feelings from the sad gaze she saw on his face every time he came home after running into them. One day, she'd decided to take the initiative, facing off with the leader of the gang, a big strong boy who had no respect for anyone; at first she'd spoken to him courteously, but then, faced with the boy's mocking laughter, she'd been forced to put matters in physical terms, with a pair of resounding blows. After that, the young master had never been mocked again, but the boys had also sought his company far less often: perhaps the cure had been worse than the illness.

This time, however, it would be different: she wasn't planning to throw a scare into anyone, nor would she establish direct contact with the person who, intentionally or unintentionally, was making her boy suffer. She'd made use of the hairdresser, a necessary but dangerous intermediary: she hoped that she'd succeeded in purchasing the woman's discretion, even though the cash price had been unreasonably high. Still, news had come in punctually, and once again, it had been good news.

Enrica, the eldest daughter of the Colombo family, couldn't stand the man that her parents had been trying to match her up with: this was a well-known fact. She didn't have the slightest intention of seeing him again one-on-one, and she'd only socialize with him when she had no alternative: which was better still.

The big news that she'd learned in the hairdresser's kitchen just an hour ago, while a cookpot on the stove exuded a terrible miasma of onions and cauliflower and the temperature rose well above 120 degrees, was that just as Ricciardi looked at her, she too was looking at Ricciardi. Or perhaps she should say,

Enrica allowed herself to be watched as she embroidered with tenderness and trepidation. And this had been going on, Rosa learned to her astonishment, for more than a year, which explained why every night, as soon as he was done eating, the young master hastily retired to his bedroom. It hadn't been easy to pry this information out of the girl, the hairdresser had told Rosa, certainly in order to persuade her to a more generous tip. But Rosa believed that Signorina Colombo liked Commissario Ricciardi more than a little, and that it would be best if he hastened to introduce himself to the family, and wasted no time in doing so, before Signor Russo had a chance to make a formal request: also because the man wasn't at all bad-looking, according to the hairdresser who had met him one night on the stairs; apparently, he was rich, to boot.

It would therefore be up to Rosa to find some way of persuading the young master to make his move, instead of waiting in silence the way he usually did: but how could she do it, if he never let slip a word or confided in her? And then there was one other odd detail: the Colombo girl had mentioned a woman that she had seen with Ricciardi. A woman described as vulgar and not as young as she used to be, dressed in a garish, show-offy style: translating from the very particular jargon of hairdressers and girls in love, Rosa had guessed that the woman in question was beautiful and much sought-after, well dressed and very elegant. Who could this woman be? And most important of all, Rosa wondered, why, if he was seeing such a lady, was Luigi Alfredo so unmistakably unhappy?

Maione was sitting at a table at Gambrinus, sweating and waiting for Ricciardi. The person sitting across from him, and behind a glass of *spuma* that was gradually losing its foam, was making him feel slightly uncomfortable.

It rarely happened that the brigadier felt uneasy in the presence of a suspect: he was accustomed to challenging individuals who were guilty of all sorts of crimes; he'd spent his life on the street, and hunger and poverty had been the only school-teachers this man had ever had, and they'd made him the policeman he'd become. He'd seen everything and the opposite of everything. But he didn't know what to think, now, of young Andrea Capece.

He'd waited outside the school, and he'd seen him come out, identical in every way to all the other youngsters swarming in the summer sunlight, finally free of their everyday duties, heading off for a Saturday of fun and relaxation. The boy was walking next to a girl, who looked over at him as she talked and talked, her books bound together with a leather strap; once again, he had occasion to appreciate Ricciardi's sensitivity—the commissario had told him to go in civilian attire to spare the boy his classmates' gossip. He'd walked over to him, touching him lightly on the arm to catch his attention; the boy recognized him, and he took great care to observe exactly what went through the boy's eyes, what crossed his brow, in search of the usual signs of fear, the surprise of an animal caught in a trap; but he'd seen none of that.

Instead, he had seen the carefree smile give way to the signs of a profound sadness, age-old, grievous, the sadness you'd expect to see only in an adult; along with a flicker of something resembling pride. Not even a shadow of repentance, much less regret. The sad eyes had glided over the newspaper package, the shoulders had hunched over slightly under the weight of what would come next; he'd waved goodbye to the girl, and she had bowed to Maione, thinking him a family member, and then she'd walked off, the smile on her face never even fading.

They'd walked the whole distance in silence; the adult didn't know what to say, the boy simply didn't want to speak. They'd arrived at Gambrinus, as previously agreed with the commissario, and they'd taken a seat at one of the tables. Maione'd asked Andrea what he'd like, and the boy had shaken his head, with a doleful smile. The brigadier had then ordered a cup of coffee and a foamy *spuma*, but the young man never even tasted the drink. Now they were waiting for Ricciardi, who hadn't wanted to have Andrea brought to police headquarters.

Maione wasn't sure he wanted to be present during that interview, because he had a son the same age, now his eldest, after Luca's death. He thought there shouldn't be sadness in the eyes of a sixteen-year-old.

XXXIX

On Friday afternoons, the city ignores the heat; it ignores the cold, the rain, and the wind.

The city, on Friday afternoons, has no weather, or perhaps it'd be better to say, it has a special weather all its own. It's the weather of anticipation, two wonderful days when the brutal pace of work slows, when you can think about yourself and your own interests for a while, at last. Two days of seeing friends, attending mass, dancing. Two days of uniformed children doing calisthenics in the middle of the piazza, guided by lovely young ladies with megaphones; two days of children at summer camp marching in double file down to the beach, shaved bald to ward off lice, squinting in the dazzling sunlight of Mergellina. Two days of sunbaked *scugnizzi*—street urchins with a rag bound around their waist, tied with a length of rope or twine, bare feet deformed, soles as tough as shoe leather, recklessly hanging off trolley cars. Two days of gypsy girls reading your palm, or counterfeit monks offering lottery numbers. Two days of singing and music.

The city, on Friday afternoons, populates its streets with anticipation: it's far too wonderful and important to wait for Saturday together, no one wants to be shut up at home. Via Toledo fills with voices and noises, the watermelon vendor promising the cool fire of his merchandise, the strolling coffeeseller with his monumental wheeled *cuccuma*, the lemon man, his merchandise dangling from bobbing branches. And focaccias with fresh anchovies and raw shrimp, mussels, and octopus, pretty farm girls with a nanny goat on a rope and an iron pitcher to hold the goat's milk.

The city, on Friday afternoons, didn't want to know about poverty and hunger. In the *vicoli*, chickens peck through the garbage, while little processions of street urchins follow the *pazzariello*, sweating in his heavy uniform and twirling his baton, beating his drum and calling the crowds to attend the opening of some shop or other. The *comari* confide secrets by shouting them from one balcony to another, as they hang laundry on clotheslines that extend the few yards separating one apartment building from another. The *guappo* leaves for the evening, dressed in white suit and two-tone shoes, with a matching hat and two enforcers, his *sgherri*, following a few feet back; as he passes, men doff their hats and women bow, and after he's gone, they all spit on the pavement.

The city, on Friday afternoons, is accommodating and generous. Along the grand boulevard where the quality stroll bloom little match girls and fortune-tellers, blind men, both real and fake, victims of every deformity, holding out their hands, begging for charity and commiseration in the form of tossed coins. But if a pair of mounted policeman appear in their dress hats topped by tall plumes, the cripples and unfortunates are miraculously healed, scampering away down the *vicoli* on legs no longer bowed and twisted, effortlessly dragging behind them huge baskets of merchandise; only to return to their places minutes later, once the danger is past, lamenting their misfortunes even louder than before.

The city, on Friday afternoons, is preparing itself for love. The girls plan out what flowers they'll pin to their hats and their necklines, when they go for a stroll in the Villa Nazionale on Sunday morning or out dancing on Saturday afternoon. They'll need to decide well ahead of time, because their best dresses have to be pressed with a coal-heated clothes iron and they have to curl their hair, lest the most important meeting of a lifetime takes place this time and catches them unprepared. And the university students busily discuss the best place to meet up later, which club or theater will feature the most enchanting soubrette or the most scantily attired dancers, polishing their shoes as if they were rifles. The fathers and mothers eagerly anticipate their Saturday mornings, when their young children will be at meetings and rallies and they will be able to enjoy, in their one- or two-room apartments, an intimacy they've awaited all week; the *scugnizzi* know it all too well, and so they'll run from one floor to another in the apartment buildings of Naples's middle class, twisting doorbells to annoy and disturb: but no one comes to open the door.

The city, on Friday afternoons, wants to forget about blood. It has the good fortune of being unable to see ghostly figures crushed by horse-drawn carriages and automobiles, proclaiming with their bleeding mouths and collapsed lungs their desire to go on living another day, or even another minute. It is the city's luck that it is incapable of seeing knives protruding from red-stained shirts, necks shattered by clubs, uttering one last, gurgling appeal to the Madonna. It has the good luck not to see the unrecognizable corpses of workers who plummeted from wobbly scaffoldings, martyrs to the construction boom, calling out to their mammas to let them live longer than their fourteen years.

The city stops thinking about it all, on Friday afternoons. Because tomorrow is Saturday.

Ricciardi was walking toward Gambrinus, enjoying the sights of both Via Toledo and Friday afternoon. He felt sure that the conversation he was about to have with Capece's son would give him the evidence he needed to solve the duchess's murder. As he strolled through the crowd, his hands in his pockets and his eyes on the ground, he thought about himself, too, and the way he'd come to know certain emotions that, until just a few weeks ago, had been completely alien to him.

Garzo, the deputy chief of police who never seemed to miss a chance to show off his limitations, used to express a concept that Ricciardi had always found particularly inane: if you want to understand the way a criminal thinks, you must, to some extent, be able to think like him; in other words, you have to be a criminal yourself, at least to some extent.

Now, in the light of these new events, the commissario came back to this idea with some concern: both because he'd seen with lucid clarity who had killed the Duchess of Camparino and because he was no doubt infected with the same disease that had triggered that murder: jealousy. Let's call a spade a spade, he thought, as he brushed past a beggar's extended hand. I've encountered a new perversion, yet another corruption of love that leads to death and to murder. And now that I've encountered it myself, I can clearly recognize it.

Love, the worst enemy to have, often traveled twisted paths: but jealousy flew straight as an arrow. Like hunger, the other great mother of crimes, it was unpredictable and violent; but it had very different roots, sunk into the soul of selfishness and possession. And jealousy also knew how to be patient.

He found Maione and Andrea sitting inside, in silence. The boy was staring into empty air, lost in thought; the policeman was staring at the door, anxiously awaiting the commissario's arrival, which would put an end to his uncomfortable vigil. It was no easy thing to be guarding such a young suspect, and to make things worse he was in civilian garb, and the location was hardly the usual police holding tank. Sitting on the table between them, like the clinching point in an argument, was the newspaper-wrapped package.

Ricciardi sat down and ordered an espresso. Andrea neither looked up nor said hello. Maione started to snap a military salute, then he remembered that he wasn't in uniform and simply waved his hand, lamely.

"Commissa', it was all exactly as you said. The pistol was

behind a brick, in the cellar wall. It's clean, and it looks like it was recently used. The youngster, here, was at school; he came along without objecting."

Without raising his eyes, Andrea said:

"So you were keeping us under surveillance. Even before you came to our apartment, you were keeping us under surveillance."

The tone in which he spoke was that of a simple statement: there was no moral judgment, no reproof. Nor was there an admission of guilt. Ricciardi set the record straight:

"No, we weren't watching you. We received a report from others. This is a city where nobody minds their own business, you should certainly know that by now. In any case, it doesn't matter how we found out: what matters is that you hid your father's pistol. Why did you do that?"

Andrea finally looked the commissario in the face, with a shrug.

"Just because. Because I felt like it, because it made a big impression on my friends. I'm a boy, right? It's the kind of thing boys do."

Sad, pained eyes. Ricciardi decided that those eyes hadn't been a young boy's eyes for years. The theft of childhood and youth is not yet a criminal offense, he mused. But it ought to be.

"Listen: this is no time for games. Not anymore. This is a very serious matter. It will take our forensics experts five minutes, tops, maybe less, to prove that this pistol ejected the shell that we found on the scene of the murder, and that it therefore fired the bullet that killed the duchess. So let me urge you, let's not waste time."

Andrea went on staring at the commissario, expressionless, his jaws clamped tight. A knot of young girls went past their table, laughing loudly. Ricciardi softened his tone of voice.

"I understand you. Whatever reason you may have had to hide that pistol, you did it to save your family, or what's left of it. You can see for yourself, we didn't come to get you in uniform, we didn't take you down to police headquarters. But if it becomes necessary, we will: because a murder's a murder, and whoever the victim might be . . ."

The boy leaned forward, turning pale and compressing his lips. His face had taken on the feral rage of a cornered animal, forced to attack in self-defense. His voice was a hiss.

"Whoever the victim, you say. But do you know who she really was, your poor pitiful murder victim? She was someone who took away the happiness of an entire family just to satisfy a whim. Now you see him crying like a baby. But do you know that that man—yes, that man: I will never again consider him to be my father—hasn't come home in months? Yes, I know what my mother told you. But she's lost her mind, and that's just one more piece of fun that the signora, her ladyship, decided to have with us. Now she's dead. Because she needed to die. And that's all."

Once he was done talking, he slumped back into his chair and stared down at the tabletop again. Maione wondered whether he'd really seen and heard it, so sudden had the metamorphosis been. Ricciardi went on, in a harsher tone of voice:

"You can think whatever you like. But we want to know who shot the duchess; and the fact that you hid the pistol tells us beyond the shadow of a doubt that you know."

A long silence ensued. All around them, the crowd was beginning to swell, the Friday night strollers were reaching some kind of crescendo. The shops were nearly all still open and the ladies with their big fans were lingering before the display windows, commenting on the prices and models of dresses and hats. At last, Andrea spoke.

"It was me. I couldn't take my mother's madness any longer, her sobbing. I couldn't take the shame that my father had heaped on us; the fact that everyone knew, even at school. I couldn't stand the fact that my little sister still loved him, after what he'd done."

Another silence. Ricciardi stared at the boy, taking in the harsh glare, the clamped lips. Maione, as always, seemed to be half-asleep; after a while, it was Maione who broke in.

"So, you waited for school to be over and you went to the palazzo, is that it? And you went all the way into the bedroom, where you shot the duchess, who was still sleeping. Four shots, you fired; and then you took to your heels."

The boy nodded, still staring into the middle distance. Ricciardi shot the brigadier a rapid glance, encouraging him to go on.

"So explain this to me, how did you manage to get away? Why didn't anyone see you?"

The boy answered in a firm voice, as if he were talking about what he'd done at school that morning:

"There was no one there. Maybe the doorman was at lunch. The front door was wide open, it was hot out, and at that time of day there was no one walking in the street."

Maione shook his head, sadly.

"*Guagliò*—youngster—the duchess wasn't killed during the day; and only one shot was fired. She wasn't killed in the bedroom, either. None of this was in the newspaper, and for once we owe a debt of gratitude to those who decided to eliminate crime reporting. No, it wasn't you."

Andrea's expression remained unchanged, as if he hadn't heard a word. But one tear did suddenly course down his cheek. Frustration, thought Ricciardi.

"What can I tell you? I could insist, say that I got my facts backwards. I'm sixteen years old, the punishment would be a slap on the wrist, wouldn't it? But then I'd get tripped up again, and again: because I wasn't there, when the bitch was murdered. So I have to admit it. It was him. It was my father."

Maione settled back in his chair. At last, the case was solved: for once the murderer was the prime suspect. He turned to look at Ricciardi and recognized his expression; he immediately realized that he hadn't understood a thing.

"No. It wasn't him. We have an alibi for him, we know where he was at the time of the murder. And we even know who it really was: who you're protecting. But we need to hear you say it. To keep you from being implicated in any of this, to make sure you come out of this story free of guilt, to make sure we can forget the fact that you hid the pistol. And also to make sure that you understand clearly that a murder is a murder: even when the murderer is perhaps more innocent than the victim. Who was it?"

In the cheerful din of Friday, as the afternoon slowly faded into the evening and Via Chiaia filled up with noise and hopes, Andrea's face resumed its age and dissolved into grief and uncontrolled sobbing. Through his tears he looked at Ricciardi and said:

"Can't you see what she's been through? Don't you see that the pain and grief have driven her insane? That she doesn't know what she's doing and she never will, my poor mamma?"

XL

Prego, Commissario, come right on in. Have a seat, Brigadier: right here, get comfortable on the sofa. Let me shine a little light in here, I'll open the curtains, the days are starting to get a little shorter; but it's still hot out, eh? Such terrible heat, you can't even breathe.

Can I offer you something? And the two policemen outside, can't they come in? Do they have to stay by the door? You know, we don't entertain as much as we used to. There was a time when this apartment was like a seaport; my husband was a hub for culture and politics. If you'd seen the prominent personalities who came to see us, you would have been astonished. The children were little, perhaps they don't even remember the comings and goings, the hubbub and bustle, right, Andrea, Mamma's little treasure? I was never done making coffee, tea, cookies, and *biscottini*. Never once did he call ahead, my husband. But I never complained, in fact, I was proud of this man that everyone wanted to know.

Have you met him, my husband? Ah, of course, you were here with him just the other day. He's a little depressed now, but you'll see, he'll be as good as new before long. Because now he's back in his place, back where he belongs. You see, Commissario, I think that everyone has their own place: and they can only be happy when they're in their place. Any other place leaves them feeling incomplete and, therefore, unhappy. My husband always used to tell me: Sofia, you are my wisdom. Because Sofia means wisdom, in ancient Greek: *Sophia*. Did you know that? That's what he used to say to me. Before. What I mean to say is, before Adriana.

Really, you don't want a thing? An espresso? You shouldn't think that I simply accepted it at first, the thing with Adriana. In fact, the first year I was miserable. How I suffered! Like a dog, the way that any woman feels when she loses her man. I fought, of course, what else would I do? At first, I was horrible, I'd make a scene every night, broken dishes, him with his head down, saying nothing. Then I tried using honey, I did my best to lure him back, you must know how a wife would try to lure back a husband, I can't explain it to you right now, with the youngster listening, but you're men and you know what I'm talking about.

And I started cooking all the things that he loved best; but he never came home for dinner, he never came home. If you only knew how many kilos of the finest food I was forced to throw away, the stray dogs in the neighborhood were feasting like kings. Here I was, night after night, sitting at the kitchen table and wondering, why, what had I done?

But I hadn't done a thing, Commissario, not a thing. I'd stayed here, in my place, in my apartment, with my children, waiting for my man to come home. I hadn't done anything. You can't imagine what happens to an abandoned woman as she waits. It's as if she's come down with some contagious disease. Everyone, friends, girlfriends, relatives—they look at you pityingly, then they try to open your eyes, then one by one they move away, avoiding you as if your sores and wounds disgusted them. And you're left alone, with no one but yourself, trying to find a reason why, a reason that doesn't exist.

The first time was a year and eight months ago. I remember it like it was yesterday—it was raining. One night, after the children were all asleep, I got dressed and went out. It just came over me, I threw on some old thing and I went out, into the pouring rain. I went and stood outside the theater, where I knew they'd be. You know, Brigadier, it's as if I'd become invisible. Like an angel. If you ask me, the Madonna, and I talk to Her every day, gave me this gift, that I can go unseen. When I want, I dress in dark clothes, I go places, and no one notices me at all. And so I'm free to watch, observe, look, all without being noticed.

That night I saw them, I was telling you. They came out the door, laughing, they'd been to see some comedy. She was beautiful: as far as that goes, Commissario, I have to say that Adriana really was beautiful. She was elegant, self-confident: how many men could have resisted her? And he was looking at her.

For me, it was a real discovery: he'd never looked at me that way, not even remotely. Lord knows, my husband loves me, absolutely; but he'd never looked at me that way—never. He was just rapt, as if he were gazing at the sun. She laughed and he was gazing at the sun.

After that night I followed them, every evening. I'd feed the children, give them dinner, and then wait for them to fall asleep: I'm their mamma, my place is to be close to them if they need anything. But then I'd go out and tag along behind them, the two of them, living their lives for a little while, watching them live. It didn't matter, I was invisible. They were beautiful and happy, the whole city revolved around them. Everyone looked at them, everyone envied them. But they loved each other, and they were happy, and I was happy too because I thought that, a little bit, I deserved credit for the fact that the two of them could be together like that. Because certain kinds of happiness are complete only if they can remain in the shadows; because it's everyday life that kills happiness.

I must have followed them a hundred times, the two of them went everywhere. I saw that my husband was happy, in a way I'd never seen before.

Then she started getting tired of him.

He didn't notice. Men are such fools, no offense, Commissario. But a woman is more diabolical, she notices. And I noticed. She started looking around, when he was distracted because he was talking with someone or saying hello, the minute he stepped away for a moment, she would smile, and wink, and take someone into her confidence. She was one of those women who liked having men like her. She attracted attention, she sent signals.

The first time that she cheated on him was seven months ago. He'd stayed at the newspaper, he had to work up a full page on the visit of the Prince of Venice or some other member of the royal family, and she went out all the same, and then she took some man home. I waited out in the street until I saw him leave, practically at dawn. And then there was another, and another still, and the pace was accelerating. Common folk, nobodies. She'd go find them in another part of town, outside of her part of the city; she wanted to make sure that Mario could never find out about them.

Where she lived, well, as you've seen: nobody cared what she did. Everyone minds their own business, in that palazzo, and everyone's careful not to step on anybody else's toes. The duke never left his bed. I asked the Madonna to gather him to Her quickly, poor man, how he suffers. The duke's son, every so often a big black car comes and picks him up, and he spends the night away from home. Who knows where he goes. The servants, they only care about a few things: holding on to their jobs and their privileges, that silly doorman with his children who do nothing but eat, the housekeeper who thinks about nothing but the duke and his son.

So I'd see her with these other men during the times of day when my husband was at work, at the newspaper. But if you ask me, Commissario, she wasn't an evil woman. It's just the way she was: she liked men. And as long as those men knew enough to stay in their place, my husband was safe and I was happy. It was my job to keep an eye on him, remember? I told you before. That's my job, the Madonna told me that I'm an angel, my husband's guardian angel.

But then, one night, I noticed something odd: she sent word to Mario that she wouldn't be going out, because she didn't feel well; I know that because I asked the florist when he brought a bouquet of roses to the building, my husband is so thoughtful, if you only knew the flowers he sent me when Andrea, mamma's little darling, was born. But instead she went out, she went to the theater with a young man. This was ten days ago. A good-looking young man, not much older than a boy, someone I'd seen escorting the occasional rich old woman to parties, when I was standing watch.

And so I started to worry. You know, it's one thing with a fisherman, it's quite another thing with a young man from a good family, a young man in a tuxedo who comes from the same social circles. And in fact, even my husband—who is a man, and men never see things until they've smacked their noses right up against them, again, forgive me, Commissario—sensed something and caused a scene. I was there, hiding behind the coat check, I told you, I'm invisible and no one ever notices me. And he even took my ring away from her, the ring he'd taken from me when he fell in love with her. And he slapped her in the face, in public.

That's not right, Brigadier; that's not right, hitting a woman. That's not typical of him. It must mean that he was suffering, that he was suffering terribly. And I, his guardian angel, couldn't let that happen.

He went off, who knows where, to get drunk; but I followed her. I waited for the play to be over, sitting in a seat in the gallery, surrounded by people who stamped their feet, whistled, and applauded, and I never once looked at the stage. I was watching Adriana, who was smiling and whispering and even blowing kisses. And the young man was responding the whole time, because after all the old woman who was with him was fast asleep, head back, mouth open. They met after he accompanied the old woman home; he caught up with her in a restaurant in the Galleria, the two of them dined alone. No one saw them, but someone could have: and my husband, what kind of a fool would that have made him look? You tell me, a man like him, a respected professional, well known throughout the city, would have become a laughing stock. And for what? For an infatuation. Because I'm sure of one thing, Commissario: once she'd scratched that itch, she could not have done anything but go back to him. He's too handsome, my husband: too important and too cultivated.

So I decided that it was time for me to do something. The angel has to intervene, and mete out justice. I ran home and got Mario's pistol. My father was an officer in the army, you know, Brigadier. I know how to clean and load weapons, my father used to let me do it when I was a little girl, sitting in his arms. And I keep my house clean and orderly, so I kept the pistol clean and properly oiled.

I certainly never meant to kill her. I only wanted to scare her, I wanted to make her understand that she had the immense good luck to have a wonderful man and that she couldn't make him unhappy. It was an important thing, you know, Commissario: he might even have done something stupid, if he found that Adriana had a lover. He might have strangled her and ruined his career, or even worse, he could have shot himself in the head. I couldn't let him do it.

And so I went. I walked through the festival of Santa Maria Regina, you tell me whether the Madonna, on Her own feast day, was likely to leave me to my own devices. Like an angel I passed through and no one even saw me. I hid in the courtyard until I saw her come home. I know the routines in the palazzo very well, I know that she opens the gate, goes inside, and then comes back out to lock up. I waited a while, to make sure that everything was quiet, and then I went in.

And this is where the odd thing happened, Commissario. I just wanted to talk to her. I wanted to explain that what she was doing was sheer folly, and I'd only brought the pistol along to frighten her, perhaps to threaten her: maybe if I could scare her enough, she'd go back to my husband and stop betraying him, so that I could see him once again with those happy eyes I used to see, those sparkling eyes I could never forget. But instead I saw her there, in the shadows, stretched out on the sofa, and I heard her breathing heavily, as if she were snoring. She was tired from the night she'd spent with that other man, maybe she was even drunk. She hadn't even made it to her own bed.

That's when the blood went to my head, Commissario. How dare she betray my husband like that? How dare she pile up and burn the happiness of a man like him, the finest, the handsomest of all the men on this earth?

At that instant, the Madonna told me that I was an angel, but that I'd been sent to bring justice. That I was the angel of death. I picked up the cushion that was lying on the floor, and I placed it on her face, and I fired. A single shot. And she stopped snoring.

And so I went home, because everyone has a place, Commissario. And a mother's place is with her children, who are sleeping peacefully because they're angels too, and you don't need the Madonna to tell you so. When you came to see me the other day, I told you the truth, because I never lie: I told you that it wasn't my husband, and in fact it wasn't. And I told you that I didn't know where the pistol was, that someone had taken it. And in fact, Andrea had taken it, mamma's little treasure, and he'd done it to protect me.

But there was no need, my treasure: because your mamma has the Madonna to protect her, and the Madonna told her exactly what she was to do.

But really, are you sure that I can't offer you anything to eat or drink? A drop of liqueur, a little homemade *rosolio*, perhaps?

XLI

They hadn't felt up to taking Sofia Capece down to police headquarters; they'd sent Camarda and Cesarano with a car, after taking careful note of the woman's unruffled composure: they decided there was no reason to fear irrational behavior from her.

Then they'd called Capece at the newspaper, alerting him to what had happened and suggesting he go home to take care of his children. On the other end of the line, the man remained silent for a long time, and then in a broken voice he had assured them that he'd return home as soon as possible: it seemed to Ricciardi that he wasn't surprised, just mortally weary. The months that lay ahead wouldn't be easy.

On the way back, Maione remained silent, lost in his own thoughts. Abruptly, he said:

"Commissa', is it really true that Sofia means 'wisdom' in Greek?"

Ricciardi nodded. The brigadier shook his head, mopping the sweat with his handkerchief.

"That's crazy. Just try telling me that everyone's name points to their destiny. If I've ever seen a raving lunatic it's Signora Capece, and her first name is Wisdom."

"Grief and pain can make people lose their minds. Haven't you seen it happen a thousand times? The poor Capece woman, beaten down by suffering and loneliness, abandoned to care for her two children, and held up to ridicule and shame, lost her mind. Understandable, it strikes me."

"Still, Commissa', you have to satisfy my curiosity on one point: when the boy, Andrea, told us that it was his father who committed the murder, why didn't you believe him? After all, the man didn't really have an alibi, and we know that very well. Couldn't it actually have been him?"

Ricciardi looked down and walked a little faster; they were passing the site of the car crash, and he didn't want to see the child nailed to the seat by a sharp piece of shattered windshield. He couldn't help sensing the boy on his flesh and in his brain, saying: "*Gelato at the Villa Nazionale, Papà promised me, a nice cup of gelato.*"

"No: the boy hates his father, everything points to the fact: the way he looks at him, the things he says. He wouldn't have lifted a finger to save him. In fact, if he'd had the time to do things right, he would have orchestrated all the evidence to put the blame on his father: he's an intelligent boy. Now the hardest task before Capece is trying to win back, if not his son's love, at least his son's tolerance. For his own good, and for the good of the boy as well as his sister."

Maione smiled wearily.

"Eh, very true, Commissa'. Poor Signora Capece got one thing right: everyone belongs in their place. And right now Mario Capece's place is with his family, and without distractions. And after all, I believe that, with a good lawyer, the signora won't have to spend long in an asylum for the criminally insane. It's still a crime of passion, isn't it? After all, the woman she killed was her husband's lover."

Ricciardi sighed.

"Yes, but for reasons that were completely different from what we had imagined. At least, from what I had imagined. If I live to be a hundred, I'll never understand the paths that love takes to harvest its victims. It tricks me every time. Listen, why don't you go ahead on home. Nothing else is going to happen tonight. We can take care of the reports tomorrow. I have a place to go, and then I'm heading home. Have a good evening."

He couldn't say just why his mind had turned to Don Pierino. Perhaps all the references that Sofia Capece had made to the Madonna, or else the sadness in Andrea's eyes; or his compassion for Mario himself, the twice-heartbroken journalist who would never be able to escape the fact that his wife was in an insane asylum, and the woman he loved was dead, and it had been his fault.

Perhaps it was because he wanted to hear the priest tell him that there *is* such a thing as a love without folly, a love without violence; and pretend to believe it, for once.

The church was deserted and shrouded in shadows, illuminated only by the candles that glowed before the altars: people who had requested the granting of a grace, offering in exchange another little bit of pain. He spotted the little priest at the far end of the aisle, seated on a front-row pew and reading a book with his eyeglasses perched on the tip of his nose. He walked up the aisle and sat down next to the man. Without lifting his eyes from the page but with a smile on his lips, Don Pierino whispered:

"Here's the ghost of the church of San Ferdinando again: the ghost that appears soundlessly and then vanishes for months on end. How are we doing, Commissario? What's happened this time?"

Ricciardi replied, whispering in turn:

"Nothing, Father. This time, nothing. We've identified the murderer, that's all. And as always, instead of making me happy, it just leaves a void inside me."

Don Pierino closed the book and, after folding his glasses, he put them away in a pocket in his tunic.

"Talk to me about it, Commissario. Tell me everything."

And Ricciardi told him. In the acrid scent of incense, as the shadows grew longer and the church remained dark, clustered around its candles, as the noises from the street grew muffled and the evening grew late, Ricciardi talked. And he told him about Sofia's madness, Mario's desperate love, Andrea's infinite sadness; but also about the desolate and illicit love affair between Ettore and Achille, the loneliness of the Duke of Camparino, the bovine devotion that his housekeeper felt for him. And without realizing it, he found himself talking about himself as well, about the evening he spent with Livia and the four Fascists; his jealousy, his discovery of the infected egotism of his solitude. He also talked about Enrica, and what an endless distance five yards can be, when it is the distance separating his window from hers. And how much he missed watching her embroider.

He couldn't believe his own ears as he listened to himself tell a priest, almost a perfect stranger, about the abyss in his soul. He stopped just short of the brink, before he told the man about the dead people who infested his solitary existence.

Don Pierino's gaze was focused unwaveringly upon him, and the expression on his face betrayed no emotion: if he'd sensed the priest's pity, he would have stopped. But now the little man said: "What a terrible jailer you are to yourself. I'd like to ask you to give yourself peace, but I can't. No one can do that. But I do want to tell you one thing: there is no redemption without grief and pain. You can only free yourself if you know that you're in chains. That awareness is the first step."

They sat in silence for a long time: a small portly priest, with dark eyes that glowed, and a policeman on the verge of despair, whose transparent green eyes seemed incapable of formulating questions for his answers. Then Ricciardi shook himself and said:

"That's not why I came, Father. I didn't come to bore you by talking about myself. Forget I did it, please. I'm here for another reason: I believe that the next few months are going to be terrible for the Capece family. The father isn't used to being with the children, and the son has some very serious reasons to feel resentment toward his father. I urge you, therefore, to stay in touch with them. You're the only person I know who can do it. I'm going to ask you as a personal favor."

Don Pierino sighed and said nothing. Then, with a smile, he said: "Rest assured, Commissario. That's my job: I thank you for bringing this to my attention. But I have something to ask you in return. And you can't tell me no."

Ricciardi looked at him quizzically.

"Ask away, Father. I've piled up a considerable debt of gratitude with you: if for no other reason than the talk I've forced you to listen to tonight."

"Actually the chat we've had tonight is the nicest gift you could have offered me. And I'll be interested to learn the upshot: neighborhood priests are curious. But what I want to ask you is something else. Do you know about the 'Nzegna festival?"

Ricciardi shook his head no.

"The 'Nzegna festival isn't a religious thing. It's held in the Borgo di Santa Lucia; it's a folk festival, and it has some truly enjoyable traditions around it. But it does begin with a religious celebration, because there's a commemoration of the finding of the Madonna della Catena, Our Lady of the Chain, an ancient painting that is kept in a church that bears the same name, a church that is of course in the quarter of Santa Lucia. It's next Sunday, at midday. This year, the ceremony will be officiated by yours truly, and in fact I've just finished preparing my sermon. I would be happy if you attended."

Ricciardi decided that he really couldn't turn down a request from that man, especially considering that he'd just asked him to look after the Capece family. Or what was left of it.

"All right, Father. I'm not working this Sunday, because I worked on Sunday last week. I'll be there."

The priest clapped his hands in delight.

"Oh. Bravo, Commissario. That's the way I like you! There will be lots of people and lots of singing and dancing: for once, you can enjoy a party. And one more thing: remember that there is something worse than remorse, and that's regret. Let me tell you, because every day, from dawn to dusk, I listen to people in confession asking God for a forgiveness they can't seem to give themselves. If it's necessary to take the initiative for once in your life, do it now. So that you don't spend all the years left to you on earth wondering what would have happened if you'd just had a little more courage."

Ricciardi got to his feet; he seemed to be about to answer, but then his mouth snapped shut. He said:

"You don't know the whole story, Father. There are other considerations, other . . . motives that prevent me from taking certain initiatives. Let it be; I already told you, forget about the raving I've done this evening. Maybe I'm just tired; this hasn't been a simple investigation. See you on Sunday, then."

XLII

When Ricciardi arrived in police headquarters the following morning, he was ready to take on the sensation he felt every time he wrapped up a murder investigation: a mixture of nostalgia, disappointment, and anger.

Nostalgia was the most absurd sentiment of the three: to some extent the commissario missed thinking about the investigation. It was always something of an obsession, something that was ongoing no matter what else he might do during the course of the day; his mind was working incessantly on the solution of the crime, and when this constant thought vanished, he missed it. It was as if a room cluttered with one enormous piece of furniture were suddenly emptied, revealing itself to be drab and deserted, just like before.

The disappointment came from the experience of once again looking out on the inferno of the human soul and the corruption of the passions: the same as before, nothing new.

Last of all, the anger came from the forced realization, yet again, of the pointlessness of what he was doing: in fact, what had he achieved by discovering that Sofia Capece had killed Adriana Musso di Camparino? He had merely ensured that now two children would have a mother locked up in a criminal mental asylum, while the duchess remained dead.

Sometimes, he thought, as he wrote up the report of the murderess's confession, the solution is much worse than the problem. And there's never a solution for the solution. By a process of mental association, the figure of the victim appeared before him, as he was condemned to see her.

This is how it always was: the following day he faced his reckoning with the Deed. Aside from confessions and evidence, proof and details, the Deed itself presented its invoice to his soul and demanded attention. He glimpsed Adriana again, beautiful and proud even as a corpse, with the bullet hole between her eyes, her arms hanging limp at her sides. And the phrase, repeated obsessively:

"*The ring, the ring, you've taken the ring, the ring is missing.*"

And so, in the end, the contest between the two dueling rings had gone to the one that Capece had torn off her ring finger at the theater. It was clear: the duchess had recognized Sofia right before dying and her mind had begun to establish a link with the object that had once belonged to her killer; before the bullet tore through her brain and put an end to this and any other thought.

And yet, Ricciardi mused, someone had torn the other ring off the now-dead duchess's finger; and Modo's autopsy mentioned signs of violence on her body, as if there had been a struggle that Sofia Capece had said nothing about. True: the woman was insane, and it might well be that the gunshot had come in the wake of a fight. Perhaps the madwoman simply forgot that part after emerging victorious, or maybe she chose not to say anything about it.

After lightly rapping, Maione opened the door and came in.

"Good morning, Commissa'. How are we doing, this fine day? That's some heat we've got, eh? Are you writing the report on the confession?"

Ricciardi greeted the brigadier with a nod of the head.

"Yes, I'm writing it. And the more I think about it, the sadder it seems to me for those two kids, who didn't used to have a father and now don't have a mother either."

Maione shrugged.

"Eh, I know it, it's a sad thing. You're right. But on the other hand, someone killed her: the duchess. And at a certain point I was afraid that it might well have been the boy, Andrea."

Sure, thought Ricciardi: Andrea. He was a strong, powerful young man, and he could certainly have helped his mother in what she did at Palazzo Camparino. And then the woman could have covered up for him, or even forgotten that he was there too. It was very possible.

Just as he was about to answer Maione, the door swung open and a euphoric and highly scented Garzo made his entrance, followed by Ponte who took turns looking at the floor and the ceiling.

"Ricciardi, bravo, *bravissimo*, a thousand times bravo! You were brilliant, I have to say it: truly brilliant. And bravo to you too, Maione."

Ricciardi looked at the deputy chief of police with his pen still in his hand, dripping ink onto the report.

"And why do you say that, Dottore? Brilliant seems like a strong word, I don't think I've done anything remarkable."

Garzo had no intention of letting his enthusiasm subside one inch:

"Brilliant is what I said and brilliant is what I meant! You have no idea how worried we were, the chief of police and I. We were afraid it would turn out that the murderer of the duchess of Musso di Camparino was actually a member of her family, one of the most important families in the city; perhaps even the son, Heaven forefend, who I hear has friends in very high places that . . . well, enough said. Or else it could have been Capece, a prolific and indiscreet journalist who might even be a dissident, and then we would have been attacked by his fellow journalists, who are just champing at the bit. But instead, who do you nail for the murder? His wife! Which means he has to shut up and take it, and all his friends and colleagues can't do anything else but pity him, while the Camparino family emerges scot-free. Bravo, Ricciardi! Once again, we're proud of you!"

Maione emitted a faint hiss, like a steam boiler whose pressure was too high. Ricciardi replied coldly:

"I'm pleased to hear how happy it makes you, Dottore, that one woman is dead and that another, the mother of two childen and a faithful, loving wife, will be confined to a criminal asylum, possibly for the rest of her life. I'm pleased that it turns out to be a relief, for you, that two families have been ruined forever, and that shame will blot their names for many years to come. And I'm sorry to inform you that it wasn't us who crafted this solution, but merely the demon of a corrupt and desperate passion."

A profound silence followed the commissario's words. Through the open window came the sound of a departing ship's horn. Ponte had turned practically purple and was staring in fascination at a patch of peeling plaster on the wall. Garzo swallowed and turned to Maione, with an air of complicity:

"Always modest, eh, our man Ricciardi. Always refusing to take credit for a brilliant solution. Of course, it's a pity that people die, and that there are still murderers, even in these times when we ought to be focusing on the luminous future that awaits us. Luckily for everyone, we're here, taking care of things; we find the guilty parties and put them behind bars. You, too, Maione, you did a beautiful job. If you come to my office and you give me the details of what happened, I'm pretty sure that I'll be able to arrange for you to receive a generous bonus."

Diplomacy was not one of Maione's gifts; his face seemed to be a billboard for disgust.

"No, Dotto', forgive me but I've got something urgent to do."

"And what would that be?" asked Garzo.

"I have no idea," Maione replied, "but it must be urgent, whatever it is. With your permission, I'll be going."

And he left the room, touching his fingertips to the visor of his cap. Garzo, pigeon-chested and all smiles, turned and spoke once again to Ricciardi, who hadn't moved in the meantime:

"All right, Ricciardi, I'll be expecting that report. Again, congratulations, and on to bigger and better things. Come along, Ponte: we have a thousand things to do."

Ricciardi's sense of unease, increased considerably by the visit from the deputy chief of police, led him to go out into the street even before lunchtime. Pensive and unhappy, he found himself in front of the hospital, just as Doctor Modo was heading out for a bite to eat.

"There you go, the story of my life. All my colleagues are greeted at the front gate by lovely women, either enchanting girlfriends or loving wives. And here I am, awaited by you: a melancholy policeman, and ugly, to boot."

"Stop complaining, Bruno: I don't recall having to stand in line to buy you lunch."

Modo tipped his hat to the back of his head and mopped his brow with his handkerchief.

"Better alone than in bad company. In any case, I swore an oath to fight suffering, and as far as I can tell you're the unrivaled champion of misery; and so, though it's with a heavy heart, I'm going to take you up on your offer. After all, you're a wealthy man, and I'm just a penniless medical examiner. Where are you taking me for lunch?"

At the trattoria the doctor, as usual, ate for two; Ricciardi on the other hand, toyed listlessly with a forkful of pasta, responding monosyllabically to his friend's efforts to draw him out in a conversation. His chosen topic, needless to say, was politics.

"Do you have any idea how low we've sunk? I find this young man in my waiting room, a student, as far as I could tell, glasses, clean but shabby clothing, the elbows of his jacket looked as thin and delicate as onionskin paper. A Calabrian, perhaps, or maybe from Lucania, I can never tell them apart. But a respectable polite young man. You know the kind, put themselves through school by working on the side, and even send a little extra money home. So I find him sitting in the waiting room, he hadn't made a sound, patiently pressing a handkerchief against his forehead. So I say to him, yes, young man, how can I help? And he shows me a five-inch cut. Probably a knife wound, and they came this close to taking his eye out, just a hair to the left and he'd have been blind in one eye. I asked him, son, who did this to you? And he said: I fell and cut myself. He fell, my foot! There'd been a meeting of freethinkers, socialists, maybe, and those guys showed up, a squad of enforcers, probably ten of them. He'd been a straggler when everyone took to their heels. Getting the story out of him was like pulling teeth. But in the end, do you know what he said? Doctor, I'll let you stitch up the cut only if you promise not to tell a soul. What kind of filthy world has this turned into? Can you answer me that?"

Ricciardi sadly shook his head.

"Bruno, I know that things aren't going particularly well. Believe me: I've experienced it personally. But you're important, for all the people you help and you protect. For once in your life, let me try to protect you, by asking you to take care. That's right, I'm asking you—I'm begging you—to be careful what you say, especially in public places. Don't ask me how I know, but I do: there are people keeping an eye on you. And if they locked you up, even if it would mean not having to look at your ugly face anymore, it would be a serious loss for everyone."

Modo slammed his fist down on the table, making the silverware dance. Heads turned to look at them.

"What's this, you too now? You're starting to talk like them? Who did you talk to about me, if I may ask? Don't I at least have the right to know my enemies?"

Ricciardi laid a hand on his arm, whispering: "There, you see: they're watching us. These are exactly the kind of situations to avoid. During the course of the investigation into the duchess's murder, you remember, your last autopsy, I had to question a person. A man who works for their secret police, to be exact: even if I find it repellent to dignify them with the name of police. Still, he wasn't a bad person, at least, that was the impression I got. And he told me to give you some advice: try to stay out of trouble. Now I've done it, at my own risk and danger. Don't make me regret it."

Modo considered the matter and calmed down, just as Ricciardi had expected. He wouldn't risk his friend's life just to make a point. Plus, it warmed his heart to think that someone like the commissario actually worried about him.

"Fine, you've talked me into it. I'll try to be more careful. By the way, I hear that you caught the duchess's murderer, or perhaps I should say, her murderess, the wife of that journalist, what's his name . . ."

"Capece, that's right. But I wanted to talk to you about that, too. Now then, this woman, Signora Capece, is crazy. Of course, there will be an expert evaluation and all the rest, but she's certainly not of sound mind. So: in your experience, can a person like that do something and then remember only a part of what they've done?"

Modo looked at him intently through the cigarette smoke.

"If you explain to me exactly what you mean, I may be able to answer your question."

Ricciardi sighed:

"Do you remember when you described the condition of the corpse to me? You mentioned a struggle. Broken fingernails, broken ribs."

"And signs of asphyxiation, of course, I remember perfectly. So what?"

"So Signora Capece told us that she came in and shot the

duchess through the cushion, and that the duchess was fast asleep. But she didn't say anything about a fight."

Modo shrugged:

"I'll say it again: so what? Did she fire the gun, yes or no? If she pushed the cushion down onto the duchess's face, whether it was for one second or thirty seconds, if she braced her knee against her abdomen so she was better able to fire the gun, if the duchess grabbed her dress, breaking her fingernails in the processs—and they were long, well manicured nails, and therefore quite fragile—well, there you are, you have your full clinical picture of the autopsy. It all lines up perfectly, as far as I'm concerned. If you tell me that she's crazy, well, as you know individuals with mental problems can wield enormous strength without even being aware of it. I remember, during the war, there was a guy . . ."

But Ricciardi was too focused to listen to the doctor's post-prandial digressions.

"And the fingers? You told me that there were abrasions on one of the fingers, as if someone had violently ripped off a ring, and the explanation for that emerged in the investigation; but the other finger, the one that was dislocated when she was already dead, given the absence of hematomas? The Signora Capece said nothing about having taken a ring off the corpse."

The doctor spread both arms wide:

"Ah, well, that's something I can know nothing about: I'm a scientist, not a seer. I can tell you with great confidence, and in fact I did, that the finger was dislocated after the poor duchess had shuffled off this miserable coil. Whether someone then took her ring or visited a strange and perverse desecration upon her corpse, I have no idea. But forgive me if I say: now you're starting to look like the lunatic in this story. Signora Capece has confessed, you've found the murder weapon, and her confession fits in with all the evidence and clues that you've found. Can you tell me what more you want?"

Ricciardi ran a hand over his face as if brushing away a fly.

"You're right. Maybe it's just that I can never seem to give up an investigation just like that, that's all."

Modo stretched out in his chair, knitting his fingers behind his neck and smiling:

"Of course. If it were anyone else but you, the high priest of crime and justice, I would suggest you come with me to sample the delights of a new bordello that just opened its doors at La Torretta, with a team of French mademoiselles who are actually from Mugnano, but trust me, they'll take your breath away. But since you stubbornly insist on being yourself, I think I'll let you go back to your muckraking. But I want to give you a piece of advice, too, in exchange for the advice you gave me: every so often, why don't you give yourself a little peace. Take some time off, do something fun. Otherwise they'll be checking you into a room next to Signora Capece, take it from your friend Bruno."

"Fine, fine, I'll just have to devote a little leisure time to my favorite pursuit: hunting for dissident doctors. Come on, let's go get a cup of coffee. And this time, it's your treat."

XLIII

Maione slowly made his way up the last part of the steep uphill street that led to his home, where lunch was waiting. Incredible as it might seem, given how hungry he was, he'd happily have skipped lunch entirely, for a number of reasons: first of all, he couldn't stand the prospect of another bowl of vegetable soup; next, last night's spat was certain to mean a chilly silence on his wife's part, and that meant he couldn't hope for the friendly conversation that was his one sure way of getting his mind off work; last of all, he'd have to walk past the fruit and vegetable shop run by that damned Di Stasio, who had greeted him with a smile that struck him as faintly sarcastic.

Things changed radically however when, still a good fifty yards, perhaps more, from his own front door, he caught an unmistakable whiff of Lucia's Genovese savory pastries. It couldn't be anything else: the meat and onion sauce his wife cooked, and no other sauce out there, would have woken him out of a deep coma, and it was famous throughout the quarter. Long before the topic of food became a minefield, Lucia used to rib him, saying that the reason he'd married her was her Genovese pastries: and he, with a laugh, would say that she was probably right.

The thought only irritated him more: it struck him that making Genovese pastries for their children, now that he couldn't eat them, was gratuitously cruel; a torture that Lucia was inflicting on him to punish him for rejecting the soup she'd made the night before. He was tempted to turn around and head straight back to police headquarters, just to deprive her of that satisfaction; then he decided that a real man faces challenges, he doesn't turn and run, so he climbed the stairs, down in the mouth but grimly determined.

When he opened the front door, the celestial odor wafted over him violently; he even thought that he could detect the scent of fried broccoli and roasted potatoes, and possibly even a rum baba. He couldn't believe it: a full Christmas banquet in the middle of August. What on earth was happening?

He noticed that none of the children came running to greet him the way they usually did. He made his way into the kitchen and stood there, openmouthed: the table was groaning with an array of food, cooked in every style imaginable. There were only two place settings, with the tablecloth and silverware that were only used on very special occasions. Lucia stood glaring at him, combatively, by the kitchen sink as she dried her hands with a dish towel. He asked her:

"Where are the kids?"

"They're down at my sister Rosaria's. They've had lunch there and they won't be back until tonight."

The brigadier pointed to the dishes arrayed on the table: "And all this food . . . who put it here?"

Lucia replied in a harsh voice, but laughter was glinting in her eyes. She was enjoying herself.

"Who do you think put it here? And you tell me, who else would I let set foot in my kitchen?"

As she spoke, she came closer to Maione and gave him a fake punch in the chest, and another, then another, punctuating the things she said:

"And you tell me, is there a woman in all Naples who cooks better than I do? And you tell me, is there a place in all Naples where you'd be more comfortable than in your own home? And you tell me, how should a woman feel when she sees her own husband not bother to come home for dinner? And you tell me . . ."

He seized her wrist to stop her from hitting him and put one arm around her waist, pulling her close to him.

"Well, while we're at it, how is a man supposed to feel when he's rejected in his own home? And you tell me, how is a husband supposed to feel when he sees his wife flirting with an idiot fruit vendor—and even if we went to school together when we were kids, it's never too late for me to pluck out every last whisker in his whorish mustache, one by one?"

And they both burst out laughing and crying, until Lucia said, sit down and eat, or else we'll have to throw out this whole banquet; and Raffaele replied, if you're thinking of throwing away your Genovese pastries, you'll have to pry them out of my cold dead hands. And they sat down and ate for an hour, and then they made love, and then they ate the rest.

Crying and laughing the whole time.

His lunch with Modo had at least helped Ricciardi to pinpoint the source of his uneasiness: the duchess's second ring. He realized that whoever had torn the ring off her finger, dislocating it in the process, had done so after she'd already been killed, but still he felt compelled to complete his picture of the emotions that had danced around her corpse that night. His sense of order demanded it.

He headed off toward Palazzo Camparino, on an afternoon so muggy that the movements of the few people out on the street seemed to be in slow motion, as if they were underwater.

In the courtyard he saw Sciarra sweeping, doing his best to stay in the shade of the columns; he had his back to Ricciardi and didn't see him coming. When the commissario tapped him on the shoulder he lofted straight into the air from a standing start, a comic sight accompanied by the loss of his hat and a high-pitched scream.

"Oooh, *Madonna mia*, Commissa', it's only you. You're going to give me a heart attack, you know, really! I was lost in thought, I was . . ."

"Forgive me. See if young master Ettore is in, I'd like to talk to him."

The little man was panting, with one hand on his chest and the hat he'd picked up from the ground in the other hand; after brushing it off as best he could, he put it back on his head. In an apologetic tone he said:

"There's so much sweeping to do, there's always dirt on the pavement out here. The young master says that I'm supposed to water the hydrangeas now, in the heat of the afternoon: but I can't do that, climbing up and down the stairs with a heavy pail of water in this heat. So I water the plants in the evening, and I just pray that he doesn't notice. Yes, Commissa', he's here. He's upstairs, surrounded by his plants, as always. Just a minute, I'll walk you up, and let him know."

Ricciardi replied:

"I just want to stop by the duchess's anteroom first."

He followed the doorman up the first flight of stairs and stopped on the landing, waiting for him to open the gate. He sensed how uneasy the man was, but that was certainly par for the course. Everyone was uneasy around him: Ponte, the other policemen, sometimes even Maione. He was the only one of his kind, he thought. From another planet, the moon or Mars, or another star. Condemned to spend his life alone, and watch the others avoid him like the plague.

He took one step into the room, which was now clean and tidy, as if nothing had ever happened; but something had happened, and evidence of the fact was Adriana's corpse, still visible, even if it was gradually fading, speaking to him in a subdued voice from the same corner where he'd first seen her six long days ago.

"*The ring, the ring, you've taken the ring, the ring is missing,*" murmured the woman's dead and swollen mouth, her strong white teeth bared, with the black tip of her tongue extended between them. Ricciardi stood still, staring at her, his hands in his trouser pockets, his shirt collar unbuttoned and his tie loose. He wondered why her last thought should have been for her piece of jewelry, instead of some final curse or a note of regret.

Turning his back on the corpse he gestured to Sciarra and followed him upstairs to Ettore's apartment. The duke's son was on the terrace, leaning over a yellow rose bush. His back was to the two men, as he worked carefully with a pair of shears to trim the branches, with the utmost attention. After a moment, without giving any sign of having noticed that Sciarra was waiting, hat in hand, to announce Ricciardi, he said:

"*Prego*, Commissario, come right on in. Do you know the story of the yellow roses? Sciarra, you're free to go."

With unmistakable relief, the doorman moved off quickly: it was clear that he enjoyed neither the commissario's nor the young master's company. Ricciardi stood at the threshold of the terrace.

"No, I don't know the story. Should I?"

Ettore stood up and turned to look at his guest, mopping his sweaty brow with his sleeve.

"No, I imagine you wouldn't. It's an Arabic story: Mohammed suspected that his favorite wife, Aisha, a beautiful woman, might be betraying him. And so he asked an angel how he could find out the truth; there are angels, you know, in almost all religions. Well, the angel told him to bring the woman some red roses, and then to dip them in water: if the flowers changed color, it meant that the woman had been unfaithful to him. Mohammed brought her the flowers and arranged for her to drop them into the river: the roses turned yellow. The color of jealousy, of love betrayed."

Ricciardi heard Sofia Capece's voice in his mind, as she claimed to be the angel of death. And he thought about jealousy, which had driven her so mad that she had decided to punish Adriana for betraying her own husband.

"And what happened to the favorite? Did someone shoot her between the eyes?"

Ettore laughed.

"No, of course not. She was kicked out of the house, that's all. She was really rather lucky, wasn't she?"

"But the duchess wasn't lucky. She met quite a different fate."

The man's expression hardened.

"She was a bitch, Commissario. A vile, stupid bitch. She did whatever her diseased appetites suggested to her, she had no interest in anyone else's feelings. If you expect thanks for having identified her murderer, don't look at me. In fact, her lover's wife has my pity and comprehension: she did what a great many of us ought to have done long ago, believe me."

Ricciardi gave him a cool reply:

"It's not up to you, or Sofia Capece, or anyone else to decide whether someone has the right to live or not. No matter how dastardly that person may be."

The young duke shrugged his shoulders and smiled.

"The fact remains that someone, as you've seen for yourself, took that right. There's another thing though: I've heard about your . . . nocturnal strolls, and a certain visit you made to a building not far from where you live. As well as a lengthy conversation."

Ricciardi nodded. He hadn't expected Ettore to make any reference to the matter that concerned him, nor had he decided what he would do if he did: it had no conection to the investigation. All the same, the man clearly felt the need to talk about it. In fact, he continued:

"You see, Commissario, in a sense it's almost a relief to be able to talk about it. I understand why Achille would do it. There are times when I want to jump out of my skin from the urge to talk about it. Like everyone who's . . . who's ever been in love, I imagine."

Ricciardi said:

"These aren't matters that concern me, Musso. I needed to understand, find out the reason for certain things, and that's all. Once I've got a clear picture, the rest is of no interest to me."

"I know, I know. And I thank you for your sensitivity. But now that you know, let me tell you something: if you keep them in long enough, eventually emotions will suppurate and poison the blood. I've always been the way I am, you know. And I've never said a word about it to a soul. I've gone to bordellos, with fellow university students, to keep the others from talking about me, making hints about me. And then, once I got home, I would vomit for hours, out of sheer disgust. My mother would come over to me and stroke my head, without a word. She knew everything, I think: a mother can guess about certain things. And she loved me tenderly, no matter what. Not my father. But, then, he might not have loved me in any case."

Ricciardi said nothing: there was nothing to be said. In the heat of the afternoon that was turning into evening, the insects buzzed and the scent of jasmine was intoxicating. Ettore went on:

"And I fought it, you can believe me. Nothing ever happened. I fell in love with colleagues, classmates, but I turned my back on love. I ran away, I broke off friendships. And I hated my own name, the name of this house, my father who was imposing upon me a nature that did not belong to me. Only my mother held me close. Only her tender love. And then she fell sick."

"And Adriana came into your home," Ricciardi added.

"That's right, the bitch arrived. And she took my mother's place, even before she was dead. Did you know, Commissario, that she slipped into my father's bed while my mother was still alive, and in horrible pain from the tumor that finally carried her off? They even gave her this extra dose of suffering. Those two filthy beasts. And fate paid them back: killing her violently, and him slowly, little by little, day by day."

Ricciardi felt a faint shiver run up his back; the horror of that hatred was far worse than the sight of the murdered dead.

"But you didn't kill her. Not you."

Ettore shook his head.

"No. I don't have that kind of strength. I'm not a man of action: I'm a damned theorist, a writer. But I hated her, no question that I hated her. I yearned for her death every minute of every day. She tried to seduce me almost immediately, which was her way of sealing alliances. I found her, half-naked, in my bedroom one night, not long after my mother died. When I threw her out, do you know what she did? She burst out laughing. First she was just surprised, and then she started laughing. She knew that if a man rejected her, he had to be . . . like me; perhaps nothing of the sort had ever happened to her. And from that day forward, she never missed a chance to humiliate me, to mock me. She even told my father, who had never noticed or had simply pretended not to notice. And we haven't spoken since."

Ricciardi asked, in a flat voice: "Talk to me about the ring."

Ettore reeled, as if he'd just been slapped.

"The ring? How do you know about the ring?"

Ricciardi replied, without changing his expression:

"The autopsy revealed a dislocated middle finger on the left hand; it also found that it had been dislocated after she was killed because there was no hematoma. Clearly, someone had removed the ring that the duchess wore, and this someone couldn't be anyone but you: the only one who returned home after she was killed."

Ettore stared into the empty air, as if he were speaking to himself.

"I love him. I love him like I've never loved anyone in my

life, in a way I never even thought was possible. We hide our love, we've tried to break it off a thousand times. I've fought against it, we've fought against it. But you can't fight love, Commissario. Because if you fight it you're bound to lose. Inevitably. And so you need to take the initiative, and you need to pluck this love, the way you might one of these flowers. When you love, then you find that you love the world as well, and you want to sing, and shout, and laugh about nothing at all, in the light of day. But instead I have to hide, leave at night and come back before dawn, like a wolf, like a criminal. That night I came home happy, and I found her there, the bitch: dead on the sofa, with a bullet hole between the eyes and the gate hanging open. And her hand dangling, with my mother's ring on her finger. I've always known that ring, as long I can remember, every caress I've ever received was with that ring. The ring my mother was married with. That woman wasn't fit to look at it, but she wore it as if it had always been hers. Yes, I tore it off her finger, with all the strength in my body. And I kept it. It's right there, in that drawer: every now and then I take it out and I polish it. But just by wearing it, that bitch made it dirty for all time. It's no longer my mother's wedding ring. It's as if she killed her a second time."

XLIV

Apparently, regulations required that any woman sitting alone at a café must and should be besieged. Livia actually found it amusing, as she sat at a sidewalk table outside Gambrinus, waiting for Ricciardi to pass by on the Via Chiaia, according to what she had learned at police headquarters.

A euphoric and deeply obsequious Garzo informed her that the investigation had been closed. When she happened to run into the deputy police chief at the main entrance to headquarters, she'd made it very clear to him that she was there to confer with the commissario; but Garzo made sure not to miss this opportunity to chat up the former Signora Vezzi who enjoyed, as he knew very well, highly placed friends in Rome. And so he unreeled a succession of phrases—"why how lovely you look" and "what a pleasure to see you again in Naples" and "the salt air must be agreeing with you" and "what's the latest news from our beloved national capital?"—but also, once he sensed the signora's interest in the commissario and the possible favorable implications that that might have for him, he unfurled a daisy chain of generous compliments for his subordinate's skills and achievements.

By the time she managed to wriggle out of the conversation, Livia had obtained the information that Ricciardi would in any case be back in his office that evening and that, in accordance with a route that had almost become a ritual with him, he'd be stopping at Gambrinus for a quick cup of coffee; if the signora wished to see him, then that was the best place for her to wait. Otherwise, Garzo concluded, he'd be pleased to send Ricciardi to see her, posthaste.

In a way, she found that man to be a much more asphyxiating presence than the men who, taking turns in a minuet of glances, sighs, and broad winks, were now vying for her attention at the café. And for that matter, the woman's beauty, elegance, and solitude were irresistible elements of attraction to the dandies and *gagà* who killed time there, smoking and drinking. A light veil dangled from her hat, covering her eyes and leaving only a view of fleshy, sensual lips painted bright red; her body was tightly wrapped in a narrow-waisted dark-blue dress with a white-leather belt: her shoes, handbag, and elbow-length gloves were likewise in white leather. Her generous bosom and long legs were also unmistakable, even if they were technically covered.

She'd chosen an outdoor table, lest she miss the commissario as he passed, and she was watching the world go by with feigned interest as at least ten men devoured her with their eyes.

Ten men and a woman, to be exact.

The first shadows of evening were stretching out into Giulio Colombo's hat shop, but he didn't even notice them; nor did he hear the customer standing across the counter from him when she asked for a discount, and in fact she was forced to repeat the request in an even more doleful tone of voice. Giulio Colombo was focused on something else: he was staring at his daughter who in turn stood, motionless, looking out the plateglass window like a tiger downwind, laying in ambush for an unsuspecting gazelle.

That girl was starting to worry him. She'd never spoken to him explicitly about her state of mind, but it wasn't hard to guess, knowing her character as he did, knowing how similar she was to him; for some time now he'd been catching her with reddened eyes, as if she'd been crying, or else with a suddenly truculent expression. She was clearly being tormented by unusual thoughts, but she seemed unwilling to talk about it; nor did her father, reserved and discreet as he was, feel able to ask prying questions. As for the girl's mother, she hadn't noticed a thing. She was dismissive when Giulio shared his worries with her: she's probably finally starting to fall in love with Sebastiano, she had replied, that's all. These are the little bumps in the road of love, she'll get over it.

But that's not the way it seemed to Giulio. As far as he could tell, the situation was steadily worsening, day after day; and it was obvious to him that the Fiore boy wasn't even slightly in tune with his daughter's state of mind. For the past few days, Enrica had been coming into the store systematically every afternoon, and she stayed for an hour, gazing out the window, coolly dismissing the young man whenever he came in on some pretext to talk with her.

Deep inside, he had already dismissed the idea of this engagement ever working out, ever since the night he'd caught the look on Enrica's face as the young man was just about to sip his espresso with the disgusting slurping noise that he always made; it was a ferocious glare, and he could hardly blame her for it: it annoyed Giulio, and no one was pushing him to marry the boy. Just then, as Enrica stood peering out throught the plateglass window, he saw that same ferocious glare in her eyes.

There she is now, Enrica was thinking. Sitting all by herself, smoking cigarettes in a public location. But where does she get it, this bottomless pool of gall and sheer nerve? And at the exact time that he comes by for his daily cup of coffee: I know it very well, since I come to the store just to see him, now that I can no longer see him from my window every night. I have to admit: she is beautiful and elegant, not a bit vulgar, even though I told the hairdresser she was, to make sure she'd convey that information to his housekeeper.

What do I have that she lacks? Why on earth should he choose me, if he can have a woman like her? Even if I were to dress the way she does, if I weren't ashamed of going out alone and having men look at me, I'd never be as attractive as her. But I love him, I love him with every fiber of my being, and I can't stand living without his gaze, the sight of his eyes, even from a distance. She's waiting for him, I know that; and he'll stop to talk with her, he might even kiss her the way he did the other time. And it will break my heart, just like the other time. But I need to be strong, strong enough to wait and see.

You can't turn your back on love.

You can't turn your back on love, thought Ricciardi as he walked up Via Toledo: that's what Ettore Musso had said. And Achille Pivani had said the same thing. And Don Pierino had said that you have to take the initiative, at least once in your life.

Now that a complete atlas of the passions that had surrounded and destroyed the Duchess of Camparino had been sketched out, the commissario was left face to face with himself, and he had nowhere to turn, no refuge from his own thoughts. You can't turn your back on love: you have to take the initiative. But what initiative should he take? Should he inflict on the person he loved the same cross he himself had to bear, the same torture he suffered? So that he could tell her, as they strolled out arm in arm some summer afternoon, forgive me, my dear, I missed what you were saying just now because, of course, dearest, though you can't see him, in that corner, right next to the florist shop, there's a little boy who fell and broke his neck, and he's screaming for his mamma and it just distracted me for a moment. Is that what a man should offer the woman he adores?

All the same, he could no longer lie to himself: the picture of Enrica with that well dressed young man was becoming an obsession, far worse than the faded images of corpses that lined every street he walked down. He couldn't live with her, and he couldn't live without her. He sighed and looked up: Libreria Treves, he read on the sign. He shook his head and walked into the bookstore.

Livia saw him coming, his eyes on the pavement and a book in his hand. She decided that she'd recognize him anywhere, with that air of lovable loneliness that surrounded him, as if he were walking down other streets, streets that no one else could share with him. A mysterious man; in fact, a mystery made human. She couldn't remember ever having been so fascinated with a person in her life. Without realizing it, she had tensed up in her chair, like a wild animal scenting prey.

At first he didn't notice Livia at all and simply walked straight to the counter. Then she stood up and caught his attention with a wave of her hand. On the other side of the street, Enrica's heart was pounding furiously in her ears. Ill at ease, darting a fleeting glance at the envious occupants of the other tables in the café, Ricciardi took a seat next to the elegant woman from out of town. She had in the meanwhile lifted her veil, revealing a pair of dark eyes, with a luminous gaze.

"At last! And yet I was told that you couldn't hold out very long without your daily espresso. I've been here for hours, waiting for you."

Ricciardi was clearly uncomfortable, as he was every time that Livia explicitly referred to the attraction she felt for him.

"I had gone . . . I had to question a person. I had no idea that you'd be here. And in any case, you understand, my work . . ."

She interrupted him, laughing:

"Don't talk to me about your work. Believe me, I know

everything, all about your investigation and the brilliant way you wrapped it all up. I had to listen to that insufferable colleague of yours, you know the one I mean, Garzo, who buttonholed me and wouldn't stop talking about your achievements. But I told him that I was well aware of what a hero you are. My hero, to be exact."

Ricciardi furrowed his brow.

"First of all, Garzo is my boss, not my colleague. And I certainly don't confide in him. Last of all, I'm no hero: the murderer confessed, that's all."

Livia dismissed his explanations with a gesture of annoyance.

"Anyway, that's not why I'm here. I wanted to give you some important news. First: I've decided to stay on for a while in your magnificent city. I called an old friend of mine, a theatrical impresario, to ask him to arrange to find an apartment for me."

Ricciardi stood openmouthed.

"What, an apartment? But why?"

The woman smiled.

"You wouldn't want me to be stuck in a hotel, would you? I'll be much more comfortable in an apartment. And then I could hire a maid and finally be able to entertain. Don't you think that a little company would do me good?"

Ricciardi shrugged, and she went on talking, carefully enunciating like a schoolteacher addressing a slightly dim pupil:

"Second: I've decided that our friendship should evolve. Since you keep pretending not to notice, I'm going to tell you clearly: I'm interested in you, Commissario Ricciardi. I'm *very* interested in you. I don't remember when a man has caught my fancy the way that you have, and I intend to get to know you much better."

Ricciardi wished he could have been anywhere but there. Above all, he had the disagreeable sensation that, at least at the four tables closest to them, all conversation had ceased as the customers listened to the two of them. But there were certain things that needed to be said, and so he said them.

Now he's stopped and he's sitting down, the girl on the other side of the street thought to herself. He doesn't look comfortable, but he's sitting down. She called him, she even stood up, he hadn't noticed her at all. How can you miss a woman who looks like her? And now what are they saying to each other? She's counting something on her fingers, first, second. What could she be counting? And now, what is he answering? She felt her head start to spin, and she leaned her forehead against the plateglass window. Enrica, do you feel all right? her father asked. Yes, of course, she replied, as her eyes welled up with tears.

Never been better.

"I'm not sure that's really a very good idea, you know. This isn't an easy city to live in, and the climate can be harmful for someone who isn't used to it. And then there's the fact that you don't really know anyone. You'd have to build up a network of friends, and that wouldn't be easy for a single woman. And just where would this apartment be? In what quarter? You'd need help, you'd want to have someone you could rely upon. And I'm not sure I'd be the right person. In fact, I'm quite certain that I wouldn't. I have no time to spare, I have no friends of my own, it certainly wouldn't be . . ."

Livia interrupted with a loud laugh; she wanted to act cheerful, but there was sadness in her eyes.

"Why, what eloquence, and so unexpected! Do you know that I've never heard you talk this much? And just to get rid of me, think of that. Well, my dear man, do you know what I say to that? I say that Livia Lucani is not about to retreat. And that the more you tell me I ought to leave, the firmer my decision to stay. Actually, though, there is one thing you could say, if you want to get rid of me. Tell me the truth: do you have a girl-friend?"

Time ground to a halt around Ricciardi. The four men sitting at nearby tables all held their breath, as anxious to hear his reply as Livia herself. He opened and shut his mouth, once and then twice. If he answered in the affirmative he'd be lying, but he'd also get himself out of this sticky situation, possibly once and for all. But was that what he wanted? Livia was beautiful, cheerful, and passionate. He liked her and being around her gave him an odd, unsettled feeling that was more than just simple queasiness. In good conscience, however, he couldn't say that his heart was entirely unfettered.

"No. I don't have a girlfriend. But . . . I do have feelings for a person, yes. She doesn't know it, but I have feelings for her."

As he whispered such a profound and personal thing, in the crowded café, his head spun: he felt as if he had a fever. It was as if a cloud passed over Livia's face, and her eyes were tinged with pain. Ricciardi felt as if he'd just beaten her. But it was over in an instant: she immediately got to her feet with a smile on her face.

"Well, then, my dear man, I'll go on fighting. It seems to me that I still deserve a little happiness, and that you have this happiness tucked away somewhere. I intend to seek it out, find it, and seize it for myself. Tell your would-be girlfriend, deep in your heart, to pack her bags and get ready to move. Now, if you'll excuse me, I'd better get going: I have some apartment-hunting to do."

And she left, her progress followed by dozens of eyes.

XLV

Sunday is a holiday. But it seems like a war.

The armies are summoned by the bells, pealing out the announcement of the seven o'clock mass in scolding tones: how could you have failed to think of God first thing, instead of lolling on your pallets, with open windows, trying to obtain the faintest whiff of a breeze? For shame!

And the armies respond, descending from the quarters inhabited by the poor to take the best seats, on the steps of the churches or in the streets popular with strollers: no one is out yet, but to lose a position means being forced to find another way to make a living, another way to fill one's belly. It's an army of a thousand colors, the army of beggars: purple mutilations, verdigris uniform jackets worn by veterans just returning from the front, gauze bandages concealing, variously, empty eye sockets or perfectly healthy eyes, parakeets in their little cages, trained to extend little notes to passersby, telling their fortunes. And an army of a thousand sounds, accordions, ocarinas, mandolins, old violins with cracked soundboards. Even wrinkled black shirts, to win the pity of the newly powerful.

Shortly after dawn, the sound of hammering began to ring out as improvised stages were built: upon which bands would play, beneath which pickpockets would buzz like bumblebees, slipping deft hands and light fingers into pockets and purses, without marring the delighted smiles on the faces of the many listeners—at least, not until they got home that night.

Sunday is a war of commerce, for the street vendors who

take the place of the shops, closed for a day. Cobs of corn, golden brown or scorched black, an irresistible aroma wafting in the air; seeds and nuts, advertised by the shrill whistle of the peanut cart; doughnuts sprinkled with silver and particolored dots of sugar, with a fat female vendor shooing away flies with a fan; juicy slices of watermelon, liquorice sticks, greasy fritters. Rattletrap old ice cream carts, shaped like a ship's prow with an umbrella to ward off the heat of the sun, and wooden penguins carved into the sides. All of them snatching the best locations, whoever arrives last is poorly lodged: Sunday is a holiday but it seems like a war.

And like all wars, here comes the cavalry riding into the fray: most of the carriages rolled in shortly after dawn, though some of them had been there all night long, with the coachmen fast asleep, hats on their faces and whips under their arms, stretching in discomfort from the dankness in their bones. The straw scattered under the dray horses, capturing their urine and feces, if not the foul smells that poison the surrounding air.

Sunday is a war, for the children as well; the luckiest ones have been dreaming of this day all week long, with ink-stained fingers, breathing in chalk dust, at their desks or behind the blackboards, on their knees in punishment. The other children have thought about it too, chasing barefoot after the rats in the *vicoli* or fighting off stray dogs for a scrap of stale bread in the garbage discarded by the well-to-do palazzi of Santa Lucia. They'll meet later at the Villa Nazionale, casting greedy glances at the toy stalls, dreaming of floating away hanging from a red balloon on a long string or making their stern fathers jump in the air at the sound of the firecrackers that can be heard going off every so often; the fathers targeted by the vendors with their smiles as they hawk their wares, the children driven off rudely with clubs and sticks.

Sunday is a war. But it seems like a holiday.

Ricciardi had slept very badly, though that was hardly a change. He recalled a chaotic dream, where he was mixing up Livia and Adriana, both women talking to him in threatening tones about rings and apartments. Behind them, Enrica's elegant and well-dressed boyfriend, looking at him and laughing at him, for who knows what reason. And he was trying to open a book that he'd bought the day before and immediately concealed from the intrusive and gossipy eyes of his *tata*, underneath a loose floor tile behind his armoire; but he couldn't do it, the pages were massive and he had no strength left in his hands.

When he woke up in the morning, his forearm tingled painfully with pins and needles: he'd slept with his full weight on it. He couldn't move it, and the anxiety of his dream spread to his waking life. On the other hand, the ghosts of the living and the dead were gone, leaving a new and unfamiliar dread in his heart.

He had been tempted to break the promise he'd made to Don Pierino, reluctant as he was to plunge into the frantic chaos of the day, in all that heat: he really didn't feel like celebrating. But he had more than one debt of gratitude toward the little priest and he didn't want to disappoint him yet again, and so he trudged off wearily toward the waterfront. Along the way he cultivated fractured thoughts: Livia and her determination to stay on, Enrica and her closed window, Adriana and her sad fate. He thought once again of the book he'd purchased and concealed, and he wondered if he'd ever have the nerve to pull it out and read it. And he thought of his *tata*, too, and how, when she saw him going out on a Sunday morning, she had smiled and made reference to what she supposed was a date the young master had, perhaps with a woman from out of town: that woman had a gift of second sight, or else some anonymous informer. He hadn't replied.

There was something different in the air: it was still oppressively muggy and humid, but the sky was gray and it smelled of damp. Maybe it would rain, eventually, he thought. As he walked, he saw the crowd swelling, families and knots of friends going to enjoy one of the city's most beloved and traditional festivals. By the time he got to Via Santa Lucia, the crowd was enormous, and the neighboring marina, where the allegorical procession would conclude, was already packed.

Ricciardi had heard something about the 'Nzegna festival, but he'd never made an effort to understand the ritual nature of it, nor had he ever bothered to go to it. He knew that the moment everyone was waiting for was the procession and that, as usual, everyone took advantage of the opportunity to dance, sing, and commit every sort of crime imaginable, under the cover of the massive crowds; the holding tanks at police headquarters during this kind of event tended to be incredibly full.

Shoved along by the crowd he found himself not far from the wharf from which, ten feet above the surface of the water, a number of *scugnizzi* were hurtling straight down in spectacular dives, to the applause of hundreds of sweaty spectators. Not all the dives were successful, though: Ricciardi saw the image of a little boy looking out to sea, standing erect on the wooden structure of the wharf. He was looking out to sea from an unnatural angle, though, because his neck was snapped a little below the nape; the translucent pallor and the wrinkly skin pointed Ricciardi to a delayed recovery of the body and an extended stay in the water before the boy died. He heard his message, loud and clear in spite of the noise:

"One last dive. Just let me take one last dive and then we can go."

And that's exactly what it was, thought the commissario. The last dive: the very last dive.

Unsuspecting, the kids kept climbing up to the dock and leaping off, each time passing through the image of the little corpse. He wondered where the mother could be, in what madness she was extinguishing her grief. In the heat and the crowd, Ricciardi shuddered and walked away.

XLVI

The entrance to the church was a double staircase, covered with beggars who clutched at the clothing of all those who passed, demanding alms. On the street, musicians and strolling vendors were raising a din, a dissonant concert of shouts and out-of-tune instruments.

The sidewalk out front was busy with *madonnari* hard at work, sidewalk artists who specialized in drawings of the Virgin Mary, their hands aglow with colorful chalk, their faces sweaty and focused: the beautiful drawings that they created reproduced the story of the chained crate that Maione had mentioned, showing it being thrown onto the beach of Santa Lucia from a tempest-tossed sea. The crowd, suddenly seized by a new respect for the visual arts, carefully avoided trampling the figures and the landscapes that were gradually covering the sidewalks and street.

It was only with some difficulty that Ricciardi made his way into the church, and more than once he considered giving up and returning home; but he'd made it that far and he wanted Don Pierino to catch at least a glimpse of him, to exchange a wave and a nod, and then leave.

Mass had just begun and the church's single aisle was packed with people: the air was heavy with incense, the scent of the enormous number of flowers adorning the main altar and many of the side altars, and the sweat of the people inside. Ricciardi saw Don Pierino celebrating mass with two young altar boys. The words, uttered in a language that had been dead for centuries, swelled and flowed in a call and response from the assembled faithful. The churchgoers mouthed the answers without any idea of their meaning; ritual is a comforting thing, thought Ricciardi. Perhaps understanding doesn't matter. Maybe understanding only makes things worse.

The heat and the murmur of prayers pushed the commissario into a sort of trance, his mind wandering over and over through the same chaotic thoughts. The faces of Livia, Rosa, Lucia Maione, Enrica, and Adriana overlapped into a single blurry, suffering image, depicting all the nuances of pain and loss, apprehension for our loved ones and melancholy; and that image increasingly resembled the face of the statue atop the altar.

After Don Pierino was done with his reading of the Gospel, he scampered with considerable agility up the narrow spiral staircase to the pulpit: a marble balcony atop four columns, overlooking the assembly. He glimpsed Ricciardi in the midst of the crowd beneath him and shot him a rapid smile, to which the commissario responded with a nod of the head.

The little priest began to speak; he had a kind, gentle way of setting forth concepts, modernizing the message of the Holy Scriptures and making it accessible to one and all. Now he was talking about the festival.

"Today we are celebrating the Madonna of Catena, Our Lady of the Chain, to whom we are all deeply devoted. It is simply a painting, ancient and very dark: it is almost impossible to make out the figure. It has traveled a long way to reach us, and it deserves all our love. But today it is not about the Virgin Mary that I want speak, though She is in my heart just as She is in all yours: I want to talk to you about the chain."

Many of the faithful exchanged glances of bafflement: where was the priest heading with this? They'd be carrying the Madonna in the procession, certainly not the chain. After a pause, Don Pierino went on:

"In fact, the chains that most of us know are bad chains: the chains of slavery, the chains of incarceration. The chains of the soul, of the senses, of wickedness and evil. But there are also good chains, like the ones that protected the Madonna of the painting in its crate, all the way to the beach of Santa Lucia nearly a century ago. But the best chain, the chain most possessed of goodness that can be imagined, is the chain that binds humanity to God, God who fashioned humanity in His image."

Ricciardi was listening, fascinated in spite of himself. He was no believer, and it seemed to him that, given the life he led, it would be impossible to be one; but faith was a balm he envied others, a comfort to the luckier ones who possessed it.

"The chain that binds God to man is strong, and it withstands nature and the elements. It is the chain that binds a father to a son, a chain that never rusts or wears away with time. A chain that God will never break, a chain that in fact He made stronger through the sacrifice of His only begotten son."

Ricciardi saw a father, ahead of him, caressing the head of a little girl who kissed his hand in response.

"And so we might think," Don Pierino went on, "that this chain which can withstand even God Himself can never be broken. Unfortunately, that is not the case. There is a way to shatter this chain: a terrible pair of shears, that can inflict this irreparable damage."

The priest sought out Ricciardi in the crowd and found him again, gazing straight into his eyes.

"This pair of shears is sin: a formidable weapon, which God himself gave to us so that we might choose not to employ it, saving our souls with free will. Sin shatters the chain: it separates us from God and lets us drop directly into hell and damnation."

With Don Pierino's eyes leveled directly into his own, Ricciardi noticed a new sense of discomfort spreading inside him; he began to feel his heart racing loudly in his throat, as if he were about to faint. He leaned against a nearby column while he tried to regain his equilibrium. What was happening to him? As if muffled by fog, the priest's voice came to him, through the subdued rustling of the women's fans—whipping back and forth incessantly:

"Sin shatters the link, the most important link in the chain. It shatters the link that cannot be replaced, and without it there is no longer any contact between us: the chain no longer exists, only two useless parts of chain exist. The most important iron ring of all those that make up the chain is the one that's missing. By committing a sin, you've removed the link."

Ricciardi's jaw dropped: before his feverish, smarting eyes, in his blurred vision, to his mind ravaged by the thousands of instances of suffering to which he was a daily witness, the truth suddenly blazed clearly in its simplest and most unmistakable form. He understood: he understood it all.

Making his way through the crowd of the faithful, while Don Pierino climbed down from the pulpit and went back to the main altar, he emerged into the open air, the gray muggy heat, and he inhaled in long, hungry gulps: the world was spinning around him dizzyingly. He felt like an idiot, a dull-witted fool who'd failed to see what was obvious, the truth that lay right before him.

He pushed past people, making his way upstream through the crowd pushing back toward the marina to enjoy the spectacle of the 'Nzegna. He walked and no one noticed him, no one seemed to see him at all as he made his way upstream through the masses. He was reminded of Sofia Capece, who was convinced she'd become invisible by divine intervention: the angel of death.

Perhaps the woman, in her madness, had had a point. Those who bring death and damnation really are invisible.

The Colombo family was getting ready for the Sunday lunch, but there was something in the air that didn't seem right.

It wasn't the humidity, nor was it the gray daylight that filtered in through the open window: it was, rather, a question of atmosphere. Even the children, who usually talked all at once in a cheerful, deafening cacophony, had fallen silent and exchanged baffled glances. There was a reason.

The reason was Enrica.

Usually the young woman was a smiling, quiet presence in the apartment, and she filled the kitchen with her serene, hardworking sweetness. She was part of the family and, in a very real sense, its true core. But today she loomed like an omen of some impending disaster: her eyes swollen, behind sunglasses, her tangled hair, her reddened cheeks.

It was obvious that she had been crying, shut up in the bedroom she hadn't left since that morning. Her mother and her sister, both worried by that unusual behavior, had gone to knock on her door, but they'd received only a terse reply; finally they'd resigned themselves to making lunch without her, exchanging bewildered glances without a word.

Giulio, for his part, was clearly glowering with grim discomfort: he was no longer willing to tolerate the fact that his daughter was manifestly suffering, and there was no mistaking the reason. He hadn't worked his whole life so he could condemn his beloved Enrica to a fate that went against her will; if he had to, he'd support her for all the years she wished, and then leave her enough to live on with all due dignity. And if his wife didn't agree with him, that would be too bad for her.

Just as he was about to put down his fork and express his thoughts aloud, Enrica beat him to it, speaking in a calm and unruffled voice:

"Mamma," she said, "I know you only want what's best for me and you're worried because at my age I'm still not engaged to be married."

One of her younger brothers stifled a nervous giggle behind one hand, prompting an angry glare from his father. Enrica went on:

"But I would beg you to consider that, precisely because I am now and have been for some years an adult, I am also capable of deciding what I want from my life. And what I do not want. Mamma, don't take this the wrong way: but I never want to see that man, Sebastiano Fiore, again as long as I live."

The phrase tumbled out into the silence of the tomb. A distant rumble of thunder came in through the window, sounding like an airplane going overhead.

Maria shot a fiery glance at her daughter, but the girl looked back with her customary tranquil determination. At that point, the woman tried on a conciliatory tone:

"How on earth can you say such a thing? Has he somehow disrespected you, is there something wrong with him? Do you think you deserve better? Don't you like his family? Or is it . . ."

Enrica raised one hand to stem the rising tide of questions.

"No, Mamma. Nothing like that. It's simpler than that: I don't love him."

"But you could get used to him, in time. Perhaps, a little at a time . . ."

"I'm sorry, but you refuse to understand." Enrica heaved a deep sigh; her whole family was looking at her, no one touched their piping hot bowls of pasta. "I know that I'll never be able to love him the way a wife must love her husband; the way you love Papà."

Her mamma sat, waiting, openmouthed: "Why on earth not?"

"For the simplest reason imaginable, Mamma: I'm in love with someone else."

In the quietest tone of voice on earth. A bomb like that, tossed in the quietest tone of voice on earth. Maria turned to Giulio:

"And you? You're her father, and you ought to have her best interests at heart; what do you have to say about it?"

Her husband straightened his back and, looking his wife right in the eye, said calmly:

"I say that this ragù looks like it must be delicious. It's Sunday, it's lunchtime, and I say: *buon appetito.*"

And with that, he dug in.

XLVII

In the silence of Sunday afternoon, Ricciardi was looking at Adriana Musso di Camparino's murderer.

He watched him move lazily in the heat, taking care of minor chores. He watched him look up at the sky, when a distant rumble announced that the weather was finally about to change; the man shook his head, sighed, and went back to pruning dry leaves off the plants.

Ricciardi's head was no longer spinning. The walk he'd taken all the way from Santa Lucia had cleared his thoughts, and he'd felt the usual miracle take place in his mind: with the new interpretive framework, every individual piece slotted into its place, every element harmonized with the others, and now, at last, they formed a picture that was fully plausible from every point of view. To a certain extent, he'd also forgiven himself: he'd been superficial and careless, he knew that; but deep down he'd also gone on thinking, investigating that murder without ever really stopping. Because he'd never really been convinced that it had gone the way everyone thought.

By the halfway point along his walk, he'd reconstructed all the various events, exactly as they had occurred. Now he needed to know the rest: the motives, the reasons why. The context of the passions, the emotions that had danced around the duchess's corpse.

He walked over to the murderer and the man saw him. He didn't seem surprised, nor did he appear to have any thought of running, no sudden impulses. The commissario greeted him with a nod of the head and sat down on a marble bench: Peppino Sciarra, the doorman of Palazzo Camparino, doffed his oversized hat and let himself sink down beside him.

They sat in silence, for a while. Somewhere, from a window not far away, several goldfinches sang sweetly to the dying summer. It was Ricciardi's turn to speak, and Ricciardi spoke:

"When Signora Capece confessed, I believed her. We all believed her; and we were right, because everything she said was true. But there were a few pieces that didn't fit, with either Sofia Capece's account or some of the things that we'd found. Still, Capece confessed, Musso was somewhere else, so was the journalist, and her new lover would have been noticed. So for all of us, it was Signora Capece, end of story. But it wasn't the end of the story."

Sciarra looked straight ahead, head bowed as if the weight of his enormous nose were simply too much.

Ricciardi went on:

"There were marks on the duchess's body: broken ribs, shattered fingernails. And the cushion, the cushion pushed down on her face. The duchess was already dying. Those were her death throes, the last rattles of her respiration: she wasn't snoring when Sofia Capece shot her."

The doorman ran a trembling hand over his eyes. Ricciardi didn't bother to look at him, but went on with his reasoning in a cold, remote voice:

"And she was dying because she'd been suffocated. The bullet hole between the eyes distracted us, kept us from understanding: in fact, when she was shot the duchess's fate was already sealed. But then, who killed her?"

He turned to look at Sciarra, who was covering his eyes with his hand. He hardly even seemed to be breathing.

"We could have seen it. I could have seen it. I had all the evidence in hand. The murderer's strength was the strength of desperation; there was no fury, there was no rage. The murderer didn't take it out on her, he didn't disfigure her. He was fighting for his life, he was afraid. He fought and he won, the murderer. The only disfigurement was Ettore's work, when he tore his mother's ring off the dead finger, dislocating it. And Signora Capece's gunshot: there was no violence, there was no rage; it was simple madness. Sofia Capece wanted to execute a guilty person. Three different acts of violence inflicted on Adriana's body. That's what confused me, threw me off. I didn't understand that the solution was a simple one: three acts of violence, three guilty parties."

Sciarra shook his head gently, almost as if he were lulling himself. The murmur of Ricciardi's voice continued:

"There were two clues I didn't understand, two clues I chose to overlook. There was a partial footstep on the carpet. A strange mark, you could only guess at it. Grit, a little mud, and it hasn't rained for two months. Where did that mud come from?"

Sciarra lowered his hand and for the first time he looked the commissario in the face. His strange eyes, set apart by his nose, were glistening like the eyes of a fawn. He said nothing.

"Then you told me that you watered the hydrangeas late at night, even though the young master scolded you for it. Water and dirt: that footprint was yours. And the other clue that I missed at first, fool that I was: the chain. The padlock was shut, the duchess would open it when she came home: but this time she came home earlier than expected, because she'd quarreled with Mario Capece, and she found the door open even though she had the keys. Why? Very simple: the hasp ring was missing."

Ricciardi heard the last lament of Adriana's dead soul, loud and clear:

"The ring, the ring, you've taken the ring, the ring is missing."

And all the while, he, idiot that he was, wondering which ring she meant, whether it was Capece's ring or Ettore's mother's ring. Instead, it was quite simply the hasp ring, which had been tampered with. With that ring removed, the chain no longer held the gate shut, and Sciarra—who had done the tampering—was able to get into the apartment when she was out and the housekeeper had already retired for the night. It took Don Pierino and the chain binding man and God, shattered by sin, to bring the truth to the surface, to make it emerge from the depths of his subconscious.

Slowly, the little man slipped one hand into his pocket and pulled out something, which he handed to Ricciardi. A circle of burnished metal, open in the middle; it wasn't steel, but a softer metal painted to look like it, perhaps lead. This was Sciarra's skeleton key to the apartment of the duke and duchess of Camparino.

Night fell over the palazzo's courtyard, lengthening the shadows and making the colors fade. At last, Sciarra spoke, and in that whisper his cracking voice seemed more pathetic than comical.

"What's my place? Do you know that, Commissa'? Can you tell me? Everyone says to me: stay in your place. Don't try to rise above your place. But no one seems to know my place, my real place. Even I don't know what my real place should be."

The goldfinch suddenly stopped singing. Then it started up again, full-throated. And Sciarra, too, went on.

"I'm from Pozzuoli. In my hometown, if you don't have a fishing boat, you can't do a thing. I met my wife when I was little more than a boy; we're simple folk, our dreams are simple ones: we're not like our masters, here, who all have a thousand things spinning through their heads. We wanted a roof over our heads and enough food to eat, for ourselves and our children. And we wanted to do an honest day's work. Where I come from, if you don't have a boat, you have only one choice, if you want to get enough to eat: you have to work for those people, you know the people I mean. And I didn't want to work for them. So we loaded our few possessions onto a cart and we came to Naples, to the big city."

Ricciardi knew from personal experience that every murderer is searching for that moment: he yearns to speak, he wants to get it off his chest. He wants to be understood. He wants the person who listens to him to support his reasons, to tell him, "Poor Sciarra, it's just the way you say it is: you're the victim, not the guilty party." The usual story.

"But instead, Commissa', we found blackest hunger here too. We slept under the cart, one at a time, otherwise the rats would gnaw away at the noses and ears of our babies, I've seen it happen, trust me. And when it wasn't rats, it was people who were even worse off than we are, who wanted to steal our few miserable rags. But then, one morning, when I came to this very piazza to ask the Madonna in the church to intervene on my behalf, I saw Signora Concetta, the housekeeper; she was talking to a shopkeeper and complaining about how it was impossible to find a doorman and a maid, and that she just couldn't keep the household going all on her own."

Sciarra's eyes lit up at the recollection of that divine grace, accorded even before he could ask for it.

"I've thanked the Lord God every day, and I thank Him still. A position, a place: I finally had a place of my own. This was it, my place. My children could grow up under a roof, and they'd be able to get enough to eat. You can't imagine how hungry we were. And what it meant to us to be able to eat, twice in a single day. My children forgot about hunger; the littlest girl never actually experienced it. But not my wife and me, Commissa'; we'll never forget it. We still wake up at night, terrified, when we dream about going hungry and spending nights under the cart, with rain splashing in everywhere and the noise of chattering teeth. We looked death in the face, Commissa'."

Looking death in the face: and he said it to him of all people. The duchess, who was dead, was looking him in the face; who knew how many years she would have still had to live.

"I can't stand it, watching my children go hungry. I can't even take it when they're peckish. If my children ask me for food, I give it to them. I'm their father: it's my duty. And maybe because when they were little they had nothing, now they always seem to be hungry; always, Commissa'. From when they wake up until night falls, they'd eat every second of the day. It's not that they're gluttons: it's just that they're hungry."

Ricciardi remembered Sciarra's two children, fighting over bread and cheese the morning the duchess was found dead.

"You wouldn't believe what's in the pantry in this house. No one eats a thing, one person goes there, the other goes here; and the duke, poor old man, lives on thin soups and broths. But from the farms they own, every delicacy imaginable comes pouring in, tons of food. They waste it, they let it go bad, they literally throw it away. It would break your heart to see the things they throw away every week: meat, pasta, fruit. With children dying of hunger in the middle of the street. It's not fair, but that's the way it is: everyone in their place. But where is everyone's place? Can you tell me that, Commissa'?"

Ricciardi said:

"Go on. Tell me about that night."

Sciarra ran his trembling hands over his face again. There was another rumble of thunder, closer this time.

"Signora Concetta, when she retires at night, locks the chain on the gate with the padlock. She goes straight to sleep, she's a heavy sleeper, and she never wakes up until morning. Much later, never any earlier than two in the morning, the duchess would come home and go to bed; she'd unlock the padlock with her keys, she'd relock it, she'd put the keys in the drawer where Concetta would find them the following morning, and then she'd go to her bed. Sometimes she'd retire with . . . with someone else, in other words. But the passages of keys and padlocks were always the same."

"And so?"

"And so, a year ago, or thereabouts, I thought to myself: who would ever notice if a little piece of meat is missing from the pantry? Sooner or later they always wind up throwing it away, after all. My son, the eldest boy, was very sick. He'd turned white as a sheet, his blood counts were low. And I made a hasp ring, a ring of lead, identical to the ring that anchored the chain to the wall. And I replaced the real hasp ring with the lead ring. And at night, before the duchess came home for the night, I'd pry it open with my hands. I'm strong, you know: nobody'd ever believe just how strong I am."

Maybe the duchess would believe it now, thought Ricciardi; since she couldn't break free of your grip, the grip that suffocated her.

"From that day on, every so often, I'd pilfer a little something to eat. Not always, Commissa'. Just now and then. I'd slip in, take a little oil, a piece of meat, some bread. A hunk of cheese. That night, in fact, I'd taken a piece of cheese. The child was hungry, she'd asked me a hundred times, and I'd promised her some. Well, I walk out of the pantry and I come face to face with the duchess, with the keys in hand. She took one look at me and said: tomorrow you're packing your bags and you're out on the street. All of you. None of your family will ever set foot in this palazzo again. It's not your place anymore. Do you see, Commissa'? Our place. The cart appeared before my eyes again, the rats, the rain. I thought about my little girl, who'd never lived in the street in her life. And I said to her, Signora Duchessa, take pity on me. And you know what she said? If you don't get out of here, I'm going to scream. After that, I just lost my mind; outside you could hear the festival, the piazza was still full of people. It would mean humiliation, the worst mortification imaginable. So I grabbed the cushion and put it on her face."

Ricciardi fell silent, picturing the scene.

"You fought; the duchess lashed out."

Sciarra looked into the empty air, immersed in the murder he was reliving.

"Like a cat. She fought like a cat. She kicked, she scratched; I was wearing my uniform jacket; if I hadn't been, she'd have ripped my arms to shreds. But then she stopped moving: she was still breathing, or at least I thought she was. I picked up the keys from the floor and I put them in the drawer, and I left. When I got home, upstairs, I realized I still had the piece of cheese in my hand. My wife started crying, and she's crying still."

Ricciardi shook his head; as incredible as it seemed, the true guilty party was hunger. Not some complicated love story, with its countless paths to murder, rage, possessiveness, jealousy; but instead none other than dull, stupid hunger, with its blind shrieking need.

By now the courtyard was almost dark; a muggy evening had fallen over the city. In the half-light, he heard the faint sound of footsteps, and Ricciardi glimpsed Sciarra's two youngest children as they approached, hand in hand.

"Papa? Mamma wants to know, aren't you coming up?"

The boy's voice was worried, clearly by Ricciardi's presence: what could that grim-faced gentleman want with their father? Sciarra replied:

"Yes, but you go up first. Tell Mamma that . . . tell her that I'll be up as soon as I can."

The two children went off reluctantly; before turning away, the girl curtsied to Ricciardi.

"They're beautiful, eh, Commissa'? My children really are beautiful. And they help me, you know. They do all the little chores around the house. And at school, they're at the head of their classes. Who knows what their place is. Who can say what their place will be now."

The thunder roared violently, and the wind picked up. Ricciardi shivered. Hunger, he thought. And the Capece family, the boy and the girl left without their mamma, with a father who was now a stranger, a father they'd have to forgive every day, though they could never forgive him entirely. And the duke dying alone in his bed, and Achille and Ettore and their love that could never see the light of day. And Sofia Capece, in the darkness of the room and the madness where she might spend the rest of her life.

How many victims had the duchess's murder taken? Who'd actually killed her? Perhaps Signora Capece's gunshot had been enough. Or perhaps the angel of death had done it all on its own.

For the Capece children it was too late; but not for Sciarra's children. Ricciardi's conscience was pitted against his sense of justice. He followed his instinct as he spoke.

"Your prison will be your children, Sciarra. If they end up badly, you too will end badly. I won't forgive you, because that's not my job: but your children need you, and they come before justice."

Sciarra hadn't raised his eyes from the pavement.

"I can never forgive myself, Commissa'. Whether I live here or in prison, I'll never be able to forgive myself. And I'll dream about the duchess every night of my life. Now I know where my place is. You've told me yourself. My place is close to my children."

When Ricciardi left, in the first drops of rain, he was still sitting there, staring at the ground.

XLVIII

Rosa's bones were warning her that the weather would be changing, and had been since the day before. The advantages of age; like wisdom. But she would gladly have done without them. While she was massaging her aching elbow, in front of the sink, she thought—as usual—of Ricciardi.

He'd come home late, damp from the first onset of rain, his face more melancholy than usual. He'd eaten without a word, answering her questions with grunts; God, how hard it was to understand him, he was so closed, so shut off.

Then he'd withdrawn to his room. Rosa glanced out the kitchen window as she washed the dishes. The rain was coming down harder; the air smelled of autumn. The seasons pass, she thought, and they never change; yet each one leaves its mark. On the other side of the *vicolo*, the Colombos' drawing room window was dark: no company tonight. That's a good sign, thought the *tata*. Everything was going exactly as it ought to.

She wondered why Ricciardi had hidden a book underneath a loose floor tile behind his armoire, thinking she wouldn't see it. What was it for? Of course, she'd found it that same morning, it was the first place she checked every day; he was so methodical, he never thought to come up with a new hiding place. She'd only been able to read the title, because she knew the big letters, not the little ones. She thought about the woman from up north that the hairdresser had mentioned, quoting Enrica's words. She couldn't say why, but the thought of that woman worried her. First of all, her presence ought to have made Ricciardi happy, but she could see he was even gloomier than usual. Then, there was the fact that she'd been described as someone quite different from the kind of woman she'd want her boy to be with. She knew who she wanted. The girl next door, she thought.

She looked out the window again, as it shivered with the impact of an especially strong gust of wind and rain. Who knows, maybe I could invite the Colombo girl over here for a cup of coffee, some afternoon. Now that it's not so hot, now that the rains have come. From Ricciardi's bedroom came the sound of a chair pushed along the floor. Rosa smiled as she dried the last dish.

As he walked into his bedroom, he'd immediately noticed that the light was on again in Enrica's kitchen window. The heavy rain made it impossible to identify the silhouette he could glimpse, sitting in the cone of light, reading or perhaps embroidering. But he needed no confirmation.

Initiative, he thought. Everyone had told him that he needed to take the initiative. An act of will. As if that were so easy. His ears echoed with the words of Modo, Don Pierino, and Ettore Musso; people who were living the lives they'd chosen, despite a thousand obstacles.

He too made certain choices, of course; and they weren't easy ones, to tell the truth. For instance, he'd just decided to let a murderer go free, just because a little girl had curtseyed gracefully.

Just a few seconds earlier, he had made up his mind to take the man in, since he was as guilty as Sofia Capece, or possibly more so; then he'd decided that it was up to him, not a judge seated behind his bench in the tribunal of Porta Capuana. It was he, Ricciardi, who had to decide whether to sentence four young children to a life of infamy and a man to life imprison-

ment for a momentary impulse, driven by the rediscovered terror of a return to poverty. And he'd made his decision.

How could that be? he wondered, as he looked out the
rain-driven window. How can the same person make a decision like that on the spot, in the blink of an eye, and then sit
here helpless, for months, looking out the window and not
knowing what to do?

He bent over and looked under the armoire, lifted the brick,
and grabbed the book. From the kitchen he heard the clatter-
ing of pots and pans; his *tata* would never find his hiding place,
he thought to himself. She was too old to bend over like that,
at her age. He shot another glance across the street, but he
could only make out the light: the rain was drumming down
too hard.

He went over to his little writing desk and sat down, turning on the lamp. He put the book on the table in front of him,
remembering the flush of shame in the bookstore when he'd
told the clerk the title: *Il moderno segretario galante*. A helpful
guide to writing modern love letters.

The initiative, he thought: he had to take the initiative. He
took a deep sigh: the man who saw dead people, and felt their
furious pain on his flesh without blinking an eye, was now
quite simply terrified.

He took a sheet of paper and dipped his pen in the ink:
Gentile Signorina, he wrote.

Then he stopped, with his pen in hand. And he sat there,
enchanted by the sight of the large raindrops streaking the
glass.

Acknowledgements

Ricciardi has several traveling companions, whom he couldn't imagine doing without.

He works according to the directions of Aldo Putignano, a brother as much as a friend, irreplaceable.

Antonio knows the destination and how to reach it; Michele knows the equipment required, and the luggage to take along. Giulio Di Mizio speaks with Ricciardi and alone knows his other gaze. My mother knows his memories, and his hidden emotions. Giovanni and Roberto are the only ones who know how to keep him company.

If you notice a new spring in his step, it's thanks to Mario Desiati, and to my dear friends, Manuela Cavallari, Manuela Maddamma, and Tiziana Triana: I wouldn't know how to think of Ricciardi anymore without them. And especially Domenico, who picked him out of the crowd.

I, however, have only one real traveling companion: my sweet Paola.

About the Author

Maurizio de Giovanni lives and works in Naples. His Commissario Ricciardi novels, including *I Will Have Vengeance* (Europa 2013), *Blood Curse* (Europa 2013), and *Everyone in Their Place* (Europa 2013), are bestsellers in Italy and have been published to great acclaim in French, Spanish, and German, in addition to English. He is also the author of *The Crocodile* (Europa 2013), a noir thriller set in contemporary Naples.